"What say to some more tennis?" Lady Dunsmore asked.

Richard raised his arm, snapped his fingers in the direction of one of the Myn servants and called, "Rackets!"

The nearest of the Myn servants seemed not to notice. It stood rooted in place, its head tilted upward toward the heavens.

Richard sighed in frustration. "You see what we have to contend with here, my lord," he said. "The Myn are so damned dreamy and distracted, forever communing with their departed elders instead of keeping their pathetic little minds on the task at hand. It's hardly a wonder that the Home Office is dissatisfied with production in the plantations."

"Indeed," said Lord Dunsmore, gazing at the immobile Myn. "Can't you get its attention somehow? Perhaps a good swift kick?"

"It would hardly help. Ah, but one of them, at least, seems to have gotten the message." Richard nodded toward another of the Myn approaching their table.

The Myn stopped ten feet away from the humans, opened the case, and stood there in front of them holding what appeared to be an automatic rifle of some sort. It looked to Lord Dunsmore like something he had once seen in a museum in Edinburgh. Curious, thought Lord Dunsmore, that such an antiquated device should turn up here. It was the last thing Lord Dunsmore ever thought . . .

DEXTA

C.J. RYAN

BANTAM BOOKS

DEXTA
A Bantam Spectra Book / August 2005

Published by
Bantam Dell
A Division of Random House, Inc.
New York, New York

Bantam Books, the rooster colophon, Spectra, and the portrayal of a
boxed "s" are trademarks of Random House, Inc.

ISBN 0-553-58776-5

Printed in the United States of America
Published simultaneously in Canada

www.bantamdell.com

OPM   10 9 8 7 6 5 4 3 2

For Cedric and his humans

DEXTA

chapter 1

"THE BEST OF TIMES, ASSUREDLY," LORD Dunsmore agreed. He was always eager to agree with anyone whose opinion was worth noting, and in this instance, he could have found no reason not to agree had he pondered the matter for hours. His host, although only a regional manager for GalaxCo, was related to the Mainwaring family by marriage and therefore had to be considered knowledgeable and, to a carefully measured degree, influential. "By any standard," Lord Dunsmore said, "clearly, the Empire is at high tide."

"But Herbert, dearest," his wife protested, "surely a high tide implies the coming of a low tide. You seem to suggest that the Empire's fortunes shall soon be on the wane."

"Not necessarily, Lady Dunsmore," their young host, Richard DuMont, quickly responded. "Here on Mynjhino, we have three moons, you know. One high tide may be quickly followed by another, which may be even higher. Rather a complex business, I fear."

The lad was clever, Lord Dunsmore decided,

although perhaps a bit presumptuous to contradict his wife in such a bold fashion. Contradicting his wife was a prerogative Lord Dunsmore embraced for himself, and it was one of his more satisfying pastimes. "It was, in any event," he pointed out, "merely a figure of speech. What I meant, of course"—he looked toward Lady Dunsmore with a peremptory glare—"was that the state of the Empire is satisfactory in nearly every respect. Young Charles is growing into his office in a most splendid fashion, and peace and prosperity are the order of the day. I confess, I had my doubts after that dreadful business three years ago—I suppose we all did, what?—but one can hardly gainsay his performance since then."

"Oh, indeed, Lord Dunsmore, indeed!" young DuMont responded, raising a glass of wine. DuMont nodded toward one of the waiters to summon another bottle. "However," DuMont continued, "I, for one, never had any doubts about the qualities of our new Emperor. You see, I knew him briefly when we were in school together, and just after. Did I mention that already?"

"Five times, at least, dear," his wife, Rosalyn, reminded him. She was quite attractive in a rather obvious way. A bit of a tart, it seemed to Lord Dunsmore, with her High Imperial pretensions. Her skimpy attire was nearly transparent, which seemed a bit much merely for Tuesday afternoon tennis and drinks at their club. Still, she presented distinct possibilities for this evening. He was not likely to find better on this isolated rathole of a planet.

The waiter arrived with a fresh bottle of wine, preceded by an unpleasant waft of pungency. The creature was about five feet tall and covered head to foot in short, rather greasy yellowish-brown fur. Naked, it seemed. It had long, sharply pointed ears jutting outward from its skull at a forty-five-degree angle, and large, liquid brown eyes set wide above a short, blunt snout. It looked like an animated teddy bear or a tall koala, perhaps, and was not unpleasant to behold. But it stank. Lord Dunsmore turned his head away in search of fresher air while the creature did its duty. He stared out from their table on the veranda across the tennis courts and toward the lush green of the plantations in the distance. When the wine was poured and the creature was gone, Lord Dunsmore looked back at his host.

"It's a wonder to me that you can stand the stench."

"One gets used to it, in time, my lord," DuMont replied. "But I do apologize for it."

"Oh, no need for *you* to apologize, Richard, dear," Lady Dunsmore responded with just the right touch of airy condescension.

"Still," said Lord Dunsmore, "one would think that at a private club such as this, one might find some relief from the locals. Can no humans be found to provide services? Or failing that, robots?"

"Robots might be preferable," DuMont conceded, "but importing them would be a problem. No local construction facilities, of course, and our concession agreement is rather restrictive in that area. We aren't to put the little fellows out of work, if we can avoid it. And as for humans, well, my lord, good luck in finding one to serve you your dinner. They are all out in the hills on the Western Continent looking for gems and ores, or overseeing the plantations here on the Eastern Continent. There are fortunes to be made on a world such as this— or at any rate, there is always the hope of a fortune. No one comes this far at such an expense just to be a menial."

"I suppose." Lord Dunsmore reluctantly nodded. "Still, one would *think* ..."

"There are only ten thousand of us here, my lord," Rosalyn DuMont pointed out.

"Yes," her husband agreed, "there's always a shortage of human labor on worlds like Mynjhino. Spirit knows, GalaxCo has its problems finding adequate staff out here. We're 862 light-years from home, and we must compete with hundreds of nearer, better-established colonies. And you are aware that Imperial policy is to make use of local labor, where it exists."

"Imperial policy? Dexta policy, you mean!" Lord Dunsmore sniffed. "Damned bureaucrats. If I have any complaint at all with our new Emperor, it is with his constant truckling to that knave Mingus and his grim, gray army."

"Oh, they aren't all *that* bad, dear," Lady Dunsmore objected. "We know some perfectly fine people at Dexta. And as for the Emperor, well, one mustn't forget that his wife—or I should say, *ex*-wife—is at Dexta. At a rather low level, I gather, but perhaps she still has some influence over him."

"I knew her, as well," DuMont couldn't keep himself from mentioning. "Perfectly stunning woman, and smart as a whip."

"If she was so stunning and smart as all that," Lord Dunsmore said with a trace of contempt, "I rather fancy she'd still be his wife instead of some drone in the Department of Extraterrestrial Affairs."

"Oh, but it was she who dropped him," Lady Dunsmore reminded her husband. "Of course, that was five or six years ago, before he had any prospect of ascension."

"And as for being a drone"—DuMont laughed—"well, Glory was anything but that. I even took a run at her myself, back in school, but that was before she met Charles. And before I met Rosalyn, of course," he added, with a quick, reassuring glance at his wife. Rosalyn returned his smile mechanically.

Lord Dunsmore was becoming annoyed at being contradicted so frequently. Young DuMont forgot himself, and even if his tart of a wife was a Mainwaring, he might do well to keep in mind that Dunsmore was a nonvoting Board member of GalaxCo. That was the only reason he would even consider coming to this drab little world, or being hosted by such unctuously common young functionaries. Spirit be praised, he only had to spend a week here, making the obligatory tours of the plantations and processing facilities. His eyes roved to the flimsy togs and pert young body of Rosalyn DuMont, and he made up his mind that he would bed the bitch before the week was up. It would be small enough compensation for such a tedious sojourn.

"What say to some more tennis?" Lady Dunsmore asked.

"Boys against girls, this time!" cried Rosalyn enthusiastically.

Her suggestion was greeted with a long moment of frosty silence by the Dunsmores. Lords and Ladies were seldom referred to as "boys and girls," certainly not by commoners, no matter how rich or well connected. Lord Dunsmore's face registered his disapproval. A slow consciousness of her blunder began to dawn on Rosalyn, and her features fell into a grimace of embarrassment and horror. Lord Dunsmore said nothing as his wife let the girl suffer a few seconds longer than was really necessary.

"Women against men, my dear," she said, breaking the tension while doing little to make Rosalyn feel any better. "A battle of the sexes, then," she added, eyeing Richard.

Lord Dunsmore didn't really want to play any more tennis, but he supposed that it would be preferable to sitting here and being insulted. "Very well," he said to Richard, ignoring his desolated young tart for the moment. "Have that—creature—fetch our rackets, if you would."

Richard raised his arm, snapped his fingers in the direction of one of the Myn servants and called, "Rackets!"

The nearest of the Myn servants seemed not to notice. It stood rooted in place, its head tilted upward toward the heavens.

DuMont sighed in frustration. "You see what we have to contend with here, my lord," he said to Lord Dunsmore. "The Myn are so damned dreamy and distracted, forever communing with their departed elders instead of keeping their pathetic little minds on the task at hand. It's hardly a wonder that the Home Office is dissatisfied with production in the plantations."

"Indeed," said Lord Dunsmore.

"I hope you'll make a point of mentioning it to them when you return home, my lord. If one hasn't actually seen the Myn, it's difficult to understand how truly impossible it is to get anything done in this place!"

"So it would seem," said Lord Dunsmore, gazing at the immobile Myn. "Can't you get its attention somehow? Perhaps a good swift kick?"

"It would hardly help, my lord," said DuMont. "Ah, one of them, at least, seems to have gotten the message." He nodded toward another of the Myn approaching their table. But Lord Dunsmore noted that it appeared to have picked up the wrong case. It didn't even look like a case for a tennis racket.

It wasn't. The Myn stopped ten feet away from the humans, opened the case, and stood there in front of them holding what appeared to be an automatic rifle of some sort. It looked to Lord Dunsmore like something he had once seen in a museum in Edinburgh. Curious, thought Lord Dunsmore, that such an antiquated device should turn up here.

It was the last thing Lord Dunsmore ever thought.

chapter 2

WHEN THE ROBOTIC COURIER FROM MYNJHINO burst back into normal space just inside the orbit of the asteroid belt and slightly below the plane of the ecliptic, Gloria VanDeen, Level XIII Dexta bureaucrat and Coordinating Supervisor for Division Beta-5, Sector 8, was staring at her computer console and trying to concentrate on the next Quarterly Resource Allocation report. The Dexta offices on the five worlds of Beta-5, one of which was Mynjhino, had already made their needs known to the five System Coordinators at HQ, and they had dutifully reported their desires to Gloria, whose task it was to sort the wheat from the bureaucratic chaff.

As usual, everyone had asked for much more than they needed in the faint hope of getting what they actually required. Pecos, a prosperous planet with a growing population, had requested authorization for eight additional Rated Staff and thirty Unrated Staff positions. Gloria skimmed the too-lengthy justification offered for the increase and arbitrarily cut the numbers to four and sixteen. By the time the QRA wended its way upward through Sector and Quadrant, Pecos would be lucky to wind up with two and eight—which was probably about what they actually needed. And as for the small, dismal mining colony on Gregson's Planet, just why, she wondered, did anyone there think they would get approval for a new node on their Orbital Station?

Gloria sighed, leaned back in her chair, and rubbed her eyes. The QRA was one of the more tedious scraps of bureaucratic effluvia that regularly came her way. But, she reminded herself—not for the first time—that she knew the job was tedious when she took it. This was routine, meat-and-potatoes stuff, and normally she cut right through it, but today she was having trouble staying focused. Her mind was elsewhere.

Specifically, it was in Rio. And the Emperor's Levee. For Spirit's sake, what could Charles have been thinking?

"His Imperial Highness, Charles V, is pleased to request the honor of your company..." Gloria shook her head slowly in lingering disbelief at the invitation. People had been known to kill for an invitation to a Levee, or, failing to get one, to kill themselves. Gloria's reaction to the invitation was not quite so extreme; she merely dreaded it.

They hadn't seen each other since she walked out on him, what seemed a lifetime ago. What did his Imperial Smugness want? And why now? And why did he think she would come?

And yet... Gloria felt some indefinable tug in her gut when she thought of Charles. It hadn't been *all* bad, and there were times when...

No, she told herself, it would definitely not do to think about *that*. Not at all. What she really needed to think about was the truly pressing issue of how many new cargo docks were actually necessary for the Gregson Orbital Station. Gloria returned to the QRA with a will.

• • •

MEANWHILE, THE COURIER FROM MYNJHINO oriented itself, then squirted out a high-intensity signal crammed with information, directed at the nearest Repeater. An hour later, having received confirmation of receipt, it used the last of its fuel to bend its trajectory away from the Sun and off toward interstellar space. Assured now that it posed no further threat to traffic in the inner solar system, the courier obligingly blew itself up, and its debris continued onward and outward at 92 percent of the speed of light.

Traveling at the speed of light, the courier's original signal, amplified by the Repeater, soon arrived at the receiving antennas of Central, a vast complex of such antennas hovering at a stable Lagrangian point in orbit above Earth. There, the signal was rerouted and beamed to another orbital complex and down to the waiting antennas of the Department of Extraterrestrial Affairs, stationed in a stunted meadow in northern New Jersey. A final change of direction allowed the information to complete the last twenty miles of its 5,000-trillion-mile journey, and it arrived at Dexta's offices in midtown Manhattan, where it was routed to the desk console of Level XIV System Coordinator Zoe Zachary, announcing its presence there with a loud, annoying electronic trill.

Zoe Zachary was currently busy elsewhere, in the women's restroom, but outside her office, Level XV staffer Gordon Chesbro heard the trill through the open door. Hidden by the low walls of his cubicle, Chesbro didn't hesitate, and, with a few deft but officially forbidden keystrokes, quickly violated at least three of Dexta's sacred IntRegs and transferred a copy of the message to his own console. The pudgy young man munched on a candy bar as he read the message, becoming the first person on Earth to learn of the deaths of Lord and Lady Dunsmore, along with fourteen other humans, which had occurred three days earlier on the distant world of Mynjhino.

Mynjhino was Chesbro's bailiwick, and no one in Dexta knew more about that planet and its inhabitants than he did—not even his boss, Zoe Zachary, whose responsibility they were. Zoe had other things on her mind much of the time, but Chesbro had no other function in Dexta—and barely any other function in life—than to absorb, process, and understand all that could be known about that rather odd planet, more than three-quarters of the way to the frontiers of the Empire. He could honestly say that he was not completely surprised by the news, although some of the details included in the report gave him pause.

Chesbro had only been in Dexta for three years, but he had already internalized the fundamental Dexta staffers' response to any piece of news that came their way from anywhere: *What does this mean for ME?* For Chesbro, in this case, it meant that his frequently written and universally ignored memos on the subject of unrest among the Myn had been proven correct. Sixteen lives seemed to him a small price to pay for such spectacular confirmation of the soundness of his expertise and instincts. Smiling as he licked crumbs of candy from his lips, he called up a particularly well crafted memo he'd written on the subject two months ago, enjoyed rereading it, then shot it over to Zoe's console, tagged to the incoming report.

He sat back in his chair and peered over the cubicle's modest walls to await the return of Zoe Zachary while congratulating himself on his foresight and good luck. Out of 2643 inhabited worlds in the Empire, Lord and Lady Dunsmore had managed to die on *his*, Spirit bless them! Things were going to start happening now.

He watched happily as Zoe Zachary returned to her office. She was a trim-looking woman of about thirty, and Gordon often had fantasies about her. She was no Gloria VanDeen, but then, who was? Zoe was of medium height, medium build, medium beauty, and there were no frills about her. She wore a very standard gray shirt, gray skirt, and gray jacket, covering what might possibly be outstanding breasts that Gordon had been sweatily dreaming about for the two years Zoe had been System Coordinator for Mynjhino. Of course, he was just a Level XV, and she was an exalted Level XIV, but a man's dreams should exceed his grasp, else what's a heaven for? He stared at her appreciatively for the three or four seconds it took her to enter her office and close the door behind her.

ZOE PAUSED INSIDE THE DOOR, SURPRISED and concerned by the alert signal wavering from her console. She knew what it meant, although it was a sound she had never heard before. It might be just some nervous bleating from that idiot of a Governor, Rhinehart, but Zoe doubted it. Couriers were expensive, and even Imperial Governors whose brains and bladders were as weak as Rhinehart's didn't expend them casually. In any case, it was much more likely that the alert had been issued by Imperial Secretary Melinda Throneberry, or her Undersecretary for Administration, Brian Hawkes, both of them reliable and competent people.

She sat down in front of her console and read the news, along with the self-serving memo Gordon Chesbro had foolishly attached to the bulletin. Chesbro had tapped into her console again, just to show how clever he was. Clever and intelligent, certainly; smart— never. If nothing else, his repeated violations of IntRegs had given her all the ammunition she required to dispose of him if the need ever arose. It might be wise to remind him of that salient fact. For now, though, he was valuable, if annoying. In an age when nearly everyone looked attractive and healthy, Chesbro had contrived to be neither, and his interpersonal skills bordered on nonexistent.

The bulletin itself was troubling, but Zoe wasted no time feeling sorry for the sixteen dead humans on

Mynjhino. She was more interested in the manner of their death, which apparently involved thousand-year-old antique weaponry that was nevertheless several centuries beyond the capabilities of either the Myn or the Jhino. When humans had first arrived on their planet eighty-five years ago, the Myn and Jhino were engaged in a war that relied on sailing vessels and primitive gunpowder projectiles, roughly equivalent to the technology employed in the Seven Years' War on Earth. The Empire had quickly ended their little war and set about civilizing and integrating the planet. The place was an oddity in that there were two separate, though related, intelligent species living on it. That circumstance presented complex but manageable problems for the Empire, and the colony had been relatively peaceful and even marginally profitable for decades.

Yet now, somehow, the Myn had acquired automatic weapons—*machine guns,* Spirit save us!—and were using them to kill humans. The report from Throneberry, with an uncredited rider obviously added by Hawkes, was as thorough as possible under the circumstances. The attack at a GalaxCo corporate club had been carried out by at least five and possibly as many as seven Myn, some of them posing as menials. Every human in the place had been slaughtered, and the eyewitness reports from the Myn workers—none of whom had been harmed—were predictably vague and contradictory.

The club was five hundred miles upcountry from the Myn capital city of Dhanj, the largest metropolitan center on the planet, with a population of about a million Myn. All told, there were about 100 million Myn on the Eastern Continent, and about as many Jhino on the Western Continent. The Jhino tended to be more focused and productive than the vague and dreamy Myn, yet it was apparently the Myn who had launched the bloody and unprovoked attack.

For some time, reports from the planet had mentioned the activities of a nativist movement among the

Myn, known as the Myn-Traha. The movement seemed to draw most of its support from among the plantation workers who tended GalaxCo's corporate fields. Some of the unrest could be ascribed to the usual labor problems that could be found on almost every colony with an indigenous population. The people at GalaxCo could be remarkably obtuse and insensitive, even where their own best interests were concerned, but in that they were no worse than any of the other Big Twelve. But GalaxCo was the major operator on Myn, and would be an obvious focus for the resentment of the Myn-Traha. Imperium, Ltd. confined most of its operations to extraction activities on Jhino, and had encountered fewer problems than GalaxCo. Servitor was active on both continents and seemed minimally affected by the nativists. None of the remaining Twelve maintained more than a token presence on the planet.

Not a great deal was known about the Myn-Traha. Ricardo Olivera, the young Undersecretary for Security, had been on the job less than a year and had yet to show any sign of exceptional competence or ability. His predecessor had attempted to establish a network among the Myn nativists, but with little apparent success, and the situation had not improved under Olivera. Zoe remembered a memo from Hawkes a few months earlier in which he mentioned having established a contact among the Myn-Traha, but there had been no follow-up.

The Myn-Traha had been no more than a vague and poorly understood irritation until now, but the real mystery was how the hell they had managed to acquire automatic weapons. They could have manufactured them domestically, although the Jhino, rather than the Myn, were the ones who had developed meaningful industrial skills. It hardly seemed likely that the Jhino would be supplying their ancient rivals with weaponry that was, by local standards, sophisticated. That left smuggling, which would make it a matter for Internal Security. But Zoe had seen no reports from the Bugs suggesting any such activity in the Mynjhino region, or, for that matter, anywhere inside the Beta-5 jurisdiction. Still, maybe Gloria knew something that she didn't. Zoe was only responsible for Mynjhino, although she tried to keep up to speed with developments in the other four systems entrusted to Beta-5.

Zoe read over the report again, then quickly scanned Chesbro's smart-ass memo that had more or less predicted trouble on Myn. She hit the Condense & Extract function, and seconds later the ten-page memo was pared down to a single page. She read over it, made a few changes, deleted Chesbro's name and inserted her own, then sent the whole package on to Gloria VanDeen.

She sat quietly at her console for a few minutes, considering what was likely to happen next. It seemed a real possibility that she would be dispatched to Mynjhino herself, an attractive opportunity for a System Coordinator. It was a chance to be Noticed, and nothing could be more important to an ambitious Level XIV. Being Noticed, however, carried with it the very real possibility of winding up holding the short end of something she would rather not be holding at all. Still, that was part of the drill at Dexta, and Zoe accepted the risks.

Mynjhino was just under nine days away for a Dexta Flyer. If Zoe got the call, she would be allowed to take along an assistant, which meant either Gordon Chesbro or Elaine Murakami. The thought of being trapped in a tiny Flyer for nine days with Gordon Chesbro was nearly enough to make her gag. Granted, no one knew more about Mynjhino than Chesbro, but that was a plausible reason to leave him behind to mind the shop. Elaine Murakami, then. She was smart and a little too obviously ambitious—a Gloria VanDeen in the making, minus the money, connections, and overwhelming physical presence. But Elaine made the most of what she had, and would surely try to show her up on Mynjhino. That didn't worry Zoe; she could handle Elaine. If it came to that, she thought, she might even be able to handle Gloria.

ZOE WALKED DOWN THE CORRIDOR TO THE office of Beta-5 Coordinating Supervisor Gloria VanDeen, Level XIII, and confronted Gloria's principal assistant and gatekeeper, Petra Nash, Level XV. Petra was a compact, mousy-cute young woman still learning the ropes at Dexta. It remained to be seen how long she would survive, but Gloria seemed to like her, so Zoe trod more lightly with her than she might have with another Level XV. Anyway, Zoe liked her too.

"Gloria's going to want to see me in about two minutes," Zoe told Petra.

"Then why don't you sit down and wait for two minutes?" Petra asked her politely.

Zoe smiled, and Petra smiled back at her. Zoe didn't appreciate being blocked by Petra, but two minutes hardly mattered. "And how has your day been?" she asked.

"Just fine, Zoe. And yours?"

"Couldn't be better," Zoe assured her. "How is Herself?"

"Busy," Petra replied vaguely.

"Is she going to that Imperial Levee tonight?"

"Watch the vid tonight and find out," Petra suggested. "I'm going to. All those gorgeous men, dripping with money! I'm going to sit down with a gallon of fudge-ripple ice cream and pig out on sensory excess."

"I have other plans," Zoe said with lofty nonchalance, although she didn't. In another world, Zoe might have asked Petra to share her fudge-ripple and the two of them would have had a fun, girly evening together making catty remarks about the glamorous nobs at the Levee. But not in the world of Dexta.

A light on Petra's console illuminated, and she

nodded to Zoe. "She'll see you now," she said. Zoe nodded back and opened the door to Gloria's office.

Gloria was staring at her console, but raised a hand toward Zoe and waved her in. Zoe closed the door and took a seat, then waited while Gloria continued reading the alert from Mynjhino.

Gloria's office was about twice the size of Zoe's, but it still seemed small with Gloria in it. Gloria was like liquid, like quicksilver; she seemed to flow and expand to fill whatever space she was in, somehow diminishing anyone else who shared it with her. Zoe felt herself shrinking in Gloria's presence.

Zoe couldn't help staring at her. Despite her Dutch surname, Gloria VanDeen's genetic heritage was thoroughly mixed, which was common enough after a millennium of global culture and several centuries of on-again, off-again flirtation with DNA sculpting. Gloria's flawless skin was the color of coffee with a little cream in it, darker than Euro, lighter than Polynesian. Her complexion was set off by long, gracefully flowing blond tresses the color of honey. She obviously had it Dura-styled, so she probably got out of bed each morning with not a hair out of place. That was an extravagance Zoe couldn't really afford—and her short, practical cut suited her just fine, in any case.

Gloria's eyes were set at an angle that was vaguely suggestive of Asia, but their intense, sky-blue color, almost turquoise, called to mind fjords and lochs. Her cheekbones were high and broad, tapering down to a narrow, delicately shaped chin. Her nose was short and straight. If she had a flaw, it was her mouth, which was a little too determined, her lips a little too thin, for perfection.

The rest of her body had no flaws at all. Her breasts were firm and globular, not especially large, but they seemed bigger than they really were thanks to her very slim waist. They were only minimally covered at the moment, since she wore nothing under the gray jacket buttoned at her waist. Her gray skirt was dangerously short, revealing the entirety of her long, taut, and well-toned legs.

There was no doubt about it: the complete VanDeen package registered somewhere beyond spectacular, and she was fully aware of it. Zoe neither envied nor resented Gloria, but simply accepted her as she was, another fact of life in Dexta. Having Gloria for a boss carried with it certain advantages and hazards, and Zoe confidently charted her course to exploit the one and avoid the other. Women tended to fade to near invisibility in her presence, but invisibility could be a good survival trait in Dexta. Gloria was smart, skilled, and successful, and all of that could rub off on those around her. Most importantly, Gloria was not likely to be around for very long. She would either move up quickly or just as quickly fall flat on her beautiful face. Fall, or be pushed. Zoe was not above providing the shove, should the right circumstances arise. This Mynjhino business might even provide certain opportunities along those lines. It bore watching.

Gloria looked up from her console and gave Zoe a quick, automatic smile. "Well," she said, "interesting development, wouldn't you say?"

Zoe returned the smile. "Interesting, indeed," she agreed.

"You think it's the Myn-Traha?"

"That would be the best bet, for the moment."

"Uh-huh," Gloria said, nodding. "I had them pegged as annoying but not dangerous. The Myn seem too otherworldly to organize themselves that efficiently. Still, I suppose it only takes one silver-tongued devil to set them in motion."

"The Myn don't have tongues," Zoe pointed out. Gloria didn't look thrilled to receive that piece of information, so Zoe gave her some more. "They have these cilia hanging down from the roof of their mouth. Pretty disgusting to see them eat, actually. But you're right, the

Myn-Traha had all the elements in place for a terrorist movement. All they needed was leadership and organization, and it would seem that someone has provided that."

"Right," said Gloria. "I suggest you cross-reference the Tai-Pings in nineteenth-century China, the Islamic fundamentalist groups in the twentieth and twenty-first, the Upang Rebellion on Ficus IV in the twenty-fifth, the Seven Dragons Movement in the twenty-eighth, and, of course, the Heavenly Uprising in the thirty-first. The Myn-Traha are religion-based, and we might find some common elements that would be useful."

"Check," said Zoe. In spite of herself, she was impressed by the way Gloria reeled off the historical analogues. Zoe hadn't thought of the Upangs until Gloria mentioned them.

"Now," Gloria continued, "any thoughts on the weapons?"

"Smuggling seems more likely than local manufacture. It would help if we could get our hands on the guns they used, but they didn't leave any behind."

"Hawkes has pretty close ties to the nativists, doesn't he? Maybe he'll be able to come up with something on that end. In the meantime, I'll check with IntSec on the smuggling angle. There have been no reports of any activity in Beta-5, but the Bugs don't always tell us everything they know. I'll lean on Bianca Warren, and you see what you can get from her Coordinator for Mynjhino."

"That would be Fred Nakajima," said Zoe. "If your skirt were on fire, Fred wouldn't tell you unless you asked him."

"So ask him. If they've got smuggling operations going on under their noses in Beta-5, they either know or don't know. Either way, this incident makes them look bad. Offer a helping hand, and look deeply concerned for poor Fred's welfare."

Zoe smiled. "Poor Fred."

"Poor *us*, Zoe. Lord and Lady Dunsmore bought the farm on *your* planet. Questions will be asked. Notice will be taken." She stared meaningfully at Zoe.

Zoe swallowed and nodded silently. Gloria turned back to her console for a moment, her perfectly formed left nipple flashing briefly into view as she did so. Zoe felt oddly intimidated.

"I'll write up something for Public Affairs," Gloria said, turning back to look at Zoe. "I'll refer them to you for details on Mynjhino, so be ready for a lot of stupid questions from the PAOs. Just make sure your answers aren't as stupid as their questions. We've got to look sharp on this thing."

"Sharp," Zoe agreed.

"And, of course, I'll bounce it all upstairs to Balthazar. And Gladys, too, since she'll have to coordinate with IntSec. But it's going to land on Grant's desk, and he's not going to be happy about it. For one thing, it will ruin Hector Konrad's day, and he'll go running to Kwan and Ringold, who will want to see blood on the floor, unless I miss my guess. What are you, Zoe, Type O?"

Zoe smiled nervously at Gloria's feeble but ominous jest. Gloria had run through the roster of all the upper echelon people who held her fate in their hands, strictly for Zoe's benefit. A gentle reminder of how low Zoe stood on the Sector 8 food chain. Zoe felt her internal organs twisting into knots. She could not recall feeling so thoroughly intimidated in all her time at Dexta. And, of course, that was precisely what Gloria wanted her to feel. Zoe decided to show that she was made of stronger stuff.

"Someone should go to Mynjhino," Zoe said, trying to sound confident and assured.

"Possibly," said Gloria. She looked Zoe up and down, as if mentally measuring her for a coffin. "You want it?"

"I do," Zoe answered.

"Uh-huh," Gloria said inscrutably. "We'll see. Now go get your ducks in a row, Zoe."

"Yes, ma'am," Zoe responded, instantly hating herself for it. She nodded to Gloria, then left her office as quickly as she could. She hurried past Petra without so much as a glance and headed for the nearest restroom. There was a very real chance that she was going to be sick.

GLORIA LEANED BACK IN HER CHAIR AND sighed. She wondered if she had been a little too overbearing with Zoe. The woman was an excellent System Coordinator and probably had a bright future ahead of her at Dexta, unless something like this Mynjhino business blew up in her face. Ripples from such an explosion would propagate all the way up the line to Sector Administrator Lars Ringold, Level VII, and maybe even on up to Quadrant. But Zoe, at ground zero, would be disintegrated by the blast, and all her competence and intelligence wouldn't matter at all. And Gloria, one rung above, could be sent spinning off into the void by the force of the shock waves.

No, she decided, she had been fair with Zoe. If anything, maybe she should have been tougher on her. If you can't stand the traffic, Gloria reminded herself, don't play in the street.

Petra stuck her head into the office. "Your mother called," she said. "I told her you couldn't be disturbed at the moment. She said she'd call back."

"Thanks, Petra."

Petra paused before leaving. "Anything wrong?" she asked. "Can I help?"

"Oh," said Gloria wearily, "alarums and excursions. Give me a couple of minutes and I'll have your marching orders for you." Petra nodded and retreated, closing the door behind her.

Gloria turned back to her console and called up the

list of victims. She didn't want to forget about the fact
that sixteen people had just died. It was too easy to lose
sight of details like that.

Lord and Lady Dunsmore, of course. Minor nobility,
minor personalities, minor lives, now ended. Imperial
would handle that end of it. Gloria moved on down the
list and saw the name of Richard DuMont, a GalaxCo regional manager. She had known someone by that name
in school, she realized. She called up the Passport Office
records and saw DuMont's face displayed. She recognized it.

He had been one of the hangers-on that Charles attracted like clouds of gnats. Friendly, eager, fawning. He
had dared to squeeze her ass once, Gloria remembered.
He probably bragged about that now—or did. Married
to Rosalyn Mainwaring, no children. Gloria knew the
Mainwarings, of course, but had never met Rosalyn.
Attractive young couple on the rise. Sad.

Gloria moved on through the rest of the list and was
glad to see that she had never heard of any of them. But
someone knew them, and would have to be notified. Re-
grets, condolences, and the official end of a life. Gloria
loved her job, but there were times when she loved it a
little less than at others.

She read through Zoe's memo that accompanied
the report from Mynjhino and realized that it was really
Gordon Chesbro's work. Chesbro knew Mynjhino inside
and out and would be a valuable resource in the days
ahead. If she sent Zoe off-planet, Gloria realized that she
would probably have to consult closely with Chesbro—
an unappealing prospect. Unless, of course, she sent
Gordon along with Zoe. She had to smile at the thought.

Gloria added a couple of paragraphs to the memo,
made a few changes, deleted Zoe's name and inserted
her own, then sent the whole package onward and upward to her immediate superiors, Balthazar Trobriand
and Gladys Pymm, and also to Deputy Sector Supervisor, Beta Division, Grant Enright, Level XI. That was as

high as she could officially communicate directly, but she expected to be hearing from Sector Supervisor Hector Konrad, Level X, before much time passed. She also shot the whole package over to Petra's console, so she could share in the fun.

Petra came in a moment later. "A real mess, huh?" she said.

Gloria nodded. "I need you to write up a notification for the next of kin, except for the Dunsmores. We are saddened, regretful, and so forth. Don't give any details. Let me see it when you're done, then send them out immediately."

"Shouldn't we wait for the official release?"

Gloria shook her head. "That should come within the hour. But I don't want those poor people to have to find out from the evening vids. Or worse, from a journalist calling to ask them how they feel about the tragic demise of their loved one. Get right on it, Petra."

"Gotcha. Oh, and your mother is on hold."

Gloria sighed. "Put her through."

Petra departed and Gloria turned to her console. "Hi, Mom," she said, trying to sound happier than she felt at the moment.

Her mother's face appeared before her on the console. She had done something rather odd with her hair, but other than that she looked great, as she always did. She was sixty-two, but looked like Gloria's slightly older sister. At the rate this job was aging her, Gloria reflected, in a couple of years Mom would be able to pass for the younger sister.

"Gloria, dear, you look tired."

"Rough day at the office, Mom. But I'm fine."

"And you're coming to the Levee, of course."

"Is that tonight? I totally forgot," Gloria lied.

"Don't give me any of your nonsense, young lady," Mom scolded. "You *be* there!"

"Mom, you know I hate those things."

"Since when? You used to be the belle of the ball at the old Emperor's Levees."

"We've got a different Emperor these days, in case you forgot."

"And Charles will expect to see you there."

"Mom . . ."

"I don't want to hear it, Glory. You'll have to see him sometime, and it might just as well be tonight. Anyway, the whole VanDeen side of the family will be there, even your great-grandparents. *They'll* certainly expect to see you. Be nice, Glory, even if it kills you."

"Mom," Gloria protested, "I just don't want to see him."

"Don't be ridiculous. He won't bite. Anyway, I know for a fact, from Lady Skylar herself, that he is looking forward to seeing you. And if you don't come voluntarily, he's perfectly capable of sending out a squad of Imperial Marines to drag you there. He'd do it, you know."

He would, too, Gloria realized.

"Okay, Mom," Gloria said at last. "See you in Rio."

Her mother smiled radiantly, then signed off.

Gloria wondered idly if everyone's ex-husband was such a pain in the ass. Probably, she concluded. But hers, alas, happened to be a *royal* pain in the ass.

chapter **3**

SECTOR SUPERVISOR HECTOR KONRAD, LEVEL X, was unhappy, so it followed that everyone else in Sector Admin had to be unhappy, too. Gloria certainly was after Konrad concluded his lengthy and unpleasant call. Konrad had never liked her, for all the obvious reasons and a few that weren't so obvious. He could hardly be expected to pass up an opportunity like this to ream her out from stem to stern, pillar to post, lengthwise, sidewise, and every other-wise. His enjoyment in the task was so obvious that Gloria had struck back with the least creditable weapon at her disposal. She hated to cut their discussion short, she had told him, but she really did have to go; she was expected that evening at the Emperor's Levee. Konrad had reacted to that as if someone had hit him in the face with a dead rat.

Gloria always felt ashamed whenever she hauled out her Imperial connections, although in this instance she didn't regret it. Konrad had it coming. Of course, he would have his vengeance sooner or later. He was Level X, she was Level XIII, and that was all that really mattered, Imperial connections notwithstanding. Unless Gloria took care to cover her ass—or, conceivably, uncover it more completely—Konrad could go a long way toward making her life a living hell.

Speaking of uncovering her ass, she realized that really did have to get moving if she was going make it to the Levee on time. She grabbed her purse and left her office, locking the door behind her, and smiled good night to Petra.

"You're going tonight, aren't you?" Petra asked. "You are, I can tell. You've got that Imperial gleam in your eye."

Gloria smiled icily, and said, "Good night, Petra."

"I'll watch for you on the vid," Petra called as her boss made her way down the corridor.

Gloria noticed the usual heads sticking out of the usual doors as she passed. What did they have, she wondered, some sort of jungle grapevine? Somehow, they always knew when she was leaving.

Gloria filed into the Level XIII Transit, waited her turn at the ring, exchanged some very small talk with fellow Coordinating Supervisors Gwendolyn Jacinto and Allen Brahmaputra, then stepped through into the main concourse in Brooklyn. Gwen and Allen, and nearly everyone else, peeled off to the right to enter the Residence, but Gloria headed left, toward the parking lot.

Dexta provided housing for nearly all of its Manhattan staff at the Residence in Brooklyn. The housing was, of course, segregated by Level, ensuring that like socialized with like. The XIII housing was quite nice—two-bedroom apartments in the West Tower, with an impressive view of the Harbor and all the usual amenities. Since most Thirteens were single, the apartments gave them plenty of room to spread out—a psychological necessity after spending ten or twelve hours in the Manhattan offices.

Dexta actively discouraged marriage, at least by the lower-level personnel, and was nearly adamant on the subject of children. Dexta people were supposed to be married to their jobs, and if they attempted to be doting spouses or dutiful parents as well, then they were clearly not giving their all to Dexta. And Dexta demanded nothing less.

Gloria's refusal to live in the Residence was counted against her by those who kept track of the score, but she considered it a relatively minor matter. They had plenty of other things to count against her and would find more if they could, so one more or less didn't seem cause for additional concern.

In the parking garage, Gloria slid into her sleek Ferrari skimmer, fired it up, and took off. In less than a minute, she was out of the Residence and cruising on auto along the Skyway East. She kicked her shoes off, turned on some loud music, and relaxed for the first time all day. Dexta slowly drained out of her and she began to feel marginally human again. She wiggled her toes, scratched her butt, and stretched like a cat.

The Levee. "Go down to the lev-ee, I said to the lev-ee," Gloria sang, the words to the ancient ditty welling up from somewhere in her subconscious. She changed the music to Mississippi Delta Blues, and sang along with it in as ballsy and bluesy a voice as she could manage. She was convinced that somewhere in her family tree, there had to have been a black, cotton-pickin', likker-lovin' blues singer. At a minimum, there was a man in her life who had done her wrong.

Gloria was only twenty-three. People who hadn't seen her personnel file thought she was at least five years older, and she didn't discourage that belief. Even young, naïve Petra was two years older than she was. But she had crammed a lot of living into twenty-three years. Married at fifteen, divorced at eighteen, an advanced degree at twenty, and three years in Dexta, rising swiftly from XV to XIII. The youngest Thirteen in the history of Dexta, if the truth be known. Somewhere along the line, she had even had something resembling a childhood.

And now Charles wanted to see her again. Swell.

If she had known the bastard was going to become Emperor someday, she would never have married him. But in those days, he was only seventh in line, then sixth, after old Darius IV finally expired. Gregory III had only been fifty when he ascended, and could reasonably be expected to live for at least another hundred years. And if he didn't, he had two sons and three other nephews who could be counted on to pick up the reins and keep Charles safely away from them. But then came the Fifth of October Plot, and suddenly there was no one left but a stunned and callow Charles. Thank the Spirit she had dumped him two years earlier!

Maybe he had grown up a little in the five years since she had seen him face-to-face. He could hardly have avoided it. News reports seemed to indicate that he had, but news reports tended to indicate whatever the Imperial Household wanted them to indicate. She would believe it only when she saw it for herself—which she was about to do, she remembered. Mom, she thought, why did I let you drag me into this?

She was coming up on her turnoff. Gloria flipped to manual, ignored the electronic protest from the Skyway, and veered sharply to the right, breezing over the marshes of southern Long Island at an altitude of about five feet. She angled southeast, toward the coast. The State Troopers no longer even bothered with her. She zipped between two houses and out onto the beach, where she revved the Ferrari up to its max and frightened the fishes as she zoomed over them. The acceleration pushed her back into the seat, and a broad grin spread across her face. Gloria turned up the blues till the instrument panel shook, and shouted "Yeeeowwww!" at the top of her lungs.

Five minutes later, she parked in the carport of her house in the dunes, got out, peeled off her jacket and skirt, then dived into the pool. She stroked back and forth vigorously for a few minutes, then rolled over on her back and watched the darkening skies above her as she floated in tranquility.

She was already running late, so she didn't have time for the full sequence of Qatsima exercises that she normally performed after her dip. The discipline, developed some five hundred years earlier by humans and the indigenous race on the world of Songchai, combined elements of ballet, martial arts, and acrobatics. She had taken it up after she left Charles, as a way of calming her mind and toning her body, but she continued it now simply because she enjoyed it and was good at it.

Gloria stood by the edge of the pool, balanced herself precisely on the ball of her left foot and toes, then slowly bent her back and left leg as she raised her right leg until it was nearly vertical. She reached up with her right hand, almost to her toes, then gently toppled over in a controlled fall that ended in a forward somersault from which she sprang up into a triple scissors kick that would have broken the neck of anyone standing there. Like, say, Hector Konrad. She repeated the move three more times, then called it quits. Her mind was as calm as it was going to get, and poor Hector had suffered enough for one day.

Getting later by the minute, Gloria ran into the house, stepped briefly into the statodryer, stepped out again, and shook her head violently for a couple of seconds. Her hair, streaming halfway down her back, responded to the signal and pulled itself back into Dura-styled order.

She had chosen her dress while drifting in the pool. Nothing too extreme, she had decided, bearing in mind that this was an Emperor's Levee and not a Sunday afternoon tea party. Gloria pulled the dress out of her closet and it floated down over her head. She smoothed it out, glanced in the mirror, and pronounced herself satisfied. The dress was made of a smart fabric that changed color in a randomly varying pattern, cycling from a deep scarlet through vermilion, purple, and violet, punctuated by starbursts of gold and silver. The wide, U-shaped neckline was deep enough to reveal twin sunrises of areola just above the fabric, which was as far as she intended to go this evening. The dress displayed as much cleavage in back as it did in front, and was slit from ankles to waist along each flank. Nothing too extreme. She added some ridiculously expensive diamond earrings and some bangles for her wrists, then was out the door.

GLORIA SKIMMED BACK TO THE DEXTA RESI-dence in Brooklyn and used the Transit facilities there. The Transit pinched together bits of the fabric of space, connecting them and permitting instantaneous travel between distant points. It worked beautifully for travel on Earth, but the power requirements were too great to make it practical for longer distances. Dexta had a Transit available for VIPs traveling to the Moon, and people who could afford it preferred reaching Earthport, out in geosynch, via Transit rather than liftship. But even a world as nearby as Mars was beyond the practical limits of Transit technology. Despite centuries of effort by scientists, interstellar Transit remained a dream; it would require all the energy output of a small star just to make a Transit to Alpha Centauri.

Gloria made the trip to Rio in two hops, and a third hop brought her to the gates of the Imperial Residence. It was one of six, one on each continent, and once a year each of them played host to an Imperial Levee. At each Levee, the local elites were given a chance to brush shoulders with Imperial nobility and the Emperor himself. She passed through a painstaking security check, then entered the grounds.

She knew the Rio Residence well, having spent a fair amount of time there when she was married to Charles. To the extent that they'd had a home at all, it was here. After Charles finally graduated and persuaded

Gloria to suspend her studies, they had spent most of their time flitting about the Empire in Charles's private yacht. It was a fun and exciting life, she had to admit, at least for a while. During their days of roaming among the worlds, Gloria developed first an affinity, then a passion, for exosociology and the study of colonial and indigenous cultures. Her decision to return to school and complete her degree had been the proximate cause of their divorce, but there were plenty of deeper causes.

The architecture of the Residence relied heavily on swooping arches and cavernous halls, including a main ballroom that could have hosted soccer matches. Gloria strolled slowly through the familiar surroundings, trying to resist the nostalgia they invoked. There were too many memories for comfort. They had once made love on that sofa, Gloria remembered, and over there on that Persian rug, and once they had even gotten a maintenance ladder, climbed up into that immense chandelier, and tried it *there*. And that had been the problem, really. Charles was too willing to try it anywhere...and with anyone. Too damn many *anyones*.

Gloria took a glass of champagne from a passing waiter and stood near one wall, watching the swarms of well-dressed—and well-undressed—people passing by. Everyone was rich and beautiful, and there were more bare breasts and bare bottoms on view than even Charles could hope to possess. High Imperial culture had always emphasized elegance and beauty, and, depending on the Emperor, nudity was considered either fashionable or nearly mandatory. Gloria remembered her early teenage years, in the waning days of Darius IV, when practically everybody who was anybody appeared at High Imperial events wearing little to nothing, including her own parents and young Gloria herself. Things became more restrictive under the dour Gregory III, but Charles's ascension seemed to herald a new era of overripe excess.

Of course, these days nearly everyone was a Spiritist, so nudity was no longer considered to be shameful or particularly shocking. The Spirit herself had been nude during each of her Seven Visitations, and Spiritist pastors were expected to address their congregations in the altogether on Visitation Days. Gloria didn't know whether she really believed in the Spirit or not, but as religions went, Spiritism had much to recommend it.

At heart, she supposed that the Cynics' explanation for the whole phenomenon was the most plausible. After more than a century of bloody religious warfare, in 2117—1099 years ago—the Spirit had made her Seven Visitations. Forty feet tall, beautiful, ethereal, and nude, she had appeared suddenly before a soccer match here in Rio, followed by other Visitations at the Rose Bowl in California, a youth rally in Beijing, a pilgrimage on the banks of the Ganges, a slum in Cairo, a carnival in France, and finally—and most memorably—in the midst of a battlefield in Central Africa. Before stunned but adoring crowds, she spoke lovingly, glowingly, of the Seven Seeds of Wisdom—Love, Compassion, Tolerance, Generosity, Knowledge, Joy, and Peace. And then she was gone, leaving behind a new religion that swept the world and helped usher in an age of global unity and peace.

If the Cynics were right, the whole thing had been a sham concocted by a group of scientists who were weary of war and believed the world needed an emphatic shove in the direction of peace. If people insisted on believing in the supernatural, the scientists decided, then they would give them a supernatural being who was at least worthy of being followed. So they invented the Spirit as an alternative to all the vengeful, bloody-minded deities inexplicably worshiped by so many for so long. The Spirit, the Cynics claimed, was nothing more than a sophisticated holographic projection, and her Gospel a collection of catchphrases devised by advertising copywriters in league with the scientists. All of that might well be true, Gloria thought, although no evidence had ever turned up to prove it. But even if it was a sham, it was a beautiful sham, and it worked.

More than 70 percent of the Empire's human population now called themselves Spiritists. Spiritism's appeal was universal, and it made few unreasonable demands upon the faithful. Unlike other religions, Spiritism was even in favor of sex ("Do not deny yourself Joy, for it is a gift unto humankind, and the wellspring of happiness") and discouraged fanatical devotion ("Believe if you will, or doubt if you must, but hear my words and think of me, for I am with you always"). Even those who still celebrated Christmas and Ramadan did so with a loving nod to the Spirit, and major sects of Hinduism and Buddhism incorporated the Spirit into their dogma. In consequence, no one had fought a religious war on Earth for more than a thousand years. What more could anyone ask of a religion?

As she mused about religion, Gloria drifted through the Residence, out to the rear lawn, and looked up toward the stars. *Her* stars. Sector 8, one of twenty-four, occupied a wedge of the cosmos extending from the south celestial pole to the celestial equator, subtending thirty degrees of arc. It was difficult to see from New York, but here it was high overhead. None of the stars in Beta-5 were even visible to the naked eye, but Gloria knew where they were and stared in their direction.

She shivered with awe. For all the absurdities of the Empire and its current Emperor, and for all the smug bureaucratic pretensions of Dexta, the Empire was a glorious and spectacular achievement. It gave her chills to realize that she was part of it, and that she played a role in shaping its destiny. At twenty-three, she already had direct responsibility for the well-being, prosperity, and happiness of over a billion sentient beings. She shook her head slowly and smiled. "Not bad, kid," she said to herself, "not bad."

"*There* you are!" cried her mother. "I was so afraid you were going to let us down again." Gloria embraced her parents. Her mother looked terrific, as always, draped with silken sashes of alternating colors and transparency, and her father was ever the healthy and hearty yachtsman. They were two warm, loving, happy, attractive, fabulously wealthy, and thoroughly useless people. She loved them dearly, but had never wanted to be like them. As far as she knew, neither of them had ever held an actual job, and they couldn't quite comprehend why their daughter should want to. They were content to live off the fat of the land and their ancestors' labors, and didn't understand why that should not satisfy Gloria as well.

Some of those ancestors were here with them. The VanDeen elders were having a family reunion, and Gloria hugged her grandparents and great-grandparents. They made quite a collection, and Gloria thought she could see bits of herself in each of them. Her grandmother was Southeast Asian—French Polynesian—and Gloria's eyes were set at the same exotic angle as hers. The blue of her eyes and the golden honey color of her hair were the contribution of her great-grandfather VanDeen, a smiling Dutchman, and her skin color was closest to that of Great-grandmother Umbeki, a tall, lithe Ethiopian. Of course, she also shared some traits with her mother's family, none of whom were here tonight. On that side of her family tree, there were Japanese, Cherokees, Zulus, Brazilians, Swedes, and Australian aborigines. And if her natural combination of African, Asian, and European features were not enough, at various times over the centuries, some genetic tinkering had occurred, bringing out the best features of each racial group.

However it happened, all that disparate DNA had combined to produce Gloria. Her mother always claimed that Gloria had popped out of the womb perfect and beautiful, and had gotten more perfect and more beautiful each day. Her mother, for once, was hardly exaggerating. Even in this august assemblage, Gloria was by all odds the most spectacularly beautiful woman present, and she attracted more than her share of stares, despite her modest attire.

"Why so conservative, dear?" her mother asked her with a disapproving frown when they had a moment alone. "There are so many luscious young men here! Don't you want to be noticed?" Her mother tugged at the fabric of Gloria's bodice and liberated her perfect nipples.

"Mom," Gloria said as she tucked them back in, "if I have to see Charles tonight, I don't want to give him the wrong idea. Or *any* ideas."

"Now, Gloria, you know you haven't seen him in five years. Don't go prejudging. I know he hurt you, but you were both very young, and now you've both grown up. Give him a chance."

Gloria saw where this was leading. "Don't *you* go getting any ideas, either, Mom! There is not a chance in hell that we will ever get back together, so just get that little notion out of your head, okay? You are never going be the Empress's mum. Not unless you and Dad get back into the baby business," she added with a grin. "Maybe the next one won't be such a tragic disappointment for you."

"Oh, now, Glory," her mother protested, "your father and I are both very, very proud of you. We just want you to be happy, that's all. And frankly, dear, I don't think that job at Dexta is making you happy."

"You're wrong," Gloria told her flatly. "In fact, just before you saw me, I was standing here looking at the stars, thinking about how much I love my job, and how happy it makes me to do what I do."

Her mother looked into her eyes. "Really, dear?"

Gloria nodded and smiled. "Really."

"Then I'm happy, too." Her mother kissed her lightly on the cheek. "Now," she added, "if you could just find yourself a good *man* . . ."

• • •

GLORIA SEPARATED FROM HER FAMILY AND wandered aimlessly across the crowded lawn, sipping champagne and humming a blues tune to herself. The warm Rio breeze felt soft and sensuous on her undraped backside. She was glad she had come, after all. She had spent much of her youth at similar gatherings, and from the time she first blossomed, she had been a center of attention. Gloria smiled to herself as she remembered the last Levee here under Darius IV, when she had strolled the grounds wearing nothing but a diamond tiara and a star sapphire in her belly button. By the time Charles spotted her a year later, at fifteen, she had already broken a thousand young hearts. Charles, a dashing and seemingly mature nineteen at the time, had set about sweeping her off her feet, and succeeded all too well. The memory was not entirely painful for her, she had to admit, and there were still long, lonely nights when she found herself thinking of him, and longing for him.

"No, Gloria," she upbraided herself, "this will *not* do!"

"What won't do?"

Gloria spun around and found herself staring at Althea Dante, Coordinating Supervisor for Imperial Affairs, Quadrant 2, Sector 8, Division Beta-5, Level XIII, and all-around bitch. "Why, Althea," she exclaimed, trading air-kisses with her, "how nice to see you here."

"And what a surprise to see you, Gloria. I thought you were boycotting Levees these days. Myself, I never miss one."

"So I hear," Gloria said dryly. Althea had famously humped her way through most of the Imperial Family, male and female, including Charles—before, during, and after his marriage to Gloria. The wonder was that she was still only a Thirteen after more than ten years at Dexta. Poor Althea must be pushing thirty-five, Gloria reckoned. If she had devoted as much time to her job as she did to bedding royals, she'd already be at least an Eleven.

Althea was wearing nothing but a confusion of white and black pearl strands that randomly covered her here and there but did nothing to hide her small, pointy breasts and very little to conceal her crotch. She was a smallish woman with fair skin, dark hair, and violet eyes. She was beautiful, perhaps, but not stunning, and wore too much makeup. Sometimes Gloria thought she could detect just a hint of desperation about her, as if somewhere along the way she had let too many opportunities slip from her grasp.

"Have you seen Charles yet?" Althea asked, not without a hint of malice.

"I expect he'll find me, sooner or later," Gloria said.

"Yes, well, I suppose he hasn't noticed you yet, dear. That dress really doesn't do you justice, you know. You should let everyone see those wonderful tits of yours, Gloria. It's such a disappointment."

"Well, I'll come to the Coordinating Supervisors meeting tomorrow topless, just for you, Althea."

"Ooh," Althea cackled, "wouldn't it just be delicious if you really did? Still, it is going to be a rather difficult meeting tomorrow, isn't it, what with your little mess on Mynjhino?"

"*Our* little mess, Althea."

"Oh, you Admin types always say that. But Imperial really has nothing to do with it, you know. Our part is limited to sending condolences for Lord and Lady Dunsmore, those poor, poor darlings. But I can tell you in confidence, Gloria, that the Household is really quite perturbed by what happened. Of course, you must know that Charles was intimate with Lady Dunsmore at one time."

"For ten minutes, I'd guess," Gloria replied. "Fifteen, if she was lucky."

"Ah, but Gloria, some women can live a lifetime in fifteen minutes!"

"How sad for them," said Gloria.

"And how sad for you," Althea said, "when all that Imperial shit starts flowing down on you. Heads may roll over this, Gloria, heads may roll!" Althea reached out and patted Gloria gently on her left cheek. "But I'm certain yours won't be one of them, dear. Until tomorrow, then, Gloria. Ta."

Gloria watched Althea walk away, her bare ass swaying. She longed to plant one good Qatsima scissors kick in that ass, but restrained herself.

CHARLES DID FIND HER, EVENTUALLY. STANDing alone next to a pavilion, Gloria saw him coming and quickly turned her back to him as she tried to get a grip on herself. Her heart was racing, and her mouth was dry. She felt his hand on her bare back, and sucked in her breath as he traced the long, subtle curve of her spine all the way down to her mostly naked buttocks. "I'd know that ass anywhere," Charles said.

Gloria turned to face him and smiled hesitantly. "Hi, Chuckles," she said, as casually as she could manage.

"Hi, Glory." Charles gave her a warm and unaffected smile, and she found herself returning it. He had grown a beard since they were married, closely trimmed and arrogantly regal. It suited him. His languid blond hair curled over the tops of his ears, and his pale blue eyes danced before her. He was tall and still slim and fit. His deep blue tunic, trimmed in gold, fit him like a glove, and his tightly tailored breeches made it very clear that he had lost none of his legendary virility.

"It's good to see you," Gloria said, meaning it.

"And you," said the Emperor. "I can't tell you how much I've missed you, Glory."

"I wrote," she said. "After— after October the Fifth, I mean. Just to say that I was thinking of you and wished you well. But I suppose you must have gotten a million letters."

"More like a billion," he said. "I think they're still busy answering them. But I read yours, Glory. I just didn't know how to answer you. So much was happening then."

"It's all right, I understand."

"It's been a rather busy three years."

"You've done well," she said.

He raised an eyebrow. "And that surprises you?"

"Well, I suppose it does, in a way," she admitted.

"Don't tell anyone I said this, but it surprises me too. It was difficult at first, but I think I'm beginning to get the hang of this Emperor business."

"Maybe you finally grew up."

Charles laughed. "Well, if you're going to be *nasty* . . ."

"No disrespect intended, Your Majesty."

"Oh, don't truckle to me, Glory. I get so sick of that. I always counted on you to point out all my flaws and shortcomings."

"I'll make up a list and send you another letter."

"And I am certain I shall profit from it." His eyes roved over her and he stroked her just under her chin with his long, bony forefinger. "You've grown up too, Glory," he said.

"I've tried."

"You've succeeded, from all I hear. Dexta could hardly survive without you, they say."

"Then what they say is ridiculous. I'm just a Level XIII, Chuckles. On good days, they let me clean out the restrooms."

"Perhaps we can do something about that."

"Don't you dare!" Gloria cried in alarm. "I mean it, Charles. The last thing I want or need is Imperial interest on my behalf. I can do this on my own—I *need* to do it on my own!"

The Emperor nodded. "I understand, Glory. I'll stay out of your way. But if there ever is a time when I can be of service, don't hesitate to call on me. I'd move heaven and Earth for you, Glory—and I can, you know."

Gloria nodded. She had lived in dread of his interference ever since he became Emperor, so perhaps it was good that she'd had this chance to tell him to keep his distance. At the moment, though, the distance between them was less than six inches, and steadily diminishing. Gloria backed away from him.

"So, Your Highness, I understand the Household is very upset about Mynjhino." She tried to sound brisk and professionally interested.

"About *what*?" Charles asked.

"Mynjhino. Lord and Lady Dunsmore . . . ?"

"Oh," said Charles. "That. Yes, yes, I suppose it has ruffled some feathers hereabouts. Tragic, very tragic. A delightful couple, and a credit to the Empire. Boring old farts, actually, but one must keep up appearances. Are you involved with that?"

"It's one of my planets," Gloria said, liking the way that sounded.

"They're *all* my planets," Charles pointed out, deflating Gloria a bit.

"Yes," Gloria conceded. "Twenty-six hundred and forty-three of them. The responsibility must be crushing at times. I only have five, and sometimes I think even that's more than I can handle."

"What's this, my dear? Doubts? Never let them see you worrying, Glory. Even when you are completely without a clue as to what to do next, always let them think you know exactly what must be done. In fact, *especially* when you are without a clue."

Gloria smiled. "Imperial wisdom?"

"Just some advice from an old friend. And we are still friends, aren't we, Glory?"

Gloria looked down at her toes and wiggled them. Charles didn't attempt to press the point.

"Have I mentioned that you look ravishing?" he asked her brightly. "Lovely dress, too, but why so conservative?" He reached for her breasts, fondled them gently, and pulled the fabric away from them.

"I wish people would stop doing that," she said. She tried removing his hands and covering herself, but Charles resisted her and began stroking her stiff, erect nipples. She gasped at his touch.

"Charles, please. I don't like being pawed in public."

"You used to," he said, continuing what he was doing.

"That was when I was still competing for your attention with about a million other women. As you may recall, I gave that up as a losing battle."

"You shouldn't have. Perhaps you might have won in the end."

"Fat chance!" She pulled away from him and felt a flush coming into her cheeks.

"You still want me, Glory," he said, a hard edge coming into his voice. "I can tell. I could always tell. I know exactly what you want, Glory, and what you like, and what I can do to you to make you come and come and come, the way you did when—"

"Stop it, Charles! Just stop it."

"Are you sure you want me to?" he asked her.

"Please."

He regarded her coolly, crossing his arms and staring at her as if he were inspecting an Imperial Marine. "How long since you've had a man, Glory?"

"Oh," she said airily, caught off-balance by the question, "you know how it is with us single girls."

"Don't lie to me, Glory. I can tell just by looking at you. You haven't been well and truly fucked for a very long time, have you?"

"Don't be absurd," Gloria protested. "Just look at me! I'm every man's dream. I walk around half-naked at Dexta and they all—"

"You haven't, have you?"

Gloria sighed and put her hands up to her face. "Spirit," she breathed. "It's so hard, it's just *so* hard!"

Charles moved to her, put his arms around her, and

drew her close. "I know, Glory, I know," he said softly. "After what I put you through, you never want to be dependent on another man, do you? You can't let yourself go. They all want something from you, one way or another, and you have to battle every instant to hold on to what's yours. Even if that means denying yourself the very thing you want most."

She tilted her head back and looked up at him in amazement. "You understand that?" she asked him.

"Of course I do! Do you really think it's any different for me? I can fuck every woman in the Empire if I want, but I can never truly let myself go. We're exceptional people, Glory. We can't be like everyone else, and we shouldn't try. It only makes us unhappy in the end."

"Charles . . ."

He kissed her softly on her lips, then pulled back and looked down at her again. "Forget about what's right and proper and expected, Glory. Tonight, you and I are going to let ourselves go. Tomorrow you can go back to being the good little bureaucrat and I can go back to being master of all I survey. But tonight—tonight, Glory, you and I are going to take what we both want and be happy about it."

Charles kissed her again, and this time Gloria kissed him back. She had known it would happen, from the instant she set foot on the Imperial grounds. And she wanted it desperately. Desperately.

chapter 4

SECTOR SUPERVISOR HECTOR KONRAD, LEVEL X,
hated women. He also hated men, although not with
quite the same intensity. In twenty-five years at Dexta,
he had come to hate everyone who was not Hector
Konrad. It was a strategy that had served him well.

He stood in the corridor in front of Gloria VanDeen's
office, waiting for her to arrive. It was early, and it
was Saturday—not that it mattered. The affairs of the
Empire could not be put aside just because it happened
to be a weekend in New York. Dexta staffers worked six
days on, one day off, and the day off was always subject
to change or cancellation. He knew VanDeen would be
in, because there was work for her to do and she was con-
scientious about seeing that it got done.

It was time, he had decided, to do something about
that Imperial slut. Getting ahead depended on a precise
knowledge of the activities of one's superiors, but staying ahead required a certain amount of attention to the
progress of subordinates. They might try to do to him

what he had already done to others, and Konrad had no intention of being caught unawares.

He saw her coming down the corridor. The arrogant bitch had the nerve to be wearing the same dress she'd worn to the Levee last night; Konrad knew, because he had watched it on the vid. Tits and ass hanging out for all to see while the Emperor himself groped her; the strumpet was nothing less than a disgrace to his Sector. Konrad had been raised as a Christian, not a Spiritist, so his views on sexual morality differed markedly from the norm. In his view, VanDeen was simply a whore.

"Good morning, VanDeen," he said as she approached. He gave her a frown of disapproval. "I've been waiting for you."

GLORIA WAS NOT SURPRISED TO SEE HIM. Konrad kept track of the comings and goings of his subordinates with punctilious interest, like the headmaster of a school for wayward children.

"Good morning, Supervisor Konrad," Gloria said. "Lovely day outside, isn't it?"

"I hadn't noticed."

Big surprise, thought Gloria. Konrad wouldn't notice if it were raining frogs. But she was in such a good mood this morning, she refused to let Konrad spoil it for her. She resolved to be friendly and charming, no matter what Konrad dumped on her desk.

"We've heard from the Prime Minister's office on the Mynjhino matter," Konrad told her. "They want a full report, and I'll expect it from you by noon, as well as another report for Quadrant."

"I've got a Coordinating Supervisors meeting this morning. I'll put Zoe to work on the Quadrant report."

"I want you to do it yourself, VanDeen. Don't think you can duck out from under your responsibility for this mess by fobbing it off on underlings."

"Yessir," Gloria answered obediently. Konrad

surveyed her carefully, and Gloria realized that he was probably aware that she had not gotten any sleep last night—not if the young Emperor was equal to his reputation. She braced herself for what was bound to come next.

"I also want you to Transit to Australia this evening to meet with Lord and Lady Dunsmore's family and give them a full explanation for this tragedy. While you're there, meet with the local media; I'll have PAO set up half a dozen interviews for you. Then Transit to Bombay to give a report to the GalaxCo Board. Corporate will arrange that. Then get back here and be prepared to brief Sector Administrator Ringold at eight tomorrow morning, and Twining, Mirabelli, and possibly Grigsby at Quadrant by ten."

Gloria carefully avoided saying anything other than, "Yessir." Konrad had obviously decided to take advantage of the time difference with Sydney and Bombay to keep Gloria on the run all night. Then, after she'd had two sleepless nights in a row, he would send her to brief the top officials at both Sector and Quadrant. Tired people make mistakes, and Gloria knew she would be very tired indeed by then.

"Finally," he said, "I want an Action Plan on my desk no later than 6:00 P.M. tomorrow afternoon, with at least three viable alternatives spelled out in detail. Tomorrow evening, you will brief Security and the Navy on your report. Oh, and don't forget that your Quarterly Resource Allocation Report for Beta-5 is due Monday morning at nine."

"You realize, don't you, that—"

"What I realize, VanDeen," Konrad cut her off, "is that all this may cut into your social life a little, but then, we all have to make sacrifices for Dexta, don't we?"

"Some of us more than others," Gloria said under her breath.

"What was that, VanDeen?"

"Nothing, sir. Have a good day."

Gloria walked past him to her office without another word. Her good mood had vanished. She proceeded onward to her office, muttering to herself.

After she had shut the door behind her, Gloria closed her eyes and went through a series of Qatsima mental exercises to help calm her mind. Sometimes they worked beautifully, sometimes they didn't work at all. This morning, they had no effect.

Gloria opened her closet door and pulled her dress over her head. She put it on a hanger and surveyed the rack for something to wear today . . . and tonight and tomorrow, it seemed. She looked for something that might give her energy and an edge, just to be wearing it, because it was clear that she was going to need all the help she could get just to make it through the next two days.

"Wow! If I had a body like that, I'd come to work stark naked, too."

Gloria turned and saw Petra standing in the open doorway. "Petra," Gloria said, "if you're going to barge in on me with no warning, at least close the door behind you."

"Oops." Petra turned to close the door, but not before Gordon Chesbro, walking past in the corridor, had gotten an eyeful. Poor Gordon, Gloria thought. This will probably scar him for life.

Gloria decided on something versatile. She pulled out a gray band-skirt, which was nothing more than a twelve-inch-wide, stretchable hoop of fabric. She pulled it up over her hips to within three inches of her navel. Then she slipped into a gray, long-sleeved pullover, tossing her head back and forth to free her long mane. She pressed a hidden contact in a seam, and the pullover contracted itself, uncovering her midriff and molding itself to her torso with immodest precision. Then she pressed another contact, and the fabric reduced its opacity by 10 percent.

"With all your money, you'd think you could afford some underwear," Petra said.

"With all the work you have to do, you'd think you could afford to spend a little less time critiquing my clothing. What have you got for me, Petra?"

"Nothing, yet. Uh...have you seen the morning newstexts yet?"

Gloria shook her head. "Why?"

"Well, the *Times* has everything on Mynjhino and the Dunsmores. Lead screen, no less. But I really think you ought to check the *Post* this morning, too."

"Oh? Okay, will do. And listen, Petra, Konrad is playing the old Run 'em and Stun 'em game with me. I'm going to be on the go for at least the next forty-eight hours, which means that you are, too. As soon as I get myself organized, I'll have a list of particulars for you."

"Okay, boss." Petra turned to go, then looked back at her. "You looked fabulous last night, Gloria, but your dress was kind of conservative for that crowd, wasn't it?"

Gloria sighed wearily. "Oh, you know me. Old Stick-in-the-Mud Gloria."

Petra grinned. "Right," she said. "Did you have fun?"

Gloria smiled back at her. "Yes," she said happily, "I did."

Settling in at her console, Gloria punched up the *Times* and scanned the main article, which was mostly just a regurgitation of the report she'd written for PAO. There was also a lengthy obituary of the Dunsmores; Gloria read it carefully, knowing she would be meeting with the family. Finally, there was a sidebar on Mynjhino itself. The reporter did a creditable job, but got a few things wrong. Gloria made a mental note to send him some background material on Mynjhino, if she had the time. Then, she called up the *Post* and immediately groaned in dismay.

Emperor Sparks Old Flame! the headline shouted. There, on the lead screen, were three vids of Gloria and Charles. In the first, he was running his hand down her bare back to her very bare bottom. In the second, he was pulling her bodice down and playing with her nipples. In the third, they were passionately kissing. On the next screen, they were walking away hand in hand, presumably toward the Imperial Bedchamber. The accompanying story described her as "the beautiful, bare-bummed bureaucrat," and dutifully reported that, "Well-informed sources at the Imperial Residence state that the couple spent the entire night together."

Spirit!

She had been so wrapped up in seeing Charles again that she completely forgot what he had become, and what it meant. There were always imagers at Levees, of course, but it simply didn't occur to Gloria that she would become their subject. But it sure as hell ought to have occurred to Charles! How could he have let this happen?

Then she realized the obvious truth. He didn't just let it happen; he wanted it to happen. He wanted her back; he had spent all night making that crystal clear. They had made love until the sun came up and Gloria had to leave, and she left thinking that it had been one of the best nights of her life. She had no intention of returning to him, but she hoped that they could meet quietly now and then and share more nights of passion. It had been so good to be with him again, to let herself be fondled and caressed and loved. She needed that more than she had realized.

But Charles wanted her back for keeps. So he made sure that everyone in the Empire knew that she was his. The Household could have easily quashed the story and the vids, but Charles wanted them on lead screens for everyone to see. The story could easily make her position at Dexta untenable and force her out ... and back to Charles. That was obviously what the bastard had in mind.

Damn him! This was precisely the kind of game he had played, on a much smaller scale, when they were married. He would create situations that would force her to respond in a particular way, and she would wind up doing exactly what he had wanted all along. *Not this time, Chuckles!*

Gloria resolved to respond by not responding. She would simply ignore the controversy and publicity surrounding their night together. She would pretend that it had never happened.

Her resolve was challenged a moment later when she received a call from Chad Enders, a Level XIII in Public Affairs. "Gloria," he said, "we need a favor. Could you brief the media this morning on this Mynjhino thing?"

"Not me, Chad," Gloria told him. "Zoe Zachary's our point person on Mynjhino. She'll do the briefing."

"Well, Gloria, the fact is that they want *you*. And not just on Mynjhino. They want an interview on your relationship with the Emperor."

"That," Gloria firmly declared, "is none of their business! And it's none of Dexta's business, either."

"It is now, Gloria," Enders told her. "They're all over us on this. Dammit, Gloria, I know it's an imposition, but we have to deal with this somehow."

"My relationship with the Emperor has nothing whatsoever to do with my work at Dexta. Speaking of which, I have a ton of it. Good-bye, Chad." She signed off and cursed Charles again.

She had spent three years devoting herself to succeeding at Dexta. She gave everything she had to the job, and she had done damned well at it. After those first awful six months, she had found herself, hit her stride, and built up a remarkable record of success and accomplishment. She had a very real and promising future at Dexta. And now, in a single night, she might have lost it all.

No, she told herself, no. It is not going to happen that way. She wouldn't let it.

• • •

GLORIA VANDEEN, LEVEL XIII, WAS COORDInating Supervisor for Administration for the five inhabited planets in Quadrant 2, Sector 8, Division Beta-5. At the same Level, Beta-5 also had Coordinating Supervisors for Agriculture, Corporate, and Imperial Affairs, all under Commerce; Banking and Currency, under Finance; and External and Internal Security, for a total of eight. With five divisions in the Sector, and five Coordinating Supervisors in each Division for each Jurisdiction, there were a total of two hundred Coordinating Supervisors in Sector 8. The Empire was composed of twenty-four Sectors, averaging five divisions each. Thus, there were some five thousand Level XIII Coordinating Supervisors in the Department of Extraterrestrial Affairs. Counting Quadrant staff, Public Affairs, and other jurisdictions, some eight thousand Level XIII staff worked at Dexta Headquarters in Manhattan. In addition, another twenty thousand Level XIII personnel were stationed off-planet, scattered throughout 2643 worlds spread through a sphere of space two thousand light-years in diameter. And of those twenty-eight thousand Level XIII Dexta staffers, as far as anyone knew, Gloria VanDeen was the only one sleeping with the Emperor.

Gloria reflected on that uncomfortable fact as she tried to concentrate on the reports she had to write for the PM and Quadrant. In the vastness of the Dexta bureaucracy, the only certain way to advance was by being Noticed. And yet, this sort of Notice could be fatal to her career. If nothing else, 27,999 Level XIII staffers would try to make certain of it. Life at Dexta was not dog-eat-dog; it was far worse than that.

Long ago, someone had invented a Dexta Bestiary, describing the forms of life that could be found in the Dexta bureaucracy. There were Lions, Tigers, Dogs, Sheep, and Moles. Almost by default, Gloria was a Tiger. Petra Nash was a Sheep who wanted to become a Dog.

Gordon Chesbro had "mutton" written all over him. Zoe Zachary would be a Lion someday, if she survived. Althea Dante was another Tiger. Hector Konrad was a Mole. Broken down by population, about 10 percent each were Lions, Tigers, Dogs, and Moles, and the other 60 percent were Sheep. Each species had its own characteristic traits and survival strategies, and each ran its own risks in the jungle that was Dexta.

Dexta had evolved over the centuries with Darwinian ruthlessness, and only the strong survived. Each year, 100 million bright and talented young people throughout the Empire took competitive examinations to win a position as Rated Staff at Dexta; only a hundred thousand were selected. The reason so many got in was that just as many left each year. There was a constant 20 percent turnover rate among the five hundred thousand Level XV staff. The system was consciously designed to test, stress, oppress, overwhelm, and even terrorize the Fifteens, and there were few limitations on what could be done to break them.

The Fifteens endured killing hours, poor pay, intentionally inferior food and recreation facilities, and atrocious living conditions, all for a chance to make careers for themselves at Dexta. While the Fourteens and Thirteens enjoyed measured amenities, such as the living quarters in the Residence, the Fifteens were required to live in Annex Fifteen, a carefully designed slum in the Bronx. They were expected to survive any way they could, and if they failed, no one would miss them when they were gone.

The rewards for those who survived the terrors of the lower levels could be lavish. Mid- and upper-level personnel were well paid and enjoyed a cornucopia of perks and privileges. Aside from the satisfactions inherent in running an empire, Dexta staffers could also look forward to receiving lucrative job offers from the Big Twelve corporates, which viewed Dexta as a training ground for executive talent.

Dexta was a world unto itself, a realm dominated by thirty-third-century technology and nineteenth-century labor conditions. Local law enforcement jurisdictions had no authority on Dexta property, and practices that had long since been discredited in society at large not only endured, but thrived. The all-seeing eyes of Internal Security's imagers made privacy nonexistent, so any felony was detected immediately and the transgressor was simply shipped off to a prison colony with no trial and no appeal. Consequently, things like theft, murder, and rape were almost unknown, but other activities that were considered criminal elsewhere were permitted and sometimes actively encouraged.

Assault, for example, was forbidden if directed against either a superior or a subordinate. But staffers at the same level could and often did resolve disputes through sheer force. And although physical rape was out of the question, sexual harassment and intimidation— illegal for centuries in the larger society—were an essential ingredient of life at Dexta. Staffers were expected to find their own means of survival in the political, bureaucratic, and sexual cauldron, with the harsh and unforgiving system quickly and brutally disposing of anyone who couldn't stand the heat.

Thus, the Lions, Tigers, Dogs, Sheep, and Moles. The numerous Sheep were the solid, unspectacular, but essential workaday staff who did most of the routine work that kept the Empire functioning. If they survived the rigors of Level XV, they slowly moved upward and became the backbone of the bureaucracy. They generally tried to avoid being Noticed by anyone but their immediate supervisors. Sheep found safety only in numbers and anonymity.

Moles preferred to work unNoticed, as well, but they worked with a purpose. They silently burrowed beneath the surface layers of the bureaucracy, virtually unseen, until one day they popped up out of nowhere, at the right place at the right time. A well-placed molehole could trip up even a Lion or a Tiger. Hector Konrad was a Mole, and had reached exalted Level X status by being good at what he did, clever in his strategy, precise in his timing, and utterly ruthless.

There were two breeds of Dogs—LapDogs and Pack Dogs. The LapDogs attempted to win the affection and loyalty of a willing superior. They fetched slippers, barked at strangers, licked faces, performed simple tricks, and displayed unlimited devotion. As the masters and mistresses moved up, their LapDogs moved with them. Petra Nash was attempting to escape the insecurity and anonymity of the Sheep herd by becoming Gloria's LapDog, but Gloria had yet to commit to the relationship. She still had some doubts about Petra's stamina and ability, if not her devotion.

The Pack Dogs roamed free, mostly in the lower levels. They savaged Sheep, and in sufficient numbers were capable of bringing down a Lion or Tiger. They were vicious, unprincipled, bureaucratic street gangs. Embittered Sheep and failed Lions and Tigers often became Pack Dogs. Dogs of either breed had low ceilings in Dexta, but good survival rates.

The Lions and Tigers took the greatest risks and reaped the biggest rewards, if they survived at all. Many did not. Lions often formed prides for mutual support, although the competition within a pride could be deadly. Solo Lions could be clawed by other cats or mauled by a pride, but didn't have to share their meals. Most Lions were males, but there were exceptions; Zoe Zachary had the instincts of a Lion, but it remained to be seen whether she could hunt successfully on her own.

Tigers like Gloria or Althea Dante were sleek and beautiful, prowling the bureaucracy with grace and arrogance. They flaunted their stripes and used sex the way Lions used power. They could rise high or fall far, and they carried the scent of danger with them wherever they went. Those who couldn't make the grade were known as Paper Tigers. Elaine Murakami, Zoe's assistant, was likely to become one. She had the stripes, but not the teeth.

In addition, there were the Eagles, soaring at Level VII and above, subject to an entirely different set of rules, as well as a handful of Mules. The Mules were Lions or Tigers who had made a bad move or been victimized so thoroughly that they were bureaucratically neutered. They hung on at Dexta but had no future. Gloria's fellow Coordinating Supervisor Dina Westerbrook, in Alpha Division, had been Muled. She was a sad, brittle beauty who had made one big mistake and had spent the past twenty years in her current position, with absolutely no prospect of advancement.

Gloria had not always been a Tiger. When she arrived at Dexta, twenty years old and fresh out of school, she began her bureaucratic life as a Sheep. Despite her sophistication in the world outside Dexta, within the bureaucracy she was as innocent and helpless as a newborn lamb. Charles was not yet Emperor, and her connection to him was little known and of even less consequence. If she were to survive, she would have to do it on her own. She almost didn't.

Sexual harassment and intimidation were simply part of the game at Dexta, and its victims could be of either sex. Gloria's stunning beauty made her a natural target, and her fierce desire to succeed at Dexta made her an all-too-willing victim. The lower-level Dogs had a field day with her, and even the more experienced Sheep took advantage. She was uncertain just how things worked at Dexta; it seemed clear that she would have to sleep with someone to gain Notice and protection and the possibility of advancement, but it was far from clear with whom she should sleep. So she slept with everyone.

She couldn't even remember how many there had been in those first dreadful months... Thirty? Forty? Once it began, somehow, there was no stopping it. She hated what was happening to her, but couldn't control it. Those at Levels XIV, XIII, and above who wanted her could have her, because her very survival at Dexta rested in their hands. And once they had had their way with her, the Level XV Dogs moved in and savaged her. They threatened to sabotage her work and get her dismissed from Dexta if she didn't put out, so she did, because there was nowhere to file a complaint, no one to take her part. Daily life at Dexta and the Annex became an unending nightmare of fast fucks and under-the-desk blow jobs. She still woke up sobbing sometimes, thinking she was still lying on the men's room floor after five of them had taken turns with her. And yet, it wasn't rape, because she had never found the courage to say no.

Finally, Viveca Kwan, then the Level X Sector Supervisor in Sector 21, where Gloria first worked, called her into her office for her first Six Month Review. Gloria was terrified, certain she would be fired. Viveca was a glamorous, successful Tiger, and she looked across her desk at Gloria with sadness and compassion.

"The consensus of the Review Panel," Viveca told her, "was that you have no future at Dexta and should be terminated. In fact, it was more than just a consensus, it was unanimous."

"Unanimous?" Gloria was stunned. She had slept with every man—and two women—on that panel. Promises had been made...

"I know what they told you," Viveca said, as if reading her mind. "And you were young and naïve and stupid enough to believe them, weren't you?"

Gloria nodded and began to cry. Viveca passed her some tissues.

"Settle down, Gloria. I saved your bacon for you. I told them that I thought you had excellent potential, outstanding skills, a brilliant mind, and that once you wised up, you could make a real contribution at Dexta. And I believe that. So I called in a few markers and saved that lovely hide of yours. Of course, we'll have to transfer you to another Sector. You've pretty well blotted your copybook in this one."

"Thank you, thank you!" Gloria had sobbed.

"Don't thank me yet. Do you think things will be any different in some other Sector, Gloria? Believe me, they're all the same. If anything is going to be different, it's going to have to be *you*."

Gloria looked up. "What do you mean?"

"Look, kid," Viveca said, "you've been going about this all wrong. Do you *want* to be a Sheep? Hell, Gloria, it's not even *possible* for you to be a Sheep and survive around here. The only thing you can be is what I am: a Tiger."

"I don't understand."

"Just look at yourself. You're gorgeous, Gloria. Yet you let yourself be a victim when you could be a predator. Don't be someone else's lunch, Gloria. Learn to hunt. Use what you've got, because in this place, that's the only way you can possibly survive. Every button you button up is just another button some bastard of a Dog will want to rip off. Do you see what I'm driving at?"

"I . . . I'm not sure."

"Well, then let me make it as clear as I can. You can sleep with any man you want in Dexta, so why lie down with Dogs? Tell them to go fuck themselves, while you go and seduce somebody worthwhile. Somebody who can actually help you, and will. Sleeping your way upward is part of the game around here, for both men and women. Either play the game, Gloria, or go sit on the bench. You could be an All-Star, you know."

"But—"

"But you want to succeed for your brains and not for your body? Hey, they're connected, you know? Use both of them. Up to now, you've been sleeping with men out of fear, Gloria. That's no way to live. My way is a hell of a lot more fun, and will get you a lot farther. I'm transferring you over to Sector 17. When you get there, be a

Tiger. I mean really *be* one. I have a feeling you'll be a great one."

Gloria took Viveca Kwan's advice, and suddenly her life at Dexta was transformed. She prowled the corridors of the Sector 17 offices unbuttoned and unafraid. Men stared at her, but the Dogs shied away from her and the Lions above Noticed her. She found one who seemed honest and sensitive, and began sleeping with him. Out in the world, he was probably not a man she would have chosen to sleep with, but the relationship was not unpleasant, and it provided her with stability and protection for the first time in her life at Dexta. She was able to concentrate on her work, and its quality improved to the point where she was Noticed for that, as well. After six months, her Lion moved up and left the Sector without even saying good-bye. But two weeks later, Gloria was promoted to Level XIV and given a System Coordinator slot in Sector 3.

There, she established liaisons with two different men at higher levels. Each knew about the other, but accepted the situation. Meanwhile, she did excellent work with her System and attracted more Notice. Within a year, she earned promotion to Level XIII, and Viveca Kwan, by now a Level VIII Assistant Sector Administrator, brought her in to Sector 8 in her present job.

On the prowl once more, Gloria set her sights on a handsome young Lion, Deputy Supervisor Grant Enright, a Level XI responsible for Beta Division. To her amazement, Enright turned her down. Enright was not only married, but happily so. He was that rarity in Dexta, a relatively normal human being. They became friends, rather than lovers.

And then, a curious thing happened. No man above her in Sector 8 made a play for her, and Gloria felt no need to seek one out. Her work spoke for itself, and she had grown confident and mature in her position. Charles was Emperor by now, and knowledge of that connection may have deterred some advances; but

Gloria's growing reputation as a Tiger gave her power of her own. She could have chosen a subordinate for a sexual plaything, as Althea Dante frequently did, but decided that she didn't really want to play that game. She didn't want scared and eager Fourteens and Fifteens looking to her as their passport to success. Nor did she want to place her own fate in the hands of some rising Lion or successful Sheep in the levels above.

What she really wanted was a relationship with an equal, where affection and attraction mattered more than sexual politics. But that was an impossible dream at Dexta—politics *always* mattered. Her fellow Thirteens in Sector 8 were a mixed bunch, in any case, and none really caught her fancy. Within Administration, there were two other Tigers, Moana Tuan and Michelle Vargas-Lopez. Moana slept with everyone, and Michelle slept with Deputy Assistant Sector Administrator for Administration Nigel Raines, Level IX, a successful middle-aged Sheep. But Gloria slept with no one, giving her an aura of mystery. Everyone assumed that such a beautiful and glamorous woman had to be sleeping with someone, probably someone very important, but no one knew for sure. As a matter of safety and self-preservation, most men looked, but didn't attempt to touch.

Gloria's sheer physical presence was overpowering in itself, intimidating to both men and women. Ironically, if she had gone around like Zoe Zachary, gray on gray and all buttoned up, men probably would have hit on her a hundred times a day, simply because she looked accessible. But in her Tiger mode, she seemed an unattainable ideal, and they left her alone. Merely by displaying her body, she avoided the necessity of actually using it. For a while, that was just fine with Gloria, but it had been going on for a year, and she didn't quite know what to do about it. When she moved up again, and on to another Sector, perhaps there would be new opportunities, but for now, she slept alone.

Or at least she had, until last night. She had been hungry, Charles sensed it, and Gloria found herself in bed with the Emperor . . . and on the lead screens of the newstexts. Spirit, how could she have been so stupid?

Sleeping with a superior at Dexta was a normal and accepted part of life, but sleeping with the Emperor went far beyond the bounds of decency. It would inspire resentment rather than envy, and make her a target for the intrigues of everyone, both above and below her. Other Thirteens would no longer cooperate and would do everything they could to see to it that she failed. Lower-level Dogs would nip at her heels, and the big cats above would claw her. Moles like Hector Konrad would set traps for her, and even the Sheep would trample her, if they could.

There were no formal rules governing sex at Dexta, but everyone knew what was expected. It was like working attire; no regulation mandated gray, but the culture somehow expected it, and so nearly everyone wore it. There were few rules to break, but the force of cultural expectation could be overwhelming.

It was expected that someone like Gloria would use her sexual power within Dexta. But using it on the outside—by sleeping with the Emperor, no less!—was a blatant violation of expectations. It simply wasn't proper, and Gloria would be punished for it.

GLORIA FINISHED THE PAPER FOR THE PRIME Minister's office. It wasn't her best work, but it would suffice for now. She was too distracted to stay focused. In a few minutes, she had to leave for the Beta-5 Coordinating Supervisors meeting. She wished she could just avoid it, find a hole in the ground and hide in it.

Another call showed her the impossibility of that strategy. Chad Enders's boss at Public Affairs, Moira Gonzalez, Level X, appeared on her console and told her flatly, "Gloria, we expect you to be here for the noon briefing. The media are already accusing us of trying to cover up for you, and we're not going to take that kind of heat for your sake. You'll excuse the expression, Gloria, but you made your bed and now you'll have to lie in it."

"I won't do it," Gloria insisted. "My personal life has nothing to do with Dexta."

"I understand your position, but this is not a request. It's an order."

"You can't give me orders, Moira," Gloria reminded her. "You aren't in Admin. If you can get my superiors to give me that order, maybe I'll do it. Maybe I won't. But if you want to lean on me, you're going to have to do it through channels."

Gloria signed off and sat there silently stewing for several minutes. If she did the briefing, that would only generate more publicity, more controversy, and more resentment within Dexta. If Konrad ordered her to do the briefing and she still refused, he could use her insubordination against her. It was doubtful that he could have her fired, but her refusal would create a still-bigger flap. Who did she think she was, defying a superior's direct order? She screws the Emperor and now she thinks she can get away with anything at all!

"Your basic no-win situation," Gloria said to herself. What she needed, she realized, was simply to get away for a few weeks until everything blew over. But if she took a leave of absence, it would look as if she were running scared.

Gloria got to her feet and started for the door to go to the Coordinating Supervisors meeting, but she stopped abruptly. An idea occurred to her, and she smiled.

"If you're going to be a Tiger, Gloria," she said aloud, "then *be* a Tiger!" She had been thinking like a Sheep, she realized. And at a time like this, she should be showing her stripes.

Gloria hooked her thumbs in her band-skirt and pulled it down to the edge of respectability, and a smidgen beyond. Then she pressed one of the hidden contacts, and the skirt retracted to a width of just six inches. She pressed the other contact four times, and the skirt's opacity decreased by 40 percent. Then she contracted her pullover another degree and pressed the opacity contact on the left side twice. She looked at herself in the closet mirror and saw that a single stray pubic hair was curling over the top of her skirt, golden and obvious against her cocoa-toned flesh. She rather liked the effect. Then, remembering what she had said to Althea the previous night, she pressed the contact on the left of her pullover six times in rapid succession.

She grinned at herself in the mirror.

"Ah, Gloria," she said. "What immortal hand or eye could frame thy fearful symmetry?"

chapter 5

PETRA BLINKED WHEN SHE SAW GLORIA EMERGE from her office. "Stick in the mud, huh?" she said.

"Stop gawking and listen up," Gloria told her. "I want you to call Chad Enders at PAO and tell him I've changed my mind. I'll do the briefing at noon. Then tell Zoe to get her ass in here as soon as I get back from the CS meeting, and to bring Elaine Murakami and Gordon Chesbro with her. And find Joe Exton and tell him he's going to have to do everything that I told you to do in the next two days. Bring him up to speed on everything else we're doing so that he'll be able to take over for you for the next three or four weeks. Then, go home and pack, and meet me at the VIP Transit rings at three."

"Pack? VIP Transit?"

"You heard me, Petra."

"Where are we going?"

"You and I, my dear, are going to Mynjhino."

Petra stared blankly at her boss. "We are? But—"

"Leave all the buts to me. Now march!"

Gloria headed down the corridor toward the

conference room, hearing eyeballs click as she passed. Feeling confident and supremely Tigerish, she reduced the opacity of her skirt another 50 percent to match her top. Let them stare, she thought; from now on, there's nothing left for me to hide. She knew what she had to do. It was merely a question of doing it.

The seven other Coordinating Supervisors had already arrived, and they stared at her as she took her place at the head of the table. The CS for Administration chaired these meetings, although everyone was a coequal Thirteen. When any dispute resulted in a four-to-four split, Administration got its way. However, the four dissenters could appeal the decision to their superiors, which the superiors didn't appreciate; it made the dissenters reluctant to appeal and the chair reluctant to force the issue. Such difficulties could have been avoided simply by giving the panel an odd number of members, but that was not the way Dexta operated. Decisions were not supposed to be easy and conflict was not to be smoothed over. It was just another way of ratcheting up the pressure and forcing everyone to be at their best all the time.

Although the Coordinating Supervisors had direct, day-to-day responsibility for much of what happened within the Empire, they were still only Level XIIIs, and very junior members of the Dexta hierarchy. Above them, the twenty-eight thousand Thirteens answered to thirteen thousand Twelves, eighty-six hundred Elevens, sixty-two hundred Tens, six thousand Nines, and fifty-four hundred Eights. And in the aeries of the Eagles, there were five hundred Sevens and above. Thus, those at the meeting were aware that nearly forty thousand people had the power to tell them what to do, second-guess their decisions, and generally make their lives miserable.

"Good morning, everyone," Gloria said pleasantly. She looked around the table and saw seven attractive, intelligent young faces. Everyone but Althea Dante was wearing standard Dexta gray, in various shades and styles. Even Gloria was in gray, although her clothing was now one part gray and nine parts Gloria. Althea was wearing a blue-gray working-girl dress that was nearly as transparent as Gloria's skirt and pullover, and featured wide Vs that exposed most of her from neck to navel and knees to crotch. She didn't wear underwear, either; true Tigers rarely did.

At Gloria's immediate left sat Fresco Terwilliger, the Beta-5 Coordinating Supervisor for Agriculture, a solid and dependable Sheep in his midthirties. Next came Nancy Nfumi, the CS for Corporate Affairs. She was a loyal LapDog of Paula Ho, the Level IX Deputy Assistant Sector Administrator for Commerce, a well-regarded upper-level Lion. Nancy monitored the activities of the Big Twelve in Beta-5, but her primary concern was making Paula Ho look good.

Althea Dante came next, sprawled lazily in her chair, her left breast completely exposed. For historical reasons, Imperial Affairs was under Commerce, but it was really something of an independent fiefdom within Dexta. Althea came to the meetings not so much as a fellow Coordinating Supervisor, but more as an ambassador from some distant kingdom where everyone was charming, sophisticated, and well dressed.

At the far end of the table from Gloria sat Raul Tellemacher for Banking, under Finance. He was a darkly handsome Lion, clearly destined for bigger things. He already tended to dominate Sector 8 Finance from below, and had the people above him running scared. He was extremely well connected, having come from an old Zurich banking family. Tellemacher was one of the very few Thirteens in Sector 8 who had made a serious run at Gloria, but she found him arrogant and boorish. In rejecting his advances, she had made a serious enemy.

In the far right corner was Kristen Kim, for Currency, also under Finance. She was a quiet Sheep whose talent for numbers had led her to her present position. A dark-haired, blue-eyed Korean-Swede, she was very attractive and a much-victimized sexual plaything of the higher-ups in Currency, who had nothing better to do with their time. Currency simply kept track of and attempted to regulate the value of the crown throughout the Empire, with reference to local economies and business conditions. Kristen always looked sad, and not without reason.

Next to her sat Phillip Benz, for External Security. In effect, he was a liaison with the Imperial Navy, which was finding peacetime to be a major challenge. The Empire's last great war had ended victoriously forty-two years ago, and now the Navy was mainly engaged in patrolling the frontiers and battling to maintain its budget. Benz, a Navy veteran, was a quiet, competent Sheep.

On Gloria's immediate right sat Bianca Warren, the Coordinating Supervisor for Internal Security in Beta-5. A Mole by nature and inclination, Bianca had the unenviable task of explaining just how the Myn-Traha had managed to get their hands on automatic weapons. If heads were going to roll over this incident, Bianca's would be the first. And Gloria's might very well be the second.

"All right," said Gloria. "Before we get to Mynjhino, let's dispose of our other four planets." Each of the remaining worlds in Beta-5 was a human colony with no indigenous intelligent species. In the entire Sector, with 123 inhabited worlds, only twelve were occupied by sentient natives. Of those, only the Klaath—a seven-system confederation—had independently acquired space travel. The Empire had fought a bloody war with them four centuries ago, and now they were loyal and productive vassals. The remaining five intelligent species (six, really, counting both Myn and Jhino) had low-order technologies and were easily dominated by the Empire. The most advanced of them, on Mynjhino, had never been any trouble until now.

"Anybody have anything to report about Gregson's

Planet?" Gloria asked. No one did. Gregson's was a dull mining planet with a population under a million.

"What about Pecos?" A thriving, multifaceted world originally settled by emigrants from Texas, Pecos boasted a population of 400 million and an economy that tended to run in boom-and-bust cycles. It was currently booming.

Kristen Kim hesitantly cleared her throat. "Uh," she said, looking down at some notes, "we're getting some indications of runaway inflation in some sectors of the economy. We're considering contracting the money supply if it goes on." Having said her piece, Kristen shrank back into her chair. Gloria looked toward Raul Tellemacher.

"We don't think it's anything to worry about," he said. "Currency is wetting its pants, as usual, and for no reason."

"If your people would stop approving so many loans—" Kristen started to object, but Tellemacher cut her off.

"Those loans are low risk and high-return And they need them on Pecos to finance the expansion of the Central Waterway project."

"Okay," said Gloria, anxious to prevent a debate, "we'll keep an eye on those inflation figures. Thank you for bringing it up, Kristen. Now, what about Othello and Desdemona? Anything pressing?"

Othello and Desdemona were colonies on planets orbiting each star in a double star system. Together, they had a population of about 300 million. The Desdemonans kept complaining that Othello was trying to strangle their economy, but Dexta didn't take the matter very seriously. No one had anything to say about either world today.

"Fine," said Gloria. "What I want to do now is go once around the table on Mynjhino. Let's hear anything that's even marginally relevant to the situation. We'll start with you, Fresco."

"Well," said Terwilliger, "as you know, the continent

of Myn has an economy that is primarily agricultural. They are self-sufficient in food, and their principal cash crop consists of antigerontological pharmaceuticals. Until GalaxCo moved in about twenty years ago, their agricultural organization was essentially communal, with the land being held in perpetuity by tribal groups. GalaxCo began buying up what they could and pressuring the tribes to enter into agreements that got them access to large sections of land suitable for the establishment of plantations. Technically, much of the land still belongs to the tribal groups, but the GalaxCo leases are ironclad. At least," he added, glancing toward Nancy Nfumi of Corporate, "that's what GalaxCo claims."

"And the labor situation on the plantations?" Gloria asked.

"Unsettled. A lot of natives have been withdrawing from the plantations, leaving them short-handed."

"Where do they go?" asked Tellemacher. "What do they do?"

"They seem to be returning to the tribal plots, where they still exist, and reverting to precontact agricultural methods. There's a strong religious element involved in tilling the soil. But their methods are not very productive, so if this trend continues, there could conceivably be food shortages at some point."

"How soon?" Gloria asked.

"Probably not for years. I don't think it's an immediate issue."

"I see. And what about the other continent, Jhino?"

"Industrialization there has taken a lot of workers off the tribal farms, but modern methods have increased production. They do import about 10 percent of their ag products from Myn, however."

"Okay. Nancy, what about Corporate? I know GalaxCo took the hit, but what do you hear from Imperium and Servitor?"

"They're nervous," Nfumi said, "but Imperium has most of its assets and people on Jhino, and they feel relatively secure. Servitor does have operations on Myn, but they are urban-based. Generally, Servitor is simply attempting to establish a position in the local financial infrastructure. They tend to think long-term, as you know."

"And GalaxCo?"

"They intend to ask for a Marine detachment to guard their plantations." Nfumi glanced across the table at Phillip Benz. "I know what you're going to say, Phil, but they're going to ask for it anyway."

"Do they actually expect to get it," Benz asked, "or are they just trying to look good for the stockholders and employees?"

"I think they have a realistic attitude," Nfumi responded. Benz nodded, satisfied. It would take a lot more than one incident and sixteen dead to get the Navy to commit its thinly stretched resources to Mynjhino.

"Anything else we should know about GalaxCo?" Gloria asked.

"Their operation on Myn is profitable, but it's not a major moneymaker. The new generation of pharmaceuticals grown there is important to them, but they could be grown on a number of other planets where GalaxCo is strong."

"So if things got too hot, they might pull out?"

Nfumi nodded. "They are a long way from that point, but it's certainly possible. I think the main thing they are concerned about is their human workforce on Mynjhino. Not just protecting them, but getting them to stay. It's not exactly a plum assignment in any case, and if things get nasty, a lot of people might decide to leave."

"Thank you, Nancy. Althea, what's the Imperial interest here?"

Althea smiled. "Well, of course, Gloria dear, you may know more about that than I do. However, aside from the tragic deaths of Lord and Lady Dunsmore, Mynjhino does not rank high on the list of Imperial concerns. Governor Rhinehart is, shall we say, not highly thought of in the Household. A political appointee, of course, and eminently expendable. If things get ugly, they'll replace him with somebody competent, but they'd prefer not to have to do that at the moment. They are counting on Dexta to apply its usual healing balm and make the problem go away. At least, that's what *my* sources say. Tell us, Gloria, what do *your* sources reveal?"

Althea leaned forward, as if she couldn't wait to hear Gloria's answer. Everyone else leaned forward a bit, too.

Gloria smiled back at Althea. "My sources," she said evenly, "have no comment. Raul, let's hear Banking."

"Not much to say," Tellemacher said. "Bank of Earth and Zumgaard, between them, have about a billion crowns out—mostly to Jhino to support industrialization. Myn is only in for about 200 mill. So far, no payment problems. The Myn are not what one would call heavy financial thinkers. The banks are concerned by developments, of course, but no one is panicking."

"Uh-huh. Anything from Currency, Kristen?"

"Not really. The local monetary unit has been stable for years. The money markets haven't really had time to react, but basically, I'd agree with Raul. No one is panicking."

"Thank you, Kristen. Phil? Does the Navy currently have any assets in the region?"

"Nothing but a revenue cutter within a hundred light-years."

"What if they had to bring in a regiment of Marines? How long would it take?"

Benz shook his head. "If it were a true emergency, they might be able to do it in a month from the day they get the orders. Possibly a little less if they shift some of the occupation troops back from the Frontier. But they'd hate like hell to have to do that."

"Understood," said Gloria. "Nevertheless, Mynjhino is only about 150 light-years from the Frontier, and nothing much is happening out that way these days. If they have to commit forces, that would be the logical place to get them."

"No argument, Gloria. I'm just saying that they won't like it."

"Of course not. They never do. They'd rather be off someplace conquering three-headed lizards on virgin worlds."

Benz nodded in agreement. "Trouble is, there are just never any three-headed lizards around when you need them."

Gloria turned to her right. "Now, Bianca, what can you tell us about smuggling? Everyone agrees that it's highly improbable that those weapons were manufactured on Mynjhino. So how did they get them and where did they come from?"

"We don't know," said Bianca Warren. Everyone waited for her to say something more, but she didn't.

Gloria nodded slowly. "Then find out," she said.

"When we know, you'll know," Warren responded.

"Just make sure that we do," Gloria told her. "Now, one final word. I'm leaving for Mynjhino this afternoon."

Heads snapped to attention around the table. It was not unprecedented for a Coordinating Supervisor to go off-planet, but it was highly unusual.

"I thought Zoe was going," said Althea.

"Zoe's taking over here in my absence, which should be three to four weeks. I'm sure you'll cooperate with her as you have with me. Let's stay on top of this thing. And Bianca, I expect you to have something on the smuggling by the time I return. I'll see what I can pick up on that end. See you soon, people."

GLORIA WAS SITTING AT HER CONSOLE IN HER office when Zoe Zachary arrived, with Elaine Murakami and Gordon Chesbro in tow. There weren't enough seats to go around, so Gordon stood while Zoe and

Elaine sat. His eyes bulged out slightly as he stared at Gloria.

"You've heard by now that I'm going to Mynjhino," Gloria said. "Petra will be coming with me. Zoe, you'll take my place here. You have about a hundred things to get done in the next two days. Petra will give you the list."

"That was supposed to have been my trip," Zoe said, not bothering to conceal her anger and disappointment.

"I never said that, Zoe. You simply assumed," said Gloria. "In any case, it's mine now." She didn't offer any further explanations.

Gloria turned and looked up toward Gordon. "What I want from you, Gordon," she said, "is everything you've done on Mynjhino since you got here. Every research report, every annual, every supplemental, every smart-ass memo. The works. Plus anything remotely relevant that may have been done by the people who preceded you."

"That's an awful lot of stuff," Gordon said.

"I'll have nine days to read it. Give it all to Petra, ASAP."

Gordon continued to stand there, staring at Gloria's more or less naked body. Gloria allowed him a few seconds of ecstasy, then said, "Hop to it, Gordon."

"Yes, ma'am!" He started for the door, glanced back, managed to collide with the doorframe, and finally stumbled his way out of the office.

"You shouldn't torture the poor boy like that, Gloria," Zoe chided her.

Gloria simply smiled. "Think of it as a reward for all his good work. Anyway," she added, nodding toward Elaine, "Murakami here tortures him every day, don't you, Elaine?"

Elaine looked uncomfortable and smiled nervously. As a would-be Tiger, Elaine was wearing form-fitting black tights and a loose, sleeveless gray vest unbuttoned to the waist. She couldn't think of a response, so she said nothing.

"Elaine," Gloria said to her, "Zoe's moving up to fill my shoes, so you're going to be filling hers for the next month. It's going to be a hot seat, there could be a lot of media attention, and there will definitely be a lot of attention paid by the higher-ups. When they want answers, you make damn good and sure you've got them ready. Work Gordon around the clock if you have to. Keep him motivated."

"Just how motivated do I have to keep him?"

"That's up to you. Just remember, he's got the brains in your shop, but he needs somebody to keep him focused. What you've got, Elaine, is a winning personality and nice little tits. Use them. This is your big chance, so don't blow it. Now, go back to your office, invite Gordon to lunch, and start motivating the poor bastard. Got it?"

"Got it." Elaine nodded. "And thanks, Gloria."

When she was gone, Zoe stared at Gloria, her features registering a degree of disgust. "Do you honestly expect that girl to fuck Gordon Chesbro?"

"I expect her to do whatever is necessary to make sure that this office functions at peak efficiency in my absence. I expect the same from you, Zoe. Don't worry, I won't ask *you* to fuck him."

"Would *you* fuck him, Gloria?"

"I," said Gloria with emphatic superiority, "don't have to."

Zoe shook her head. "Sometimes I wonder about you, Gloria. I mean, what in Spirit's name goes through your head when you dress like that?"

"One, that it's fun. Two, that at times, like now, it can be essential to my job. After that business with Charles and the media reaction, my head is on the chopping block, and if I can use my tits, tush, and twat to save it, then that's what I'll do. This job means everything to me, Zoe, and I'll do whatever I have to do to keep it. And you're going to have to learn to be every bit as tough and determined as I am if you expect to succeed in this place. I wonder about you sometimes, too, Zoe. I wonder if you're really as tough as you think you are. I wonder if you really understand just how tough you need to be. There aren't many women who make it as Lions, you know. Do you think maybe there's a reason for that?"

"So what are you saying? That I should tear off all my clothes and try to be a Tiger instead?" She said it with evident contempt.

"You could, you know. You might stand a better chance that way. All I'm saying is that doing it your way requires every bit of strength at your command. And I don't just mean the strength to stand up to someone like Konrad. I mean the strength to throw someone like Elaine at someone like Gordon, if that's what it takes to get the job done. If you can't do that, Zoe, then you might just as well go stand in line to be sheared along with the rest of the Sheep, because that's all you'll ever be."

"We'll see," said Zoe.

Gloria nodded. "And sooner than you think. I am handing you a red-hot potato. You get to be me for the next month. See how you like it. This is your big chance, too. Blow it, and you'll never get another. Come through the way I think you can, and you'll be a Thirteen in six months. Now, on your way. I've got things to do."

Zoe got to her feet, paused at the door, and looked back at Gloria. She hesitated, then finally said, "Have a safe trip, Gloria."

Gloria smiled at her. "You stay healthy too, Zoe."

THIRTY OR SO MEDIA REPS HAD GATHERED IN a small auditorium to hear the noon briefing on Mynjhino, but they were really there to see Gloria VanDeen. Some of the regulars already knew about Gloria, who had a considerable reputation within Dexta, despite her relatively low level. The others couldn't care less about Mynjhino, but were eager to question the Emperor's newest bedmate.

Gloria knew why they were there, but was determined to handle the briefing on her own terms. If she was going to salvage her position at Dexta, she had to go on the offensive and take control of the situation. If she were defensive in any way—in word, deed, or manner—all would be lost. Her almost transparent attire was an essential part of her strategy; the media vultures wanted to see where the Imperial penis had been last night, and she intended to show them. The PAO introduced her, and Gloria strode confidently to the dais and stood nearly naked before the eyes of the Empire.

Gloria looked out at the media reps, who were staring at her in frank disbelief. "Before we get to Mynjhino," she said, "I'd like to make a few brief remarks on a personal matter. As you know, I was once married to the Emperor. We were divorced five years ago and I had not seen him following the divorce until last night at the Imperial Levee. What may or may not have happened last night is an entirely personal matter, and no one's business but our own. But in answer to the storm of speculation that has resulted from that meeting, let me say that there is no truth whatsoever to the suggestion that the Emperor and I plan to reunite. To the contrary, I would say that last night was simply a passing encounter between two people who were once close but no longer are. It may very well be another five years before we see each other again. My relationship with the Emperor, such as it is, has no bearing on my work here at Dexta, and I will have no further comment on it."

Media hands shot up and there was a flurry of people calling out, "Ms. VanDeen! Ms. VanDeen!" Gloria ignored them and forged ahead.

"Concerning Mynjhino," she said, raising her voice as the media reps slowly returned to order, "we have nothing new to report. But I can tell you that the situation is viewed with concern and that we are making every effort to determine the facts and formulate our response. To that end, I will be leaving for Mynjhino this afternoon on a fact-finding tour of that world. I will be meeting with Governor Rhinehart and Dexta personnel on the scene, and will report on what I learn there upon my return to Dexta in some three to four weeks. I will be happy to answer your questions at that time. Until then, I have nothing more to say. Thank you, and good day."

With that, Gloria turned and marched out of the auditorium, ignoring the shouted questions from the media reps. She had been in and out in under a minute.

GLORIA WAS PLEASED WITH HER PERFOR-mance. With her bold, not to say shocking, appearance, she had put to rest any notion that she was simply the Emperor's latest conquest. If anything, it would appear that it was Gloria, and not the Emperor, who was the sexual predator. She could have any man in the Empire, her appearance implied, and Charles simply happened to have been the lucky one last night. And it might be years before he got so lucky again. For his part, Charles would be forced to play it the same way Gloria had and let it be known that their encounter had been of no significance.

Secondly, by announcing her trip to Mynjhino, she had conveniently taken herself out of the limelight for the next month. By then, the media storm would have subsided and the vultures would be circling some other body.

Only one minor detail remained. Gloria had no authority to go zipping off to Mynjhino on her own. When he heard the news, Hector Konrad would go ballistic, but Gloria knew how to handle that. She arrived at the office of Deputy Supervisor Grant Enright, smiled her way past his assistant, and entered his inner sanctum.

Enright looked up from his console, stared appreciatively at Gloria, and grinned.

"Deftly done," he said. Enright was a handsome, solidly built man of forty, with short dark hair and intelligent brown eyes.

"You understand why I had to do it that way, don't you?"

"Of course. If you'd asked Konrad for the trip, he'd have turned you down. Now, you've mousetrapped him with the media, and he has no choice but to approve it. I'll get started on the paperwork, and you should have your authorization as soon as we scrape Konrad off the ceiling. Want to sit down and have some coffee?"

"Thanks, but I have to run. Konrad overscheduled me for the next two days, and now I get to dump all of that in Zoe's lap. I want to be sure I give her everything she needs."

Enright got to his feet and approached Gloria. "Are you all right?" he asked her. Gloria noticed a look of concern on his face.

"Fine," she assured him. "I think I managed to get Charles off my back with that briefing. The son of a bitch wants me back, and tried to use the media to force me back into his waiting arms. Now, the media will play it as if I raped poor Charles, then dumped him. Hopefully, that will reassure people around here that I'm not playing Imperial games behind their backs. By the time I return from Mynjhino, everything should be back to normal."

"I'm not so sure," Enright cautioned. "You made quite an impression with that briefing, kid. It's not everyone that stands in front of the media in transparent togs."

"Nonsense," Gloria laughed. "They aren't transparent at all. Just 90 percent."

"I stand corrected. How does that thing work, anyway?"

"There are little contact switches here and here."

Gloria showed him and demonstrated. "See? *Now* they're transparent."

"Ah. A subtle but important distinction. Well, in any case, I'll get you that authorization. Have a good trip, and for Spirit's sake, be careful out there. You're going into what could be a combat zone, Gloria. This isn't going to be just some public-relations lark."

"I know," she said. "Thanks for worrying, but I'll be fine." She leaned forward, planted a kiss on Enright's cheek, then turned to go.

"I know you will," Enright said as she left. "But be careful anyway."

PETRA CAUGHT SIGHT OF GLORIA AT THE FAR end of the corridor. She quickly pressed a button on her comm panel. A moment later, heads started popping out of doorways as Gloria walked past. They chipped in ten crowns a week for Petra to signal them when Gloria arrived or departed. She felt slightly disloyal about it, but no harm was done and ten crowns was ten crowns. Anyway, Petra knew that although Gloria would never admit it, she *liked* being stared at.

As Gloria approached, Petra noticed that her attire was now completely transparent. She wondered if she should start asking for twenty.

"I could have sworn you were actually wearing some clothing when you left here," Petra said, staring at Gloria. "Speaking of clothing, what should I pack for Mynjhino? What's it like there?"

"Warm," said Gloria. "Humid too, they say. Pack the way you would for a trip to the Congo."

That was not very helpful for Petra, to whom everyplace outside of Greater New York was the Congo. She decided not to mention to Gloria that she had never been off-planet before.

"Why don't you take off now, Petra? Grab some

lunch, go home to pack, then meet me at the Transit at three."

"Okay. The stuff from Gordon is on your desk, Zoe has her schedule, and Enders from PAO called to say thanks. See you at three."

GLORIA STOOD THERE FOR A MOMENT AND watched as Petra departed. She liked her a lot, but wondered how she would perform in the coming weeks. Petra was still relatively new to Dexta, and had a lot to learn.

Gloria went into her office to make sure she had everything before going home to do her own packing. Out of curiosity, she called up a newstext on her console to see how the media had played her briefing. Predictably, they had made the most of her stunning appearance, led with her statement about her relationship with the Emperor, and barely mentioned her trip to Mynjhino. Mission accomplished, she told herself. In a month, the beautiful bare bureaucrat would be old news, long since forgotten.

"Pardon me for coming in unannounced. There was no one outside."

Gloria looked up and saw a man standing in the doorway. It took a moment for it to register just who the man was: Norman Mingus, Secretary of the Department of Extraterrestrial Affairs.

Level I.

Gloria got to her feet and tried not to gawk, or salute.

"Yessir," she said. "Please, come right in. Will you have a seat?"

"Not necessary," he said. "I just wanted to have a quick word with you before your trip. A pleasure to meet you, Ms. VanDeen." He held out his hand and Gloria took it in hers. She tried not to pump it too hard. Adrenaline was surging through her.

Norman Mingus had been Secretary of Dexta for forty years, ever since the general reorganization of the Department following the last Imperial war. He was 130, which made him look like a man of sixty-five. His frame was tall and spare, with narrow, bony shoulders and a slight stoop. His hair was snow-white and his face pink and unlined. He looked kindly and gentle; nothing could have been further from the truth.

"It's a pleasure to see you too, sir," Gloria said as she released his hand. "Actually, we met once before."

"Oh? I'm surprised I don't remember."

"Well, it was about fifteen years ago, sir. I went to summer camp on Melampus IV with your daughter, Judy. We met when you picked her up to go home. How is Judy?"

"Thriving," Mingus said with a pleasant smile. "It seems I'm to become a grandfather, yet again."

"That's wonderful," said Gloria.

"Yes, I suppose. Although I can't keep track of them all, as it is. One of the hazards of having had a long life and five wives. Tell me, Ms. VanDeen—that little media circus act you just performed. Do you think it was entirely wise?"

"I thought it was necessary, sir. I needed to make it clear that I have no ongoing relationship with the Emperor. Otherwise . . ."

"Otherwise," he nodded, "people around here would think you were using Imperial influence to get ahead, and they wouldn't like it."

"That's right, sir."

"A clever maneuver, in that case. Still," he said, gazing frankly at Gloria's fully exposed charms, "I can't help but think that you may have made a somewhat more lasting impression on the media than you may have supposed."

"They'll have forgotten all about me by the time I get back."

"I wouldn't count on that, Ms. VanDeen. I understand your intent, however. You wanted to make it clear that you are not merely an Imperial plaything, but a formidable woman in your own right. Well, I would say that perhaps you now appear a little too formidable. You can never go back to being an anonymous Level XIII bureaucrat. Whether you realize it or not, you have just crossed a personal Rubicon, Ms. VanDeen. From now on, that lovely face and beautiful body are public property. Are you prepared for that?"

"I hadn't . . . I hadn't exactly thought of it that way, sir. I suppose you may be right. But I can live with it. All I really want is to be able to go on doing my job here at Dexta. What the media and the public think doesn't really matter."

"In a narrow sense, that's true. But here at Dexta, we are so insulated that people sometimes forget that the public and the media *do* matter. You have just made a considerable impression on them, Ms. VanDeen. Still, we may be able to make use of that. Our public image is that of a bunch of gray, secretive, but remorselessly efficient bureaucrats. That may have served us in the past, but times are changing. It may be useful for us to put a more human—and attractive—face on our public endeavors. Come and see me when you get back, and we'll discuss this more fully."

"Yessir," Gloria said. She wondered what he had in mind.

"In the meantime, I have a question. Our friends at GalaxCo are concerned by this incident on Mynjhino and intend to ask us for some Marines. What do you think about that?"

"It would take a month to get a regiment to Mynjhino," Gloria told him, glad that she had raised the matter at the CS meeting.

"What about a smaller contingent? Say, a company, mainly for show?"

"Perhaps two to three weeks from the date the orders went out, sir. They'd have to take them from the Frontier garrisons, however, and the Navy would resist that."

"Leave the Navy to me," said Mingus with a hint of impatience. "My question is, would it be wise? And will it be necessary?"

"Well, sir . . ."

"Just tell me what you think, Ms. VanDeen. Forget about channels and protocol. You know this planet better than anyone at higher levels. I want to hear what you think, from your own lips."

"Yessir. In my opinion, there will be more incidents. Whoever has those weapons probably can get more of them, and they have already shown that they are willing to use them. It's unlikely that they'll stop after the first attack."

"Just so. And the Marines?"

"A company or two would reassure the human population. But their very presence might inspire more incidents. As a practical matter, I suppose a company could ensure the security of the Imperial Compound. Beyond that . . . well, sir, we're talking about a planet with a population of 200 million."

"And would you recommend deployment of a company at this point?"

Gloria couldn't believe that Mingus was asking her for policy recommendations. Matters of such importance were far beyond the normal purview of a lowly Thirteen. And yet, Mingus had asked the question, and she had to come up with an answer.

"Sir," she said, trying to sound confident in her own judgment, "I think we'll end up sending Marines there at some point. Better too early than too late."

Mingus nodded. "Very good, Ms. VanDeen. Thank you for your input, it has been most valuable. And may I say," he added, looking her up and down and smiling, "that you are very lovely. Please do come and see me when you get back. Have a safe trip."

"Thank you, sir. I will."

Gloria watched him go, then exhaled slowly. It seemed like hours since her last breath.

"Wow," she said to herself.

chapter 6

INTERSTELLAR TRAVEL IN THE THIRTY-THIRD
century: step into a sealed, windowless tube, then step
out of it nine days later, 862 light-years away. For Gloria,
it was a familiar experience, but she knew from the personnel files that Petra had never left Earth before. She
supposed that for Petra, the trip probably lacked the element of romance that most people associated with going off-planet.

They had taken the VIP Transit from Manhattan to
Earthport, where Dexta functionaries quickly ushered
them into their Flyer. A Flyer was the smallest and
fastest form of interstellar vehicle available for human
transportation. Once they were aboard, the computer
piloted the ship away from Earthport, cut in the fusion
drive, and rapidly accelerated to 92 percent of the speed
of light. At that point, the fusion engine diverted its
power to the Ferguson Distortion Generators, and a
bubble of Yao Space formed around the Flyer, causing it
to squirt through normal space like a watermelon seed,
at a rate of a hundred light-years per day.

A complex balance of mass, energy, and fuel requirements dictated what was possible. A tiny courier vessel, with no life-support equipment and a small mass, was able to travel about three times as fast as a Flyer, although it lacked sufficient fuel to decelerate after arrival at its destination. A troopship, carrying a company of Marines, would take seventeen days to make the same journey from Earth to Mynjhino. A luxury liner would take a month.

The Flyer was anything but a luxury liner. With no crew, Petra and Gloria were the only occupants of the vessel. Their quarters consisted of a cylindrical tube twenty feet long and ten feet in diameter. Beds were built into the sides of the tube, with a narrow aisle between them. Forward, there were two small work consoles, along with chairs, a table, and food-processing facilities; aft, a small, waterless bathroom. There were no windows, and not even any viewscreens, since there was nothing to see outside but the featureless gray haze of Yao Space.

Once they were under way, Gloria stripped off her minimal clothing and stretched out on her bed. "You might as well take your clothes off too, Petra," Gloria said. "One of the most important things to know about going off-planet is that you can't count on there being any decent laundry facilities when you get to where you're going. No point in using up nine days of clean laundry just getting there."

Petra sat on the edge of her bed and dubiously eyed her unclad boss. "I don't know," she said. "If I have to spend nine days staring at your naked body, I'm going to wind up with a terrible inferiority complex."

"Nonsense. You've got a cute little body, Petra."

"Right," she said. "Cute. Little."

"I'm sorry, Petra. I didn't mean to sound patronizing. I just meant—"

"I know what you meant. It's okay, Gloria. Us cute little people are used to left-handed compliments." Petra pulled off her gray sweater, her gray skirt, and her shocking pink panties, and stowed them in her travel bag. She had short, straight, brown hair, and smooth white flesh that had rarely seen the sun.

Gloria looked at Petra's small, round breasts and pleasantly curved hips, and asked, "You got a man in your life these days, Petra?" Gloria rarely inquired about her coworkers' personal lives, but she was going to be spending nine days in close proximity with Petra and figured that this would be a chance to get to know her better. If she were going to take Petra on as a permanent LapDog—an assistant who would accompany her not just to Mynjhino, but on her continuing journey through Dexta—Gloria wanted to know her as well as possible.

She already knew a few things about her. Petra had been born in New Jersey, had gone to school in New York, and after two failures, finally passed the Dexta qualifying exams. Her first months at Dexta had been a horror story much like Gloria's own. They had worked together on a couple of projects, and six months ago Petra had come to her, begging for a chance to be her assistant. Up until then, Petra had been working under a Fourteen who used her like tissue paper and enjoyed passing her around to the other members of his Dog pack. It was nothing less than bureaucratic rape, a common enough rite of passage for an attractive and naïve Fifteen. Gloria knew that Petra had been close to the breaking point, but after trying so hard to get into Dexta, she was determined not to give up. Gloria was her last hope.

Feeling empathy for Petra, but harboring some doubts about her abilities, Gloria reluctantly took her on. Since then, Petra had shown herself to be competent and energetic, and thoroughly devoted to Gloria, who had rescued her from a nightmare existence. She had a smart mouth and a sense of humor that Gloria secretly enjoyed, but she had yet to prove herself capable of meeting more than routine, everyday challenges. This trip would be a chance to test her, and see what her limits were.

"Not really," Petra admitted, in answer to Gloria's question. "There's a cute guy over in Epsilon Division that I wouldn't mind spending nine days naked with, but I think he's spoken for. One of Patsy Saito's Lost Boys."

Gloria nodded. Patsy Saito was an Associate Supervisor, Level XII, who kept a harem of handsome young Fourteens and Fifteens at her beck and call. Patsy was the worst sort of Tiger, the female equivalent of the Dogs who had once savaged both of them.

"Well," Gloria pointed out, "there *are* a few men in the Empire who don't work for Dexta. Maybe you'll meet one or two of them on Mynjhino."

"You mean we're going to have time for extracurricular activities?"

"Never can tell," said Gloria. "And you don't have to wear gray all the time, you know."

"I don't own anything that isn't gray. Except my underwear. Underwear are those little things that some women wear under their outerwear."

"I think I've heard of them." Gloria smiled. "And I may have a few things you could borrow that might fit you, Petra. If you don't mind showing some of that cute little body of yours."

"I don't know," Petra said, shaking her head. "I'm not sure I could walk around with everything hanging out, the way you do."

"It's not such a big deal. Growing up around the Court, casual nudity was pretty commonplace."

"Seems kind of dangerous, if you ask me."

"Let me tell you a secret, Petra. Most men are scared to death of sexy, intelligent women. That's why they act like such jerks. The less you wear, the more power you have over them. It's a way of letting them know who's the boss."

"You may be the boss, Gloria. Me, I'm just a pathetic, cowering underling."

• • •

GLORIA CAUGHT UP ON HER SLEEP, THEN SPENT most of her time studying the material Gordon Chesbro had compiled on Mynjhino. She urged Petra to study it, too. There wasn't much else for either of them to do, other than play computer games and indulge in some virtual-reality diversions.

Gloria also spent time thinking about her encounter with Norman Mingus, and what it might mean for her future at Dexta. His comments made her wonder if he had it in mind to transfer her to some slot in Public Affairs. She hoped not. She enjoyed having her hands on the actual gears and levers that made the Empire function, and didn't want to be shunted off to some show-and-tell position.

There was also the question of her sudden fame. The fact that Charles V had once been married was not exactly a secret, but the Household had soft-pedaled that aspect of the Emperor's past; Gloria had never been more than a footnote to history. Now, her night with the Emperor and her news briefing had made her, as Mingus pointed out, public property. She hoped and expected that the sensation would soon fade and that she could quickly settle back into comfortable obscurity. But what if it didn't?

She supposed that she could always reverse course—start wearing underwear and dressing like Zoe Zachary—but she honestly enjoyed being a Tiger and didn't want to surrender the power and, yes, the fun, that went along with it. She still felt an unabashed sexual thrill when she thought about her nearly naked performance in front of the media. But being a Tiger within the cloistered walls of Dexta was one thing; being a Tiger out in the world might be quite another. She resolved to test the waters on Mynjhino and dress even more dangerously than she did on Earth. That might add some spice to what was, by all accounts, a pretty boring planet.

Aside from the fact that people were being killed.

SHE AND PETRA CHATTED OCCASIONALLY AND shared a few secrets. Petra hesitantly quizzed her about the Emperor, but Gloria initially offered little on that subject. Finally, she admitted that the Emperor was, in fact, as well endowed as rumor had it and was, despite an essentially selfish nature, a marvelous lover. "That's why I stayed with him as long as I did," she confessed. "He was screwing every woman he could get his hands on, and I knew it, but he still managed to keep me satisfied in bed. But when I wanted to make something more out of my life, he couldn't handle it. Absolutely forbade me to return to school. So I left him, and never looked back."

"Do you ever think about what would have happened if you had stayed? I mean, you'd be Empress now."

"What a horrifying thought *that* is." Gloria laughed.

"Yeah," said Petra. "Why live a life of pampered luxury when you can work fourteen hours a day for Dexta?"

"Petra, I grew up rich. I spent the first eighteen years of my life in pampered luxury. You know what? I got bored with it. I get more enjoyment and satisfaction from those fourteen-hour days at Dexta than I ever did or ever could have from being rich and useless."

"Whew," said Petra. "Thank the Spirit I managed to avoid all that! I was smart enough to grow up poor and desperate."

Petra had a talent for shooting off zingers that were sharp and accurate. This one had found its target. "I suppose," Gloria said, "that poor people must get a little sick of hearing rich people talk about what a burden and a bore wealth is."

"Oh, no," said Petra, "we love it. It makes us feel superior."

"Some of you," Gloria said with a warm smile, "*are* superior. Not one of the girls I grew up with could have survived what you went through at Dexta, Petra."

"*You* survived it," Petra pointed out. "And from what I've heard, it was a lot worse for you than it was for me."

"What have you heard?" Gloria asked.

"Oh . . . just things."

"What things?" Gloria was curious to learn what people at Dexta thought of her.

"Well," said Petra, "they say you . . . how shall I put this? That you, uh, spread your legs for half the men in your Sector. That they took turns with you in the men's room."

"I did and they did," Gloria admitted. "I was too scared to say no."

"I was, too. I almost quit."

"But you didn't."

"Neither did you, Gloria. And you had a lot more to go back to than I ever did. I stayed because I couldn't afford not to. But you could have gone back to your dreadful life of ease and luxury anytime you wanted. Why didn't you?"

"Two reasons," Gloria said. "First, because Viveca Kwan showed me a way to survive at Dexta. The whole Lions, Tigers, and Sheep thing always seemed like some kind of silly Dexta mythology to me, but it's not. Dexta is actually a complex ecosystem in its own right, and there are very real niches within it that must and will be filled by someone. If you fired everyone but the Sheep, pretty soon some of the Sheep would start growing claws and fangs. The system demands it. And Viveca helped me to realize that I could choose my own niche. So can you, Petra."

Petra considered that. "Woof," she said.

Gloria laughed. She reached across the aisle between their beds and patted Petra on the head. "Good Petra," she said.

"What's it like being a Tiger, anyway? I mean, what do you feel like when you walk into a room in your invisible bits of nothing and everybody stares at you?"

"I feel powerful," Gloria said. "A tiger's stripes are like an advertisement, I think. They tell everyone else in the jungle, 'Watch out for me. I'm beautiful and powerful, and I can be dangerous. Cross me, and I'll have you for lunch.' When I see people staring, I know I have power over them. And I can use that power to do my job better and secure my own position in the jungle. And, I admit, it makes me feel sexy and alive. The truth is, I love it. You know, there's nothing in the *Dexta Code* that says you can't have fun."

"Fun," said Petra. "What a concept!"

"Maybe you should try having a little more fun, yourself."

"Hmmm... Petra Nash—Tiger! Naw, it just doesn't work."

"It might," Gloria suggested. "Have you ever tried it?"

She shook her head. "I don't think Tigers can be 'cute' and 'little.' I think I'm more the Dog type."

"Doesn't mean you have to be a mutt."

"Is there such a thing as a tigerdog?"

"Maybe there could be. Maybe you could make a brand new niche for yourself, Petra. But Tiger or Dog, whatever you are, enjoy it."

Petra thought about that in silence for a while. "Gloria," she asked after a minute, "you said there were two reasons you stayed. What was the second reason?"

Gloria got up from her bed, walked a few paces to her work console, and came back with a memory cube. She tossed it to Petra.

"That's the second reason," she said. "Know what that is? That's Mynjhino. An entire planet, or everything we know about it. You're holding a planet in your hands, Petra, and all 200 million sentient beings on it. What you and I do in the next few weeks will directly affect their fate. If we mess up, there could be terrible consequences for them and for us. Do it right, and maybe we save thousands of lives and make a better future for them. That's why I stayed. What could be more important than what we're doing? What could be more meaningful and fulfilling? We're helping to run a galactic empire, Petra. I get chills when I think about it."

"You know what?" Petra said. "I do too. We're pretty lucky, aren't we?"

"Damn right," Gloria said.

THE FLYER BURST BACK INTO NORMAL SPACE

200 million miles from Mynjhino and began decelerating. It sent out a signal to the Mynjhino Orbital Station announcing its impending arrival and another signal to the Imperial Compound on the surface, alerting them that important visitors were on the way. Inside the Flyer, Gloria and Petra couldn't see what was happening, and didn't know that their journey had ended until a gentle thump informed them that their vehicle had docked at the Orbital Station.

The Flyer's door slid open and they emerged into the Station, where they were greeted by the Station Manager and his assistant, as well as by two robots to carry their baggage. The Station personnel, who had some of the more tedious and boring jobs in all of Dexta, had been expecting two gray and overbearing big shots from HQ. They were pleasantly stunned to find two smiling, attractive women who met their expectations only in the matter of gray. For this first day, they both wore standard Dexta gray—Petra a jacket, shirt, and skirt, and Gloria a jacket, no shirt, and hardly any skirt. The Station Manager invited them to stay for lunch and was crushed when Gloria politely declined and said that they really did have to get to the surface as quickly as possible. Less than fifteen minutes after arriving, Gloria and Petra took their leave aboard a liftship shuttle.

"Now this is more like it!" exulted Petra, staring out of the passenger compartment windows as they began their descent into the atmosphere of Mynjhino. Below them, the planet was immense and blue, with swirling white clouds floating above broad oceans. Eighty percent of the planet was covered by seas, with two relatively small landmasses. The Imperial Compound was located on the Eastern Continent, Myn, in the coastal capital city of Dhanj, just visible from orbit as a brownish-gray enclave on the edge of a lush, green upland.

The descent was quickly accomplished, as the shuttle's computer guided it downward. Unlike the Flyer, the shuttle did have a human pilot, because Dexta rules required it, but he had nothing to do other than monitor the computer's performance and wait for something to go wrong. Nothing ever did. Spaceflight was too precise and unforgiving a business to be left to the limited skills of flawed human beings. Far from being a daring and romantic profession, piloting in the thirty-third century was a pedestrian and boring occupation.

The shuttle soared low over the harbor area of Dhanj and touched down in the Roads a mile offshore. The port was the busiest on the planet, which meant that once or twice a month a freighter would splash down there. Only one was currently in port; a bright yellow GalaxCo vessel snugly docked at the commercial wharf, where it was being loaded with pharmaceuticals from the company's processing facilities. The shuttle cruised smoothly into the passenger wharf and docked.

Gloria and Petra had arrived on Mynjhino.

They stepped out of the shuttle and into the sunlight and bracing air of Mynjhino. The planet's surface gravity was .92 G, and the atmospheric oxygen content was a little higher than Earth's; the combined effect made new arrivals feel light and energetic. The air was warm and humid, and carried a thousand exotic and unfamiliar scents.

A small delegation from the Compound welcomed them. Imperial Secretary Melinda Throneberry had come to greet them and introduced Undersecretary for Security Ricardo Olivera and two assistants. She didn't introduce the four Myn porters who fetched their baggage. The Myn were barely five feet tall and Petra, who was not much taller, stared at them in wonder.

Gloria chatted briefly, pleasantly, with Throneberry and Olivera. The Imperial Secretary was a tall, somewhat harried-looking blond, probably about forty, with gracious manners and an air of intense efficiency. Olivera was young and more expansive, with a gleaming smile and the look and enthusiasm of an assistant tennis pro. Throneberry was in standard Dexta gray, but Olivera wore tight black trousers and white short sleeves. He unabashedly ogled Gloria, whose open jacket and too-short skirt rippled revealingly in the gusty oceanside breeze.

Pleasantries out of the way, Gloria asked Throneberry, "Have there been any more incidents?"

Throneberry, with a sidelong glance at the Myn porters, said, "We'll talk in the car. Right this way."

Gloria and Petra got into a nearby limo skimmer along with Throneberry and Olivera, while the two assistants and the porters piled into a second vehicle. Once they were under way, Throneberry said, "Sorry, I didn't want to get into a discussion out in the open. You may have noticed, the Myn have long ears. In answer to your question, yes, we've had two more incidents. Another seventeen dead. Things have gotten very tense around here."

Gloria turned to Olivera. "The same sort of thing? Automatic weapons?"

Olivera nodded. "That's what the eyewitnesses claim. Of course, the only surviving witnesses were all Myn, so it's hard to get precise details. We still haven't gotten our hands on a weapon."

"Where were the incidents?"

"Upcountry, in the plantation regions," said Throneberry. "One at a bar frequented by GalaxCo employees, the other at the gate of a processing facility."

"But nothing in urban regions yet?"

Throneberry gestured toward the passing city scenery. "As far as urban regions go, this is about it. A million Myn here, no more than about fifty thousand in any other town. No incidents here or in the other towns, but a lot of tension."

Gloria looked out of the limo and watched the streets of Dhanj for a few moments. The buildings were generally less than four stories, constructed from a tan, adobe-like substance, and there were not a lot of Myn visible in the streets. Skimmer traffic was light. It seemed a sleepy, lethargic sort of community.

"What's the reaction back home?" Throneberry asked.

"They're taking it seriously. I'm here to appreciate the situation and report back. I'd like to meet with you and all your Undersecretaries before I meet with the Governor."

"Fine, I'll call in everyone when we get back to the Compound. But Hawkes is upcountry, and I'm not sure if he'll be back today. As for the Governor . . . perhaps tomorrow. He is currently indisposed. Migraine."

"I see," said Gloria. She turned to Olivera. "The major question we want answered is how the Myn are getting these weapons. IntSec has nothing on smuggling operations in Beta-5, but no one thinks the Myn are manufacturing the weapons themselves. What do you think?"

"It's unlikely," said Olivera. "The Jhino might be able to do it, if they put their little minds to it, but the Myn?" He gave a derisive snort. "Not in a hundred years."

"So where do they get them?"

Olivera looked uncomfortable. "We're looking into various possibilities," he said vaguely.

"Which are?"

"Why don't we wait until we get to the Compound?" suggested Throneberry. She looked uncomfortable, too. "We'll give you a full report."

Gloria already had her doubts about that. She settled back into the seat of the limo and stared outside at the threadbare world of the Myn.

THE IMPERIAL COMPOUND WAS NOT QUITE AS grand as its name, but it was the most impressive place Gloria had seen so far in Dhanj. Surrounded by an electronic fence and ten-foot stone walls, the Compound consisted of three main buildings and a handful of smaller outbuildings. The largest building was the Governor's Residence, a sprawling three-story conglomeration that called to mind Spanish-Moorish architecture. It was apparently made from the same dun-colored adobe that was so common in the city. The pair of two-story office buildings were of the same construction, but less ornate in design. The skimmer came to a stop outside one of them.

Olivera led Gloria and Petra inside to their rooms on the second floor, while Throneberry went to her office in the administrative building. The two assistants and four Myn porters trooped along behind them with the luggage. While Petra got settled in her room, Olivera lingered in Gloria's and attempted to engage her in small talk. He smiled a lot, and stared at her nearly naked legs and breasts. Gloria decided it would be worth her while to indulge him, although on a purely personal level she found him a bit too oily and adolescent. But she already suspected that Olivera was keeping secrets, or was at least reluctant to say everything he knew in Throneberry's presence. Later, alone, she would have no trouble getting him to tell her everything he knew, which probably wasn't a lot.

As she leaned over to open a suitcase on the bed, intentionally giving him an unobstructed view of her right breast, she asked, "Is there a place where we can meet for dinner? I'd like to talk to you some more, Ricardo."

"Everyone goes to Blaine's," he said, smiling broadly. "It's a charming little place a block from the Compound, with loads of atmosphere. I'd be delighted to have dinner with you, Gloria. May I call you Gloria?"

She stood up and faced him. "Certainly. Petra and I will see you there at eight."

His smile wavered a bit and froze. "Ms. Nash? She'll be coming too? Of course, of course. That will be wonderful." He obviously didn't think so, but was stuck with it.

"Now," said Gloria, dismissing him with a subtle nod of her head, "if you'll excuse me, I'd like to freshen up. I'll see you in half an hour in Secretary Throneberry's office."

Olivera made an obedient exit, and Gloria sat down on the bed and leaned back. Spirit, it was so easy.

AS GLORIA WALKED ACROSS THE DUSTY COM- pound to the administration building for her meeting with the staff, she pondered the fact that her presence on Mynjhino had created a situation charged with institutionalized ambiguity. By law, all Imperial Secretaries throughout the Empire were Level XII. That put every world on an equal footing, bureaucratically speaking. It also prevented Imperial Governors from inflating their own importance by surrounding themselves with high-ranking staffers.

At the same time, although the Imperial Secretaries were Twelves, they reported back to System Coordinators at Headquarters who were all Fourteens and Coordinating Supervisors who, like Gloria, were Thirteens. As their job titles implied, they simply coordinated and supervised; all directives, instructions, and policy decisions emanated from higher up. In addition, the System Coordinators and Coordinating Supervisors were routinely rotated to new positions every two or three years, preventing them from accumulating too much power and establishing their own mini-empires within Dexta. During the early days of Dexta and the Empire, before these rules had been put in place, such abuses of power had been all too common.

What all of this meant, in practice, was that Gloria could not issue any orders to Melinda Throneberry and her staff, although her opinions were likely to carry considerable weight. For her part, Throneberry could not issue any orders to Gloria, who was outside the local chain of command and responsible only to Headquarters. Gloria was well aware that these tangled lines of authority could sometimes lead to problems and could only hope that things would go smoothly on Mynjhino. If not, conflicts would likely be resolved through sheer force of personality; life at Dexta was not for the timid or faint of heart.

Gloria and Petra entered the administration building and were directed to the Imperial Secretary's office. Throneberry introduced them, and they sat down on a plush sofa. Petra sat next to Gloria, ready to make notes on a palm pad. Seated on chairs in a semicircle around the sofa were Throneberry, Olivera, and the Undersecretaries for Commerce and Corporate Affairs, and Finance: Tatiana Markova and Sonia Blumenthal. Gloria knew from their files that Blumenthal was fifty-five and had been on Myn for nine years, twice as long as anyone else on the staff. She was regarded as a burn-out, common enough for someone of her age in Dexta, but still competent and reliable. Markova, on the other hand, was just twenty-seven and had been transferred to Mynjhino from Headquarters eighteen months ago. She was an up-and-coming Tiger, and eyed Gloria with suspicion. Like Gloria, the Undersecretaries were all Thirteens.

Each of them gave brief, formal reports that didn't really tell Gloria anything she didn't already know. The banks and money supply were stable, GalaxCo and the other corporations were deeply concerned, and the ten thousand humans on Mynjhino were frightened. What was missing, Gloria realized, was any appreciation or understanding of the Myn themselves.

"Tell me about the Myn leadership," Gloria said. "How are they reacting to events?"

"Leadership?" sniffed Olivera. "It's hard to dignify it with that term!"

Throneberry gave Olivera a look of impatience, then turned to Gloria, and said, "As you know, the Myn are loosely organized in a quasi-federal system, based on the eleven major tribal groups. The tribal council, known as the Tandik, meets here in Dhanj on an irregular basis. They are not currently in session, however. The Primat is a Myn named Quan, who is rather elderly and appears to have little support from the younger Myn. He is not very comfortable with humans, and is frankly somewhat confused by modernization and integration. I think he wishes we would all just go away, and thinks that if he ignores us long enough, we will."

"That would suggest that he's in basic agreement with the nativists, wouldn't you say? Does he have links with them, particularly with the Myn-Traha?"

"Nothing we've been able to put a finger on," said Olivera. "He just sits there in his Palqui—that's a sort of combination temple and government center—and meets with occasional visitors."

"Who are the visitors?"

Olivera smiled wanly. "Hard to say, exactly," he said. "We do keep a watch, but they all look alike, you know."

"Probably not to each other," Gloria suggested. "Don't you have any help among the Myn, themselves?"

"Well, of course. We have some Myn on staff... those little fellows who took your bags, and some others.

But as for recruiting them for intelligence purposes, I'd say that's unrealistic. You'd have to know them, Gloria."

"I'd like to. Can I meet with some of them?"

"We might be able to arrange something," said Throneberry. "Give us a day or two to set that up."

Gloria nodded. If it took a day or two just to arrange a meeting with anyone in the local population, the situation was worse than she had supposed. She was already forming a picture of an isolated, out-of-touch human community on this world. That was a sadly common circumstance throughout the Empire. Gloria looked at Sonia Blumenthal, who had been on Mynjhino the longest.

"Sonia," she said, "you must know some Myn personally. What can you tell me about them?"

"They are shy, friendly, happy, sad, intelligent, ignorant, competent, incompetent, simple, complex...a population of individuals, in other words. Like humans, only they're shorter and smell worse. I've been here nine years, and have friends among them, but I can't really claim to know or understand them. You see, we're not entirely real to them. They live on two planes, one in the here and now, and one in some mystical otherworld, where they converse with their revered ancestors. You can be in the middle of a conversation with them, and they'll stop dead, tilt their furry little heads upward, and spend the next five minutes listening to advice from their great-great-great-grandfathers."

"I see," said Gloria. "What about the Jhino? I gather that they are a little more connected with the present."

"They're a lot easier to deal with," said Tatiana Markova. "Spirit knows why we didn't put the Compound there instead of here. As it is, our consulate in Jhino conducts more actual business than we do here. In fact, the Jhino have been suggesting that we move our main operation over to the Western continent. Some of us," she added, glancing at Throneberry, "would like to do just that."

"Not feasible," said Throneberry coldly. "Unless you can go back home, Gloria, and get our budget tripled."

Gloria smiled, and said, "Make a note of that, Petra. I take it there has been no similar trouble with the Jhino?"

"None," said Olivera proudly. "Relations are rock solid."

"Might we be able to get some intelligence from the Jhino?"

"They don't know much more than we do, Gloria," Olivera explained. "The two races don't like one another. They were at war when humans got here eighty-five years ago, and would be again if we left."

"And since the Myn-Traha want us to leave, that raises an interesting point, wouldn't you say?"

If it did, Olivera didn't get it. Blumenthal did.

"The Myn-Traha," she said, "would like nothing better than to be able to finish their interrupted war with the Jhino. Their ancestors seem to insist on it, in fact."

"What's the Jhino attitude?"

"They think the Myn are foolish and primitive," said Throneberry. "They don't like them, but they've kept the peace. They don't seem to want another war."

"What if they did?" Gloria asked. "What kind of show could they put on, if they got serious?" She looked toward Olivera.

The Undersecretary for Security dismissed the notion with a casual shrug. "I can't see them trying. But if they did, they could certainly develop better weaponry than the Myn. Remember, when we arrived they were shooting at each other with cannonballs. Today, the Jhino might manage something more like nineteenth- or twentieth-century technology."

"Like automatic weapons?"

"Conceivably," Olivera conceded. "But Gloria, it's the Myn who have been shooting at us, not the Jhino."

"I'm just trying to cover all the possibilities. You're

convinced that the Jhino are not the source of the weapons?"

"I don't see how they could be."

"And that estimate is based on what? Intelligence, or intuition?"

Olivera took a moment to answer. "We have no intelligence indicating that," he said at last.

"So if it's not the Jhino, where are they coming from?"

No one had a ready answer. An uncomfortable silence hung in the air for several seconds.

"I saw a GalaxCo freighter in the harbor today," Gloria said. "Could someone be using corporate ships to smuggle in arms?"

"Why would they do that?" Markova asked, sounding a little indignant.

"I didn't ask why," said Gloria. "I asked if it's possible. Are incoming freighters inspected or searched in any way? Do the Myn have effective Customs control? Do we?"

"It's never been an issue," said Markova.

"It is now," Gloria told her.

"I'll look into it," Throneberry said, casting a disapproving glance at Markova.

"What do we know about the weapons themselves?" Gloria asked next. "I know you haven't found any, but what about the bullets? Have you learned anything from them?"

"We're not exactly set up to do ballistic analysis around here, Gloria," said Olivera. "We have no laboratory facilities, and I can't think of anyone who would know the first things about antique bullets."

Gloria nodded. "Well, then, get me some samples, and I'll take them back to Earth with me when I leave."

She got to her feet and looked around at Olivera, Markova, and Blumenthal. "Thank you very much for your input," she said. "I'm sure I'll be seeing a lot of you in the next several days, and we can talk some more. Now, I'd like to have a few words alone with Melinda."

The Undersecretaries looked at Throneberry, who nodded to them. They got up and filed out of the office annex. Gloria looked at Petra, and she got up and followed them out.

Throneberry rose, walked to a window, and stared outside for a few moments. Then she turned to Gloria, and said, "I'm sorry. I know that didn't look very good."

"It looked like shit, Melinda," Gloria told her bluntly.

"Look, Olivera and Markova haven't been here long, and Blumenthal has been here too long."

"And the Governor has a migraine."

"You see what I have to work with? Honestly, Gloria, we do all right around here most of the time. But nobody was prepared for this."

"And that's the problem. Why weren't you?"

Some color came into Throneberry's cheeks. "Do you think it's easy out here?" she demanded. "You've been Beta-5 CS for what, a year? What the hell can you possibly know? Everything looks so clear and simple in Manhattan, but we're 862 light-years from Times Square."

"Calm down, Melinda. I'm not here to take scalps. But I can tell you this much about the view from Manhattan. Mingus is personally interested in the situation here. He talked to me before I left."

The color quickly drained from Throneberry's cheeks. "Mingus? Spirit! That's all we need."

"Look at it this way, Melinda. It's a chance to get some serious Notice at Dexta if you handle this well. And as for your personnel problems, you may be getting some help soon. This is for your ears only, and it's not definite, but I think Mingus intends to send a company or two of Marines."

"He *does*? Spirit, that would—"

Throneberry broke off abruptly and looked toward the door. A man had just entered the annex. He wore boots and khaki field gear. There were dark red stains on his shirt; they looked like blood.

"It's happened again," he said.

chapter 7

THE MAN WAS BRIAN HAWKES, UNDERSECRE-
tary for Administration, and the blood was not his own.

He walked into the annex, found a chair, and sat
down. He leaned forward, elbows on his knees, and
rubbed his hands over his eyes and forehead and through
his medium-length dark hair. After a few moments, he
looked up at Throneberry, then noticed Gloria. He ran
his eyes over her quickly, without apparent interest, then
turned back to Throneberry.

"The GalaxCo plantation at Zinkan," he said.

"That's just sixty-five miles from here!" Throneberry
looked alarmed.

Hawkes nodded. "I got there about ten minutes after
it happened. Five or six of them showed up outside the
operations office. Four dead, three seriously wounded. I
don't think one of them's going to make it, but the other
two might. Fortunately, GalaxCo had a med team on-site.
No Myn casualties, and the attackers got away clean."

"Did you manage to get a statement from the
wounded?" Gloria asked him.

"They were too busy bleeding." Hawkes looked up at Gloria. "Who are you?"

"Brian, this is Gloria VanDeen, the Beta-5 CS. She just arrived from Earth. Gloria, Brian Hawkes, Undersec for Admin."

"Welcome to our happy planet," he said. He was a big man in his mid-thirties, with massive shoulders and a bronzed, outdoors appearance. Gloria had read his file and the memos he had written, and knew that he was the one person in the Compound who actually got out into the country and spent time with the Myn. She was eager to talk with him, but could see that now was not the time.

"You two have things to do," Gloria said. "I'll get out of your way and let you do them." She nodded to Throneberry and Hawkes and left the annex.

Gloria went back to her room, shaken by what she had seen. It was real now, not just a sterile report from a courier and a spate of bureaucratic assessments. She had seen the blood.

She lay back against the pillows on her bed and tried to make sense of Mynjhino. The Imperial operation here was obviously a shambles. Whom to blame and how to fix it were questions beyond her competence at the moment. Throneberry was right about one thing, though; everything had looked much simpler in Manhattan.

"WE'RE GOING TO DOUBLE-TEAM HIM," GLORIA told Petra later that evening as they prepared for dinner. "I want him dazzled and babbling. He'll share all the local secrets with us if he thinks he's going to wind up in bed with one or both of us."

"Is he?" Petra asked warily.

"Of course not," Gloria assured her. "Not with me, at least. What you do is up to you, Petra, but sleeping with Olivera is not part of your job description."

"He's kind of cute, though," Petra said. "A dreamy smile."

Gloria looked at her assistant. "What's this? Hormones, Petra?"

"Hey, I've got some. I think."

"Well, feel free to indulge them. I told you, it's not against the law to have some fun while you're here. Why don't you pick out something to wear from my closet? Some of the smart fabrics are retractable and ought to fit you."

Petra went to the closet and gazed in wonder at Gloria's wardrobe. Gloria knew that the least expensive item in it would have cost her a week's salary. "What are you going to wear?" Petra asked.

Gloria had already stripped off her skirt and jacket. She picked up a dress she had laid out on the bed, and said, "This." She pulled it over her head and slipped into it. The gauzy white confection featured long, flared sleeves and a wide, plunging neckline that left her breasts almost completely uncovered. If she didn't move, the hemline provided a little more than minimum coverage in front and a little less than minimum coverage in back. The fabric was just transparent enough to hint at the presence of what little the dress didn't already reveal.

"Maybe I'll just stay home and hide under my bedcovers," said Petra.

"Nonsense. Why don't you try that band-skirt?"

"Uh . . . Gloria, I think I'll just go with what I have on."

"Scaredy-cat. At least do something to make yourself look a little more available. Give him a reason to look in your direction once in a while."

Petra undid the top button of her gray shirt, hesitated, then unfastened the second button.

"Well, don't stop now," Gloria told her.

Petra gave Gloria a dubious look, then reluctantly undid the third button. She looked at herself in the mirror and saw that the undercurve of her breasts was clearly visible from some angles. "Gulp," she said.

"Lovely," Gloria declared. "We'll make a Tiger out of you yet."

THEY GOT DIRECTIONS TO BLAINE'S FROM THE single Security man at the front gate of the Compound. Gloria noticed that he was armed with a plasma pistol. She wondered what other weapons were available in the Compound, should they become necessary.

It was a short three-minute walk to the restaurant. The night was warm and muggy, with unfamiliar stars and two moons visible in the sky overhead. The streets around the Compound were completely deserted, and the only sound was the clop of their own heels on the rough pavement. Gloria wondered if that was normal, or if the locals were avoiding the Compound because of the troubles.

They found Olivera waiting for them in front of the restaurant, decked out in a blue tunic, tight, white Imperial breeches, and black boots polished to a high gleam. "Ah, ladies," he cried, "you look exquisite!" He turned his head, noticed Petra, and added, "Both of you."

Inside, the owner, having been alerted by Olivera, greeted them with fawning smiles and compliments. His establishment featured the same ersatz Spanish-Moorish architecture that seemed to be the norm in Dhanj, with red tile floors and a profusion of strange plants hanging from the low ceiling. A Myn waiter led them to their table. Gloria noticed that the small, bear-like creature was heavily perfumed to cover his normal scent, which was offensive to humans. She wondered how the Myn felt about the lilac aroma he was required to adopt.

Perhaps, as Olivera had said, everyone came to Blaine's, but only three couples were dining there at the moment. As they were being seated, Gloria caught sight of Sonia Blumenthal alone at a table in the corner with a book and a bottle of wine.

Olivera smiled happily as he ordered wine and made inane small talk. He asked about Earth and people he had known during his one year at Headquarters in Manhattan. He had spent most of his time at Dexta off-planet, Gloria knew, performing relatively simple tasks with enough efficiency to win him promotion to the Undersecretary for Security slot on Mynjhino a year ago.

Under Gloria's gentle questioning, he was soon describing the social scene in Dhanj, such as it was, complete with salacious tidbits about some of the more prominent members of the human community. He seemed aware that he had not exactly covered himself with glory during the meeting in Throneberry's office, so he was eager to make up for it by proving that he really was in the know, and that whenever Gloria wanted to know something about life on Mynjhino, he was the man to whom she should turn.

When the waiter brought them their menus, Olivera described what was good and what was to be avoided. "All of our beef, lamb, and poultry is imported from Pecos," he explained. "The Myn are vegetarians, except for seafood, of course. There are one or two local dishes that might interest you—what they call lobster is actually a sort of shellfish, and the clams are pretty much the same as the clams back home. But most of the native foods are what you might call acquired tastes."

"So the human community gets most of its food from off-planet?" Gloria asked.

"The majority of it," said Olivera. "The GalaxCo plantations do grow a little wheat, and the natives have a few crops that are palatable. Some of their fruit is rather delicious, in fact. We've been trying to get them to start exporting it to the other Beta-5 worlds, but they have some odd religious scruples about that, it seems. A curious people, in many ways."

Olivera ordered beefsteak, Petra the chicken Kiev,

and Gloria opted for the local lobster. The wine, also imported from Pecos, was ordinary, at best. Gloria kicked Petra under the table to get her to open up a little bit; Olivera had all but ignored her so far.

"What do you do for fun around here?" Petra asked.

"Precious little of that, I'm afraid," he said. "Some folks are big on sailing. The Myn are proficient at it, and have some interesting little vessels. Then there's tennis, Servitor is building a golf course, the GalaxCo people have softball and soccer leagues, and there's a drama group here in Dhanj that puts on the classics from time to time. I was Mercutio a couple of months back."

"Not Romeo?" Petra asked, leaning forward slightly to show a little more of her small, pert breasts.

Olivera noticed, and smiled at her. "Another case of crass nepotism. Governor Rhinehart's nephew got the part."

"And who played Juliet?" Gloria asked.

"The lovely Tatiana Markova, of course," said Olivera. "She has most of the star power around here. Or did, until you beautiful ladies arrived, bless the Spirit."

"She is very attractive," Gloria agreed. "I suppose she snaps up all the good men."

Olivera smiled knowingly. "Tatiana is not shy," he conceded. "In fact, I probably shouldn't say this, but the Rhineharts think very highly of her, if you take my meaning."

Gloria smiled and nodded. Interesting, she thought.

"Sounds pretty juicy," said Petra eagerly. "Are there any other good scandals we should know about?"

"Oh, nothing terribly scandalous. The usual Compound intrigues, one might say. Melinda has had an on-again, off-again thing with Hawkes for some time, I gather. Currently off, it seems. And poor, sad Sonia, over there in the corner, is said to have some secret lover who works for Imperium, but no one ever sees him. Some of us doubt that he even exists, but it would be nice to think so. Sonia's only other constant companion is the bottle."

"I see," said Gloria. "That reminds me, there were a couple of things I wanted to ask Sonia about. Would you mind? Petra will keep you company. I'll be back in a few minutes."

"Not at all." Olivera sprang to his feet, pulled Gloria's chair out for her, clearly enjoying the view from the rear as she made her way to the corner of the restaurant.

Gloria looked down at Sonia Blumenthal, and said, "Would you mind a little company?"

Sonia glanced up from her book. "Suit yourself," she said, nodding toward the empty chair at her table. "But those tits of yours won't get me babbling the way they did with young Olivera. However," she added, "another bottle of wine might do the trick."

Gloria seated herself, motioned to a waiter, and indicated she wanted another bottle. "You've been here longer than anyone else, Sonia," Gloria said. "I'd be interested to know your opinion about what's happening."

"Imagine that. Someone wants my opinion." With a full course of antigerontological treatments, a woman Sonia's age could have looked thirty if she worked at it, but she obviously hadn't. She looked closer to forty. She was not unattractive, but carried herself with an air of glum resignation.

"How long has there been this nativist movement, Sonia? And why did it erupt into violence now?"

"Some of the Myn," Sonia said, "have resisted us ever since we got here, eighty-five years ago. But it wasn't a serious thing until GalaxCo started grabbing their land and putting them to work on their plantations, about twenty years back. Since then, the resentment has gradually escalated. I suppose it finally reached a critical mass."

"Relations with the Myn have never been very good, I take it?"

"Oh, some of them don't seem to mind us. They like

some of our technology, but reject a lot of it. They are a highly moral and spiritual race, and some of their taboos make little sense to us. Generally, humans and Myn have gotten along reasonably well, but these damned GalaxCo people treat them like serfs. Or cattle. They resent that. I would, too."

The waiter arrived with the wine and poured glasses for each of them. Gloria looked at him and found that she had no idea what he was thinking. His large brown eyes avoided hers.

Gloria took a sip of the wine. "So, you think most of the opposition is directed against GalaxCo rather than the Empire itself?"

"All of their attacks have been against GalaxCo people or facilities. Draw your own conclusions."

"What about the other corporates?"

"All of Servitor's operations are right here in Dhanj. Imperium does a little mining up in the mountains to the north, but they haven't been bothered. Neither one employs a significant number of Myn."

"And where do *you* think the weapons are coming from?"

Sonia drank some more wine. "Spirit knows," she said. "As you surmised, there's no effective control on what arrives here. Aside from the corporate freighters and the occasional independent, there is a fair amount of light traffic from the other Beta-5 worlds. Nothing much from beyond that. They could be coming from anywhere."

"Who would have an interest in gun-running? And how would the Myn pay for the goods? From your reports, I gather that they don't have a lot of capital floating around."

"You actually read those reports?" Sonia shook her head. "I always assumed they wound up in some decomposing memory cube, unseen by human eyes."

"I've read every one you've submitted, Sonia. Good, sound reporting. Very helpful."

"Well, then you know that the Myn think of money as sort of a perishable commodity. Spend it before it goes bad. They don't quite grasp the notion of interest, or investment. What comes in from their few exports or the corporate fees goes out right away for technical goodies they like, most of which are inconsequential. The equivalent of glass beads and trinkets. They have a very primitive economy. Think of American Indians trading with Europeans in the sixteenth or seventeenth century."

"It wasn't long before those Indians started trading for guns, you know."

"Well," said Sonia, "there's that. Look, Gloria, I have a doctorate in economics from London, but I can sum up everything I ever learned in one sentence. If someone wants something, and someone else has it, sooner or later they'll find a way to strike a deal."

Gloria nodded and got to her feet. "Thanks, Sonia," she said. "You've been a help."

"Anytime." Sonia picked up her book, found her place, and began reading again.

Gloria made her way back to her table through the increasingly crowded restaurant. Maybe everyone *did* come to Blaine's.

Their food arrived, and Gloria found the local lobster, or whatever it was, very tasty. She noticed that Olivera was concentrating more of his attention on Petra.

A tall, prosperous-looking man from another table came over to theirs, cleared his throat, and said hello. Olivera introduced him as Roland Belvoir, the director of GalaxCo's operations on Myn.

"Forgive my intrusion, Ms. VanDeen, but I heard that you arrived from Earth today, and I was eager to make your acquaintance."

"Please join us," Gloria said.

"Just for a minute. I wanted to tell you that we are grateful that Dexta has responded so promptly, and that if there's anything we can do to help you, just let us know."

"Thank you, Mr. Belvoir. I'm sure I'll be getting in touch with you in the next few days. I can tell you that Dexta is very concerned about developments here, and we intend to do everything possible to bring the situation under control. And I'm very sorry about your losses."

"Well, our production has only been minimally impacted, to this point. We can pick up the slack, I think, and make our normal export quota."

"I meant the four GalaxCo people who were killed today," Gloria said.

"What? Oh, yes, of course. Thank you. A terrible thing. We have good people here, Ms. VanDeen, and we want to do all we can to protect them. This is something of a backwater, as you know. It's hard enough to keep our people here, without having them get shot at. Damned little buggers."

"Why do you think the little buggers are singling out GalaxCo for their attacks?" Gloria asked him.

Belvoir frowned. "The usual reasons, I suppose. We are a major employer, so I suppose they focus their resentments on us."

"You also own or occupy a lot of their land," Gloria pointed out.

"Neither here nor there, Ms. VanDeen. Most of that land would lie fallow, in any case, if we weren't growing pharmaceuticals on it. And we pay them well for it. They have no legitimate cause for complaint."

"Legitimately or not, some of them are clearly complaining, wouldn't you say?"

Belvoir turned to her, a look of impatience on his features. "Look, Ms. VanDeen, I realize that it is currently popular in some quarters at Dexta to blame the Big Twelve for everything that goes wrong in the Empire. But I can assure you, GalaxCo's practices and procedures do not differ in substance from any of the other eleven's.

Just take a look at what goes on in Imperium's mining operations over on Jhino."

"I intend to," Gloria told him. "I'd also like to get a look at your plantations."

"That can be arranged," he said. "Just get in touch with our office, and we'll set it up for you. A pleasure to meet you, Ms. VanDeen, Ms. Nash." Belvoir got up and walked back to his table, giving Gloria the distinct impression that it hadn't been such a pleasure for him, at all.

Gloria looked around the restaurant and noticed Brian Hawkes standing at the bar. He was drinking alone.

"Would you excuse us for a moment, Ricardo?" Gloria made a head motion to Petra, and they both got up.

A few moments later, in the women's restroom, Gloria said to Petra, "You seem to be making some progress."

"Uh-huh. I think I've got him convinced that if he so much as kisses your hand, the Emperor will have him chopped into very tiny pieces and fed to the Imperial swine."

"Charles *is* the Imperial swine." Gloria laughed. "Listen, Petra, I'm going to go see what I can find out from Brian Hawkes. Make my apologies to Ricardo, would you?"

"You mean he's all mine now?"

"For as long as you want."

"You know, I think that chicken Kiev did something to my hormones."

"Well," said Gloria, "I'm going to see if I can do something to Hawkes's hormones." Standing before the mirror, she pulled some fabric farther apart, completely exposing her nipples.

"That works, huh?"

"Try it and see for yourself."

Petra looked at herself in the mirror and unbuttoned the fourth button of her shirt. She experimented with various motions and discovered that her own nipples were available for Olivera's inspection. She took a deep breath, and said, "Grrowwll!"

Outside, Petra returned to the table and Gloria approached Hawkes at the bar. "Buy a girl a drink?"

Hawkes looked at her, saw everything there was to be seen, and motioned to the bartender.

"Lousy day for you, I guess," Gloria said.

Hawkes nodded and drained his Scotch. He indicated that the bartender should bring two more.

"Look," said Gloria, "I'll understand if you don't want to talk right now. I just wanted you to know that I've read all your reports, and it's clear to me that you know more than anyone else around here about the Myn. I'd be very interested in hearing anything you have to say."

"Right. Listen, Ms. VanDeen—"

"Gloria."

"Gloria. I appreciate the fact that you've read my reports, I appreciate your interest, and under any other circumstances, I would appreciate the excellent view of your breasts. But I just lost two rather close friends today. One of them died in my arms. So I'm not really in the mood for company or conversation. Not even yours."

"I'm sorry," said Gloria. "Bad timing on my part. I'll leave you alone."

"Stay. Finish your drink, at least. You know how much good Scotch costs around here?"

"All right," said Gloria. She took a sip of the Scotch.

She looked at Hawkes and tried to identify him with the sharp, perceptive, and meticulous man who had written the reports. They might have been written by a scholar, but Hawkes looked more like a mining engineer, perhaps, or a rancher. His chiseled features were deeply tanned, and his rolled-up sleeves revealed powerful, well-muscled forearms. His broad shoulders were hunched as he leaned over the bar, and his green eyes looked sad and tired.

Gloria felt herself responding to Hawkes's presence. Now, here was a man that actually might be worth pursuing. She wondered what it would feel like to run her hands over those broad shoulders and feel those big hands caressing her own body.

"I've been trying to place your accent," Gloria said. "Woolamura, right? I was there once, years ago. Settled by Australians, wasn't it?"

"I don't have an accent," Hawkes said. "*You* have an accent. And yes, Woolamura. But then, you know that from my file, don't you?"

Gloria shrugged. "I was just trying to make conversation." She took another sip of Scotch.

"Sorry," said Hawkes. "Even on my good days, I tend to be abrasive."

"I'd like to meet with some of the Myn," Gloria said. "Not the tame, urban Myn that Melinda's lining up for me. I want to go upcountry and meet some of the nativists. I know you have contacts with them."

He looked at her. "I'm not sure you're the upcountry type. It's not exactly Manhattan."

"Try me," she said.

Hawkes seemed to think about it for a few moments. He sipped some Scotch, then said, "All right. Tomorrow morning, early. And wear something a little more practical. That getup wouldn't impress the Myn in any case, at least not in the way you'd expect—they aren't even mammals. They think we're ugly."

"Practical it is. Sorry about the dress."

"Don't apologize. I didn't say it didn't impress *me*. I *am* a mammal. Just a distracted one, tonight."

"I understand," Gloria said. She smiled at him. "Thanks for the drink. I'll see you tomorrow morning, early."

She didn't see Petra and Olivera at their table, so she walked back to the Compound alone. Upstairs in her room, she got out of her dress, hung it up, then crawled into bed, set her alarm, and turned out the lights. She closed her eyes, thought about Hawkes for a few minutes, then tried to shut off her mind and get to sleep.

Noises from Petra's room next door woke her. She listened for a moment, and there was no doubt what was causing the noises. Petra's high-pitched giggle penetrated the walls.

Gloria couldn't help noticing that there was no one else in her own bed. Some Tiger you are, she thought.

chapter 8

GLORIA ROSE WITH THE LOCAL SUN, HAD A quick light breakfast in the cafeteria downstairs, and was outside waiting when Hawkes pulled up in a battered bush skimmer. He was dressed in khakis, boots, and a blue baseball cap with a Dexta logo on it. He got out and looked at Gloria.

She was wearing a loose, nearly transparent white shirt, unbuttoned and knotted at the waist, and that most practical and enduring of nineteenth-century inventions, denim blue jeans. Gloria's were tight and rode low on her hips, a fetching five inches below her navel. Hawkes took in the view, nodded, and said, "Practical."

"Where are we going?" Gloria asked him.

"About five hundred miles upcountry. Get in and make yourself comfortable."

Gloria climbed into the hovering skimmer and sat next to Hawkes. Like Gloria's much sleeker Ferrari back home, the skimmer worked on a mass-repulsion principle that she didn't understand but took for granted. The closer a skimmer got to the ground, the harder the ground tried to push it away, and the faster it went. Skimmers could achieve a maximum altitude of a few hundred feet, but their efficiency declined and fuel consumption rose with altitude, making roads a practical necessity.

They exited the Compound and followed city streets for a few minutes. Soon, the urban clutter gave way to suburban sprawl, then open countryside. Hawkes accelerated and followed a narrow, dusty road that led to the northeast. Once they were clear of the city, there was almost no other traffic. A few dun-colored houses dotted the roadside, and Hawkes slowed down to pass through a couple of small villages.

"The Myn aren't much for road-building," Hawkes explained. "We'll have to cut cross-country in a little while. Before we got here, they had nothing but narrow footpaths between their towns. GalaxCo has cut some roads connecting their plantations, but where we're going, there aren't even many paths."

"Why no roads?" Gloria asked. "Are the Myn basically homebodies?"

"To an extent. But the main thing is that this planet didn't have any beasts of burden for them to domesticate. Nothing like horses or camels. If the Myn wanted to travel, they had to do it on foot. Or by boat—they are excellent sailors."

"How do they get around now? Do they have many skimmers or ground vehicles of their own?"

"Very few. What little traveling they do is still mostly by foot or boat."

"Which raises the question of how the terrorists move from place to place."

Hawkes nodded. "I've wondered about that, myself. There have been four attacks, including yesterday's, spread over a range of about five hundred miles. Of course, each attack could have been carried out by a different group."

"That still leaves the question of their weapons. Someone would have to be distributing them."

"Someone would," Hawkes agreed.

Gloria's wristcom beeped. "VanDeen," she said.

"Hi, Gloria. Petra here. I got your note, but you didn't say when you'd be back."

Gloria looked at Hawkes, who said, "By nightfall, most likely."

"Hawkes says this evening, Petra. You've got the day free."

"No, I don't. I found a guide to take me on a grand tour of Dhanj." Gloria heard a giggle, making the identity of her guide apparent.

"Have fun, then," said Gloria. "I'll try to check in with you this afternoon."

"You have fun, too, Gloria."

"That's the woman I saw you with last night?" Hawkes asked. "With Olivera?"

"Petra Nash, my assistant. Will she be all right with Olivera?"

"Depends on how you define 'all right.' I don't think there's much likelihood of any trouble in Dhanj. And Olivera isn't quite as big an idiot as he seems."

"That's reassuring," said Gloria.

"He's young, and he's only been here a year. In time, he might become marginally competent."

"You've been here four," Gloria pointed out. "You could have rotated out a year ago. Why did you stay?"

Hawkes shrugged. "Believe it or not, I like it here. They offered me a Coordinating Supervisor slot in New York, but I'd rather be staked out on an anthill. Spent a year there a few years back. Dreadful place."

"It's not so bad," Gloria responded.

"Yes, the Greatest City in the Empire. The most exciting, dynamic, and stimulating urban center in two thousand light-years. Home of culture, commerce, and the most beautiful women in the galaxy." Hawkes glanced at Gloria. "That much, at least, seems to be true."

"But . . . ?"

"But it's filled with *people.*"

"And you don't like people?"

"I like freedom," Hawkes said. He gestured toward the open, green landscape rolling past them. "The more people, the less freedom. Dexta HQ is nothing but a big cage, a zoo for bureaucrats. A place like Mynjhino, a man can spread his arms and take a deep breath now and then. Anyway," he added, "if I left, the Compound would fall apart. Not to overstate my own importance, but no one else on staff can even speak the local language. I'm needed here, so I stay."

"Melinda seems competent," Gloria said.

Hawkes nodded. "Melinda is, but she's in the wrong place. Give her a human colony with human problems to deal with, and she'd be a star. But she's wasted here. Dexta mass-produces people like Melinda, then sends them forth to administer the Empire, with little or no thought given to the realities on the ground. By the time Melinda really understands this place, they'll rotate her back to Manhattan and bring in a new body to fill her slot here. And it can't happen soon enough to suit her."

"I understand you and Melinda are pretty close."

Hawkes gave her a sour, disgusted look. "Pumped Olivera for all the local gossip, I see. Look, I'll make you a deal, Ms. Coordinating Supervisor. Don't ask me about my personal life, and I won't ask you about yours."

"Fair enough," said Gloria.

After about twenty minutes, Hawkes went off road and piloted the skimmer at high speed over broad, open fields of tall, green grasses, broken by small clumps of lazy, swaying trees that resembled palms. He took the skimmer up to two hundred feet, and Gloria saw isolated villages and intricate geometric patterns of cultivation in the distance. Once, they skimmed over a large lake and she saw hundreds of small sailing vessels plying the languid waters.

They reached the plantation district, and the character of the land changed. The hexagonal and star-shaped fields of the Myn gave way to huge rectangles of uniform green plants arrayed with military precision. Gloria saw hundreds of yellow-brown Myn making their way along the endless rows of crops, stooping to attend to each individual plant.

"Pharmaceuticals," said Hawkes. "They need a lot of care. GalaxCo finds it cheaper and easier to use the Myn than robotics, and the Myn wouldn't be happy about mechanization. They have religious ties to the land itself and believe that automated agriculture would defile it."

"And yet, they don't seem pleased about working the plantations," said Gloria. "I know a lot of them have been leaving to go back to their ancestral fields."

"They don't object to plantation work, in itself," Hawkes explained. "One of their sacred dicta—a Commandment, of sorts—translates as, 'The land must be happy.' The land itself, that is—the dirt and rocks. And the land is happy as long as something useful and harmonious is growing on it. The Myn don't mind growing pharmaceuticals that are of no use at all to them, just to keep wrinkles off the faces of their human overlords. What they do mind is the kind of regimentation that GalaxCo imposes on them. The land isn't happy about that. They say the land speaks to them through their ancestors, and their ancestors are upset by the depersonalization of the plantations. Each Myn should have a one-on-one, personal relationship with each plant they grow. GalaxCo's methods make that impossible."

"Do the GalaxCo people understand that?"

"Some of them do," said Hawkes. "On the way back, we'll stop and meet a few of them. They've studied the local agrarian practices and have made a number of sensible recommendations to their superiors. Which, of course, have been completely ignored. Corporate bureaucracies tend to be even more rigid and stupid than Dexta's."

The skimmer rose to pass over a range of broken hills and small mountains. Hawkes pointed to the land ahead of them. "Different watershed, different tribal region," he said. "We're over Dhabi lands, now. They're the people we're going to see. Of the eleven tribal groups, the Dhabi are the most independent."

"Strong nativist sentiment?" Gloria asked.

"Very. The Myn-Traha are based here. On the other hand, there haven't been any attacks in the Dhabi region. Of course, the GalaxCo presence here is pretty minimal."

"So you think the attacks are directed specifically against GalaxCo, and not against humans in general?"

"That's one of the things I intend to ask about," he said. "We're going to meet with a Myn named Pakli, sort of a local wise man or shaman. He's an old friend, and I think he'll be honest with us."

"Do you have many friends among the Myn?"

"Not many, but some."

"How did you manage that?"

Hawkes looked at her. "Radical procedure," he said. "I spent time with them and listened to what they said."

THEY APPROACHED A LARGE MYN TOWN. Hawkes took the skimmer up to five hundred feet to give Gloria a good view. The town sprawled along both banks of a river and seemed much busier and more alive than the great city of Dhanj. The skimmer slowly descended toward an open area, a kind of town square, near the right bank of the river. Dozens of Myn stopped what they were doing and watched as the skimmer came to a halt at the edge of the square and slowly settled to the ground.

"Before we get out," said Hawkes, "I want to warn you. The stench is pretty overpowering, if you aren't used to it. The Myn realize this, and won't be offended as long as you don't actually throw up. If you feel that you have to, ask permission first, and they'll direct you to an acceptable spot. The same applies if you have to relieve yourself. Human effluvia makes the land unhappy."

Gloria nodded and took a deep breath. "Let's go," she said. Hawkes opened up the skimmer, and Gloria stepped outside. The stench hit her immediately, and made her eyes water. Hawkes took her by the elbow and led her into the streets.

"The Myn evolved when the climate was a lot colder," Hawkes explained. "That's why they have fur. But about ten thousand years ago, the star began to heat up, and the climate became semitropical. So they tend to sweat a lot, and that's what causes the odor."

"How do we smell to them?" Gloria asked.

"Bland. And they find our clothing rather curious. Yours should amuse them," he said, granting her one of his rare smiles. "They aren't used to so much bare human skin."

"How would they feel if I took it off?"

"Are you serious?"

"Sure, why not?"

"To tell you the truth, I think they would feel honored. Comes to that, so would I. For entirely different reasons, I hasten to add. The Myn regard human clothing as a cause for suspicion, as if we had something to hide. What was it Twain said? 'Man is the only animal that blushes, or needs to'? The Myn don't blush. Of course, all their sexual apparatus is internal."

Gloria looked at the Myn in the streets and confirmed Hawkes's observation for herself. The Myn's small furry bodies all looked alike, and she could not tell males from females, although she knew that they had a two-sex biological system.

"How do they do it?" Gloria wondered. "I haven't read anything on Myn reproduction."

"They are sort of egg-laying marsupials," said

Hawkes. "Their internal sex organs slide out of slots in their lower abdomens. Six weeks after copulation, the female lays an egg and deposits it in the male's pouch. He hatches it and nourishes the young for about three months, at which point it emerges into the big, bad world and fends for itself."

Gloria noticed a background hum in the streets, a musical sound, almost like a flute. She realized that it was Myn speech, which she had not heard at all in Dhanj. One of the Myn, passing in front of them, stopped, made a facial expression that might have been a smile, and said, clearly and distinctly, "Good morning."

"Good morning to you," Hawkes responded, then added something that sounded like a fragment of an Italian aria.

"They can speak human languages?" Gloria asked in surprise. "I thought they didn't even have tongues."

"They don't," said Hawkes, "but their oral cilia are remarkably adept at mimicking any sound they hear. The Myn we're going to meet speaks standard Empire English as well as you do. We have a much tougher time with their language. Lots of clicks and trills that are hard for us to reproduce."

"You seem to manage."

"They tolerate my pathetic attempts. I can understand it much better than I can speak it."

"And they seem to know you here."

"I've spent a lot of time among the Dhabi," Hawkes said. "I like them. They're intelligent, independent, and they have a sense of humor. You'd like them too, if you took the time to get to know them."

Gloria noticed that most of the buildings here were made of wood, rather than the dun-colored adobe that was common in the coastal regions. The palmlike trees lined the streets. Although it was difficult to be sure about such a thing, it seemed to Gloria that the Myn bustling past them were happier and more full of life than the sullen and silent Myn she had seen in Dhanj.

The sight of two humans in their streets was cause for mild interest, but didn't seem reason for alarm.

They came to a two-story house set back from the street. Hawkes paused in front of the door and emitted a loud phrase of something that sounded like birdsong. A moment later, the door opened and a Myn poked its head out.

"Brianhawkes!" it exclaimed. It made a series of excited trills and clicks, and Hawkes responded in kind. He gestured toward Gloria and introduced her in the Myn language. Gloria nodded to the Myn, and the Myn tilted its head toward her, then turned to Hawkes and trilled some more. They conversed for a bit, then Hawkes told Gloria, "This is Dushkai, my friend Pakli's wife. She understands a little English, and says that she is happy to meet you."

"And I am happy to meet her." That established, Dushkai led them inside. Gloria looked around in the dim candlelight and saw floor cushions instead of furniture, and many beautifully carved wooden ornaments on the walls. Dushkai continued on, through the house, and brought them to an enclosed garden area. There, another Myn was seated on a red-and-gold cushion, smoking a small pipe.

The Myn saw them, put his pipe down, and got slowly, laboriously, to his feet. The usual yellow-brown fur was frosted with silver and white, and it was obvious to Gloria that the Myn was elderly. Yet he greeted them with apparent pleasure and enthusiasm.

"Brianhawkes," he said, "it has been far too long since you honored my home."

"Greetings, Pakli," said Hawkes. "Too long, indeed. But to make up for my absence, I have brought another friend, who would very much like to make your acquaintance. Pakli, this is Gloria VanDeen, who arrived here yesterday from Earth."

Pakli made an attempt at a bow, but the stubby Myn body was not capable of bending the way humans do.

Nevertheless, the intent was obvious, and Gloria bowed back to Pakli.

"I am delighted to meet you, Gloriavandeen," said Pakli, "and you are welcome in my home. Come, sit down, and we will smoke and eat and drink together. Dushkai, fetch us refreshments."

Pakli returned to his cushion, and Gloria lighted on one next to him, with Hawkes on her right.

"So," said Pakli, focusing his large, liquid brown eyes on Gloria, "you have only been on our world a day, and yet you abandon the pleasures of the great city of Dhanj to visit my humble village in...what is the word...the boondocks?"

"Gloria wanted to meet the real Myn," Hawkes explained, "and not the city-bred Myn of Dhanj."

"Wise of you, Gloriavandeen, and very flattering to us. The Myn of Dhanj are sad creatures, much oppressed by their reliance on humans. Here, we live as our ancestors did...with a few improvements, of course. I enjoy your vids, and have learned much of this Earth of yours. You come from Dexta, do you not?"

"I do," said Gloria.

"No one but Dexta people comes here," said Pakli. "Even the GalaxCo fools avoid us, which is well for them, and for us. You have come about the troubles, I have no doubt."

"That is true," said Gloria.

"There's been another attack," said Hawkes. "Four more human dead. Two of them were my friends."

"Sad tidings," said Pakli. "Let us smoke some jigli and wish them a safe journey to their ancestors." Pakli offered his pipe to Hawkes, who took it and inhaled a lungful. He passed it to Gloria.

"What will it do to me?" Gloria asked, looking warily at the pipe and its smoldering contents.

"It depends," said Hawkes with a slight cough. "It makes it easier for the Myn to talk with their ancestors. For them, it's a mild euphoriant, about like marijuana.

For us, it can have a variety of effects, none of them harmful."

Satisfied, Gloria took a puff and coughed. She passed it to Pakli, who inhaled deeply, then gave it back to Hawkes. The pipe went around three times, and Gloria noticed no effect at all.

Dushkai came out to the garden with a wooden tray filled with fruit and four glasses. She sat down on a fourth cushion and put the tray in the center of their circle. Hawkes immediately took one of the glasses and drank from it, so Gloria did the same. It tasted like weak beer. She sampled one of the fruit and found it tangy and delicious.

Gloria noticed that Dushkai was staring at her. The female Myn trilled for a moment, and both Hawkes and Pakli laughed.

"Forgive us," said Pakli graciously. "We rarely see human females. My wife is very interested in your garment. She says that she can see right through it, so you must be an honest woman with nothing to hide."

"Please tell Dushkai that I thank her for her kind words."

"And *are* you an honest woman, Gloriavandeen?" Pakli asked, his eyes fixed upon hers.

"I will speak only the truth to you, Pakli. And I hope you will do the same with me."

"That is good," he said. "We understand each other. And you will believe me when I tell you that I cannot truly answer the questions you will ask about the Myn-Traha and the sad incidents that have occurred. I am old, and the young ignore me these days. There is much I do not know, and don't care to know."

"Do you know who is making these attacks?"

"I do not know their names. I know there are foolish young Myn who speak of ridding our world of the humans. They are angry about many things. About the plantations and the way the GalaxCo fools have made the land unhappy. About the way the humans have protected the Jhino from the righteous wrath of our ancestors, in whose name we act and whose wisdom nourishes us."

Pakli tilted his head back, looked skyward, and seemed to be listening to something. Gloria glanced at Hawkes, who turned his eyes upward, indicating that Pakli was busy conversing with his ancestors. This went on for several minutes, and Gloria and Hawkes said nothing.

Finally, Pakli looked back at Gloria. "My fathers," he said, "would like to know what the mighty Empire intends to do about the incidents."

"If the attacks continue," Gloria told Pakli, and his fathers, "the Empire will send soldiers here. Imperial Marines. And they will do whatever is necessary to protect the humans on Myn, and their property."

"Humans and their property," said Pakli. "They always seem to go together. Our concepts of property differ from yours, Gloriavandeen. I believe that I understand what you mean by the term. But do you understand what we mean?"

"Please tell me, Pakli. I would like to understand."

"The land belongs to us, and we belong to the land. Some of our people entered into what the GalaxCo fools call leases. They think these leases give them the right to do as they will with our land. We are pleased that they wish to grow crops and make the land fruitful, for that makes the land happy. But it does not make the land happy when hundreds of Myn are put to work on it, all at once and all in the same place. How can the land know the Myn, and how can the Myn know the land? It makes the land very unhappy to be treated in such a way. Our ancestors tell us this, and it makes the Myn unhappy, as well."

"Unhappy enough to kill humans," said Gloria. "Do the unhappy ones want to kill all the humans, or just the GalaxCo fools?"

"Some," said Pakli, "would gladly kill all humans,

but most would be happy if the GalaxCo fools simply disappeared. But I suppose they will not, will they, Gloriavandeen?"

"It's unlikely," she told him.

"Pakli," said Hawkes, "we need to know where the Myn are getting their weapons. If we could cut off their supply of weapons and ammunition, perhaps we could end the bloodshed before it grows worse. If the Imperial Marines come, it is likely that many Myn will die. We can prevent that from happening if we can find where these weapons are coming from."

"That," said Pakli, "I do not know. If I did know, I would tell you, my friend. But the Myn-Traha know this, and so it is a dark secret. Nevertheless, I will attempt to find out for you. I would not see my people massacred by your Imperial Marines. I see your vids, and I know what they can do, and have done to others who opposed the mighty Empire."

"Thank you, Pakli," said Hawkes. "You have a comm, and can reach me anytime. Let me know what you learn."

"I shall, my friend, I shall. Now, let us smoke more jigli and thank our ancestors for this day, and for our friends."

The pipe went around the circle three more times. This time, Gloria did begin to feel something, but she wasn't sure what. She looked at Hawkes and found that he was staring at her in a new way. He was perspiring in the muggy Mynjhino air, and his face shone in the sunlight. A good face, she thought, strong but not too impressed with itself. Intense green eyes that peered right into her. Big shoulders, straining against the fabric of his khaki shirt.

Gloria tugged at the damp fabric of her own shirt. She felt warm, and her flesh tingled strangely.

Pakli struggled to his feet and held out his hand to Dushkai. "Come," he said, "let us leave our friends Brianhawkes and Gloriavandeen to themselves. Humans prefer to be alone at moments like this. Stay as long as you wish, my friends. We will talk again before you leave." With that, Pakli and Dushkai disappeared inside the house.

Gloria looked at Hawkes. "Moments like what?" she asked.

Hawkes grinned at her. "Have some more jigli, Gloriavandeen," he said, holding out the pipe to her. Gloria took it, smoked a little more of the oddly scented leaf, and passed the pipe to Hawkes. He took a mighty puff, then put the pipe down.

Hawkes stared at her. "An honest woman," he said. "With nothing to hide." He reached for her, unknotted her shirt, and pulled it over her shoulders. The tingling in Gloria's flesh became so intense she could barely stand it, and when Hawkes threw himself on top of her and began kissing her, she didn't resist. A few seconds later, she joined in, and began unbuttoning his shirt.

His big hands found her breasts and caressed her nipples, and his hot breath on her face carried the insistent scent of the jigli. Gloria lost herself in the moment and in the strength and power of Brian Hawkes. His hand moved on down across her belly and slid beneath the top of her jeans, bringing gasps of pure pleasure as he stroked her. A few moments later, when their clothes were off and he thrust into her with smooth, arrogant confidence, Gloria thought she could hear the happy and approving laughter of her ancestors.

chapter 9

"PROBABLY THE STRONGEST NATURAL APHRO-
disiac in the Empire," Hawkes said to Gloria as they
walked back to the skimmer. He pointed toward the
pouch of jigli that Dushkai had given her. "They trust
you to keep quiet about this. If word got out..."

"I can imagine," said Gloria. "I'll be careful where I
smoke it."

"It works just as well if you make a tea from it," said
Hawkes.

They got into the skimmer and floated upward, then
headed southwest at treetop level.

"You didn't have to use this stuff on me, you know,"
Gloria said.

"I just wanted to provide you with a convenient excuse," Hawkes told her. "Sophisticated New York ladies
generally climb all over us rough-hewn colonial types
anyway, but the jigli lets them pretend that they had no
choice."

"I'm not like that," Gloria said. "If I needed an

excuse, the Scotch last night would have been enough. But the jigli certainly added something to the experience."

"I've never seen anyone react to it as strongly as you did."

"That wasn't just the jigli," Gloria told him. "That was mostly me."

"Oh?" Hawkes eyed her with new interest.

"The Curse of the VanDeens," Gloria explained. "A few generations back, there was some genetic enhancement done. Something to do with nerve ganglia and pleasure centers. The VanDeen males are all preternaturally potent, and the females...well, you may have noticed that I enjoy sex *a lot*."

"I did notice something along those lines." Hawkes grinned. He leaned over to her and kissed her. "You were fantastic, Gloria."

"You weren't so bad yourself, for a rough-hewn colonial type." Gloria settled back in her seat with a smile and closed her eyes as Hawkes piloted the skimmer. She had wanted Hawkes almost from the instant she first laid eyes on him, and last night she had made it obvious that she was available to him. Still, she was pleased that he had made the first overt move. The men at Dexta HQ were so intimidated by her that few even tried anymore. But Hawkes was not a man to be put off by Tiger stripes.

"You were right," Gloria said. "I liked Pakli and Dushkai. It's hard to picture beings like that engaging in cold-blooded murder."

"They are old and mellow," Hawkes said. "Younger Myn are more passionate. Pakli is 120 years old, and was a fierce and dedicated soldier in the war against the Jhino, before humans arrived."

"It sounds as if he still bears a grudge. Why the enmity between the two races?"

"There are reasons why it's rare to find two intelligent species on the same planet. Humans wiped out

Neanderthals, our closest competition. Eventually, the Myn would have done the same to the Jhino, or the other way 'round, if we hadn't intervened. The whole thing goes back about two hundred thousand years. The Myn first evolved here on the Eastern Continent, and gradually spread westward along an archipelago in the north. But then an ice age came along, blocking passage between east and west, and the two groups evolved independently after that point."

"I see," said Gloria. "And when the ice age ended..."

"They bumped into each other and started fighting. At first it was just skirmishing along the northern archipelago. But eventually both sides developed deep-sea sailing technology, and things got serious. They had been fighting for about five hundred years when we came along. And they would fight again if we left."

"But even the angry young Myn must realize that the Empire is not going to pull out."

"Fanatics have their own strange logic. And who knows what their ancestors are telling them."

They recrossed the low mountain range and returned to plantation country. The land here was unhappy, and watching the scores of Myn trooping along the regimented rows of pharmaceuticals, Gloria could sense that unhappiness.

"The people we're going to see now," Hawkes told her, "run an agricultural research station on the fringe of the plantation lands. They work for GalaxCo, but they've developed their own ideas about how things should be run. Naturally, their superiors don't appreciate that."

"What ideas?" Gloria asked.

"They'd like to see the plantation system replaced by something more like sharecropping. Each Myn family would be responsible for a particular plot of land. That way, the personal relationship would be restored, and the land would be happy again. Their research shows that production would only decline by about 6 or 7 percent."

"Seems like a small price to pay for happy land and happy workers," Gloria said.

"'Happiness' is not a recognized category on the GalaxCo corporate ledger," Hawkes pointed out.

"Still, given what's happening, maybe they'd be willing to make some concessions to maintain the peace."

"You might try suggesting that to them," said Hawkes. "I have, and they ignored me."

"I will," said Gloria.

"There's the research station," Hawkes said, pointing to two small buildings ahead of them. "Just four people, two couples. Nice folks, but a little lonely out here. They'll probably invite us to stay for dinner. We can, if you want, but I think we ought to get back to the Compound."

"We'll see," said Gloria.

Hawkes brought the skimmer down close to the ground and angled toward the two buildings. Gloria caught sight of two Myn in a field to the right, apparently engaged in digging a hole. She didn't see any humans.

The skimmer settled to the ground and Hawkes and Gloria got out. The air was pungent with the aroma of the pharmaceutical fields, stretching away from the buildings in every direction. Gloria followed Hawkes to the door of the larger of the two buildings. Hawkes banged on the door, and called out, "Fred! Polly! Visitors!" There was no answer.

"Must be over in the lab, or out in the fields," said Hawkes. They walked around the first building and headed for the second. Hawkes suddenly slowed down.

"Something's wrong," he said. Gloria noticed broken glass in the windows of the second building. Hawkes cautiously approached the open door of the laboratory and looked inside.

"Spirit!"

"What?" Gloria demanded.

"Stay back! Don't go in there." Hawkes looked back inside the lab, and Gloria maneuvered around him to see for herself. She immediately wished that she hadn't.

Four human bodies were sprawled on the floor of the laboratory. Blood was everywhere; shattered skulls, brains, viscera. Gloria had never seen a newly dead body before, let alone four that had been chopped to pieces by automatic-weapons fire at close range. Hawkes wrapped his arm around her and firmly pulled her away from the open door. Gasping for air, struggling to maintain control of herself, Gloria let him lead her away.

Hawkes abruptly stopped, and Gloria looked up. Two Myn stood in front of them, pointing weapons directly at them.

For an agonizingly long moment, Gloria was certain that the end had come, and she waited for it with a mixture of fear and resignation. Mom. Dad...

Hawkes trilled something to the Myn in their own language. The two Myn looked at him, surprise registering on their alien faces. One of them spoke, the musical language of the Myn sounding unnaturally harsh and peremptory. Hawkes replied. The two Myn consulted with each other in low tones, then looked back at Hawkes. The one on the right trilled out something that sounded like a command.

"This way," said Hawkes, steering Gloria toward the open field to their left.

"Hawkes, what—"

"Just stay calm. I think they're as surprised as we are."

Her legs unsteady, Gloria let Hawkes move her along, the two Myn trailing a few feet behind them with their weapons at the ready. They climbed a slight rise and came to the beginnings of a hole in the ground. Stretched out on the ground next to it lay a dead Myn.

One of the Myn said something, and Hawkes turned around to face him. They exchanged several phrases, and Hawkes nodded. He looked at Gloria.

"They want us to dig the hole for them," he said. He pointed at two shovels lying next to the hole. "Human-sized tools are awkward for them, and they have to get this done in a hurry."

Hawkes looked up toward the sun, not far above the horizon in the late afternoon. "It looks like Fred or Jack took one of the Myn with them. Bashed him on the head, from the looks of it. He has to be buried before the sun goes down, or he won't be able to find the way to his ancestors. His friends figure we can get the hole done faster than they can. Pick up a shovel and start digging. Don't give up—we'll think of something."

Gloria knelt and took a shovel. She looked at the Myn and saw that they were keeping a safe distance, their guns leveled. It was impossible for her to read anything in their large brown eyes or the expressions on their alien faces.

"Dig," Hawkes told her. They started at opposite ends of the hole the Myn had begun. Gloria stabbed at the dirt with the shovel and began to dig. Hawkes worked with a will and Gloria tried to keep pace. Soon, they were both dripping with sweat. The hole steadily deepened and expanded.

"What are they going to do with us when we finish?" Gloria was certain she already knew the answer, but she wanted to hear it from Hawkes.

"Their first order of business is seeing to it that their friend has a proper burial. Nothing matters more to them than abiding by the proper forms. They'll tend to the dead first and probably have us fill in the hole."

"And then?"

"My guess," said Hawkes, pausing to wipe some sweat from his brow, "is that they'll move us away from here before they do anything. It would make the land unhappy to spill blood on freshly consecrated ground."

One of the Myn trilled a sharp command. "They want us to stop talking and work faster," Hawkes told her. "Just stay with it, Gloria, and don't try anything stupid with your shovel. You saw what those weapons can do."

Gloria nodded and resumed digging. The hole was deep enough now that they had to step down into it. The soil was soft, but there were rocks in it, and she frequently had to bend over and toss them out. She thought about throwing one at the Myn. Maybe if they both threw together, and hit both Myn in their heads at the same instant ... She caught Hawkes's eye and tilted her head toward the rock in her hand. Hawkes emphatically shook his head. He was right, she realized.

The hole grew deeper as the sun sank lower. Gloria wondered just how deep the hole had to be. Six feet was supposed to be the prescribed depth for humans, but she didn't know about the Myn. She wondered what would happen if they didn't finish before the sun dipped below the horizon.

She was developing blisters on both palms, and her back ached. Gloria tried to remember the last time she had dug a hole of any kind, but couldn't. Rich girls didn't spend much time digging holes. Maybe at summer camp on Melampus IV, when she was eight. Hadn't they buried a dead bird they had found?

Hawkes, with his rippling muscles, was excavating two shovelfuls to her one by now. She tried to stay out of his way in the deepening hole. Still, she was managing to make her own contribution to the work. At least she was in excellent physical shape, thanks to her devotion to the Qatsima exercises.

When the hole was shoulder deep, one of the Myn said something, and Hawkes looked at Gloria. "He says it's deep enough." Hawkes boosted Gloria out of the hole and scrambled out after her. They stood there, breathing hard and dripping sweat. The Myn trilled and pointed at the body of their fallen comrade.

Hawkes picked up the dead Myn by the shoulders, and Gloria took its feet. They lowered it into the hole as easily as they could, but the body slipped and dropped the last couple of feet. The living Myn didn't seem to mind. They motioned Hawkes and Gloria to get away from the hole, and they stepped back a few paces.

While one of the Myn kept its weapon aimed at them, the other stepped to the edge of the hole and began to sing. It was a high-pitched, hauntingly beautiful melody, and Gloria found herself oddly moved by the scene. She could see tears in the eyes of both of the Myn. The dirge continued for several minutes, then the Myn stepped back from the hole and leveled its weapon at them. The second Myn stepped forward to the edge of the grave and began its own sad song.

When the ceremony was at last complete, the first Myn looked up at the sun, which was sinking toward the tree line on the horizon. He trilled a command, and Hawkes and Gloria picked up their shovels. They scooped dirt from the piles they had made and began heaving it into the hole. It pittered down on the body of the fallen Myn. Too soon, the hole was filled. Another command, and they put down their shovels. Gloria felt her stomach muscles tighten and her mouth go dry.

The Myn said something and gestured in the direction of the falling sun. "They want us to walk that way," said Hawkes. "Toward the trees. Just do as they say, and at the right moment, I'll make my move. Be ready to run."

Gloria didn't know what Hawkes had in mind, and decided not to wait to find out. She had an idea of her own.

She stopped and turned toward the Myn, who raised their weapons. "Tell them I have to sing my own prayersong to let my ancestors know that I am coming." Hawkes looked at her, hesitated, then turned back to the Myn and trilled something at them. The Myn looked puzzled.

"Tell them that we observed their ceremonies, and now they must observe ours, or our ancestors will be angry with them."

There followed a lengthy exchange between Hawkes and the Myn. Hawkes gestured extravagantly toward the freshly dug grave, the sun, and Gloria. Finally, one of the Myn trilled something with seeming reluctance, and Hawkes turned back to Gloria. "They don't like it," he said, "but I think they bought it. What are you up to?"

"Just watch and be ready," she said.

Gloria took a deep breath, then assumed the beginning position for her Qatsima exercises. It would be difficult to perform the maneuvers in her tight jeans, she realized, so she kicked off her sneakers, slipped out of her shirt, and snaked her jeans off. "Tell them I am purifying myself for my prayers," she said. Hawkes nodded and trilled something to the Myn. The Myn's large eyes seemed to widen a bit at the sight of her. Their interest was not sexual, but they had never seen a naked human before and were naturally curious. They stood a few feet away, staring at her in rapt fascination.

Gloria took her position again and began a slow, side-to-side swaying motion that blended into a series of balletic leg raises and graceful twirls. Thinking something more might be needed, she began to sing the first thing that came into her mind. It was "Amazing Grace." As she sang the ancient hymn, she shut her eyes and concentrated on the sequence of Qatsima moves. To her surprise, Hawkes joined her in the song, his rich baritone complementing her flowing alto. The Myn watched in respectful silence as the humans continued their prayersong.

When she was certain that the Myn were convinced that her free-form ceremony was legitimate, she faced them, balanced on the ball of her left foot, and raised her right leg toward the sky. She stretched to reach for it, then slowly began toppling forward. She tucked in her leg and head, rolled through a somersault, and sprang out of it into a triple scissors kick.

Her right heel smashed into the snout of the Myn on the right. Before the other could react, she had come down and bounced up again to knock his weapon away with the side of her left foot. Then her right heel again found its target, and the second Myn collapsed. It was over in two seconds.

Hawkes wasted no time and quickly picked up their weapons, then turned to look at Gloria with an expression of awe and admiration on his face. Gloria caught her breath and looked down at the two fallen Myn.

"This one's dead," Hawkes said after checking the one on the right. "Must have snapped his neck." He knelt by the second Myn, searched for its pulse, and said, "Still alive."

Gloria gathered up her clothing and started putting it on. She stared at the Myn she had killed and didn't know what to think. She had never killed anything larger than a mosquito before. Her Qatsima exercises had been designed long ago to kill, if necessary, but to Gloria they had never been anything but a way of focusing her mind and staying in shape. She was stunned by what she had done.

When she had her shoes back on, Hawkes handed her the two automatic rifles. He knelt and hoisted the living Myn over his shoulder in a limp bundle. Gloria started to follow him toward the skimmer, but stopped and looked back at the Myn she had killed. The sun was setting behind the tree line.

She felt something she couldn't quite identify, then realized that it was sorrow for what she had done. "Shouldn't we . . . ?"

"Bury him?" Hawkes demanded, amazed. "Gloria, we have dead of our own, and we can't stop to bury them, either."

"I just . . . I don't know . . . his ancestors . . ."

"Fuck his ancestors," Hawkes snorted. "Come on, let's get the hell out of here!"

•   •   •

WITH THE UNCONSCIOUS MYN IN THE REAR compartment of the skimmer, his arms trussed behind his back by Hawkes's belt, they headed back toward Dhanj at maximum speed. Hawkes called the Compound, got in touch with Melinda Throneberry, and told her what had happened. "Find Olivera and have him get his Security people to set up a place we can use as a jail cell and interrogation room. And if you know anyone at all who has knowledge of ancient weapons, get them."

The call completed, Hawkes reached for Gloria and wrapped his hand around hers. "Are you okay?" he asked her.

"I never killed anything—any*one*—before," she said. "I'm not sure how I feel about it."

"Feel lucky and alive. They'd have killed us without a second thought."

"I know, I know. It was kill or be killed. I've just never been in a situation like that before."

"You think I have? Let me tell you, this rough-hewn colonial was every bit as scared as the big-city girl. I was just going to rush them, throw a cross-body block, and hope for the best. Probably would have gotten us both killed. What was that, anyway, some Oriental thing?"

"Qatsima," Gloria said. "Ancient discipline from Songchai in Sector 7."

"Well, whatever it is, you're damned good at it." He looked at her and saw that she was still disturbed by what she had done, so he added, "You sing pretty well, too."

She smiled at that and leaned over to kiss him on the cheek. "So do you, my rough-hewn colonial."

THEY PASSED THROUGH THE COMPOUND GATE and pulled up in front of the administrative building where a small crowd had gathered. They got out in the growing twilight, and Hawkes spoke to Olivera while

Petra dashed up to Gloria and gave her a hard hug. Two of Olivera's Security men pulled the still-unconscious Myn out of the skimmer.

"We've got something fixed up in the basement," Olivera told Hawkes.

"Good. And get Dr. Levin over here. He knows something about Myn physiology. I don't know how badly hurt this one is, but I want him awake and talking as soon as possible. The rifles are in the skimmer. Did you find anyone who knows about those things?"

"Sonia says she knows someone from Imperium who's a history buff. She called him, and he's on his way in."

Petra let go of Gloria and looked at her. "Are you all right?" she asked.

"I'm fine, I think." Among the small crowd of Compound personnel, she noticed an unfamiliar face. The man was pointing an imager at her. "Who the hell are you?" she demanded.

"Bryce Denton, Empire News Service, just got here from Pecos."

"Spirit, that's all we need!" Gloria looked down at herself and realized that her breasts had spilled free from her sodden, dirt-stained shirt, and that she had never gotten around to refastening the fly of her low-slung jeans. Her nipples and nether hair were there for all to see. The Empire was going to get another good look at Gloria VanDeen.

"Can you tell us what happened, Ms. VanDeen?" Denton asked.

"No," Gloria told him. She brushed past him and marched into the administrative building.

Over coffee and sandwiches, Gloria and Hawkes described what had happened. Melinda Throneberry, the three other Undersecretaries, and Petra sat with them at the table and hung on every word. When Hawkes described how Gloria had dealt with the Myn, every eye focused on her with amazement. She looked down at her coffee. What she had done was necessary, but she didn't feel comfortable accepting kudos for it. She thought of the dead Myn and the four dead humans she had seen that afternoon, and wanted to be able to push her face into her pillow and cry. But there was still work to be done, so she pulled herself together and tried to deal with it.

The doctor arrived and checked over the Myn. Sonia Blumenthal's history buff came in, and they gave him a look at the captured weapons. He examined them more thoroughly than the doctor did the Myn and reached a tentative conclusion.

"They look like AK-47s," he said. "Note the long, banana-shaped magazine. I don't think they've been altered to fit the Myn; they seem full-sized to me. The AK was the guerrilla weapon of choice in the late twentieth and early twenty-first centuries back home. Cheap to manufacture, durable, and easy to use. Serious firepower."

The doctor told them that he thought the Myn had a concussion and would live, but would be in no shape to answer questions until at least tomorrow.

"Speaking of tomorrow," Gloria said, "Tatiana, I want you to set up a meeting with the local heads of GalaxCo, Imperium, and Servitor. Make it for lunch, here. I assume you have facilities for that?"

"You can't just order them in here," Markova protested.

"Then say please; just get them here. Ricardo, I want to meet with you and all your Security people tomorrow morning early. And Melinda, I'm going to see the Governor tomorrow morning, migraine or no migraine."

"Gloria," Throneberry said, "I hate to ask this, but that guy from Empire News wants a statement. I can handle it, if you'd prefer, but—"

"But I'm going to have to talk to him sooner or

later," said Gloria. "Okay, I might as well get it over with now."

"I never thought I'd say this," Petra said, "but you're a mess, Gloria. Why don't you go get cleaned up first?"

"Why bother? He already imaged me on the way in." Gloria checked to make sure her fly was fastened and her breasts more or less covered by the thin shirt, then wearily walked back outside to face the media rep. Before answering his questions, she had a few of her own.

"You get six-day messengers at Pecos, don't you? Have you heard anything new from Earth?"

"Not before I left," Denton said. "We're only half a day from here, by Flyer. But we did have word from a freighter captain about the attacks here, so my editor sent me. And you arrived yesterday from Earth? You're Dexta's Coordinating Supervisor for Beta-5?"

"That's right. I'm here on a fact-finding tour."

"Are Imperial Marines being dispatched?" He aimed his imager at her.

"I have no word on that," Gloria said, speaking honestly if incompletely.

"Do you expect more attacks by the Myn?"

"We have—look, put that thing down for a second, will you?"

Denton reluctantly lowered his imager.

"How soon can you get this story to Earth?" Gloria asked him.

"We have three messengers with us. Six hours to Pecos. Then six days to Earth." Messengers were robotic probes similar to the couriers, except that they carried enough fuel for deceleration, making them reusable and much cheaper than the couriers. The additional mass also made them slower. Messengers were the standard means of delivering news within the Empire.

"You can't use a courier from Pecos? That would get the news home in three days instead of six."

Denton laughed. "You expect *us* to use a courier? Use one of your own."

Gloria had already checked, and knew that there were only three couriers available at the Mynjhino Orbital Station, and she was reluctant to expend one of them for anything short of a true emergency. In any case, she would have to get the Governor's authorization to use one.

"Look," she said, "this is important news, and should go out as quickly as possible. We've got captured weapons that look like ancient AK-47s, and we need to get that information back to Dexta. Can't you use a courier?"

"I hate to burst your bubble, Ms. VanDeen," said Denton, "but this is *not* important news. It's a pretty big story locally in Beta-5, but the Home Office will tag it as back-screen stuff. It's just a minor rebellion on a two-bit planet, and it's definitely not worth expending a courier. However..."

He let the "however" hang there and stared at Gloria.

"What?"

"However," Denton continued, "*you,* Ms. VanDeen, definitely are a big story. By now, everyone in the Empire has seen that statement you made about you and the Emperor."

"Oh, no," Gloria said flatly. "If you saw the statement, then you know I've already said all that I'm going to say on that subject."

Denton shrugged. "Your choice," he said. "Still, we might work something out, if you're game."

Gloria pursed her lips in response to the sour taste in her mouth. She eyed the media rep with suspicion. "What do you have in mind?" she asked him.

"One question on the Emperor. You can simply restate your no comment. For the rest of it, well, the shots I already have of you arriving are good stuff, but we'll need something more if I'm going to talk my editor into using a courier. Here, take a look." Denton tapped a couple of buttons on the imager and held it up for her to see. Gloria watched ten or twelve seconds of herself as she got out of the skimmer and approached the building—with her breasts bare and her fly undone.

"Give us boobs and bush again, and you'll get your courier. We'll cut it to make it look as if I interviewed you immediately after you arrived, before you had a chance to fix yourself up. What do you say?"

"I say you're a weasel. But you'll guarantee the courier?"

"That's the deal."

Gloria nodded reluctantly and opened up her shirt and unfastened her fly to match her earlier exposure. She didn't particularly mind the nudity, but she didn't like the way Denton had maneuvered her into it. Most of all, she didn't like the fact that she would once again become lead-screen news throughout the Empire. Her strategy of getting out of the limelight had come unraveled. Mingus had told her that it might not be easy for her to go back to being an anonymous Level XIII; it was beginning to look as if he were right.

Denton began the interview with questions about the day's events. Gloria described them without mentioning how she had dealt with the Myn. She went on to recount briefly the series of prior attacks, and make an obligatory statement about how all necessary steps were being taken to protect the human population of Mynjhino. Finally, Denton asked his question about the Emperor, and Gloria said, quickly and simply, that she had nothing more to say on the subject. Denton tried to sneak in another Emperor question, but Gloria cut him off.

"I want you to go inside," she told him, "and image those AK-47s in as much detail as you possibly can. Tell them I authorized it. They need to know everything they possibly can about them on Earth."

"Right," said Denton. "Thanks, Ms. VanDeen. I'll be around. Maybe we can do this again."

Gloria smiled sweetly and thought, Don't count on it.

She saw Hawkes emerging from the building. She went to him and wrapped her arms around his waist.

"I am in serious need of a drink and some personal attention from a rough-hewn colonial type."

"You're in luck," he said. "I happen to know where you can find both."

chapter 10

RICARDO OLIVERA AND HIS SECURITY STAFF of six—five men and a woman—sat at the table in the conference room in the administrative building, along with Gloria and Petra. Olivera and Petra exchanged a lot of quick smiles and meaningful looks, Gloria noticed. She was happy for Petra, but hoped that her mind would remain on her job. Gloria had a little difficulty staying focused, herself. Her night with Hawkes, or perhaps just the jigli hangover, had left her feeling sexually charged, and she dressed the way she felt, in her shortest skirt and most transparent blouse, completely unbuttoned. Olivera's Security men were staring at her, and she didn't mind. At least she had their undivided attention.

"Anything new to report?" Gloria asked after a Myn servant had brought in coffee, then departed.

"One of the wounded at Zinkan died last night," Olivera said. "That brings the total, counting yesterday, to forty-two."

"And the reaction from the human community?"

Olivera nodded to one of his men, Franklin. "We've

had some reports of GalaxCo people leaving the plantations and coming into Dhanj," Franklin said. "Hotels are packed."

"We should probably expect more of them," said Olivera.

Gloria nodded. "That brings me to the first item I wanted to raise," she said. "If we have to bring every human into Dhanj and the Compound, can we do that? How do we stand on transport, lodging, and food?"

Olivera looked troubled. "I've been thinking about that," he said.

"And?"

"There are 5,385 humans on Myn, Gloria. Less forty-two, now. Many of them have their own transport or can gain access to it. About fifteen hundred are in and around Dhanj, but that leaves thirty-eight hundred out in the boonies."

"How do they break down?"

Olivera checked some notes. "Uh, that would be roughly twenty-five hundred men and thirteen hundred women. Fewer than fifty children, thank the Spirit. Mynjhino isn't exactly a family-friendly assignment."

"How many work for GalaxCo?"

"They have a total of about three thousand employees on Myn, probably about five hundred of them in Dhanj. Imperium has maybe three hundred, mostly in the mines up north. Servitor, only a hundred, all of them in Dhanj."

"Okay," said Gloria. "How long would it take to round them all up and bring them into the city?"

"I think," said Olivera, a note of uncertainty in his voice, "that it could be done in two to three days. We'd need to make use of GalaxCo's freight haulers and every skimmer we can lay hands on. But between what we have or can get, and the private skimmers already out there, I'd say we could do it inside of three days."

"And once we get them here, what do we do with them? Obviously, we don't have room in the Compound for five thousand people, and you say the hotels are already packed. Food could be another problem. I'd rather not set up a refugee camp, if we can avoid it. They're depressing and tend to contribute to a siege mentality. Any ideas?"

Gloria looked around the table and saw that none of the Security people had anything to contribute on that point. She felt a rising anger. A Security staff worth its salt ought to have created contingency plans for something like this long before the present crisis developed. Olivera had only been here a year, so it wasn't solely his fault. He had obviously inherited the ambient inertia from his predecessor, and had failed to do anything to improve upon it. Still, she was annoyed by the sleepy, backwater-colony mind-set that prevailed here, even now.

"Gloria?" said Petra. "I have an idea."

Pleasantly surprised, Gloria said, "Let's hear it."

"Why not send the refugees over to Jhino via Transit?"

Gloria's eyebrows rose a fraction of an inch, and she turned to Olivera. "I didn't realize you had Transit facilities here."

"*We* don't," said the Security chief. "But GalaxCo, Imperium, and Servitor went together on one to facilitate movement between Myn and Jhino. Opened six months ago."

"Ricardo showed it to me yesterday on our tour," Petra explained.

"The other end is in Phanji, the capital of Jhino," said Olivera. "The Transit is used almost exclusively by humans, although the Myn and Jhino have used it occasionally for trade and diplomatic missions. It's located downtown, near the corporate offices."

"So we could take the overflow and Transit them to Jhino?" Gloria asked. "Would they have facilities for them in Phanji?"

"I imagine they could make do," said Olivera. "Hadn't considered the possibility, to tell you the truth. But at least our people would be safe over there, and we wouldn't have to worry about housing and feeding them here." He smiled at Petra, and added, "Good idea, Pet."

Gloria looked at Petra and silently mouthed the word, "Pet?" Petra made a face at her, then looked down at her palm pad, a hint of a blush on her face.

"Okay," said Gloria. "This sounds like our best option. Ricardo, I'd like you to get in touch with our consulate in Phanji and start making arrangements, just in case. If we have to do this, I want it to come off quickly, and without a hitch. I'll bring it up with the corporate directors when I meet them for lunch."

As Gloria was speaking, Melinda Throneberry entered the room and stood just inside the doorway. She caught Gloria's eye, and said, "I thought you'd like to know. The Myn you captured is conscious. Hawkes is in with him now."

"Is he getting anything?"

"Too soon to say."

"Thanks, Melinda." Gloria turned her attention back to the Security people, and Throneberry continued standing where she was.

"Now," said Gloria, "the next point I wanted to bring up concerns the physical security of the Compound itself. I noticed that you only have one person on the gate."

"Gloria," said Olivera, "we just don't have a big enough staff for any more than that. My people take four-hour shifts on the gate. If we doubled up, that would mean two-thirds of my people would be up half the night."

"In light of the present emergency," Gloria said in measured, even tones, "I think we can afford to lose a little sleep. I want the guard doubled, starting tonight."

Olivera hesitated, glanced at Throneberry, then looked back at Gloria, and said, "Very well."

"On a related point, what sort of weapons do we have available in the Compound?"

"We have eight Mark V plasma rifles, and about

twenty plasma pistols. There may be a few more pistols that we don't know about in private hands, and some of the GalaxCo people have begun arming themselves."

"Could you defend the Compound with what you have? Men on the walls, covering every approach?"

"Why...I think so. We have more weapons than trained Security people to use them, though. We'd have to draft some people. And we don't have an actual *plan* for defending the Compound. It just—"

"Never came up before," Gloria interjected. She suppressed a sigh. "Ricardo," she said, "I want you to walk the perimeter today and come up with a defensive plan. Take Hawkes with you; I'd like his input on this. I want to see a detailed plan by tomorrow morning. And find your draftees *now*, before we actually need them. If we come under attack, I don't want people wandering around wondering what to do. Once we have a plan in place, we'll conduct training exercises."

Gloria got to her feet. "I don't think I have to tell you," she said, fixing her gaze on each of the Security people in turn, "that the current state of readiness around here is unacceptable. I won't go into what should have been done in the past. My concern is to make certain that we are prepared for whatever may happen in the future, beginning right now. Let's get it done, people."

• Gloria marched smartly out of the conference room. Melinda Throneberry caught up to her in the hallway. "A word with you?" she asked. "My office."

"Fine," said Gloria. She could tell from Throneberry's stiff, forceful gait that she was angry. That suited Gloria; she was angry, too.

Throneberry ushered Gloria into her office, then firmly closed the door behind them. Fists on her hips, Throneberry confronted Gloria.

"Just what the hell do you think you're doing, giving orders to *my* people?" she demanded.

"*Your* people, Melinda, haven't done shit around

this place. Hawkes told me you were competent, but I'm beginning to wonder about his judgment."

"That makes two of us!" Throneberry snarled, immediately regretting it.

"Ah," said Gloria. "You want to make it personal."

"Fuck you, you Imperial bitch! It's not bad enough that you come sashaying in here with your tits and ass and New York attitude. No, you have to make sure that everybody knows that *you're* in charge here! The fucking alpha female. You go off into the weeds with Hawkes and throw your cute little assistant at Olivera. The only other man in the Compound who matters is the Governor, and I can see you're all set to bag *him*, too!"

"My tits, ass, and New York attitude have accomplished more around here in a day than you have in a year, Melinda. What the hell do you think is happening here? Just another bureaucratic catfight? For Spirit's sake, people are *dying*! And I came that close to being one of them. Why don't *you* try looking down the barrel of an AK-47 before you complain about the way I'm taking charge? *Someone* has to, and if you can't or won't, then I will!"

"Let me remind you, I'm still the Imperial Secretary around here. A Twelve, and you're a Thirteen."

"And let me remind you that Mingus didn't send me here to sit in the corner and take notes." Mingus, in fact, hadn't sent her here at all, but Throneberry didn't need to know that.

Having been trumped by Gloria's ace, Throneberry reined herself in and walked briskly past Gloria to her desk. She sat down primly, shuffled officiously but aimlessly through some papers on her desk, finally looked up at Gloria, and said, "In the future, I'd appreciate it if you'd at least consult with me before you issue orders to my staff. Even if things are as bad around here as you think, they won't get any better by you riding roughshod over the existing organization."

"Point taken," said Gloria.

"And when you meet with the Governor," Throneberry added, "it might be helpful for you to know that Tatiana already has him wrapped around her little finger. You can fuck him till you both turn blue, for all I care, but he'll listen to her before he listens to you. Just thought you should know that."

"Thanks for the advice, Melinda," Gloria said as she turned to leave. "But, as it happens, I think I'm developing a migraine of my own."

IMPERIAL GOVERNOR VLADISLAV RHINEHART was looking forward to meeting Gloria VanDeen, and at the same time, dreading it. She was said to be beautiful beyond description, and the vids he had seen of her certainly confirmed that. But her relationship with the Emperor was difficult to judge, and potentially dangerous. He didn't know how much influence she might have with Charles, and whether she might use it on his behalf, or against him. Many years ago, Rhinehart had done a favor for Emperor Darius IV, and that had won him a series of appointments to Imperial positions, culminating five years ago when Gregory III named him Imperial Governor of Mynjhino. But Rhinehart had never even met Charles V, and Imperial gratitude did not necessarily carry over from one generation to the next.

The Myn servant announced Gloria VanDeen in his singsong English and led her into the Sitting Room. Rhinehart had decided to meet with her here, rather than in his office, in hopes of keeping things light and informal. Dexta bureaucrats, particularly those from New York, could be impossibly businesslike, and Rhinehart preferred a more relaxed atmosphere, particularly when he was meeting with beautiful women.

The Governor got to his feet and smiled when he saw Gloria. She did not disappoint. Her round breasts and erect nipples were fully visible, popping out of her open, transparent blouse as she moved, and her skirt could hardly have been a millimeter shorter. He gave her a token bow, then took both of her hands in his.

"Delighted to meet you, Ms. VanDeen, absolutely delighted!"

Gloria nodded formally, and said, "Excellency, thank you for seeing me. I hope you're feeling better today."

"What? Oh, yes, yes, quite. Damned pesky migraines. I'm only sorry that my wife couldn't be here to greet you, but she's back home on Earth, visiting family. I believe Dora and you have mutual acquaintances in Rio. In fact, I'm quite certain that she mentioned knowing your parents. Tell me, is your father still winning all those yacht races?"

"All that he can," said Gloria.

"In any event," Rhinehart said, leading Gloria to an ornate sofa upholstered in gold satin, "I'm all alone here in this monstrously huge house at the moment, so it is a very real pleasure to have such charming company. Please, sit down, my dear." Rhinehart was careful to get a good look before Gloria adjusted her skirt, then sat next to her at an angle calculated to give him a perfect view of her exposed right breast. He smiled happily.

GLORIA SMILED BACK AT RHINEHART AS HE drank in the view. She was consciously making maximum use of her physical assets, and was content to let him stare all he wanted. She knew from his file that he was, to be charitable about it, a somewhat-over-the-hill rake. If she was going to get what she wanted from him, it wouldn't hurt to get him steamed up about the prospect—nonexistent, she had already decided—of bedding her. And if that didn't work, she would threaten and intimidate the poor, bubble-headed bastard.

"I understand that you had yourself a little adventure yesterday," Rhinehart said. "I trust that you are fully recovered from the excitement and suffered no ill effects."

Gloria had to pause a moment before attempting to respond. Little adventure? Either he didn't fully grasp what had happened, or he was more remote and disconnected from reality than she had supposed. She decided to play it light, for now. She could always bludgeon him with reality later.

"I'm fine, Excellency," she said. "No damage."

"Oh, I'm very glad to hear that, my dear. I would hate for you to form a negative impression of our little planet. It really is quite delightful in many ways, you know. This recent trouble is upsetting, of course, but I'm sure it's nothing to be deeply concerned about. The Myn are charming little creatures, once one becomes accustomed to their, uh, distinctive aroma. We keep them perfumed around the Residence, of course."

"Of course," Gloria agreed.

One of the "charming little creatures" came in with a silver tray and tea service, placing it on the table in front of them. He smelled of apple blossoms. The Governor poured for her, and Gloria slid forward to accept it, hiking her skirt up just enough to make the cup and saucer tremble in Rhinehart's hand.

She sipped a little of the tea, then put it down on the table. "Excellency," she said, "there are some matters that we should discuss."

"Business? So soon? I had hoped we could chat about New York and Rio. And the Emperor's Levee, of course. I do so miss them."

"Perhaps another time," Gloria suggested. "I have to meet with the local corporate directors later this morning, and I need to prepare."

"I'm certain they will be as charmed by you as I am, my dear. Good men, all of them. The kind of men the Empire needs. It's no easy task, minding the store out here in the Imperial wilderness, I can tell you."

"I'm sure they have good people to help them,"

said Gloria, "just as you do, Excellency. Melinda Throneberry strikes me as a very competent and devoted person."

"Melinda? Couldn't live without the dear! If we had trains here, she'd make them run on time, I've no doubt of that. Tells me what to sign, and where. Doesn't bother me with all the niggling little details, you know. Very considerate of her."

"And Tatiana Markova," Gloria said, carefully observing Rhinehart's face. "She seems to have very good relations with the corporations."

"Oh, the best, the very best! Dear Tatiana, such a marvelous young woman. Since she's been here, I don't believe I've heard so much as a single complaint from any of the corporations. Takes a load off, what? Before Tatiana, they were always pestering me about this and that, you know, concerned about their roads and their labor contracts and leases and whatnot."

"Brian Hawkes seems a good man," Gloria offered. The smile on the Governor's face became a little more tepid.

"Hawkes? Yes, a robust young man. Always out in the field with the Myn. Makes me wonder whose side he's on, at times. Even speaks their lingo. Remarkable, that. Always sounds to me like a robin and a blue jay arguing over a worm!" The Governor laughed at his own wit, and Gloria smiled.

"It's good that you have confidence in your staff, Excellency," Gloria said, "because we may have a bit of rough water ahead of us. As I'm sure you are aware, people are very concerned about the violence directed against humans."

"Yes, I know. Dreadful stuff. Perfectly dreadful."

"Some of the GalaxCo people have been coming in from the plantations. It's safer for them here in the city. In fact, it might become necessary for you to issue a decree bringing all the humans on Myn into Dhanj. If that time should come, I know you'll do everything in your power to support your staff in the things they'll have to do."

"Oh, of course, of course. But do you really think it will come to that? Seems a radical step to take, to say the least."

"I'll be honest with you, Excellency," Gloria lied with all the sincerity she could muster. "I spoke with Secretary Mingus before I left, and he expressed serious concern about the situation on Mynjhino. He urged me to do whatever I could to protect our people and resolve the situation peacefully. And he told me that I could rely absolutely on your support. He thinks very highly of you."

"Does he, now?" Rhinehart looked relieved to hear it. "Well, my dear, of course, you can count on my support. Whatever you think is best, you may rely on me to see that it is done."

"I knew I could count on you, Excellency," Gloria told him. "When I report back to Secretary Mingus, I'll be certain to mention your generous support and unstinting cooperation. He can't bear those fractious Governors who are always insisting on doing things their own way."

"Tell him he need have no fears about Vladislav Rhinehart, my dear. I pride myself on being a team player."

"I can see that," Gloria said. She decided that she'd gotten everything she needed from him for now. And telling lies always wore her out.

"Now," she said, "I really must go and prepare for my meeting. Thank you for your time, Excellency." Gloria got to her feet and extended her hand to him. He bent forward and kissed it.

"It has been my pleasure, I assure you, Ms. VanDeen. My very real pleasure. Seeing you brings back memories of Rio, under the old Emperor. Darius, I mean. The beautiful ladies all used to dress the way you do, my dear. In fact... Spirit, now that I think of it, I believe...

yes, I'm certain of it! I saw you once before, my dear, at the old Emperor's last Levee. You were the lovely young girl wearing the star sapphire in her navel, weren't you?"

"And nothing else," Gloria said, giving a good imitation of a blush.

Rhinehart laughed conspiratorially. "You were charming and beautiful then, my dear, and you are even more so now. Perhaps you'll favor us with an equally inspired ensemble on Friday, what?"

"Friday?"

"The Emperor's Birthday, my dear! Surely you can't have forgotten. It's the highlight of our social calendar. I'll expect you at the reception. In fact, I insist on it. Perhaps you can find another star sapphire between now and then, what?"

Gloria left him laughing, with a promise to attend the reception. Rhinehart reminded her of so many of the charming, vacuous fools she had met in her days at Court. She couldn't help liking him a bit, but wondered if he would be able to stand up to what was coming. She shook her head in wonder. "Little adventure," indeed!

PETRA CAME INTO THE OFFICE GLORIA HAD borrowed and told her that the corporate directors had all arrived. "Good," Gloria said. "Now, we'll let them wait a few minutes. How's it going with Olivera?"

Petra grinned, as if she were embarrassed by how happy she was. "He's a dreamboat. So handsome and suave! I know, I know, I've got a case of raging hormones here. But I'm having the best time of my life with him, Gloria, I really am!"

"I'm glad, Petra. You deserve it. Just remember, you can't take him back to New York with us. And by the time we get out of Yao Space, he'll have found someone else."

"I know. He told me that himself. I'm just another trophy on his wall."

"And he's one on yours. Try looking at it that way."

"I'd like to see *your* trophy wall sometime."

"You'd be disappointed if you did, believe me. Subtract the Dogs, the passing fancies, and the Emperor, and you're left with—"

"Brian Hawkes?"

It was Gloria's turn to grin. "I guess we both did pretty well this trip."

"We really ought to travel more," Petra suggested.

"I'll mention it to Mingus," Gloria said. "Now, I think I've let them wait long enough."

Gloria got to her feet and deliberately mussed up her hair. Then she pulled her shirttails partly out of the waistband of her skirt and arranged things so that her right breast was completely exposed. Finally, she pulled up her skirt just enough to provide a glimpse of what she hoped would become the object of the executives' desires.

"Might one ask . . . ?" Petra said, wondering what her boss was up to now.

"I want them to think I'm late because I was busy fucking the Governor, and that I might fuck them, too, if they play their cards right."

"Ah," said Petra, "of course."

"This is what being a Tiger is all about, Petra," Gloria told her. "If everybody thinks I'm fucking everybody else, then I don't actually have to fuck *anyone* unless I want to."

"What if they insist? I mean, really insist?"

"Then," said Gloria, "they get a foot in the face. Or points south."

Petra shook her head. "You're a hard woman, Gloria VanDeen. When I grow up, I want to be just like you."

"Petra, my dear, I'm afraid you are about as *up* as you're going to get." Gloria gave her diminutive assistant an affectionate kiss on the top of her head, then was out the door.

"I'M SORRY I WAS LATE. I WAS BUSY WITH THE Governor."

The three executives stared at Gloria's disarray and nodded knowingly.

"Mr. Belvoir, a pleasure to see you again," she said, shaking the GalaxCo director's hand.

"And you, Ms. VanDeen," said Roland Belvoir. "Allow me to introduce my friends and competitors, Julius Omphala of Imperium, and Randall Sweet of Servitor." Gloria shook hands with them, giving each an extra squeeze as she stared into their eyes. Omphala was a compact, sharp-angled man of mixed African and Indonesian descent, and Sweet a somewhat portly, pink-faced Anglo-Swiss.

"Why don't we sit down and have our lunch while we talk? Perhaps we can have some wine while we wait to be served." Gloria took charge of the wine and poured for the three men, being sure to give them a good view as she did so.

"Now then," she said after she was seated, "first let me thank you for coming on such short notice. Secretary Mingus made a point of telling me to be sure to consult closely with the corporate leaders on Mynjhino." Gloria wondered what would happen if all the lies she had told on Mingus's behalf ever got back to him.

"We're anxious to do whatever we can in the present crisis," said Belvoir. "I was very concerned to hear about the incident yesterday, Ms. VanDeen. I'm grateful to see that you returned safely. I gather you managed to capture one of the terrorists."

"He's being questioned as we speak," Gloria confirmed. "We also came up with two automatic weapons modeled on AK-47s, from about twelve hundred years ago. Hopefully, analysis of them may give us some clues as to where they are coming from. I don't suppose you gentlemen have any ideas on that subject?"

"Ms. VanDeen," said Omphala, "as you know, Imperium, Ltd. does most of its business on Jhino. We keep an ear to the ground, but we have no indication that such weapons are being manufactured there."

"But the Jhino have the industrial sophistication to make them, don't they?"

Omphala nodded. "I would say that they are capable of it, yes. And clearly, the Myn are not."

"So they have to be coming from Jhino, or offplanet," said Gloria. "Gentlemen, I'm concerned about the possibility that they may have been smuggled in aboard corporate freighters. There don't seem to be many controls on imports here. How does that possibility strike you?"

"Unlikely," said Belvoir, "but I suppose it's possible. Our ships generally come in half-empty, so there's certainly room for unauthorized cargo."

"It's about the same with us," said Omphala. "Most of our traffic comes into Jhino, in any case, so even if the guns were smuggled in aboard our freighters, there would remain the problem of getting them across the ocean to Myn."

Gloria looked at Sweet. "We deal mostly in financial services, software, and the like," said Sweet. "On the rare occasions when we have to bring in equipment, we usually rent space aboard GalaxCo freighters."

"What about independents? Do any of you utilize their services?"

All three shook their heads.

"Please understand, gentlemen, that no one is pointing any fingers. It's possible that the weapons come in via the smaller regional traders. Still, we have to cover every possibility. To that end, our Security people are going to be making a nuisance of themselves, I'm afraid. They're going to be inspecting your warehouses and any ships currently in port. That policy will continue until further notice. I'm sure you understand the necessity."

They understood, but they didn't seem very happy about it. As businessmen, their instinctive response to any form of governmental scrutiny was negative.

Two Myn servants arrived with lunch. These two smelled like roses. They never made eye contact with any of the humans and seemed intent on their labors. Gloria couldn't help thinking of Pakli and Dushkai; the friendly and funny Myn of Dhabi seemed like an entirely different species from the silent but fragrant Myn of Dhanj.

As they ate, Gloria discussed the possibility of bringing all the humans on Myn into Dhanj for their safety. Belvoir, whose people were at risk, was aghast at the prospect. With no one to oversee the plantations, GalaxCo's operation on Mynjhino would be ruinously—perhaps fatally—impacted. Still, he was forced to admit that his employees were frightened and that some of them had already tendered resignations. What was really needed, he insisted, was Imperial Marines deployed throughout the countryside, actively protecting GalaxCo's investment. Gloria didn't mention the possibility that Marines might already be on their way. If Belvoir thought Marines were coming, he would dig in his heels on the evacuation issue, despite the fact that a single company of Marines could do little or nothing to guard the plantations. At last, Gloria managed to extract a commitment from Belvoir to cooperate, should an evacuation be ordered.

All three executives agreed that the safest course would be to Transit the evacuees to Jhino. Their Transit facilities would be made available, and Omphala said that Imperium could probably find lodging and support facilities for the refugees on Jhino. Gloria arranged for a tour of Jhino the following day. Omphala and Sweet said they would be happy to accompany her, but Belvoir had too much to do in Dhanj to spare the time.

Gloria formed a generally positive impression of the executives. Belvoir was under the most pressure, and was not a very likable man in any case, but he struck her as competent. Omphala, an engineer by training, was briskly efficient and Gloria thought she could rely on him. Sweet was friendly but enigmatic. Servitor's stake on Mynjhino was small by comparison with GalaxCo and Imperium, and Sweet seemed willing to go along with whatever Gloria recommended.

The meeting ended with handshakes and the promise of cooperation all around. As Gloria walked away, she could feel the men staring at her partially bared bottom. Sex was one of the principal arrows in her quiver, and she knew she had scored a hit on each man. Convinced that she had already been intimate with the Governor, they would conceive the possibility that she might be available to them as well. As long as that possibility existed, they would treat her with deference, respect, and caution, rather than as some pretty young functionary of no real importance. But they were not stupid men, and probably knew full well that they were being manipulated. She hoped that, their desires notwithstanding, they would feel uneasy to realize that Gloria VanDeen had power over them.

And that, from Gloria's perspective, was the whole point.

THE MYN SAT ON A CHAIR, HIS SHORT LEGS NOT quite reaching the floor. Brianhawkes sat on another chair, facing the Myn, speaking Myn language in a quiet, determined trill. The Myn felt ashamed, and his ancestors spoke to him with tones of reproval and disappointment. He was disoriented and confused by what had happened to him, and the fact that a human was speaking to him in his own language frankly amazed him. He had always believed that the humans, despite their magical inventions, were too stupid to master the subtle and sophisticated music of Myn.

Lately, his ancestors had been telling him that the humans did not, in fact, invent the machines that had brought them to this world, or the strange implements they used to dominate it. Rather, they had stolen them from an older, wiser race that had been too trusting and had let the humans overcome them. The humans themselves, despite their size and strength, were a weak and foolish people who had no courage or wisdom. They could be frightened away by determined Myn.

The Myn, whose name was Oshki, stared at the human named Brianhawkes, and wondered what he should do. So far, his ancestors had offered no useful advice. He wished that he had some jigli, so that he might hear them better and benefit from their knowledge and wisdom.

The human kept asking him questions about the weapons. Oshki knew only that they had been provided to the Brotherhood of the Myn-Traha by a sympathetic friend. Oshki would have revealed nothing about their origin, even if he had known where they came from. If he betrayed the Brotherhood, his ancestors would punish him in this life and all the lives to come. The human seemed to realize this, finally, and stopped asking about the weapons.

Instead, Brianhawkes began trilling questions—hard to understand, but comprehensible once he had become accustomed to the human's barbaric distortions—about the Myn-Traha, and what they wanted. Why were they killing humans? he asked. That he could even ask such a foolish question merely showed once again how stupid humans truly were. It was like asking why the Jhino must be killed. No wonder the land was unhappy under the humans' heavy footsteps. The land nourished and revered wisdom, and the humans had none.

Oshki's ancestors often spoke to him of the time before the humans, when Myn were the masters of their own fate and the scourge of the Jhino. For almost as long as he could remember, Oshki had labored in the fields of the GalaxCo fools, following their arrogant and ignorant instructions and tending their strange plants. There were too many of the plants, and too many Myn tending them; Oshki was a stranger to the plants, and they to him. How could the land be happy when it was used in such a way? His ancestors told him of the land's unhappiness, and it was echoed by his own.

But at night, in the human-built barracks where the plantation workers lived—hard, unfeeling buildings that also made the land unhappy—friends spoke to him of the Myn-Traha. His ancestors told him to listen to their words. The Brotherhood was not afraid of the humans, and Oshki drew strength from the ancient songs they sang at night. Finally, his ancestors told him that the day had come when he must leave the plantation and join the Myn-Traha in the forests and hills where the land was happy and the Myn were their own masters. Oshki walked away one night and never returned.

Among the Brotherhood, Oshki began to feel a sense of his own strength and understood the wisdom of his ancestors with new clarity. The Old Days could come again, he realized, if the living Myn could summon the courage and resolve of those who had gone before. The humans could be swept from their land; all that was lacking was the means to accomplish this feat.

And then, the weapons arrived. Oshki didn't ask where they had come from; it was enough that they were here. He learned to use the heavy, awkward devices, and knew that his ancestors were pleased. When he killed the humans at the research station, he felt a surge of such joy that he wept to think how pleased the land and his ancestors were by what he had done.

But one of his comrades, Planksho, was killed during the attack. One of the humans had hit him in the head with a shovel. The human died seconds later, but it was too late to save Planksho. They had cleverly used

Brianhawkes and the other human to dig Planksho's grave before the sun set, assuring him of a quick and safe journey to where his ancestors were waiting to welcome him.

Then the humans began acting strangely. Oshki had never realized that humans had their own prayersongs and duties to their own ancestors. It seemed prudent to let them carry out their devotions, for it might be dangerous to anger the ancestors of the humans—who knew what they might be capable of doing? So they had watched, fascinated and even a little frightened, by the humans' rituals and their strange but oddly beautiful song.

And it had all been a trick! Suddenly, the naked human's foot was flying at his face, and the next thing Oshki knew, he was in this room and Brianhawkes was asking him questions in his ignorant and awkward trill. Oshki was mortified, and his ancestors were deeply disappointed.

The human would not be quiet. Oshki assumed that the questions would continue until he died of thirst or starvation, since the human had not yet offered him any nourishment. Perhaps, if he asked . . .

His ancestors were upset by the very notion. No, he would ask nothing of the human, and if he died, then he died. But would the humans bury him before the sunset? Would he be able to find his way to his ancestors? It was that thought, and not death itself, that frightened Oshki.

Finally, Oshki summoned the courage to speak to Brianhawkes. "I will tell you the most important thing I know," he said, "if you promise to bury me quickly after you kill me."

Brianhawkes looked at him in what seemed to be surprise. Then he agreed to do as Oshki asked. Oshki didn't know if he could trust this human, but it didn't really matter. Oshki would speak the truth, and the human could make of it what he would.

"The most important thing I know," Oshki trilled, "is this. It does not matter what you do to me, Brianhawkes, because the Brotherhood is powerful and our ancestors are wise. They have told us what we must do, and it will be done."

"And what is that?" Brianhawkes asked him.

"Every human on Myn must die," Oshki told him, speaking the plain and simple truth that his ancestors had revealed to him. "Only then will the land be happy again."

"All of us?" Brianhawkes asked. "Or just the GalaxCo fools?"

"All of you," Oshki told him. "All of you must die. And you will, Brianhawkes. You will."

chapter 11

GLORIA RAN HER HAND THROUGH THE DENSE, dark hair on Hawkes's broad chest, and said, "You could almost pass for a Myn, yourself. Except for your size."

"And my external sex organs," Hawkes added. "Don't forget about them."

"Never!" Gloria laughed, reaching down beneath the sheets to fondle the organs in question.

They were lying in lazy comfort in the bed in Hawkes's rented rooms above a tavern near the Dhanj harbor. The tavern was run by human and Myn partners and catered to both species in the hurly-burly environment of the docks. Hawkes could have lived in the Compound, but preferred to mingle with the inhabitants of the world he was supposed to be helping govern.

"I wouldn't make a very good Myn, though," Hawkes said. "Most of my ancestors were drunks. Cowboys, well-riggers, roustabouts. You could put their collective wisdom in a thimble and still have room left over for all the compassion in GalaxCo's corporate heart."

"You seem to have turned out pretty well, in spite of your disadvantages. How did you manage that?"

"Sheer desperation. I'd have done anything to get off Woolamura—even study. You said you were there once. Didn't stay long, I'll wager."

"About two days, I think. Charles had to stop there to make some repairs on the yacht. That was in my carefree, Empire-roving days."

"You turned out pretty well, too, in spite of *your* disadvantages," Hawkes told her.

"You mean being rich and useless? I suppose I was as eager to get away from that as you were to get away from Woolamura. I won't pretend it was any great hardship. But I just didn't want to spend my whole life being useless."

"You've been pretty damned useful around here," said Hawkes. "You've got people motivated and moving. Melinda could never manage to light that kind of fire. Of course, Melinda doesn't normally go around three-quarters naked. You have a unique management style, Gloria, but it seems to get results."

"I use what I've got," Gloria said. "You spent a year in Manhattan, so you know how things work."

"You mean the Lions, Tigers, and Sheep business? Always thought that was kind of ridiculous."

"I suppose it is," said Gloria. "But it works. The whole system is designed to apply maximum pressure to everyone, all the time. That, in turn, produces peak performance. I fill a necessary niche in the ecosystem. If there were no Tigers, male Lions would dominate everything and women would never get anywhere. Tigers are a potential threat to the Lions—we keep them honest. Walking around three-quarters—or completely—naked gives me a kind of power that isn't available to the men. And I use it to do my job. Melinda is a would-be Lion, and has to compete with the men on their own terms, which means the deck is always stacked against her. She has to be better than they are at their own game, and that's not easily done. Some women succeed at that, but most don't. I prefer my way because it works for me." She looked at Hawkes. "Does it bother you?"

"I understand what you're doing, Gloria. You want every man to think you might be available to him, whether you are or not. That's a bit cruel, but then, it's a cruel world, isn't it? Anyway, you're not in everyone else's bed, you're in mine. That's enough for me."

"Then you understand why I can't go to the Governor's Reception with you Friday night? If I show up on your arm, that will just create resentment. I need to spend the entire evening being dazzling and seductive to all, but when it's over, I'll wind up right back here with you. That's a promise."

"Unless *I* get lucky, of course."

Gloria punched him hard in the ribs, then raked her fingernails across his chest. "Don't mess with Tigers," she warned him. "We've got claws."

In typical human fashion, Hawkes's external sex organs responded to the stimulus, and in short order he was on top of her, thrusting with a leonine power and grace of his own. Gloria cried out with the urgent ecstasy of the moment, and finally exploded in spasms of primal pleasure. Afterward, she nuzzled up against Hawkes, and if she had really been a tiger, she would have purred.

THE NEXT MORNING, GLORIA DECIDED TO WALK the mile from the Compound to the Transit facility. She wanted a good look at downtown Dhanj, and not simply from a passing skimmer. Except for giving orders to waiters, she had not even spoken with the local Myn. Her attempts to strike up conversations with Myn on the streets all met with failure; they either didn't understand English, or pretended that they didn't. She got the impression that it was rare for humans to speak to the Myn of Dhanj, except to issue orders. The urban Myn, it seemed to her, had as much reason to resent the humans as did the plantation workers, yet so far they had shown no signs of rebellion.

For her trip, Gloria had chosen to wear another very short skirt, lemon-yellow, with a sleeveless top and a deep scoop neckline. She had set the smart fabric at 70 percent transparency. She had decided to leave Petra behind to give her more time with Olivera, not that he would have much to spare.

The few humans walking the streets stopped and stared at her, and even some of the Myn paid closer attention to her than they did to other humans. She had already become known in Dhanj, to both species, and that was according to her plan. When she met with Quan, the aging Primat of the ruling Tandik, she didn't want to be just another anonymous bureaucrat from Earth. She wanted to be known as an honest woman with nothing to hide.

Back at the Compound, things were finally beginning to take shape. Olivera had shown her the defensive plans he had worked out with Hawkes's help. Gloria knew nothing of military matters, but she did know that almost any plan was better than no plan, so she gave her approval to Olivera's scheme. Meanwhile, Hawkes had sent one of the captured weapons to the Imperium metallurgical laboratory in Jhino, where a detailed analysis might reveal something about the guns' origin. Olivera was ready to send mixed teams of Security and Commerce people to inspect the ships and warehouses in the harbor region.

Hawkes, unfortunately, had learned practically nothing from his interrogation of the captured Myn. What little he did learn was not comforting; the Myn-Traha were planning to exterminate all humans on their world and not simply the GalaxCo fools.

The Myn she saw in the streets might have been secret sympathizers with the Myn-Traha, Gloria realized, and yet she felt no sense of threat or hostility. She felt as safe as she would have in Manhattan, perhaps even safer, considering how she was dressed. At an open-air market, she stopped to purchase a cup of fruit juice, and attempted to converse with the vendor, to no avail. But when she said that the juice was very good and thanked him, the Myn nodded politely and seemed to appreciate her words. She did not get the sense that he wanted her dead and gone from his world.

Humans' expansion into the galaxy had brought them in contact with 276 different intelligent species. They had fought wars, large and small, with forty-three of them. Add in brushfire rebellions and localized insurgencies, and more than half of those races had in some way opposed the advancing human tide. Perhaps the true wonder, Gloria thought, was that there had not been even more wars and rebellions. Yet on a day-to-day basis, and strolling through the streets of an alien capital, humans and other species like the Myn seemed perfectly capable of conducting their relations with mutual honesty, dignity, and tolerance. If xenophobia was instinctive to all species—as some scholars argued—the evidence indicated that it was also a condition that could be overcome by the constructive and well-meaning efforts of individuals belonging to every race.

Gloria pondered the Big Picture as she walked along the streets of Dhanj, but felt no wiser for the effort. Perhaps her mistake lay in expecting to find sense in it all; perhaps there was none to be found.

SHE FOUND OMPHALA AND SWEET WAITING for her at the Transit facility, across the street from the six-story GalaxCo headquarters and a block from the building that housed the local offices of both Imperium and Servitor. The Bank of Earth building stood on the opposite corner. She noticed armed security personnel standing in front of the entrance to the GalaxCo building.

They greeted her and showed her inside, where the Transit ring stood ready and waiting. Gloria stepped through first and found herself inside an almost identical room in the city of Phanji, five thousand miles and an ocean away from Dhanj. As Omphala and Sweet followed, she was welcomed by Alphonse Buranski, the Imperial Consul in Jhino, and by an official from the native government.

His name was Kenthlo, and he was the first Jhino Gloria had met face-to-face. His resemblance to the Myn was more immediately apparent than his differences—the same large, widely set brown eyes, stocky body, and short stature. But the Jhino's fur was more brown than yellow, his ears less elongated than those of the Myn, and his snout a bit sharper—more like a fox and less like a bear. He also seemed to be a couple of inches taller than the typical Myn.

"Welcome to Jhino, Ms. VanDeen," Kenthlo said to her in letter-perfect Empire English. "We have already heard a great deal about you, and we are pleased that you have decided to pay us a visit. May I congratulate you on your courageous escape from the cowardly Myn terrorists? Let me assure you that you need have no fears of such an incident on these shores. Unlike the Myn, we are a civilized and responsible people."

"Thank you," Gloria said as she shook his small, furry hand. "I'm certain my visit here will be peaceful and productive."

"We have a skimmer waiting to take you to Government Center. I know it was not on your agenda, but when Prime Minister Veentro heard that you were coming, he insisted on meeting you. I hope it's not an imposition."

"Not at all," said Gloria, pleasantly surprised. "I would welcome the opportunity to meet with him. I admit that I've been preoccupied with Myn, but Jhino is equally a part of the Empire, and equally deserving of Dexta's attention."

All five of them got into the limo skimmer, and they started off through the streets of Phanji. The architecture of the city was nothing like that of Dhanj, where the Spanish-Moorish adobe style was almost universal. Phanji seemed more like a contemporary human city, with a mix of sizes and styles, some of which would have looked at home in Manhattan. It was a distinctly modern city, and much of its core area had been constructed since the arrival of the humans. The Jhino Gloria saw on the streets were as naked and furry as the Myn, but some of them wore rucksacks on their backs and carried computers, attaché cases, and handbags. And if Kenthlo was a representative sample, they didn't smell nearly as bad as the Myn.

Government Center was an imposing modern structure, where the Parliament met and high governmental offices were located. Fountains and small arbors enhanced the broad plaza leading to the main building. Inside, Kenthlo led them up to the sixth floor; he asked Omphala and Sweet to wait in the lobby area while Gloria met privately with the Prime Minister.

Veentro greeted her effusively and sat next to her on a comfortable couch. His English was as good as Kenthlo's, and he seemed almost excessively eager to be her friend. He, too, congratulated her on her escape from the cowardly Myn, and promised her unlimited cooperation from the citizens and government of Jhino.

He chatted up the sophistication and achievements of the local economy and culture and spoke of the expansion of Imperium's mining operations. Revenues from the mines were being poured into various modernization and education projects, and he repeatedly expressed the hope that the Imperial presence in Jhino would increase in the years to come.

What he really wanted, it seemed to Gloria, was for the Compound to transfer its operations to Phanji. Tatiana Markova was an advocate for that, and on the face of it, the idea made sense. The Jhino were a dynamic, forward-looking culture, much more attuned to the human presence than the Myn. The Imperial Compound had been established in Dhanj simply because it was the largest city on the planet, not because the Empire favored the Myn over the Jhino. It was an historical accident, really, and it could easily be rectified. The current problems with the Myn added some impetus and urgency to such a transfer.

Gloria realized that Veentro was attempting to take advantage of the problems on Myn. That was natural enough; any good politician would do the same. Still, there were enough unknowns in the situation to make her reluctant to accept anything at face value. She asked him about the possibility that the automatic weapons could have been manufactured on Jhino.

"Are we capable of it?" asked Veentro. "Certainly! But would any Jhino do such a thing? Never! Ms. VanDeen, aside from the fact that we scrupulously abide by every aspect of Imperial weapons policy, Jhino would never in a million years do anything to strengthen the Myn. They are our ancient rivals, you must realize. A savage, primitive, and irrational race. Always mooning about their damned ancestors!" Veentro made what, for a Jhino, was apparently an expression of contempt and disgust.

"Really, Ms. VanDeen! I realize that the Empire must strive to be even-handed in their dealings with both Myn and Jhino, but isn't it obvious which of us makes a better partner for you? We stand ready to assist the Empire in any way that we can. We are willing and fully prepared to offer shelter and sustenance for human refugees, should Myn become untenable for you. Please believe me when I tell you that we are your only true friends on this world!"

Gloria took her leave from Veentro's office with mutual expressions of gratitude and goodwill. The whole meeting had been handled with polish and aplomb, as if it had been scripted by a public-relations team. Still,

Gloria couldn't help thinking that for all Veentro's slickness and sophistication, she had liked Dushkai and Pakli better.

From Government Center, Gloria, Omphala, and Sweet took an Imperium skimmer out of the city on a four-hundred-mile trip to the mining regions. There didn't seem to be any particular point to the journey, given her present concerns, but Omphala was eager to show off his operation, and Gloria reminded herself that she would be making a report on the entire planet, not just Myn.

The land of Jhino was more rugged and mountainous than Myn. The minerals and soil chemistry made the land unsuitable for the pharmaceutical crops that GalaxCo grew on the other continent; but it was rich in things like manganese, tungsten, tin, and chromium.

Chatting idly with the executives during the journey, Gloria learned that Sweet had once been at Dexta. "Ten years and out," he said. "I was a Thirteen when I left, a Coordinating Supervisor like you, off in Sector 4."

People like Sweet were the reason that it was possible for people like Gloria to move up without encountering a logjam at the midlevels of the bureaucracy. Aside from the annual 20 percent attrition at Level XV, Dexta also suffered a steady loss of people between Levels VIII and XIII. Some simply burned out from the unceasing pressure of the job. Others decided to start families and opted out of Dexta. And some, like Sweet, accepted lucrative offers from the Big Twelve. Dexta-trained managers were highly prized by the corporations, both for their detailed knowledge of the Empire and for their demonstrated ability to perform under pressure. Sweet had been with Servitor for twelve years, four of them on Mynjhino, and admitted that he was looking forward to a promotion that would take him back to Earth.

At the mines, Gloria met the site manager and his foreman, then donned a hard hat and descended into the subsurface of Mynjhino. Without much comprehension, she observed a seemingly efficient operation involving a few humans, a good many Jhino, and a lot of automated equipment. Unlike the Myn, the Jhino seemed adept and comfortable with the machinery. It was easy for her to imagine them cranking out AK-47s in a secret factory somewhere; it was just hard to imagine why they would do it.

On their return to Phanji, Gloria met with the upper-management personnel of Imperium and a handful of Servitor people. They shared a civilized afternoon tea, and Gloria was eagerly ogled by one and all. Everyone had seen her statement about the Emperor, it seemed, and although no one was impolite enough to ask her about it directly, she was the focus of intense interest. If the sensation she had created was going to fade, as she hoped and expected, there were no signs of it yet.

Finally, Gloria asked Omphala to take her to the Imperium metallurgical lab, where one of the AKs was being analyzed. Sweet took his leave, and returned to Dhanj on his own, leaving Omphala alone with Gloria. In the back of the limo skimmer on the way to the lab, he seized his opportunity and wrapped his arm around her. He pulled her close, attempted to kiss her, and grabbed her exposed crotch with his free hand.

Gloria had been expecting something like this, but had supposed that Omphala would be a little more accomplished in his approach. There was no room for scissors kicks in the back of the limo, so Gloria simply went limp and passive and let Omphala have his way with her for a minute. He squeezed her breasts and stroked her groin industriously, but when she neither fought him off nor dissolved in ecstasy, Omphala broke off his advance and stared at her in confusion. "What?" he demanded. He had expected a variety of possible reactions, but not no reaction at all.

"If you're through," Gloria said placidly, "I'd like to

discuss possible means by which the weapons could be transported to Myn, assuming they are manufactured here."

"Well," said Omphala, looking and sounding thoroughly embarrassed, "there is a substantial merchant fleet of seagoing vessels." He released his hold on her, straightened his necktie, and continued in a businesslike manner. "They have largely converted to thermoelectric propulsion, although a few of the old sailing ships remain in service. Very much like nineteenth-century clipper ships, really. Trade with Myn is light but regular, perhaps a dozen vessels a month. There's not much scrutiny of the cargoes, I'm afraid, so I think smuggling would be a real possibility."

They arrived at the laboratory with no further difficulty. Given what she had endured during her first months at Dexta, Omphala's assault made little impression on Gloria. Tigers had to expect an occasional unwanted grope, and Gloria had been handling situations like this since before her marriage to Charles. If Omphala had been a little smoother, she might even have played along with him for a bit, confident that not much could happen in the back of a limo on a short trip through the middle of the city. But she was annoyed by his clumsiness and his arrogant assumption that she would naturally respond to his manly maneuvers. Getting out of the limo, she pressed the hidden contact and increased the transparency of her clothing to 90 percent, just to make Omphala suffer a little more.

"We have some results, Ms. VanDeen," an Imperium chemist told her in the laboratory. "We took some scrapings from the weapon and did a spectrographic analysis. Then we repeated the process as a control. There can be no doubt about the results. The match is perfect. The metal in this weapon unquestionably comes from Jhino."

• • •

"SO WE'VE NAILED DOWN *WHERE*," SAID Hawkes, after Gloria had returned to the Compound and told him the news. "Now we need to know *how* and *why*."

"*Where* isn't exactly nailed down yet," Gloria said. "Jhino's a big place. It won't be easy finding the factory. Veentro has assured us full cooperation, but I have to admit that I have some doubts about him."

"Why? It doesn't make much sense for the Jhino to be arming the Myn."

"I know. But Veentro is very eager to get us to transfer the Compound to his side of the ocean. What if he's arming the Myn just to cause us enough problems over here to push us into making the move?"

"Hmmm," said Hawkes.

"I admit, it's a reach. But what's the alternative? Some private gunrunning operation? I don't see how the Myn could hope to manage that in Jhino."

"Third party?" Hawkes suggested. "A human comes in, sets up the factory in Jhino, and smuggles them to the Myn."

"An awful lot of risk for not much reward," said Gloria. "The Myn don't have much money, and the number of weapons involved couldn't be large enough to make much of a profit. Your third party would have to have some motive beyond making a quick killing. I mean, the costs of setting up the factory would be more than they'd be likely to make on the sales to the Myn."

"True, although the factory wouldn't have to be a big operation. The AK-47 was obviously chosen because it's cheap and easy to make, and a proven weapon for resistance movements. Plans for it are available in the historical archives—I know, I checked."

"They'd need more than just the guns themselves, though," Gloria pointed out. "They also need ammunition. The Myn-Traha would need to shoot off a lot of it just to train their people. That implies a second factory, perhaps, and a continuing supply route."

"Well, we don't have enough resources to police ten thousand miles of shoreline. We could track the transoceanic trade from orbit, but we'd need the active cooperation of the Myn to check every vessel that comes into every port."

Gloria got up from the desk in her borrowed office and walked to a window. Outside, she could see Olivera leading his Security team and a handful of draftees through some sort of defense drill. Petra stood next to him, staring worshipfully at her man.

There was a knock at the door, and Melinda Throneberry came in. She glanced at Hawkes, then said to Gloria, "We just got a response from the Chancellor's office. Your meeting with Quan is set for tomorrow morning."

"Good," said Gloria. "Melinda, I'd like you to come with me."

"My pleasure," she said, and left.

"Melinda," said Hawkes, "is not happy."

"Too bad for her," Gloria said, approaching Hawkes. "I am." She put her arms around his neck and pulled him close. Hawkes reached under her short skirt and ran his hands over her smooth, bare buttocks. The couch in the office was too small for them, but there was a soft Myn rug on the floor.

GLORIA SAT NEXT TO THRONEBERRY IN AWK-ward silence in the back of the limo on the way to the Palqui, Myn's combination government center and temple. She was used to a certain amount of hostility from other women, just as she was used to occasional impulsive advances like Omphala's. Whether Melinda Throneberry liked her or not was a matter of little consequence to Gloria, as long the friction between them didn't get in the way of their jobs. Since her outburst the other day, Throneberry had been cooperative and efficient, and that was all Gloria asked of her. Still, life might be easier for everyone in the Compound if they could manage at least a veneer of civility.

Gloria attempted to make small talk about the Governor's Reception that evening, and Throneberry made a game effort to hold up her end of the conversation. She even complimented Gloria on her choice of apparel for her visit to the Palqui. She was wearing what was, for her, a modest blue wrap dress, tied at the waist by a salmon-colored cord. "I'm glad to see you're wearing something appropriate for a visit to a head of state," Throneberry said, "instead of a Manhattan singles club."

"You don't really know very much about the Myn, do you, Melinda?" Gloria asked, not in an unfriendly way.

"What do you mean?" Throneberry said, offended by the question. "I deal with them every day."

"But you don't really *know* them."

"And I suppose you do, after three or four days?"

"I've had the opportunity to learn a lot in those days, Melinda. I only mentioned it because of what you said about what I'm wearing being 'appropriate.' What's appropriate to the Myn is very different from what it seems to be to you. Haven't you learned anything about how they think? About how they view the world—and us?"

"I think I know them pretty well. I've become well acquainted with their many quirks and oddities, believe me."

"Melinda, those quirks and oddities are the Myn culture and personality. Haven't you ever tried to see things the way they do?"

"I'm too busy being Imperial Secretary to take up exosociology in my spare time. It all seems exotic and fascinating to you, Gloria, because you just got here. Stick around a while and deal with the day-to-day realities, and you might take a more realistic attitude."

The limo halted outside the gates of the Palqui. Unlike the modern, humanistic Government Center in

Phanji, the Palqui was an ancient structure. Imperial archaeologists had estimated that the inner part of the Palqui was begun some five thousand years ago. The outer rings had been added over time, with the most recent dating from about a thousand years ago. The low adobe buildings formed a complex geometric pattern within a series of concentric walls, with Quan's home and office at the center in a hexagonal hall supported by heavy wooden beams.

The Chancellor, who would also serve as translator, was a Myn named Shoon. He greeted the two women at the exterior gate, and with few words led them into the Palqui. They walked along a crushed-stone path that led them past a series of meditation gardens between the concentric walls. Each garden belonged to one of the eleven tribal groups. Gloria noticed a number of Myn seated on the ground in the gardens, apparently staring off into space and communing with their ancestors.

They entered the inner hall, and it took a moment for their eyes to adjust to the gloom. The room, about forty feet on a side, was lit solely by candles. At its center, seated on cushions on a raised hexagonal platform, sat Quan, a thin and frail-looking elderly Myn with silver-tipped fur and one eye that looked clouded and blind.

Shoon looked at Gloria, and said, "Quan will see you now." He trilled something loudly in Myn, and Quan looked up, as if in surprise, then nodded. "Come forward," said Shoon.

"Wait here and hold this," Gloria said to Throneberry. She unknotted the cord at her waist, pulled open the wrap dress, and handed it to an astonished Throneberry. She kicked off her shoes and strode forward to stand before Quan wearing nothing but a look of deep respect on her face.

"Greetings, Revered One," she said, bowing formally at the base of the hexagonal platform. "I am Gloria

VanDeen of Dexta. I have come from Earth to speak with you about important matters that concern both of our worlds. I am an honest woman, and I have nothing to hide. I will speak only the truth to you, and I know that you will speak only the truth to me."

Quan focused his good eye on her and remained silent for at least two minutes while Gloria stood waiting. Then he trilled something, and Shoon turned to Gloria, and said, "Quan bids you welcome, Gloriavandeen. He says that he has met many representatives from Dexta, but you are the first that he trusts. He will speak the truth, as well, for he knows that neither of you has anything to hide."

"The land is unhappy," said Gloria. "We both know this is true, Revered One. Together, we must do whatever we can to make the land happy once more."

"Some of my people," Shoon translated, "believe that the land will never be happy until all of the humans are gone. My ancestors are unhappy, as well, but they tell me I must listen to your words and treat you with respect. I know the power of the Empire, and it is possible that the ancestors of the Myn who kill the humans do not understand it as I do."

"How can we help them to understand, Revered One? For you know it is true that humans will not leave your world, and that they will do what is necessary to protect themselves. I fear that many humans may die, and many Myn will join their ancestors, if we cannot find a solution to our problems."

"You speak the truth, Gloriavandeen," Quan replied through Shoon. "I fear what the anger of the young and the ignorance of their ancestors may bring."

"Some of your young have acquired dangerous weapons, Revered One. You and I must find a way to get them to give up their weapons and restore the peace. I must tell you that we have learned that those weapons are made in the land of the Jhino. Surely, those who are providing these weapons cannot have the best interests of the Myn at heart."

Quan looked surprised after Shoon had translated Gloria's words. "Is this so?" he asked. "I have heard of these weapons, but no one has told me that they come from Jhino."

"It is so, Revered One. There can be no doubt of it. We are attempting to find the source of the weapons and prevent any more from reaching your land. But the weapons that are already here must be given up. If they are not, I fear great harm will come to your people. I speak of Imperial Marines, Revered One. If the violence does not end, they will come and surely bring even greater unhappiness to the land."

"I know of these Imperial Marines," Quan said, and Shoon tried to convey the sadness in his voice. "When I was young and the humans first came to our world, the Imperial Marines came with them. I did not like them. I have been told what they have done on other worlds. I hope they will not come here again."

"Then you must do all you can to end the violence, Revered One," Gloria pleaded. She wondered if Shoon's translation captured the urgency in her own voice.

"It is a difficult matter, Gloriavandeen," said Quan. "I must speak of it with my ancestors, and trust in their wisdom to guide me. I thank you for coming, Gloriavandeen, and for your honest words. It is a pleasure to meet a human who has nothing to hide. I hope you will come again."

Gloria nodded, retreated a couple of steps backwards, and turned to take her leave. But she looked back as Quan said something more.

"Quan asks," Shoon said, "that you will bid your Emperor a happy birthday."

Smiling, Gloria said, "I shall, Revered One."

She walked back to where Melinda Throneberry stood, took her dress and shoes from her, then marched out of the building.

"That," she said to Throneberry, "is what *I* mean by appropriate." Gloria got dressed and walked ahead of her along the crushed-stone path.

Throneberry shook her head, and muttered, "Spirit help us!"

chapter 12

GLORIA SAT ON A CHAIR IN HER ROOM, NAKED, sipping a cup of jigli tea. She had asked one of the Myn servants to prepare it; he seemed surprised, but did as she asked. By now, he was probably spreading the word that the woman from Dexta Headquarters was consulting with her ancestors.

What Gloria actually had in mind was something on a somewhat less elevated plane. After four days of incessant activity since arriving on Mynjhino, she was more than a little tired, both mentally and physically. She thought that she owed herself an evening of fun and relaxation, and the Governor's Reception was a convenient excuse. Between the jigli and the outfit she intended to wear, she figured that she would be about ready to explode by the time she got back to Hawkes's rented rooms.

She was tired of thinking about guns and Jhino and the Myn-Traha. There was too much to consider—too many possibilities, too many unknowns—for her to make any further sense of the situation. Instead, she pondered her own position.

Denton, the ENS correspondent, had told her that his editor had agreed to the courier, and the story ought to be arriving on Earth about now. He had played the final version for her, and she was annoyed to find that Olivera had given him a breathless secondhand account of how Gloria had actually escaped from the Myn terrorists. The man just couldn't seem to keep his mouth shut—not the best trait for someone in Security. Between Olivera's account and the partially nude scenes Denton had extorted from her, the story was bound to be a sensation, and would no doubt spread quickly on lead screens throughout the Empire. Coming on the heels of her now-famous statement concerning her relationship with the Emperor, the story would go a long way toward making her name, face, and body known in every human home on 2643 worlds. She was public property, as Mingus had said she would be.

Her out-of-the-limelight strategy had backfired, and it was already too late to do anything about it. She would become as notorious throughout the Empire as she had already become on Mynjhino. Her (nude) escape and her (nude) appearance before Quan were already the talk of the human community, and it was commonly supposed that she had slept with the Governor. She had consciously chosen to exploit the power conferred on her by her looks, and she would have to live with the consequences. Fair enough, she thought; there was nothing for it but to go with the flow.

Gloria got up and prepared for the evening's festivities. A little color for her lips, some subtle eye shadow, and she was ready to don her apparel. It consisted of nothing but two narrow strands of beads and gems. The gems were starburst diamonds from the great mines on Windhoek, and the beads were of lapis lazuli. They nearly matched the color of her eyes, which was why Charles had bought them for her as a second anniversary present.

She fastened one strand low around her hips, and the second strand hung vertically from the first, down to her knees, providing concealment that was no more than symbolic. She added matching earrings and bracelets, and was as dressed as she was going to get on this evening.

She had worn this outfit at one of Gregory III's Paris Levees, although by then, styles had changed from Darius's day, and it was considered a tad outré. She had seriously considered wearing it to the Rio Levee, now that skin was in again, but had decided against it because she didn't want to put ideas in Charles's head—not that it had mattered, in the end. It would undoubtedly cause a stir among the provincials at tonight's reception, but she was at least certain that the Governor would like it.

She sat down again and sipped some more of the jigli tea. She could already feel it working on her, and she closed her eyes and thought of Hawkes.

Petra knocked and entered, interrupting her pleasant contemplation. "It's Cinderella," said Petra. "I've come for my dress, Fairy Godmother."

"Finished scrubbing the floors, have you?" Gloria asked. "Very well, then. You can find a rag to suit you in my closet."

"What are you going to wear?" Petra asked.

Gloria got to her feet and spun around gracefully.

"Holy sh— I mean, gosh, Gloria, that's—that's—no, I think I had it right the first time. Holy shit! Are those real diamonds?"

Gloria nodded. Petra came closer and examined the strands of alternating lapis and starbursts. "You could buy Weehawken with that!"

"It was a gift from Charles," Gloria explained.

"And you just threw that in your luggage with everything else? Spirit, I will never understand rich people!"

"Don't try. We're beyond rational comprehension. Go get yourself a dress, Petra. And remember, you and I are the wicked women from New York, Center of the

Known Universe. The provincials will expect us to put on a show for them."

"Well, at least you're putting on *something*. Me, I'm going to put on some actual clothes."

Gloria sipped more tea while Petra gaped and dithered in the closet. She finally emerged with a filmy blue gown in a smart fabric that would contract to fit her. She stripped off her gray Dexta exterior, hesitated, then dispensed with her shocking pink underwear, as well. She slipped into the gown and gazed in awestruck wonder at her own reflection. Thin straps looping around her neck held up the gown, which dipped below her navel in front and halfway down her bottom in the rear. The skirt was slit in front, baring her legs almost all the way up from the floor.

Petra stared at herself for a few moments, then said, "Gasp! This is ridiculous!" She started to take the dress off.

"Petra," Gloria snapped. "I'll have no cowards on my staff! You look absolutely beautiful. Let's have no more nonsense."

"Well," Petra admitted, "it does sort of go well with my eyes. Is this the transparency gizmo?" she asked, fingering one of the seams.

Petra played with it, cycling twice from zero through 100 percent. She came back again to 40 percent. Then 50.

"Save something for later," Gloria advised.

"Whew!" Petra sighed. "If Ricky doesn't ravish me ten seconds after he sees me in this, I'm going to demand my money back. Is that tea? Can I have some?"

Gloria hesitated, then smiled, and said, "Sure, why not?" Petra sat down, poured herself some of the jigli tea from the small pot, and sipped it.

"Odd taste," said Petra. "What is it?"

"Local blend," Gloria said. "I think you'll like it. Just don't be surprised if you wind up ravishing Ricardo. We're going to relax and have fun tonight, kiddo."

• • •

OLIVERA'S EYES NEARLY POPPED OUT WHEN
he showed up to escort Petra across the Compound to
the Governor's Residence. Gloria tagged along with
them as they made their way past the skimmers that
were delivering the cream of local society to the affair.
She noticed only one person on the gate, but decided
not to make an issue of it.

The crowd for the reception filled the spacious Governor's Residence and spilled out into the garden area
behind it. Rhinehart greeted Gloria with joyous enthusiasm, and she gave him a friendly kiss on the lips. "I
couldn't find a star sapphire," Gloria explained. "I hope
this will do, Excellency."

"Oh, my dear girl," Rhinehart cried, "you do us
proud! Of all the parties in the Empire on this auspi-
cious day, none will compare with this. Takes me back to
the days of Darius!" He leaned close to her, and whispered, "Frankly, these provincial women can be a bit of
a bore, if you know what I mean. But you are the very
soul of sophistication and elegance, dear Gloria."

None of the provincial women was as nearly nude as
Gloria, but she was not alone in her extravagant exhi-
bition of epidermis. The Emperor's Birthday was the
annual excuse for women throughout the Empire to
pretend that they were as chic and *avant garde* as the
noblewomen at Court, and High Imperial style was the
order of the day. Bosoms and bottoms were bared with
abandon, and glittering gems were retrieved from storage for the occasion. If Dhanj was not Rio, on this night
the colonials and corporate wives did their utmost to
make it seem like Rio. Gloria took in the scene and
smiled; it *did* remind her of Rio, at least a little.

For their part, most of the men were decked out in
"Imperials"—tunic, breeches, and boots. There were
more bulging bellies and flabby thighs in evidence than
one might find at the well-toned Court, but the men

contrived to look dashing nonetheless. The women seemed to have more time for tennis, and were generally slimmer and more attractive than their men, but nearly everyone seemed pleased with their own appearance. In the area of smug narcissism, at least, the provincials were the equal of the High Imperial mavens at Court.

The Governor took Gloria's elbow and led her around, introducing her to one and all. Everyone congratulated her on her escape from the Myn and complimented her on her stunning attire. Whenever anyone attempted to question her on the troubles with the Myn, someone else—usually the Governor—gave them a stern look of disapproval. This was not a night for mundane concerns, even if those concerns were enough to frighten everyone there. Gloria thought it was a form of denial, but under the strained circumstances, it was probably a healthy thing. Just as much as everyone else, Gloria needed a temporary reprieve from grim reality.

With champagne tickling her nose and the jigli tea tingling her nerves, she circulated throughout the throng, feeling lighter than air and glad to be alive. Considering what had nearly happened with the Myn, life had rarely seemed so precious to her as it did now. She felt everyone's eyes on her, like sunshine striking her bare flesh, and enjoyed the sensation she was creating. Maybe it wouldn't be so bad, after all, being public property. Her face and body opened doors for her; it would be foolish not to go through them.

Other women were also using what they had on this evening, to good effect. Gloria saw Tatiana Markova standing with Randall Sweet, whispering to him. Tatiana, with her long black hair and dark eyes, was wearing a gauzy harem-girl outfit that bared her breasts and belly. Even Melinda Throneberry had loosened up a bit, and was wearing a black gown with a deep V to the waist; she was chatting with the local gentry and looked as if she had just returned from a particularly enjoyable funeral.

She noticed Petra and Olivera together, staring longingly into each other's eyes. Olivera was strikingly handsome in his Imperials, and the jigli seemed to be having an effect on Petra. Gloria noted that her blue dress was now at least 70 percent transparent. She was glad for her little assistant from New Jersey, and only hoped that Olivera wouldn't wind up breaking her heart.

Gloria searched for Hawkes, but hadn't found him yet. She hoped he wasn't boycotting the affair, just to be perverse. She wanted him to see her like this, and to have him handy just in case the jigli got to be overwhelming. There were some tall shrubberies in the garden that might serve.

A small orchestra began to play dance music. Two of the seven musicians, Gloria was surprised to see, were Myn. One of them was handling the percussion generator, and the other, despite the absence of a tongue, was somehow managing to perform on the vibraflute. The Myn were a musical race, and they seemed to have a talent and appreciation for the music of humans, as well.

Gloria soon found herself dancing with a succession of colonial gentry and Big Twelve executives. It was fun, and she didn't really mind the way they stroked her bare bottom and rubbed up against her naked breasts on the slow numbers. On the fast tunes, she consciously put on a show, writhing suggestively and twirling the hanging strand of beads and gems to fully reveal what little it had hidden. She even threw in a few Qatsima moves, with leg lifts, spins, and a graceful cartwheel.

She was dancing slowly with a young GalaxCo exec when someone cut in and she found herself in the arms of Brian Hawkes. "About time you showed up," she scolded him. "I was just about to dash off to the shrubberies with a guy who mulches pharmaceuticals."

"Tell him to go mulch himself," Hawkes said, and pulled her close. Gloria closed her eyes and floated around the floor with him, feeling incandescently happy.

What could possibly be better, she wondered, than to be Gloria VanDeen at this moment?

IMPERIAL GOVERNOR VLADISLAV RHINEHART stood on the bandstand and announced that the time had come to toast Emperor Charles V on the occasion of his birthday. Myn waiters circulated throughout the crowd and recharged every glass for the toast. But first, the Governor had a few words to say.

Without quite making direct reference to the troubles on his world, he praised the courage, solidarity, and patriotism of the human community. He went out of his way to say kind things about the Myn and Jhino, as well, but it was not really their Empire, and everyone knew it. Throughout a sphere two thousand light-years in diameter, *Homo sapiens* was the only species that really mattered; all the others survived and flourished only because of human generosity and forbearance.

In this, the 695th year of the Empire, the human race was established on 2643 worlds and steadily spreading to others. Charles was the fifth of his name and the forty-seventh of his line to hold the Imperial Throne, in an unbroken succession dating back to Hazar the Great. He was the youngest Emperor in more than two centuries, and one of the most popular, if only because he had not been in office long enough to make any significant mistakes.

When faster-than-light technology was developed, back in the early twenty-second century, and humanity began its epochal expansion to the stars, Earth was only beginning to recover from two centuries of global warfare—hot, cold, political, economic, ideological, cultural, and religious. The rise of Spiritism had fostered an Era of Good Feeling, and a tenuous world government had been established. It sponsored and oversaw the initial wave of expansion and adequately served the needs of the mushrooming population. But late in the century, mankind encountered the first of many hostile alien races, and the Terrestrial Union was hard-pressed to meet the challenge.

During the three centuries of desperate warfare that followed—centuries in which Earth was directly attacked five different times, with billions of human casualties—the Union struggled to hold together the many different factions and competing interests of a human community that extended to dozens, then hundreds, of star systems. Willy-nilly, Earth was building an empire, without quite intending it and without quite knowing how to handle one. The Union creaked and sputtered under the growing stress, and finally collapsed altogether.

There followed fifty years of chaotic rebellion and civil war, with humans once again pitted against other humans. Finally, a general named Hazar managed to conquer or intimidate all the warring factions and establish a lasting era of peace among humans. In the year 2522, Hazar declared the Terran Empire, and proclaimed himself Emperor. Many were displeased by this turn of events, but no one had the power to oppose him effectively, and in time, humanity came to accept the fact that it comprised an Empire, ruled by an Emperor. Hazar's rule proved to be popular and efficient, and upon his death in 2543, no one seriously disputed the right of his son, Baslim I, to succeed him.

The long reign of the House of Hazar had not been free of conflict. According to the history texts, no fewer than twelve Emperors had been assassinated. From what she had learned during her time at Court, Gloria knew that the history texts were wrong, or at least incomplete. In truth, a minimum of eighteen Emperors had been dispatched by one means or another, and there were unanswered questions concerning five others. Charles himself had come into office on the heels of a botched conspiracy, the Fifth of October Plot.

Despite the intrigues, the Emperors presided over

an age of unbridled expansion. One after another, rival species were assimilated or vanquished, until, with the conquest of the Ch'gnth Confederacy in 3174, a new era of peace and security was born. In the forty-two years since the fall of the Ch'gnth, humanity had not been compelled (or tempted) to fight a single new war against another species. Moreover, long-range exploration had revealed no evidence of another species within a thousand light-years of the Empire that was likely to present a major challenge to continued human expansion.

Humanity had every reason to feel proud and confident, and the Emperor's Birthday was an annual occasion for another round of self-congratulation and speechmaking. Governor Rhinehart considered himself to be no slouch in that department, and kept the revelers waiting a full twenty minutes before he finally got around to proposing the toast. At last, the champagne was quaffed, and the cheers and huzzahs had barely faded when the celebration was punctuated by a staccato burst of automatic-weapons fire.

It was not a familiar sound, just a rapid, muffled *pop! pop! pop!* coming from somewhere outside, in the direction of the front gate. The sound repeated itself, closer this time.

"Stay here and keep down!" Hawkes told Gloria, then began running toward the front doors of the Residence. Olivera was in motion at the same moment.

"Everyone get down!" Olivera screeched, his voice rising to a higher than normal register. "And someone put out those lights!"

Gloria started to follow Hawkes to the doors, but came down flat on her face an instant later, tackled from behind. Angered, she looked around and saw Petra clinging to her legs.

"Stay *down*, Gloria!" Petra shouted. Gloria tried to shake her off and get back to her feet, but an instant later another round of firing echoed throughout the Compound and windows in the Residence shattered.

Women screamed, men shouted, and two hundred well-dressed people were suddenly facedown, clutching the expensive carpet. A moment later, the lights went out.

HAWKES GOT TO THE DOORS AT THE SAME TIME as Olivera. The Security chief saw two of his people coming up behind them through the darkness. "Get to the other doors and make sure they're locked!" he ordered. "Barricade them if you have to. If they get inside..."

Kneeling in front of the doors, Hawkes hesitated before opening them. "Are you armed?" he asked Olivera.

"The rifles are locked up over in the basement of the administrative building," Olivera said. "I've got three people with pistols outside, one on the gate and the other two patrolling the Compound."

More firing rattled the air, and another window shattered. There was a flash of light outside and a loud *whummp!* Hawkes risked opening the door a crack and stayed low as he peered outside. He saw a skimmer ablaze at the front gate, and as he watched another, nearer the Residence, exploded in an orange fireball.

"I don't see your people firing back," said Hawkes. "One of us has to get to those rifles."

"I'll go," said Olivera, almost cheerfully. "My legs are longer than yours. Anyway, I've got the key."

It was at least fifty yards from the Residence to the administrative building, most of it across open ground that was illuminated by the flames of the burning skimmers. Hawkes didn't like the odds, but there was nothing for it.

"Stay low," he said, "and don't stop for anything." Olivera nodded, and when Hawkes pulled the door open, he scrambled out onto the front portico and rolled down the short flight of stone steps. He crawled to a line of low shrubbery and peered out into the Compound. Small dark figures were in motion near the gate, and another burst of gunfire came from the right of the Residence, on the opposite side from the administrative building. Olivera hurdled the hedge and paused again behind a skimmer that was parked there.

Hawkes didn't want to leave the door, but decided that he should do something to cover Olivera. As the Security chief sprang from behind the skimmer and began sprinting across the open space, Hawkes went out the front doors, shouted incoherently to attract attention, then dived to the bottom of the steps as bullets stitched a line across the heavy wooden doors of the Residence. He rolled and came up crouching behind the hedge just in time to see Olivera go down.

Olivera pitched forward and lay still. Hawkes was about to go after him to get the key, when he saw Olivera slowly creeping forward. Olivera looked back toward the Residence, and Hawkes held up his hand, with three fingers raised. He shook the hand once and lowered a finger, again and lowered another, then made a decisive motion with it. Olivera sprang to his feet and, dragging one leg behind him, floundered onward toward the administrative building while Hawkes shouted again and dived to his right. There was more firing, and when Hawkes risked another look, he couldn't see Olivera in the Compound.

Another skimmer went up, quickly followed by two more. Windows shattered in the Residence again, and Hawkes thought the gunfire was getting closer. There was still no sign of return fire from the Security people in the Compound. That could mean only one thing, he realized.

Why don't they just charge the building? he wondered. If they did, Hawkes didn't see any way of stopping them.

Another burst of fire sounded from the other side of the skimmer parked by the hedge. Hawkes's ears rang from the noise. If he could surprise the Myn and get his weapon, there might be a chance. At least it would change the odds. Hawkes crept to the left, toward the rear end of the vehicle, as another spasm of gunfire issued from the front of it. Springing from his crouch, he made a low, flat dive over the top of the hedge and rolled out of it into another crouch at the rear of the skimmer. He paused and listened.

Suddenly, a searing blue bolt coursed across the Compound and sliced through the front of the skimmer, as well as the hedge behind it and a brick in the corner of the Residence. It was followed instantly by a loud thundercrack, as air rushed in to fill in the ionized trail left by the plasma discharge. Hawkes looked across the Compound and saw Olivera lying prone in the doorway of the administrative building, aiming a plasma rifle for another shot.

"Turn down the power, dammit!" Hawkes shouted to him. Set on full, the rifle could burn a hole right through the Residence. Olivera gave him a jaunty salute, and a moment later fired again. This time, the plasma trail was thin and focused, and was aimed at something out near the gate. Hawkes couldn't tell if he had hit his target or not.

He crept warily from behind the rear of the skimmer and looked to his right. A Myn lay on his back, staring blindly upward toward two of his world's moons. A hole the size of a soccer ball had been cut through the Myn's midsection. There was no blood; the wound was self-cauterizing. Hawkes scrambled on hands and knees, grabbed the Myn's weapon, and ducked back behind the skimmer as Olivera fired another sizzling blue bolt.

Half of the AK-47's stock was missing, vaporized by the plasma discharge, but it seemed to be functional. Hawkes had studied the captured weapons well enough to know how to operate the device. He leaned around the fender of the skimmer and fired a short burst in the direction of the gate. It would give the terrorists something new to think about.

Hawkes and Olivera continued firing at random intervals. The AK felt lighter in Hawkes's hands, and he realized that he must be running out of ammunition. With no more available, he decided to save the rest in case the Myn should charge the Residence.

But they didn't. Two minutes went by without another burst of gunfire, then three. Hawkes moved to the front of the skimmer and looked toward the gate, but could see nothing other than the burning vehicle there. Across the Compound, Olivera got to his feet and limped into the open.

"They're gone!" Olivera shouted gaily. "We won!"

IN THE DARKNESS, THE SOUND OF TERRIFIED whimpers and sobs became almost too much for Gloria. She had to do *something* . . . and yet, she knew that there was nothing that could be done. She held on to Petra's hand and endured the slow march of the minutes, until finally the windows stopped shattering and the sound of gunfire died away. People gradually got back up and began moving around.

When the lights abruptly came back on, Gloria saw a small throng of men pressing forward toward one wall. Backed up against the wall, a dozen Myn servants were under assault by angry humans.

Gloria got to her feet and pushed her way through into the melee. The men paused what they were doing at the sight of her. "Stop it!" she shouted, seeing three Myn already on the floor, unconscious or dead, and a fourth in the grip of a GalaxCo exec she had danced with not a hour earlier. He was holding the Myn by the scruff of its neck and methodically pounding its face with his right fist. "Let him go!" she yelled, but the man would not stop.

Slipping out of her shoes, Gloria unleashed a

sidewinding Qatsima kick that caught the man in the rib cage. He went *oof!* and staggered back, dropping the Myn, who collapsed to the floor and didn't move.

Gloria whirled around and faced the other men. "Just stop it!" she roared. "What the hell do you think you're doing?"

"They're Myn!" someone said, as if that explained everything—and, in a way, it did.

"There are 100 million Myn!" Gloria retorted. "Are you going to kill them all? For Spirit's sake, these are just servants. If they were armed, we'd all be dead by now. Get a grip on yourselves!"

The men all retreated a step, as if the force of Gloria's words had repulsed them. She stared at them a moment, then looked toward the frightened Myn cowering by the wall.

"Take your friends," she said, gesturing to the motionless Myn on the floor, "and go to the kitchen. Stay there and don't move. Do you understand me?" One of the Myn nodded, and together, they dragged their fallen coworkers away, as the human mob reluctantly cleared a path for them.

The men turned away from Gloria in ones and twos, and returned to their women. Gloria looked toward the front door and felt her heart skip a beat as she saw Hawkes coming back inside, an AK-47 in one hand, and his other arm wrapped around Olivera. A bright red stain mottled the left thigh of Olivera's breeches. Petra screeched and ran to him.

"We need a doctor here!" Hawkes shouted as he and Petra maneuvered Olivera onto a sofa.

"I'm fine," Olivera insisted, but his face was unnaturally pale. Petra clung to him, crying and laughing simultaneously as she clutched him.

Dr. Levin, from the Compound, made his way to Olivera, and Hawkes turned to Gloria, who threw her arms around him and held him tightly. "It's all right," he said, "they've gone."

An excited, relieved babble erupted from the crowded room, and people began shouting out questions and demanding protection. Governor Rhinehart made his way through the congestion and looked helplessly at Hawkes and Gloria.

"What are we to do?" he asked, his voice sounding thin and unsteady. "What are we to do?"

"Good question," said Hawkes.

chapter 13

THE LEADERS OF THE HUMAN COLONY ON
Mynjhino sat scattered around the Governor's office in a
state of shock and exhaustion. With the coming of day-
light, Hawkes and three Security people had gone out
into the Compound and found the bullet-riddled bodies
of the remaining three Security staffers, two men and a
woman. No one else had been killed or even injured,
other than Olivera. The smoldering wrecks of five skimmers sent up thin columns of dark, acrid smoke into the
morning air. Hawkes put two of the surviving Security
people on the front gate, armed with plasma rifles, told
the other to patrol the Compound, then returned to the
Governor's office.

Undersecretary Blumenthal sat quietly in a corner,
keeping her own counsel. Tatiana Markova sat alone on
a sofa, staring off into space. Gloria had managed to find
time to put on jeans and a shirt, but Petra had never left
Olivera's side, and was still wearing what little there was
of her party gown. Olivera was stretched out on a sofa,
his leg bandaged and propped up, looking years older

than the callow young bureaucrat he had been a day earlier. Hawkes sat down on Gloria's sofa and gave her a
quick squeeze on the thigh. She grabbed his hand and
smiled wanly.

Melinda Throneberry paced compulsively back and
forth in front of the Governor's desk, where Rhinehart
sat, looking stunned and baffled. His silvery hair was
disheveled, and he seemed to have shrunk inside his
Imperials.

One of the household staff came in, looked toward
the Governor, then immediately shifted his focus to
Throneberry. "Excuse me," he said, "but the people out
there are getting hungry."

"Then feed them!" Throneberry barked impatiently. All two hundred guests from the Reception were
still in the Residence, none of them daring to venture
out into the suddenly hostile world around the Compound.

"Yes, ma'am," the staffer said, and hurried from the
room.

"We're going to have to deal with all these people,
somehow," said Throneberry.

"These, and five thousand more," Hawkes said.
"We're going to need a decision, and I think we all know
what it has to be."

"If we can't protect them in the Compound, we sure
as hell can't protect them all over the continent," Olivera
said glumly. Protecting them was his job, and he had
been unable even to protect his own staff. The three
deaths had clearly left him feeling a failure.

"What I don't understand," Hawkes said, "is why
they didn't just charge the Residence. If they had, we
couldn't have stopped them. They could have killed
everyone."

"Maybe they didn't want to," Gloria suggested.

Hawkes looked at her. "What do you mean?"

"Look," said Gloria, "the Myn we captured talked
about how they had to kill every human on the planet.

But the attack last night wasn't just some crazed murder spree. None of the attacks have been. They've all been well planned and well executed."

"It's true," said Olivera. "Counting last night, the score is forty-five dead humans, and just three dead Myn, with one captured. Each time, they've done exactly what they wanted to do."

"Which suggests to me," said Gloria, "that last night, they weren't trying to kill us. They were trying to scare us. Someone a lot smarter than the Myn we captured planned this thing, and they knew perfectly well what would happen if they massacred the government and civilian elite."

"Imperial Marines," said Olivera.

"At least a regiment," Gloria confirmed. "And they'd have come here looking for blood."

"So," said Throneberry, "they just wanted to scare us."

"They succeeded," said Sonia Blumenthal. "I, for one, am wonderfully scared."

"And it's obvious that what they want us to do is evacuate Myn, which you," Throneberry said, looking at Hawkes, "seem to want us to do."

"Do you see an alternative?" Hawkes asked her. "I sure as hell don't."

"We'll have to consult with the corporates," Tatiana pointed out.

"Then go get them." Throneberry sighed. "We'll consult." Tatiana got up and walked to the door. She was still in her revealing harem-girl outfit, looking inappropriately gaudy for such a downcast morning.

Throneberry found a chair, sat down, and looked at the Governor. He had not spoken a word since the meeting began and no longer looked capable of it.

"Could you get me a cup of coffee, Pet?" Olivera asked.

Petra kissed him on the cheek, and said, "Coming right up." She went to the coffee tray and poured him a cup, glancing at Gloria on her way back. She looked scared.

Gloria was scared, too, but felt reasonably confident that there would be no more attacks in the immediate future. The Myn-Traha had made their point, and would now pause to see how the humans reacted. What remained to be seen was whether they would stand back and let the evacuation proceed, or resort to more attacks and kill just for the sake of killing.

"We need to send a courier to Earth," Gloria said. "They need to know about the attack and the evacuation." She glanced toward the Governor, then turned to Throneberry. "We'll need authorization."

Throneberry nodded. "You'll have it," she said.

Markova returned, with Belvoir, Omphala, and Sweet at her heels. They looked angry and dazed, and wearily slumped into chairs. Tatiana got coffee for them, then returned to her sofa.

"We've decided on an evacuation to Jhino," Throneberry told them.

"Dammit, you cannot do that!" Belvoir snarled. "We'd lose the entire season's crop!"

"You'll lose a hell of a lot more than that if you try to stay," said Hawkes. "Anyway, after last night, how many of your people do you think are going to remain?"

"Then bring in the Marines! They should already be here, protecting the plantations." He looked at Gloria with angry eyes. "What the hell has your pal Mingus been doing, anyway?"

"As it happens," Gloria said calmly, "there's a good chance that he's already ordered them here. But no more than a company, and at the earliest, they couldn't be here for another week."

"A company? What the hell good is a company? How are they going to protect the plantations with only a company?"

"They aren't," said Gloria. "They'll secure the Compound and the city, but even a regiment would have a hard time covering all of GalaxCo's holdings, even if they wanted to. And it would be two or three more weeks before a force that size could get here. In the meantime, we've got five thousand people out there that we can't protect."

"It's a disgrace," Belvoir bellowed. "A Spirit-forsaken disgrace!"

"Oh, calm down, Roland," said Sweet. "It's not the end of the world."

"Easy for you to say. What have you got to worry about, a hundred people and a couple of offices in the city? GalaxCo stands to lose its entire investment on this planet. If we pull out of the plantations, how do we know we'll ever be able to take them back?"

"That's a long-term question," Throneberry pointed out. "We've got a short-term emergency to deal with now. What we need is your complete cooperation in executing the evacuation. Can we count on that?"

Belvoir continued to resist. "I want to hear what the Governor has to say about this," he said. But when he looked at Rhinehart, he knew that the Governor would have nothing at all to say about it. He was staring blindly off into space, oblivious to the conversation around him.

"You can count on Imperium to do whatever is necessary," Omphala put in. "I'll contact Phanji and get our people busy lining up housing. I'll have them pass the word to Veentro and the government."

"Thanks, Julius," Throneberry said. She looked again at Belvoir. "And GalaxCo?"

Belvoir stared at the Governor for another moment, as if waiting for him to snap back to life and come up with a better solution. When he didn't, Belvoir looked at Throneberry, frowned as if he had been forced to eat something he didn't like, and said, "I suppose I have no choice."

"None," said Hawkes.

"Very well," said Belvoir. "We'll evacuate our people. We have some freight haulers that we can use. I'll have our office get on the comm and contact everyone we can. But this isn't something we can do in a day, you know."

"We figure three days," said Throneberry. "So we might as well get started now. I suppose I should go out there and make the announcement." She looked at Gloria, and added, "Unless you'd rather do it."

Gloria shook her head. "You're in charge here, Melinda," she said. "I'll do whatever I can to help. For now, I think the best thing I can do is get to work on that report for the courier."

"Fine," said Throneberry. "Hawkes, I want you to get started on planning the evacuation. Find all the skimmers you can, work out the best routes and the timing."

"That's me, too," said Olivera, pushing himself up from the couch.

"Are you sure you're up to it?" Throneberry asked.

He grinned. "Try and stop me."

"If I can suggest something," said Gloria, "I think you should tell everyone here that if they live in the city or nearby, they should simply go home. If they're from outlying regions, it would be better if they didn't try to go back. See if the city folk can provide temporary housing for them. And try to recruit drivers and skimmers. We're going to need all we can get."

"Another thing," said Hawkes. "As soon as we announce the evacuation, some people are going to run straight to the Transit. Belvoir, can you get GalaxCo security ready to handle that?"

"Should we stop them?"

"If they want to go now, let them. Just don't let it turn into a stampede. Keep it calm and organized."

"That, I think, should be our watchword for the coming days," said Throneberry. "Calm and organized. The last thing we need is a panic. All right, people, let's go do what we have to do."

• • •

THE CONTINENT OF MYN WAS SHAPED LIKE A fat banana, curving from northwest to southeast over the course of four thousand miles. Nowhere was it more than fifteen hundred miles wide, and a range of high mountains isolated most of the sparsely populated east coast. Dhanj sat at the balance point of the banana, on the west coast. Nearly every human habitation or plantation was within seven hundred miles of the city. The southern part of the continent was too hot for the comfort of either Myn or humans, and was virtually uninhabited. Most of the plantations were in the rich plains to the west of the mountains and east of Dhanj.

Hawkes and Olivera stood in the Security office, staring at a wall map and plotting routes and schedules. Petra was with them, taking notes and keeping an eye on Olivera, who was soldiering on through little more than willpower. He had lost a good deal of blood and was obviously in considerable pain as he stood before the map. The bullet had pierced his thigh and gone straight through, without hitting bone or artery, but it was not a minor wound.

As they worked, comm calls came in from other staff members, as well as from the offices of GalaxCo and Imperium. After last night's losses, and counting Gloria, Petra, and the Governor, the Compound had only twenty-one people left on staff, exclusive of Myn servants and domestic help. Some of those Myn, Hawkes believed, were almost certainly spying for the Myn-Traha, but he thought it best to leave everyone in place. For now, it was probably to their advantage to let the terrorists know what was happening.

If the Myn wanted to make trouble, they could turn the evacuation into a bloodbath, and there was little the humans could do to prevent it. Hawkes intended to send people with plasma rifles to ride shotgun on the freight haulers, which should be able to take up to thirty people per trip, but most of the skimmers would be going out with no protection at all. It was doubtful that the Myn-Traha had armed units scattered all over the continent, but if they concentrated their forces at the approaches to Dhanj, they could wreak havoc. And if they had enough troops to seize or destroy the Transit, they could prevent any escape at all.

Hawkes trusted Gloria's instinct that last night had been a warning. It seemed likely that the Myn-Traha would simply let the humans go on their way, rather than provoke a full-scale response from the Marines. On the other hand, blood had already been shed, and he would be surprised if they could pull off the entire evacuation without incident. Humans were likely to be as big a problem as the Myn. Some of the GalaxCo people had their own weapons, and they might be tempted to get a little payback before they left.

As soon as he had a chance, Hawkes intended to reach Pakli by comm and explain the situation to his friend in Dhabi. Pakli, in turn, could spread the word that the humans should be allowed to leave in peace. It was the one line of communication they had with the Myn-Traha, and it might well turn out to be vital to the success of the evacuation. Hawkes had never been in a war before, but his study of history told him that even the most implacable of enemies had to have a way to talk to one another.

GLORIA FINISHED HER REPORT FOR THE COURIER and returned to the office, feeling better for having done at least something, little as it was. She looked at the wall map for a few moments. Compared with terrestrial continents, Myn was a small place, but there was still a great deal of ground to be covered. As they stood there, GalaxCo was sending out word of the evacuation to their people, scattered all over that map, and far away, frightened and panicky people were gathering up their possessions and waiting to be rescued. They were depending on people like Gloria to do their jobs swiftly and efficiently.

It was a different sort of responsibility than she had ever felt before. Technically, bureaucratically, Gloria had direct responsibility for over a billion lives in Beta-5. But the crisis on Mynjhino had nothing in common with fussing over the money supply on Pecos or trade disputes between Othello and Desdemona. This was about life—human and Myn—and how to preserve and protect it. Her fiercest battles and bitterest rivalries within Dexta couldn't hold a candle to what was happening on this out-of-the-way world, 862 light-years from her comfortable office.

She had always thought she wanted power and responsibility, and had persevered in the face of appalling degradation and intimidation just to save her place at Dexta. She had wanted to be a player, someone who made a difference in the Empire and the lives of its citizens. But none of her dreams and ambitions had included anything remotely like what she now faced. Helping to preside over a desperate and bloody flight for life was not something she had ever imagined or aspired to. And yet, here she was.

"We've got to do this right," she said aloud.

Hawkes looked at her and saw the deep concern on her face. "Don't worry," he said. "We will."

"I'll tell you one thing," Gloria said. "The next time some Level X like Hector Konrad tries to pressure me, I'll laugh in his face."

She handed Hawkes her pad. "That's the report to Dexta for the courier. Take a quick look and see if there's anything you want to add."

Hawkes walked away with the pad and Gloria turned to look at Olivera and Petra. Her assistant was still in her party dress, looking beautiful and determined. She scarcely reminded Gloria of the funny, flighty girl she had known. It seemed to Gloria that both of them had grown up a bit in the last few days.

She looked at Olivera and saw that he, too, looked older and graver. Three kids in their twenties, she thought, playing at running the Empire. The game had suddenly become very serious.

"Your leg is bleeding again," she said. "Petra, take him back to the doctor, then get him into bed. Preferably alone."

"Oh, you're no fun," Petra said. She put her arm around Olivera, and said, "Come, my wounded hero. I'll be back in ten minutes, Gloria."

"Make that twenty," Olivera said.

Gloria looked at the two of them, and said, "Better make it thirty. I don't want to be accused of standing in the way of true love."

"In that case," Petra said as she helped Olivera out of the office, "see you in an hour or two."

Hawkes handed the pad back to Gloria. "Looks good to me," he said. "But I think you should explicitly request a courier from Earth. We need to know when and if the Marines are coming. It could make a difference in how we handle things. We still haven't addressed the question of what we do about the Compound after we've evacuated the rest of the population."

"Right," said Gloria. "If the Marines are coming soon, we should try to hold on to the Compound if we can."

"We should maintain a presence here as long as we possibly can," Hawkes agreed. "There are still going to be humans on Myn who could need our help, even after we get all the GalaxCo people out. There are about three hundred humans over on the east coast, and we just can't spare the skimmers to go get them. They'll have to make their own way here, or stay put."

"And there are bound to be some people who just refuse to leave. There must be some who have good relations with the Myn and won't be harmed."

"That reminds me. I should try to call Pakli and see if he can give us any help at his end. Why don't you go see how Melinda's doing? With the Governor in the state he's in, she'll need all the help you can give her."

Gloria walked back across the Compound to the Residence. Scores of people were still milling around, inside and out; a sense of aimless confusion had replaced the initial panic. Several people stopped Gloria and asked her questions about their property or their pets, and she could only try to reassure them that everyone was working hard to address their concerns. She felt frustrated and ineffectual.

Throneberry was still in the Governor's office, but Rhinehart was not to be seen. "He started to snap out of his daze," Throneberry said, "and immediately developed a migraine. I don't think he's going to be much help."

"As long as he doesn't get in our way," Gloria said. "Any problems with the guests?"

"Nothing more than you'd expect. I'd say about half of them have already gone back to their homes. The others are at loose ends. I think we should expect that several dozen will wind up spending the night here. I've already got the domestics making arrangements. Gloria? I need a favor from you."

"Anything," Gloria told her.

"You're obviously better at diplomacy than I am," Throneberry said, smiling slightly. "Can you go over to the Palqui and see what you can accomplish? If Quan knows we're leaving, he might be willing to give us some cooperation. Keep the Myn out of our way, clear the streets near the Transit, that sort of thing."

Gloria nodded. "Maybe I should run over to Jhino, too. Veentro will be overjoyed to see that we're pulling out of Myn and will probably expect us to transfer all of our operations over there. But Hawkes and I think we should hold out here as long as we reasonably can, especially if the Marines are coming."

"Agreed," said Throneberry. "I certainly don't want to be the one to haul down the Imperial flag. I'll call the Chancellor here and Veentro's people in Phanji to let them know you're coming. Give Quan anything he asks for, within reason, and let Veentro know how grateful we are, but don't make any promises."

"Gotcha."

"And Gloria?" Throneberry said. "I know we got off on the wrong foot, but I'm glad you're here." She smiled hesitantly.

Gloria returned her smile. "Sorry I gave you such a hard time," she said. "You're doing a good job, Melinda."

"Everyone is," said Throneberry. "I just hope that's enough. What we really need if we're going to pull this thing off is some good luck. You know, I can't recall a similar situation in Imperial history, certainly not within the past two centuries. There have been rebellions on recently conquered planets, of course, but we've *never* fought the Myn, and we've lived here in peace for eighty-five years."

"I guess that means that we have to make it up as we go along," Gloria said.

Tatiana Markova came into the office. She had changed back into Dexta mufti and looked briskly efficient. "Has the courier gone out yet?" she asked.

"Not yet," said Throneberry.

"Good. We need to piggyback some corporate communications for GalaxCo and Servitor."

Throneberry shook her head. "You know that's against regs, Tatiana. But . . . under the circumstances, I suppose we can bend the rules. Why, what have you got?"

Tatiana smiled. "Big stuff," she said. "Randy Sweet just made an offer that Belvoir jumped at. If their Boards approve, Servitor is going to buy out all of GalaxCo's leases and holdings on Mynjhino. The works."

Throneberry whistled. "Big, indeed," she said. "What brought this on?"

Tatiana helped herself to some coffee, looking pleased with herself. "Well," she said, "you know the two companies have differing philosophies. GalaxCo rarely looks beyond the bottom line and the price of their stock on the New York Exchange. Servitor tends to take the long view. Randy made an offer of twenty cents on the crown, and Roland fell all over himself accepting it. Roland figures it might take years to restore the plantations, and in the meantime, they'll drown in red ink, depressing stock values and enraging the investors. Randy sees it as a cheap investment that may reap huge profits five or ten years from now."

"Will their Boards go for it?" Throneberry wondered.

"I don't see why not," said Tatiana. "It suits the needs of both companies."

Gloria wasn't concerned about anyone's stock prices, but she had questions about how this would affect their immediate future. "I take it," she said, "that this means the GalaxCo people will not just be leaving Myn, but the entire planet."

Tatiana nodded and sipped some coffee. "Kit and kaboodle," she said. "They'll go through with the evacuation to Jhino for now, but they want to get all of their people off-world as quickly as they can. They have a half-loaded freighter in the harbor right now, and Roland thinks they can get about five hundred people aboard it by tonight. They'll be uncomfortable, but it's only a day and a half to Pecos via freighter. They plan to set up a shuttle using that freighter and get everyone out within a week."

"This all happened awfully fast," Gloria pointed out.

"Randy's a sharp guy," said Tatiana. "He saw his chance and took it. And Belvoir's no dope. This gives him a chance to show the Board in Bombay that he managed to salvage something from what could have been an unmitigated disaster for GalaxCo."

"Well," Gloria said, "this ought to make Quan and the rest of the Myn happy. They all regard the GalaxCo people as fools who have made the land unhappy. Maybe this will satisfy them for now and make them think they've won a great victory. When things have settled down, though, Servitor could have a hard time getting their people onto those plantations."

"Leave that to Randy," Tatiana said happily. "Man's a genius." She put down her coffee cup and turned to go. "I'll drop off the corporate messages in the Communications Room," she said over her shoulder.

Gloria and Throneberry turned to look at each other after she was gone. "Nice to see someone looking so cheerful on a day like this," said Gloria.

"That's our little Tatiana," said Throneberry. "The only question is whether she'll wind up working for Servitor or GalaxCo. Either way, Dexta will be better off without her. Forget about Lions and Tigers—that woman's a Snake."

A moment later, Sonia Blumenthal entered the office. "You heard?" she asked.

Throneberry nodded. "Tatiana just told us. Something of a stunner."

"Yes," said Sonia. "Consider me officially stunned. Any coffee left?"

"Help yourself," said Throneberry.

"What about unofficially?" Gloria asked her.

Sonia pulled a small flask from her handbag and added some of its contents to her coffee. She held the flask up to see if there were any takers, found none, and added a few more drops to her cup. She put the flask away and took a long, contented sip of her coffee.

"Unofficially," she said, "I would point out that our darling Undersecretary for Corporate Affairs has been living up to her job description. Corporate affairs are, indeed, her specialty, not to mention Imperial affairs. Whatever gears and cams have been whirring between

GalaxCo and Servitor, you can be certain that Tatiana provided the lubrication."

"And your unofficial conclusion?" Gloria asked.

"I think something smells," Sonia said. "And for once, I'm not talking about the Myn."

chapter **14**

GLORIA DECIDED TO MAKE A STOP AT SERVI-
tor's offices before going on to the Palqui to meet with
Quan. She had changed to a pale pink, nearly transparent wrap dress, already partly unwrapped, and Randolph
Sweet smiled at her in appreciation as she entered his
office.

"An unexpected but very welcome pleasure, Ms.
VanDeen," Sweet said as he ushered her to a chair near
his desk. Gloria smiled at him as she sat and crossed her
legs, causing the dress to fall almost completely open. If
Sweet was already screwing one woman from Dexta, she
calculated, he might welcome the prospect of bagging
another. That might put him in a boastful mood, and
Gloria wanted to get him talking.

"I'm on my way over to see Quan," Gloria said, "and
in light of developments, I thought I should talk to you
first. By the way, congratulations on your coup."

"Coup?" said Sweet as he perched on the corner of
his desk, where he had a good vantage point for staring
down the front of Gloria's dress. "Thank you, but I

wouldn't consider it a coup. Just a logical move, from our point of view and GalaxCo's, as well."

"Still, it happened awfully fast, didn't it? I mean, I always thought that these things took months of careful planning and analysis."

"Not necessarily, Gloria. May I call you Gloria?"

"Certainly . . . Randy, isn't it?"

"Please. While what you say may be generally true, sometimes it's best to strike while the iron is hot. I offered Roland twenty cents on the crown, and after what happened last night, he was only too happy to accept. If I had waited, I might have had to offer twenty-five or thirty."

"So the attack last night might have saved Servitor millions."

"And that bothers you? Gloria, the Big Twelve don't play badminton with each other. Each of us looks for an edge, and when we find one, we take advantage of it. Last night's attack was tragic and frightening, but life does go on, after all. Here, let me pour you some tea."

"Thank you, Randy," Gloria said. "And I'm sorry if I sounded disapproving. As I said, it was certainly a coup. Tatiana seemed to think so."

"Well, you know, Tatiana is a very smart lady. Sees her future very clearly. Understands the advantages of working closely with the Big Twelve." Sweet poured tea for Gloria from a small porcelain kettle on a sideboard. "I'm sure you understand that as well, Gloria."

He handed the cup to her, holding it at just the right distance to force her to lean forward enough to expose her nipples for a moment. Gloria did as she was expected to, and shifted her weight so that when she leaned back again, her left breast was still exposed. She smiled at him.

"What I understand, Randy," she said, "is that you seem to know more about what goes on around here than anyone else. You're a good man to know."

He smiled modestly. "I only hope you'll be here

long enough for us to get to know each other even better."

"Never can tell," Gloria said. She took a sip of tea. The familiarity of the taste and aroma surprised her, and it took a moment for it to register. It was jigli tea.

On reflection, there was no reason why Hawkes should have been the only human to know about jigli, although he was certainly more familiar with the Myn than anyone else. Sweet had been on the planet long enough to have learned about it, she supposed, and under the circumstances, it was natural enough for him to want her to have some of the stuff. Still, it was a definite surprise.

"Interesting taste," she said.

"It's a special local blend," Sweet said. "Not many people know about it, but those who do swear by it. Enjoy it, Gloria, I've plenty more."

Gloria obligingly took another swallow. She already felt the familiar jigli tingle in her flesh. It seemed that the more often you used jigli, the faster it worked. But it would take a least a gallon of it before Gloria felt so much as a particle of desire for the pink-faced, vaguely porcine Sweet.

"What I'd like to know," Gloria said, "is something about your plans for the future. Something I can tell Quan."

"Well, it's very early innings yet, Gloria. We need to see how the present situation is resolved, and how soon order can be restored. Still, I can tell you that Servitor intends, long range, to turn a profit on the GalaxCo lands and leases. Exactly how we do that remains to be determined. I have to say that GalaxCo was not terribly intelligent in some of their practices. I doubt that we'd be in our current mess if they had not managed to alienate most of the Myn."

"Their plantation system is very unpopular with the Myn," Gloria said. "In fact, some of GalaxCo's own people suggested converting to something more like sharecropping. As the Myn see it, that might make the land happier."

"Ah, yes"—Sweet laughed—"by all means, the land must be happy if the Myn are to be happy. Roland always called that the 'Myn's mystical malarkey.' He might have been wiser to pay more attention to it."

"And Servitor will?" Gloria took another sip of the tea.

"As I said, we intend to turn a profit. That may mean restructuring the production methods." Sweet took a sip of his own tea and smiled. "It may even mean raising entirely different crops. There's nothing sacred about antigerontological pharmaceuticals. Not that a beautiful young woman like yourself has any need to be concerned about antigerontologicals yet."

"Actually, Randy," Gloria said, "I'm seventy-two. But I think it's really sex that keeps me young. Could I have some more of this delicious tea, please?" She leaned forward and handed him her cup. Sweet took it, laughing at her little joke, and eagerly refilled it.

"There you are," he said. "Quite good, isn't it?"

"Wonderful," Gloria agreed, taking another sip. She was feeling the full force of the jigli now, and deliberately recrossed her legs to give Sweet an unobstructed view.

"Tell me, Randy," she said, trying to stay focused, "do you have any thoughts on where the Myn's weapons are coming from? I'm going over to Jhino after I see Quan, and I suppose you know that Imperium's lab established that the AKs are made from metal native to Jhino."

"So I heard," he said. "Interesting development. But no, I don't think I know any more about the weapons than you do, Gloria. I suppose it's just the usual case of supply and demand. When there's a crown to be made, someone will find a way to make it."

"But I have a hard time seeing how anyone could make much of a profit on an operation like this. The costs of the factory would be much greater than the potential income from sales to a handful of Myn terrorists."

"Perhaps," said Sweet. "For the present, that's probably correct. But maybe they're thinking long term. First arm the Myn..."

"And then arm the Jhino?"

"It's been known to happen."

"But that would be a violation of Imperial weapons policies."

"That's been known to happen, too. But I don't pretend to understand the criminal mind, Gloria. All I'm saying is that it's obvious that someone at least *thinks* that they can make money from this. Spirit knows what the reality might turn out to be."

Gloria nodded and smiled. Her head was spinning, she realized. Sweet's brand of jigli seemed to be much more powerful than what Pakli and Dushkai had given her. Perhaps it was a different strain, or a more highly refined version. Whatever it was, it was making even Randy Sweet look good to her. She decided to leave before she did something she'd hate herself for doing. She was already a little disgusted even to have thought about it.

She got to her feet, her loosely tied dress coming almost completely undone in the process. Sweet took a good look, and Gloria stood there for a moment and let him. Then she extended her hand, and said, "Thanks for your time, Randy. I really have to be on my way now."

Sweet clasped her hand in his and stroked her wrist with his other hand. Gloria involuntarily shivered at his soft touch on her tingling skin. "Are you sure you won't stay?" he asked. "Perhaps have another cup of tea before you go?"

"I think I've had enough...for now. But I'd like to talk with you some more, Randy. You're an interesting man."

"What about tonight? Are you free for dinner? We could go to Blaine's, before they close down."

"I don't think I'll be free," Gloria said, pulling her hand away from his. "A crazy day, lots to do. When are you planning to leave for Jhino?"

"I'm not," said Sweet. "I have responsibilities, and I think I'll be safe enough here in the city. I take it you aren't planning on leaving, either?"

"I'll be around," she said. "I'm sure I'll see you again, Randy."

THE LIMO SKIMMER STOPPED IN FRONT OF THE Palqui, and Gloria got out. Hawkes had insisted that she take the limo and an armed driver, even though Gloria protested that it was a waste of resources needed elsewhere. But Hawkes remained adamant, so Gloria wound up in the limo.

Chancellor Shoon promptly came out to greet her and escort her through the meditation gardens to the hexagonal inner building where Quan awaited them. Before they went in, Gloria spoke briefly to Shoon about the need to keep the streets around the Transit clear. Shoon agreed and assured her that appropriate measures would be taken.

Inside, Gloria removed her dress and walked forward to the low platform where the elderly Myn leader sat. He was apparently communing with his ancestors at the moment, and Gloria waited patiently.

"Gloriavandeen," Quan said at last. Gloria recognized the Myn trill that signified her name. Shoon translated as the Primat continued. "I am not surprised to see you. My ancestors told me that you would be coming, because of what happened last night. I am glad to see that you are safe."

"Thank you, Revered One," Gloria answered. "But other humans have died, and more may die if you cannot control your people. Many Myn will die, too."

"And yet," Shoon translated, "your people are leaving."

"We are," said Gloria, "but we would like to be able to leave in peace. Revered One, you must do everything in your power to see that we can."

"My powers are limited," Quan said with what Gloria perceived as a hint of resignation. "I am old, and the young no longer listen to me. I have counseled peace and patience, but as you see, my words have not been heeded. Still, I will do what I can to see that your people depart in safety."

"Thank you, Revered One. It will interest you to learn that GalaxCo has sold its interests in Myn to Servitor. GalaxCo is leaving, and will not return. This should make the land happy and give the Myn cause to rejoice."

"Is this truly so?" Quan asked. "Then my ancestors will be pleased. The GalaxCo people are fools, and it is well that they are leaving. But what of Servitor? Do they intend to continue the foolish practices of GalaxCo? Will they stay when all others go?"

"Revered One," said Gloria, "I tell you truthfully that it is too soon to say exactly what Servitor will do. Their leaders have told me that they may change the system GalaxCo has employed, and that they are contemplating new methods that will not make the land so unhappy. And I cannot say when the Servitor people will come to claim their property. For now, most of the humans on Myn are leaving your lands, but some will stay and others may return someday. Those of us in the Imperial Compound intend to remain in Dhanj. Myn is part of the Empire, and the Emperor intends that it should remain so."

Quan emitted something that sounded like a sigh. "Yes," he said, "the Empire is always with us. I hope that the Emperor will consult with his ancestors and find greater wisdom. And may the humans of Servitor do the same. But their time lies in a future I shall not live to see. For now, I can only rejoice that the GalaxCo fools will be gone from our land. Go in peace, Gloriavandeen, and I shall seek to assure that the other humans may do the same. May my ancestors and your Spirit grant that it be so."

THE LIMO SKIMMER HAD TO STOP TWO BLOCKS from the Transit building. The streets were jammed with crowds of human refugees and Myn who had come to watch the show. Gloria estimated that there were at least three hundred people lined up, waiting their turn at the Transit. Some few seemed to have come directly from the Residence and were still dressed in their party attire. Others seemed to be trying to carry all of their possessions with them; some had apparently hired Myn as porters. The scene looked like a sidewalk bazaar, with cases, trunks, and even birdcages strewn throughout the area. Some of the Myn appeared to be buying human possessions that might otherwise have been abandoned. There was an undertone of angry human voices and sharp Myn trills.

Gloria got out of the limo and walked toward the Transit building. The wind from the harbor flapped her flimsy dress around freely and Gloria, still feeling the effects of the powerful jigli, frankly enjoyed the stares she was receiving from Myn and human alike. People obligingly made a path for her and called out her name. GalaxCo guards opened the double glass doors for her, and she descended several steps to the broad, open floor area, where at least a hundred more people stood in a queue extending all the way to the Ring, directly ahead. She went to the front of the line and presented herself to the GalaxCo security men, who were trying to keep order in the face of the confusion. No one objected when Gloria stepped ahead of the waiting refugees and Transited to Jhino. She was privileged, and she knew it; there were times when being who and what she was could make her job and her life much easier. She wasted no time feeling guilty about her special status.

On the other side of the Ring, Kenthlo greeted her and welcomed her back to Jhino. Things were a little better organized here, and the refugees were being escorted out of the Transit building quickly and efficiently by Jhino police. Kenthlo led Gloria to a waiting limo, and a few minutes later, they arrived at Government Center.

Veentro was pleased to see her, his manner as polished and slick as always. He expressed his shock and dismay at the events of last night, and pledged his full cooperation in the evacuation. The people and government of Jhino were eager to serve. Gloria thanked him, and they briefly discussed some of the details of the evacuation.

When she told him about the GalaxCo sell-off to Servitor, he seemed neither surprised nor particularly interested. "GalaxCo has few interests in Jhino," he said, "so the impact of the sale should be minimal. We have worked well with Servitor over the years, and I am certain the transition will go smoothly. Tell me, Ms. VanDeen, when will the Governor and Imperial staff be coming?"

"We won't," Gloria told him. "We intend to remain in Dhanj for as long as possible."

"You do?" Veentro sounded crestfallen. His pointed snout twitched from side to side. "Forgive me for being blunt, Ms. VanDeen, but this makes no sense! The Imperial position in Myn is untenable, at least for the foreseeable future. Certainly, the Empire will return to Myn at some point, of that I have no doubt. The Empire cannot afford to be seen to cave in to the threats and atrocities of a savage and primitive race. I'm certain that your Imperial Marines will presently teach them a lesson they won't soon forget. But in the meantime, surely you must relocate to Phanji!"

"Only as a last resort, Prime Minister," Gloria told

him. "We have responsibilities in Myn, and we have no intention of being forced out. Some humans are bound to remain in Myn, and they'll need our help. For that matter, the government of Primat Quan is also entitled to our continuing support."

"Quan? That dithering old fool?"

"The Empire," Gloria said firmly, "does not take its commitments lightly. We will stand by Quan in a crisis, just as we would stand by you, Prime Minister."

"Yes, yes, I suppose that you must. Still, as a matter of your own safety, I urge you to reconsider and relocate to Phanji. I intend to communicate directly with Governor Rhinehart on this matter."

"That is your privilege, Prime Minister. We appreciate your concern, but we intend to remain in Dhanj as long as possible. Tell me, sir, have you made any progress on the matter of the munitions factory?"

Veentro spread his arms in a gesture of frustration. "We have looked high and low, and we shall continue to search with diligence and care. But Jhino is large, and such a factory may be quite small. Perhaps we shall get lucky."

GLORIA WAS NOT A GREAT BELIEVER IN LUCK, and returned to Myn thinking dark thoughts. The line outside the Transit building seemed just as long as it had been when she left. The crowds of Myn had diminished somewhat, so perhaps Quan and Shoon had managed to assert some control over their people. On the other hand, maybe the Myn had decided that it might not be safe to remain so close to so many humans. Gloria shuddered to think what would happen if the Myn-Traha staged another attack here.

Back at the Compound, Gloria physically dragged Hawkes away from what he was doing, maneuvered him back to her room, and quickly and emphatically released the sexual charge that had been building within her ever since she sipped Sweet's jigli tea. Hawkes marveled at her energy and overcame his own fatigue long enough to join her in a mutual climax that left them both drained and panting.

As soon as he had recovered, Hawkes attempted to get out of bed and go back to his labors, but Gloria wouldn't let him. "We both need a few hours of sleep," she insisted. "If we burn ourselves out the first day, we'll be useless by tomorrow or the next day."

Hawkes allowed her to pull him back into bed. "I suppose you're right," he said. "We need to pace ourselves." They arranged themselves comfortably, with Gloria's head nestled on Hawkes's shoulder.

"Did the courier get off all right?" Gloria asked.

"On its way. The first wave of skimmers is already back, the GalaxCo freighter is loading, and so far, everything has gone pretty smoothly. I estimate we'll have gotten out twelve hundred people by the end of the day. Not a bad start. How did your day go?"

Gloria briefly recounted her meetings with Sweet, Quan, and Veentro. The more she thought about what she had learned, the more it all bothered her. The role of the corporates smelled as bad to her as it did to Sonia Blumenthal. Yet GalaxCo was on its way out, and Imperium's position seemed unaffected by events. In any case, she didn't see Julius Omphala as a plotter. His approach to everything seemed straightforward and unimaginative, as he had demonstrated in the backseat of their limo. Randall Sweet, on the other hand, was more subtle.

"Sweet gave me some jigli tea," she said. "I guess it's not such a big secret, after all."

"Some people know about it," said Hawkes. "The stuff only grows on the slopes in the lee of the eastern mountains. The coastal tribes around Dhanj don't use it at all. But humans who have spent time upcountry have generally heard of it. They've just been sensible enough to keep quiet. But Sweet . . . that surprises me a bit."

"Me too. He dropped some broad hints about how Servitor might change some things when they get control of the plantations. Said that they weren't wedded to pharmaceuticals. You don't think he plans to grow jigli commercially, do you?"

Hawkes shook his head. "It wouldn't work. The Myn would never stand for it."

"Why not? I'd think it would make the land happier."

"Growing it would. Selling it off-world wouldn't. Just the reverse."

"I don't get it," Gloria said.

"It's hard to explain. There isn't even an English word to describe the concept. Look, you know that fruit we had with Pakli and Dushkai?"

"Uh-huh. Delicious."

"Very," said Hawkes. "For years, we've been trying to get them to export it. A distributor on Pecos would love to handle it. But the Myn won't agree. Sending the fruit off-world would upset the land and their ancestors."

"But they have no problem with exporting the pharmaceuticals," Gloria pointed out.

"That's different. The pharmaceuticals are not native to Mynjhino. But the fruit and the jigli are. It would somehow disturb the equilibrium of the land if its products were to leave the planet."

"Then why did Pakli and Dushkai give me a pouch full of jigli to take home? Wouldn't that cause the same problem?"

"No," said Hawkes, "because that was a gift to a friend. Look, suppose I cut off a lock of my hair and give it to you as a keepsake. No problem, right? Now, suppose that I cut off one of my toes and sell it to you."

"That's sick!"

"Exactly. And that's how the Myn would feel about exporting their fruit or their jigli on a commercial scale. It would be profoundly offensive to them. If Sweet thinks he can get the Myn to grow jigli for him, he's in for a rude shock."

"You'd think he'd know that."

"He probably does. Whatever he's planning for the plantations, I doubt that it includes jigli."

"Hmmm." Gloria hummed in frustration. "That seems to shoot down my theory."

"You've got a theory? Let's hear it."

Gloria frowned. "It's not much of a theory, in any case. More like a set of connected suspicions."

"Then let's hear your suspicions," Hawkes said. "At this point, even bad ideas are better than no ideas, which is what I've got so far."

"Okay," said Gloria, "here goes. It's a *cui bono* kind of thing—who benefits? So far, the beneficiaries of the attacks are the Myn-Traha, Servitor, and Jhino. GalaxCo's leaving, so the Myn-Traha will be happy. Servitor landed GalaxCo's holdings at fire-sale prices, so somewhere down the road, they stand to reap big benefits. And with the human presence on Myn reduced to practically nothing, that makes Jhino more important to us, so Veentro gets what he wants. However..."

"Go on," said Hawkes.

"The downside is that the Myn-Traha may wind up being hunted down by Imperial Marines. The Compound is staying where it is, so Veentro is frustrated. And if Sweet can't grow jigli on the plantations, then he's stuck with pharmaceuticals and, for now, no one to grow them. It just doesn't hold together very well."

"So," said Hawkes, "what you're suggesting is that Servitor built the munitions factory in Jhino, with Veentro's help, in order to grab GalaxCo's holdings and set up the Myn for Imperial retribution. That's not bad, Gloria. The jigli may not matter, assuming Sweet has some other commercially viable crop in mind. And Veentro simply miscalculated in assuming that we'd pack up and move the Compound to Phanji."

"Yes, but I still don't like it," said Gloria. "For one

thing, it makes Randy Sweet complicit in mass murder. The man's a bit of an ass, and he told me himself that the Big Twelve don't play badminton, but still . . ."

"I know," said Hawkes. "Arming terrorists to kill humans is pretty extreme, even for one of the Big Twelve. Especially when you consider that it might take Servitor years to get those lands into production again. There'd have to be more to it. We're missing some pieces."

"Or maybe we're just trying to put pieces together that don't fit in the first place. Maybe the Jhino set up the factory on their own, and Servitor is just taking advantage of the situation. Or maybe Veentro is as innocent as he wants us to think he is, and the Myn are smarter than we give them credit for. Maybe they've got a network operating in Jhino, running the factories and smuggling in the weapons."

Hawkes stretched his arms and yawned. "We're both tired," he said. "Maybe it will make more sense after we get a few hours of sleep."

"And maybe it won't," said Gloria unhappily.

Hawkes ran his palm over Gloria's breasts and down across her belly. "Then," he said, "maybe it will make more sense if we screw our overworked brains out first, and *then* get a few hours of sleep."

Gloria smiled. "It's worth a try."

chapter 15

THE *DEXTA CODE* WAS A COMPLEX, PROLIX,
and stupefying volume of laws, edicts, rules, regulations,
ordinances, precedents, and instructions that, over the
course of centuries, had evolved into a three-thousand-
page document that Dexta staffers used to run the
Empire. Dexta itself could trace its lineage all the way
back to a United Nations Subcommittee on Space Law,
originally formed in the year 1965, and the *Code* faith-
fully reflected twelve and a half centuries of legal, political, and bureaucratic experience. During the next two
days of the evacuation, the Dexta staff on Mynjhino had
frequent occasion to call up the *Code* on their pads and
refer to its all-encompassing wisdom—it was their way
of consulting their ancestors. It had turned out that even
people who were fleeing for their lives still insisted on
what they perceived to be their rights. "You can't make
me do that!" refugees retorted when told to leave behind their antique harpsichords or twelve-foot murals.
Staffers checked the *Code*, found chapter and verse,
and said, "Yes, I can."

Part of the complexity involved in governing the Empire resulted from the overlapping jurisdictions of Imperial Governors and the Department of Extraterrestrial Affairs, which was a branch of the civil government under Parliament and the Prime Minister. Governors were appointed by the Emperor and had broad but ill-defined authority to do whatever was best for the Empire; Dexta staffers were civil servants who lived by the *Code* and had little latitude for deviating from the sacred texts. Well-connected citizens could and often did get Governors to overrule Dexta decisions; at the same time, Dexta could weave a web of legal and procedural entanglements that could and often did frustrate even the most independent of Governors.

During the evacuation of Myn, however, appeals to the Governor bore no fruit; Governor Rhinehart remained incapacitated with a migraine. The Dexta staffers, under Imperial Secretary Melinda Throneberry, ran the show and kept it on the road. Brian Hawkes spent much of his time in the field, sorting out procedural traffic jams and keeping the fleet of skimmers as close to their schedules as possible. Sonia Blumenthal was put in charge of keeping an accurate and comprehensive tally of the evacuees and their possessions. Tatiana Markova stayed close to the harried GalaxCo executives as they coped with their retreat, offering advice and serving as liaison with the Compound. Ricardo Olivera hobbled around the Compound, dispensed weapons to the guards on the freight-hauler skimmers, and stood guard each night with the rest of his depleted Security staff.

Gloria and Petra went where they were needed and did what had to be done. Not much of what they did appeared anywhere in the *Dexta Code*. Petra changed the diapers of screaming infants while their mothers coped with equally unhappy toddlers. She found food for hungry travelers and relieved panic-crazed drunks of their drinks. She carried luggage, tracked down lost puppies, and soothed jangled nerves. Gloria took a turn as a skimmer driver, until Hawkes gently informed her that her driving was scaring the pants off the people she was rescuing. She relieved Melinda Throneberry and Sonia Blumenthal when they needed sleep, and got precious little herself. She made decisions she had no legal right to make and made them stick through sheer force of personality. She charmed angry men, shouted down hysterical women, and sang lullabies to babies. She had never worked so hard in her life, or enjoyed it more.

Through it all, the Myn-Traha watched from windows and roadsides and forests, and held their fire. Hawkes managed to defuse one confrontation in a small upcountry hamlet, when drunken GalaxCo workers started shooting up Myn homes with their plasma pistols. As he quieted the humans and dispersed the Myn, he noticed three Myn with weapons standing on a nearby hillside, watching but doing nothing. Hawkes stared at them for a long moment, then went on with his work. The evacuation proceeded.

By Monday night, nearly everyone was gone. Sonia's count showed some forty-nine hundred evacuees, either to Jhino or the GalaxCo freighter that had lifted off on Saturday night, bound for Pecos. That left some four hundred humans missing, unaccounted for, or determined to stay, come hell or high water.

The tavern where Hawkes rented his rooms had not shut down. The human and Myn partners who ran the place saw no reason to leave; they figured that business would pick up as soon as the Imperial Marines arrived. Everyone assumed that they were on their way, but there was still no word from Earth.

Hawkes, Gloria, and Petra met there for drinks and a late dinner Monday night with the rest of the senior staff, except for Tatiana Markova, who was off somewhere with the corporates. They were dog-tired but proud of the job they had done. Nearly five thousand humans had been evacuated, and not one additional life had been lost.

Gloria, in her jeans and a tight, nearly invisible tee

shirt, grinned as she raised a mug of beer and proposed a toast. "Here's to the best damn colonial staff in the Empire," she said, meaning every word. "You've been fantastic, guys!" She drained half of her mug and wiped foam from the corner of her mouth.

Melinda Throneberry raised her own mug. "And here's to the best damn Coordinating Supervisor any overworked, underpaid, downtrodden, and oppressed colonial staff could ever hope to be annoyed, criticized, and terrorized by," she said. "Here's to tits, ass, and a New York attitude!" They drank more beer, and now Gloria found that she had to wipe away a tear from the corner of her eye.

"Ahem!" Ricardo Olivera interjected. "Aren't we forgetting someone? Mighty senior staffers and beautiful Coordinating Supervisors have their roles to play, but we all know who *really* makes Dexta run. I refer, of course, to the *little* people. The *cute* little people. The cute, beautiful, sexy little people."

"Hear, hear!" everyone cried as Olivera grabbed the blushing Petra and gave her a kiss that lasted a good thirty seconds.

The Myn coowner of the establishment came to the table with another pitcher of beer. "Happy humans," he said. "It is good to see happy humans again."

"How do the Myn feel these days, Kequa?" Hawkes asked him.

"They are happy, I think," he said, "but also confused. They wonder how they will make money now that the humans have gone. And, I think, some will miss the humans. There are good humans, just as there are bad Myn. It is a confusing time."

Kequa left the humans to their party, but his words had subdued some of their merriment.

"He's right," said Hawkes. "It *is* a confusing time. I wish I knew what the hell is going to happen next."

"We've been so busy with the evacuation," Melinda said, "I don't think anyone has had much time to give it any thought. All the GalaxCo people are gone, and it will take months before Servitor can hope to get enough people here to staff the plantations. Maybe even years. It could get very lonely around here."

"Maybe we'll wind up moving to Jhino anyway," said Olivera.

"If we do," said Melinda, "it's going to be because we get an order from Earth telling us to, not because a bunch of furry little bandits chase us out. Until we get that order, we stay."

"Hear, hear!" said Hawkes, and they drank another round.

A little later, Bryce Denton, the ENS correspondent, came in, looking as tired and dusty as the Dexta staffers. "Wondered where you guys were," he said. "Mind if I join you?"

There was an awkward moment of silence before Hawkes finally said, "Sure, pull up a chair, have a beer." Kequa brought him a mug, and Denton quickly sloshed down his beer.

"Thought you'd like to know," Denton said, "that we just got a messenger from Pecos. The evacuation story is big news, and my editor is going to shoot off a courier to Earth as soon as he gets my wrap-up. It's great stuff. Tears, pathos, heartbreak, and a determined band of Dexta staffers fighting against the odds to save human life in a colony suddenly gone mad, et cetera, et cetera. You're all going to be famous." He looked at Gloria, and added, "Some of you, even more famous."

"I imagine this won't hurt your career, either," said Sonia.

Denton grinned. "Just doing my job. What's a decent apartment rent for in New York these days? Listen, folks, now that things have calmed down, I'd like to do a one-on-one, in-depth interview with each of you. True tales of the evacuation, personal anecdotes, your emotional response, that sort of thing. No hurry. We could do it at your convenience over the next few days."

"So you'll be sticking around?" asked Hawkes.

Denton gulped some more beer, then nodded. "My editor wants more, anything I can give him. What he'd really like is an interview with one of the Myn-Traha leaders, but I don't suppose that's possible."

"It might be," said Hawkes, after a moment's thought. "Not an actual Myn-Traha, but someone close to them. Suppose I could put you in touch with him? How would you play it?"

"Straight," said Denton. "I'd give him a chance to state the Myn position in all of this. They need to get their side of it out, and they look so damned cute and harmless that a good interview could win them some support. That could be important when the Marines get here. People won't want them slaughtering animated teddy bears. What about it, Hawkes? Could you set something up?"

"I think so," Hawkes answered. He turned to Gloria. "I need to get in touch with Pakli anyway. You want to come along?"

"Tomorrow?" She looked at Throneberry. "Melinda, you need us for anything?"

"We can manage without you, I think," she said. "And I think it would be an excellent idea to open up communications with the Myn-Traha. They've kept the peace during the evacuation, and we should let them know that we appreciate it. We're going to have to deal with them in any case, and you two are obviously the ones to do it. They know you, Hawkes, and they trust you, Gloria. Your meetings with Quan apparently impressed the hell out of them."

Denton looked at Gloria, a gleam in his eye. "I don't suppose . . . ?"

"No," said Gloria.

Denton shrugged. "Just a thought," he said.

"Tomorrow morning in the Compound," Hawkes told him. "Early."

"I'll be there," said Denton.

• • •

HAWKES PILOTED THE BUSH SKIMMER OVER the now-deserted plantations. The humans were all gone, and even the Myn had disappeared. Denton, in the backseat, aimed his imager at the neat green fields, and asked, "Where did they all go?"

"Back to their ancestral villages, probably," said Hawkes. "But without income from GalaxCo, I don't know how they're going to manage their economy. They're tied in to the Imperial Standard now, but crowns are going to get scarce, and a lot of Myn are effectively unemployed. I doubt that they planned for success so quickly."

"The perils of victory," said Gloria. "They've got their land back, for the moment, but now they have to manage it. I don't think Quan and the Tandik are prepared for this, and who knows what the Myn-Traha have in mind?"

"How are they going to react to the Servitor takeover?" Denton asked, pointing the imager toward the two in the front seat.

"I don't know," said Hawkes. "But I think they'll recognize that some form of economic integration has to be restored. They'll probably want concessions and a renegotiation of the original GalaxCo leases before they consent to a Servitor presence. All that will have to be worked out, but there's no urgency about it. I suppose we'll have to put Sweet in touch with them."

"What about Sweet?" Denton asked. "He's a pretty cagy character, from what I hear."

"He'll represent Servitor's position with skill and imagination, I expect," Gloria said carefully, conscious of the imager.

Denton put the imager down. "Right," he said. "Now tell me what you *really* think. I know Sweet's boffing your cute Undersecretary for Corporate Affairs, who happens to be boffing Governor Rhinehart in her spare time. Some folks might get the notion that Sweet is using Markova to control Rhinehart."

"Rhinehart still has his migraine," Gloria pointed out. "Melinda's running the show for now, and Tatiana is not her favorite person."

"He's still the Imperial Governor," said Denton. "Now that you Dexta folks have done all the heavy lifting, it wouldn't surprise me to see him make a miracle recovery. He's an ass, but he's not an idiot. He's just presided over a disaster, you know. Unless he has cards he's not showing, he's going to be in big trouble with the Household. He'll be looking for some way to restore his standing."

"Like what?" Hawkes asked.

"Maybe a peace agreement with the Myn-Traha? If you two can negotiate something that looks good, Rhinehart could make a big show out of signing it and restoring peace to his troubled land."

"Let him," said Hawkes. "That's politics, and Dexta doesn't get involved in politics."

"Of course not," said Denton. "Perish the thought."

HAWKES BROUGHT THE SKIMMER TO A GENTLE halt in the town square of the Dhabi village beside the river. The town looked much busier than it had during their previous visit, and as the humans got out of the skimmer, pedestrian traffic came to a halt. The Myn stared at the humans and the humans stared back at them.

"Are we safe here?" Denton asked as he imaged the street scene.

"I guess we're about to find out," said Hawkes. He started walking toward Pakli's residence, with Gloria at his side and Denton nervously bringing up the rear. Myn stepped aside to clear a path for them, and a few trilled something at them. Hawkes smiled and trilled back, but kept moving.

Gloria was wearing a bodysuit, made from smart polymers no more than a dozen molecules thick; she looked as if she had been spray-painted with white watercolor. She'd had it set at 50 percent transparency, but as they approached Pakli's home, she fingered the control contact.

"I'm doing this for the sake of the Myn we're meeting," Gloria told Denton, "not because I want to be the star of your show. Keep that in mind, would you?" She pressed the contact, and her bodysuit quickly became 100 percent transparent. Denton turned on his imager, casually holding it at thigh level, as if nothing particularly interesting were happening.

Dushkai greeted them at the door and exchanged happy trills with Hawkes for a moment. "Gloriavandeen!" she exclaimed in English when she saw her. She trilled to Hawkes, who laughed, and said to Gloria, "Dushkai says that some of your ancestors must have been Myn."

"Tell her I'm happy to see her again, and that I thank her for her compliment. I would be proud to have Myn ancestors."

Dushkai led them inside; the humans ducked their heads as they went through the low doorway and followed her out to the enclosed garden. Pakli was ensconced on his cushions and did not attempt to rise to greet them.

"Forgive me, Brianhawkes," he said, "but it is a bad day for my old bones. They would rather remain where they are. But please, sit down and join me. Gloriavandeen, I am pleased to see you again, and very honored by your appearance. I know that my old friend Quan was pleased and honored, as well. You have made a very good impression upon my people."

"Thank you, Pakli," Gloria said as she settled onto a cushion. "Allow me to introduce Bryce Denton, who is a correspondent for the Empire News Service."

"Ah, yes," said Pakli. "I recognize you from the vids,

Brycedenton. Have you come to make me famous?"
Pakli laughed.

"I have come to give you a chance to tell your story
to the Empire," said Denton. "The Myn deserve to be
heard."

"I do not speak for the Myn, or for the Myn-Traha,
or for anyone but myself and Dushkai, and even she
sometimes tells me that I am a foolish old man without a
brain in his head. Dushkai, stop looking at me that way
and go fetch refreshments for our friends, while we
smoke jigli and give thanks for this day." Pakli passed his
pipe, already smoldering, to Hawkes, who passed it on
to Gloria. Denton was busy imaging and declined.

"Passing the peace pipe!" Denton laughed. "Damn,
this is great stuff."

"It will amuse your audience?" Pakli asked.

"They'll love it," Denton assured him.

"Then we must not disappoint them." Pakli inhaled,
then passed the pipe back to Hawkes. When it had
made the prescribed three rounds, Dushkai came in
with a tray of fruit and drinks.

Pakli put the pipe down and focused his large eyes
on Hawkes. "Much has happened since last you were
here, my friend. Not all of it good."

"Humans and Myn have died," said Hawkes. "And
now, all but a few of us are gone from the land of the
Myn. We must look to the future, Pakli."

"Indeed. And what can you tell me of this future,
Gloriavandeen?"

"I can tell you that the Empire wants peace with the
Myn, and is willing to listen to anything that the Myn—
and the Myn-Traha—have to say. We want the land and
the Myn to be happy again."

"And Servitor, of course," Pakli added. "They must
be happy as well, is this not so?"

"They have an interest here now," said Gloria, "but I
believe that they will be willing to negotiate with the
Myn. They know that GalaxCo's methods have brought

unhappiness, and they are smart enough to know that things must change."

"They are not fools, then?"

"I think not," said Gloria. "It would be wise for the Myn to talk with them."

"Pakli, my friend," said Hawkes, "I don't ask you to tell me names or locations, but can you get this message to the Myn-Traha leadership? Let them know that we want to talk with them?"

Pakli nodded. "It shall be done," he said. "I believe that they are already aware of your presence here, and that they are eager to hear your words. But can you tell me, are the Imperial Marines coming, and what will they do when they arrive? Human blood has been shed, and I know that the Imperial Marines will have it in their hearts to shed Myn blood in return."

"There is a chance," said Gloria, "that the Marines may arrive within the week. We don't know this for certain, but it is what I think will happen. As to what they will do, that will depend on the Myn-Traha. The Marines are powerful, but they are subject to the orders of the Imperial Governor. They will do nothing on their own."

"Has Governor Rhinehart recovered his health, then? We were saddened to hear of his illness."

"You don't miss much, do you, my friend?" said Hawkes, smiling.

Pakli tilted his head modestly. "We are a primitive people, it is true, but some of us have managed to learn how to operate the remote control of a vid. We have our own comms."

"And some of you have AK-47s," Denton said.

Pakli looked toward the correspondent and his imager. "Many of us deeply regret what has happened," he said. "Those who took human lives did not act on behalf of the great majority of the Myn. Nevertheless, what is done is done, and cannot be undone, no matter how much we wish that it could be so. But now that GalaxCo has gone, even the most angry of our young people realize that the time for violence has passed. They let your people depart in peace, did they not?"

"They did," said Gloria, "and we want them to know that we deeply appreciate it. We take this as a sign of goodwill, and we are eager to build on that hopeful beginning. The sooner we can begin formal talks with the Myn-Traha leadership, the sooner the land and the people will be happy again."

"Talking is better than fighting," Pakli agreed.

"What will your people ask for?" Denton said.

"I am only an individual," said Pakli, "and as I have told you, I speak for no one but myself. However, if you are interested, I would be willing to share my thoughts with you and those who watch your vid."

"Please do," said Denton.

For the next hour, Pakli spoke almost without pause. He knew that it was a chance to speak directly to the human population of the Empire, and to the Emperor himself. Only once did he stop briefly to consult with his ancestors. He spoke of the history of his world and the beliefs of the Myn. He spoke as he would to a friend, or perhaps to the child of a friend, who needed instruction and information. He sought only to teach, and to heal.

"And now," he said at last, "I find that I have grown weary of the sound of my own voice. Forgive me, my friends, but I must rest. Dushkai, please show our visitors out, and bid them farewell. Brianhawkes, Gloriavandeen, my good and honored friends, you are always welcome in my home. It is my fondest hope that I will see you here again before I go to join my ancestors, which may be sooner than I would wish. Go in peace, my friends."

Hawkes shook his hand gravely, and Gloria leaned forward to kiss his fuzzy cheek. "A human custom," she explained. "I hope it wasn't inappropriate."

"I know about kisses." Pakli laughed. "I told you, I

see your vids. I am honored to be kissed by such a beautiful human woman, Gloriavandeen. But you must go now, before Dushkai becomes jealous. And farewell to you too, Brycedenton. I shall look for you on the vid."

Dushkai led them out of the garden and to the front door. Hawkes trilled to her at length, asking about Pakli's health. He was not reassured by her reply. They said their farewells and walked out onto the street.

"Fascinating," said Denton. "My editor's gonna love this stuff."

"How much of what he said will you use in your story?" Gloria asked.

"Oh, we can edit it down to three or four minutes. The newstexts can use the entire transcript if they want, but ENS will have to trim it."

"That's not very much time, considering everything he had to say. That was important."

"There's important, and then there's effective vid," said Denton. "Don't worry, we'll get the gist of the old boy's message across. I don't think—hey, what the . . . ?"

Five Myn carrying AK-47s suddenly surrounded them. They raised their weapons toward the humans.

chapter 16

THE THREE HUMANS FROZE IN PLACE AND watched the Myn as they hefted their weapons and trilled sharply to one another. Hawkes tried to say something to them in their own language, but a harsh, peremptory trill from one of the Myn cut him off. In the street around them, other Myn had paused to watch, but all kept their distance.

Another Myn approached, unarmed but obviously in charge, from the bearing of his small body and the confident and impatient tone of his trills. The armed Myn stepped back a couple of paces from the humans, making way for the leader. He looked at each of the humans in turn, then looked back at Denton, and said, "You. Go."

"Go?" Denton asked, his voice an octave higher than normal.

"Go," the Myn repeated. He pointed toward the skimmer parked in the square.

"Get back to the Compound and tell them what happened," Hawkes said. "I think we'll be all right."

Denton nodded, then made his way past the armed Myn, his imager recording the scene as he went. The lead Myn watched him go and said nothing more until Denton had gotten into the skimmer and slowly made his departure.

"Brianhawkes. Gloriavandeen," the leader said. "You come." He gestured toward a side street. Gloria and Hawkes looked at each other, then started walking in the direction the Myn had indicated. The armed Myn closed ranks around them.

"What do you think they want?" Gloria asked Hawkes.

"I don't know," he replied, "but if they meant us harm, I think we'd already be dead. At least they know who we are."

The Myn herded them along toward an old skimmer parked on the side street. The leader told them to put their hands behind their backs, then bound their wrists with heavy twine. He removed their wristcoms, then shoved them toward the back of the vehicle. With some difficulty, they managed to get themselves seated. The leader got into the front, next to the Myn driver, then leaned over the seat to put dark hoods over the heads of their captives. A moment later, the vehicle was in motion.

Hawkes and Gloria both began working at the twine around their wrists, but neither made much progress. The Myn leader noticed and told them to stop it, so they did.

"It'll be all right, Gloria," Hawkes said, his voice muffled and indistinct under the hood. The Myn leader told them to be quiet.

Gloria found that she wasn't really scared, just baffled and annoyed. This was an unnecessary complication, and it made no sense. They had already declared their willingness—eagerness—to talk to the Myn-Traha leadership. Why kidnap them? Why not just invite them to meet at some specified location? But maybe they didn't simply want to talk—maybe they had something else in mind. It was a disquieting thought.

Time was impossible to measure, but it seemed as if at least two hours had passed before Gloria felt the skimmer settle to the ground. The high whine of its engines cut out, and the doors opened. Small Myn hands clutched at them and pulled them outside, then shoved them forward into a building. Hawkes banged his head on the low doorframe as they went inside.

They went through at least two rooms before someone told them to sit. They knelt and came to rest on a bare, uncushioned wooden floor. Soft Myn footsteps came and went, a door closed, and they were left alone.

"How are you doing?" Hawkes asked.

"So far, so good," said Gloria. "Maybe we can untie each other."

Hawkes thought about it for a moment, then said, "Not a good idea. They'd just tie us up tighter the next time. We're unarmed, and we don't even know where we are. There's probably not another human within a hundred miles of us. I think we should just sit tight and see what develops."

So they sat. Another hour went by. Gloria began to feel a desperate need to scratch her nose, but nothing worse than that happened. She and Hawkes chatted idly from time to time, but there really wasn't much to say.

Finally, they heard the door open and the sound of shuffling Myn footsteps. The hoods were yanked from their heads, and they blinked in the sudden brightness. They saw three Myn standing before them, looking down at them with unreadable expressions on their alien faces.

They were in a bare, windowless, candlelit room, with no furniture other than three cushions on the floor opposite them. Two of the Myn sat down on the cushions, while the third continued to loom over them.

"I am Kleska. That is Dilanth, and that is Quetra.

We are the Guiding Eyes of the Brotherhood of the Myn-Traha. You are our prisoners."

"We figured," said Hawkes. "What do you want from us? You obviously know who we are."

"Of course. You are Brianhawkes, Imperial Undersecretary for Administration, and Gloriavandeen, Coordinating Supervisor for Division Beta-5, Sector 8, newly arrived from Earth. You are important humans."

"Then you should realize," Gloria told him, "that taking us hostage was a mistake. We are officials of the Empire, and the Empire has an inflexible policy regarding hostages. No negotiations, no compromise. But if you release us now, we can talk with you, and no harm done."

Dilanth trilled something at Kleska, who turned and responded sharply. Kleska looked and sounded annoyed.

"We will talk, Gloriavandeen," said Kleska, "but we will not negotiate. And *we* will not compromise."

"This makes no sense," Hawkes said. "You've already gotten practically everything you want. GalaxCo is gone and there are hardly any humans left in Myn. This will only undercut your own position."

"There is a large difference between 'hardly any' and 'none.' And 'none' is what we will have."

"Some humans have refused to leave," Gloria pointed out.

"Then they will die," Kleska said flatly. "As I said, we will not compromise. We let you conduct your evacuation because it was easier that way, and it saved us ammunition. Now the evacuation is complete, but humans remain in our land. This is intolerable. We realize that some humans are beyond the mountains on the eastern coast, and others are scattered about our lands. We will give them five more days to leave. If they are still here at the end of that time, we will kill them. That also applies to the humans in the Imperial Compound. They must leave, as well."

"They won't," said Hawkes.

"Then they, too, will die," said Kleska. "However, I believe that they will leave, in spite of what you say. Certainly, they will leave if they hope to see either of you alive again."

"You don't understand," said Gloria. "By taking us hostage, you have guaranteed that they will stay. They would have no choice. Imperial policy in a case like this is absolutely inflexible."

"Yes," said Kleska, "I know." Something resembling a smile played at the corners of his mouth. "But in *this* case, I believe that Imperial policy may bend slightly. You see, I know who you are, Gloriavandeen. You are not simply another Dexta bureaucrat who has come here to tell us how we must live. You are also the former wife of Emperor Charles V."

Gloria and Hawkes looked at each other. She had never expected anything like this. Her identity as the Emperor's ex-wife was a burden she bore at Dexta, but that it should suddenly become a factor of importance on this faraway world was an absurdity. She looked back at Kleska.

"It's true," she admitted. "But the key word is *former*. We were divorced five years ago."

"Yes," said Kleska, "but not three weeks ago, you spent the night with him. You see, we watch the vids and read the newstexts too. We are not the ignorant primitives you take us for. And it would seem that five years have not diminished the Emperor's affection for you, Gloriavandeen. He will want you back, I think. And in order to get you back, he will do as we say. Every human must leave Myn, and they must agree never to return."

"You're just cutting your own throats," Hawkes told him angrily.

Kleska turned on him. "If anyone's throat is to be cut, Brianhawkes, it will be yours."

"You don't understand," Gloria insisted. "Even the Emperor has no choice. He *must* abide by Imperial policy. It was laid down centuries ago, and it cannot be altered. Fifteen years ago, a cousin of Emperor Darius IV was taken captive by bandits on the world of Weelah. They demanded a ransom. What they got was Imperial Marines. The Emperor's cousin died, but so did every one of the bandits."

"Unfortunate," said Kleska. "But a cousin is not a wife, nor even an ex-wife. Our young Emperor's blood runs hot, they say. His passion for you, Gloriavandeen, is well known. I think he will find a way to save you."

"No," Gloria told him. "He can't and he won't. As soon as word gets out that you've taken us hostage, Imperial Marines will come to Myn, and they will turn the land upside down to find us. And they won't be gentle about it. Thousands of Myn may die, Kleska. If they have to, the Marines will go through this continent house by house to get us back."

"And if they do," Kleska replied in a harsh, threatening tone, "then the Emperor *will* get you back—piece by piece."

Gloria stared into Kleska's large, uncompromising brown eyes and realized that he meant exactly what he had said. For the first time since they had seized her, Gloria felt fear.

WHEN BRYCE DENTON ARRIVED BACK AT THE Compound with the news, late that afternoon, Melinda Throneberry called an emergency meeting of the senior staff. She asked Petra to attend, as well.

"I'm going over to the Palqui as soon as we finish here," Melinda said. "I don't know how much help Quan can give us, but we obviously can't conduct a search on our own. I need to make it clear to Quan what this is going to mean for the Myn. If he realizes what the Imperial Marines will do when they get here, maybe that will get him to take some meaningful action."

"What *will* they do?" Petra asked.

"Whatever it takes," Melinda told her.

"But—"

"Petra, you know the policy as well as I do. We'll do everything we possibly can to get Brian and Gloria back safely, but we have to do it before the Marines arrive. After that, it will be out of our hands."

"But what *can* we do?" Petra asked. She turned hopefully to Olivera. "Ricky?"

Olivera reached out and clasped Petra's hand. "I'm sorry, Pet. I only have three people left on the Security staff—Franklin, Holst, and Quesada. They can't very well search the entire continent. What we can do is question every Myn on staff in the Compound. Hawkes thinks, and I agree, that some of them are spying for the Myn-Traha. We'll find out which ones, that I can promise you. There are drugs that we can give them to force the truth out of them, although, frankly, I don't think we've ever used them on Myn before. Spirit knows whether or not they'll work. If they don't . . . well, there are other methods."

"No need to go into that," Melinda said quickly. "Do what you have to do, Ricardo, and I'll back you. But suppose you get information out of our spies. What then?"

"If we can find out where Brian and Gloria are being held," said Olivera, "then we mount up an expedition, and we go get them."

"But that could get them killed!" Petra protested.

"Petra," Melinda said softly, "I think we have to accept the fact that the odds are against us here, no matter what we do. If Quan can't get them freed, then we'll have to try to do it ourselves, assuming we can even find them."

Melinda looked at Sonia Blumenthal, who seemed more depressed than usual and had said nothing. "Sonia," she said, "I know you have some friends in the Myn community. I want you to go to them, explain the situation, and make it crystal clear to them what will happen if we don't get Brian and Gloria back safely."

"I'll do it," said Sonia, "but I don't think they know anything."

"Then maybe they know someone who does. Shake them up. Scare them. Make them understand that the future of the Myn depends on this."

Melinda turned next to her Undersecretary for Corporate Affairs. Tatiana Markova had also sat quietly throughout the meeting.

"Tatiana, what can you add?"

She shrugged. "Not much. If GalaxCo were still here, there would be people who knew the boonies and might be able to give us something useful. But they're gone."

"What about Servitor?"

Tatiana shrugged again. "You know they stay in the city."

"Well, dammit, *some* of them must have gone up-country. They didn't buy a pig in a poke. Sweet must have some reason to think he can strike a deal with the Myn-Traha or he would never have made the offer to GalaxCo."

"Randy doesn't know anything about this."

"Well, you tell Randy to get off his fat ass and find out something! If he doesn't, his leases aren't going to be worth shit. Listen to me, Tatiana. I don't care what games you've been playing with Sweet or the Governor or anyone else. I don't care what kind of juicy deal you've got cooking with Servitor. You are still on staff at Dexta, and Dexta is your one and only loyalty and priority. Do you understand me?"

Tatiana remained unruffled. "Calm down, Melinda. I'll go talk to Randy. But it won't help."

Melinda glared at Tatiana and started to say something about her attitude, but decided against it. She had to stay focused on the task at hand.

"Petra," she said, "I know how difficult this is for you. But you're going to have to pinch-hit for Gloria now. I want you to prepare a report on what has happened and where we stand. When I get back from the Palqui, we'll go over it together and send out another courier. We only have two left, and I hate like hell to expend one, but Earth has to know about this as soon as possible."

Petra nodded. "I'll have it ready," she said.

"Ricardo?" Melinda said. "Is there anything else I haven't thought of?"

"I'm a little concerned about Sonia and Tatiana leaving the Compound unescorted. It's possible that they intend to grab the entire Imperial staff, if they can. I'll send Quesada out with them."

"Good idea," said Melinda. "I'll go along, he can drop me at the Palqui and Tatiana at Servitor, then take Sonia wherever she needs to go. We'll keep in touch by comm, and Quesada can pick us up again, as needed. Anything else? All right, people, let's do whatever we have to do. Brian and Gloria would do the same for us."

GLORIA SPENT A SLEEPLESS NIGHT, HER HANDS still uncomfortably tied behind her. She rested her head on one of the cushions, with her body stretched out on the hard wooden floor, but it was not physical discomfort that kept her awake. Fear was slowly spreading through her, taking root in her very bones, and she wanted to be able to wrap her arms around Hawkes and feel his warmth and strength. But they couldn't move.

Somehow, it had been different the first time she was captured by the Myn. Then, death had never been more than moments away, and after the initial fright had passed, she had kept busy digging the grave and thinking about how she could escape. She had not been tied up then, and there was at least the possibility of taking some action to save herself. Now, she was helpless, and faced the prospect of days, perhaps weeks, of captivity, with nothing to wait for but death—or worse.

That afternoon, Kleska had brought in an imager and made a recording to be sent to the Compound. He told them what to say, and they had said it, grudgingly, sullenly. When Hawkes tried to add a few extra words, Kleska walked over to where he sat and unceremoniously kicked him in the ribs. Then they started over and finished the recording.

Dilanth and another Myn came in with plates of food. He untied their hands while the other Myn watched, an AK-47 at the ready. The food consisted of the weak-beer drink she'd been served by Dushkai, fruit, nuts, and a cheeselike substance that tasted bland and slightly salty. She asked Hawkes what it was, and he told her that she didn't really want to know.

After dinner, they were escorted separately to a place outside where they could relieve themselves. Gloria fingered a control contact on her bodysuit, and a seam opened up in front, allowing her to get out of it and do her business. Getting back into it, she realized that the transparency was still set at 100 percent. Under the circumstances, she wanted to set it at zero, but was afraid that the change would disturb the Myn. They might think that she was trying to hide something, despite the fact that hiding anything under the microns-thick, form-fitting garment would have been impossible. She felt no xenophobic repulsion regarding the Myn, but she didn't want their furry little hands running over her body. She left the setting where it was.

They were tied up again and left alone. "From what I saw outside," Hawkes told her, "I think we're somewhere pretty close to the coast. The vegetation was coastal, and the air was more humid than it was in Dhabi."

"So we might be close to Dhanj?"

"It's possible. But I don't think we should count on any rescue attempts. The people at the Compound don't even know where we are, and there aren't enough of them to do much, anyway."

"So we'll have to find a way to escape."

"Let's keep it in mind," said Hawkes. "But I don't

think we should try anything immediately, unless some opportunity presents itself. We still have time to argue our way out of this. Or try to."

"Okay," Gloria agreed. "But I still have some Qatsima moves these guys haven't seen. We got away from them once before. We can do it again."

She wanted to believe that. But she wasn't sure that she did.

MELINDA THRONEBERRY ALSO SPENT A SLEEP-less night. She had borne the weight of responsibility for the evacuation without difficulty. It was a straightforward, practical problem that could be dealt with in a systematic fashion. But this was different, and she felt no less helpless than Gloria.

For thousands of years, enemies had been taking each other hostage, and no one had ever worked out a good way of dealing with the problem. The Imperial policy on the matter at least had the advantage of being clear and unambiguous. It had the disadvantage that it seldom got hostages back alive. All it did, really, was discourage someone else from taking hostages at some other time, some other place.

But at this time, this place, the problem was Melinda's responsibility, and she felt a sick sensation in the pit of her stomach when she contemplated it. It might have been easier if she didn't have to face it alone. During all her time on Mynjhino, Brian Hawkes had always been at her side, rock solid and relentlessly competent. She had relied on him more than she realized. It hurt to think of their personal relationship, which had vacillated between hot passion and frosty resentment, but their professional relationship had never wavered. Now, Brian was gone, and Gloria with him.

She had resented Gloria for more reasons than she could count, not the least of which being that she had been absolutely right in her criticisms of the state of the

Compound and its staff. Melinda had been lax and complacent, partly because the Governor's attitude inevitably filtered downward and became a model for all, and partly because lax complacency seemed to be all that was required on this sleepy backwater of a world. She had spent too much time thinking about her next job and not enough about this one.

And she couldn't ignore the fact, try though she might, that Gloria had taken about ten seconds to snap up Hawkes. The predatory Tiger from Manhattan had marched into Melinda's territory and made off with the one prize worth having.

Yet it was hard for Melinda to stay angry with Gloria. Connected to those perfect tits and ass was a sharp and perceptive brain, and a strong and willing heart. One way or another, Gloria got the job done, and Melinda couldn't help admiring her.

Gloria's way was not Melinda's, but it worked. That evening at the Palqui, Melinda had been forced to try Gloria's way, and had found it an excruciating experience. After Gloria's nothing-to-hide appearances before Quan, Melinda realized that she could do no less. Cursing Gloria under her breath, she had stripped down to her underwear before approaching Quan. The Primat didn't even seem to notice, and had been as disengaged and distracted as ever. He spent more time conversing with his ancestors than with Melinda. Quan was sorry to hear about what had happened, and would consult with his ancestors about what might be done. Perhaps they knew where the hostages were being held. As for the possibility that Imperial Marines might ransack his land in search of the hostages, Quan could only sigh and say that this would make the land very unhappy. You have no idea, Melinda thought.

Twice during her wakeful night, Melinda was roused from her bed by the arrival of important news. After the second time, she made no further attempt at sleep. When the staff arrived in her office for an early-morning meeting, they found her already there.

"This was delivered to the gate last night," Melinda told them. She hit a button on her desk and the vid screen behind her played the recording made by Hawkes and Gloria. The two looked unharmed but seemed wary of their captors. The message was quite simple: all humans, including the Imperial Compound staff, must leave Myn within five days and agree never to return. If the Emperor wished to save the life of his ex-wife, he would comply absolutely and without exception. As for Hawkes, the news was equally dire, but more immediate.

"The Myn-Traha have told us," Gloria said on the recording, "that if Imperial Marines set so much as one foot on Myn land, they will kill Brian immediately. I believe that they mean it."

"And that," Melinda said, shutting off the vid, "brings us to our second bit of news. A courier from Earth arrived last night. It officially informs us that a company of Imperial Marines has been ordered to Mynjhino, and that it should arrive here on Saturday morning, our time. That's three days from now. That's how long we have to find Gloria and Hawkes. After that, it will be up to the Marines."

"And Hawkes will be dead," said Sonia.

Melinda looked around the conference table at her staff. "So far," she said, "no one knows about this except the people in this room. I want it to stay that way, understood? At this point, the only hole card we have is that no one knows when or if the Marines are coming. The uncertainty can work in our favor. This information does not leave this room."

"But we have to tell the Governor," Tatiana objected.

"The Governor is in no condition to—"

"Oh, no!" Tatiana interjected. "He's fine. This morning he—" Tatiana broke off abruptly. She felt everyone's eyes upon her, then realized that it didn't really matter. Everyone already knew.

"He felt fine this morning," Tatiana concluded. "He has to be informed."

"I'll tell him, then," Melinda said. "Does anyone else have anything to report? Sonia?"

Sonia shook her head. "I passed the word. No feedback yet."

"We found our spy," said Olivera. "Kitchen worker named Kooshk. But he didn't know anything useful. He reports to someone he doesn't know, says they contact him and he can't contact them. The next time they do contact him, we'll be ready and waiting. But we don't know when that will be. Spirit willing, it will be before Saturday."

"Are you sure he was telling the truth?" Petra asked eagerly. "Are you sure you got everything from him?"

Olivera looked at Petra and smiled wanly. "I'm sure, Pet. Don't ask me any more, all right?"

"So," said Melinda, "there it stands. Tatiana, I don't suppose you got anything from Sweet?"

"I told you, he doesn't know anything."

"Just like the rest of us," said Sonia.

MYN'S BRIGHT SUN CUT A PATH THROUGH THE sky and sank into the western sea, ending a day in which the Imperial Compound staff had learned nothing. Melinda shared a late dinner in the administrative building with Petra and Olivera. Each of them glumly shoved the food around on their plates, but they ate little and talked even less.

Olivera wanted to be able to say or do something to comfort Petra. He knew just how much Gloria meant to her. Petra had told him a little about her life at Dexta before Gloria had taken her on as an assistant, and Olivera could fill in the missing pieces easily enough. Petra was fiercely loyal to Gloria, and felt as if she were somehow letting her down by failing to rescue her. For his part, Olivera had already lost three of his staff to the Myn terrorists, and was prepared to do absolutely anything that was necessary in order to save Hawkes and Gloria. He had proved that to his own satisfaction—and disgust—during his interrogation of the Myn spy.

For twenty-eight years, Ricardo Olivera had never been entirely serious about anything. He was bright and capable, and things came easily to him. Everyone liked him and women adored him. He coasted through his years at Dexta, never failing, and never really being challenged—until now. In the last two weeks, Olivera had suddenly become a serious person.

People who had worked for him were dead. Two people he considered friends were captive and facing death. The sleepy, placid world around him had become a dark and bloody arena where good looks and a toothy smile no longer counted for anything. All that mattered was getting the job done, by any means necessary.

He found, to his surprise, that he was even serious about Petra. He had had too many women to remember, many of them more attractive and experienced than the cute little girl from New Jersey. Perhaps it was just that they had shared so much in so little time, with so much riding on their own abilities and resolve. Maybe serious times made for serious relationships. Such things happened in wars, according to all the romantic vids, and they were in a war of sorts now. Whatever had brought it about, Olivera was grateful that he had found Petra, and he didn't want to lose her.

Franklin, one of Olivera's Security staff, came running into the room. "There's gunfire coming from downtown!" he shouted. "It sounds like AKs."

Olivera was on his feet and out the door as quickly as his wounded leg allowed. He paused outside in the Compound and listened as Franklin and the others joined him. After a few seconds, he heard a distant *pop-pop-*

pop off to the southeast, echoing dimly in the damp night air.

"Damn. The Transit! Go get two plasma rifles, and do it fast!"

Franklin dashed off, and Melinda said, "I don't get it. Why seize the Transit now? Everyone's already gone."

"Maybe they don't want anyone coming back. Melinda, make sure the Compound is buttoned up tight after we leave. And I mean *tight*!"

"You're not going *out* there, are you?" Petra gasped.

"We can't let them take the Transit." Franklin reappeared, clutching two Mark V plasma rifles. "Get in the skimmer," Olivera told him. "I'll drive."

"It'll be okay, Pet," he told Petra as he gave her a quick, hard hug. He pulled away from her and got into the skimmer.

"You be careful, dammit!" Petra called to him.

"Always!" he shouted as the skimmer sped toward the Compound gate.

Olivera kept the skimmer's lights out as he maneuvered through the darkened streets of the city. He kept a window open, but heard no more firing, although the whine of the skimmer might have masked it. The city, now empty of humans, seemed ghostly and silent, like a graveyard at midnight. Olivera felt a tickle of fear run down his spine.

He parked on a side street two blocks from the Transit facility. The two of them got out of the skimmer and slowly walked in the direction of the Transit. They paused at a corner and stared down the street into the darkness. Olivera mentally kicked himself for neglecting to bring along his night-vision glasses; one of those things that you never thought about until you needed it.

Olivera pointed across the street. "You take a position at the corner, then cover me as I advance along this side," he told Franklin. "When I get to the next corner, I'll cover you and you advance. Just like training. Got it?"

"Got it," Franklin said. Olivera slapped him on the shoulder and Franklin darted into the street. Olivera held his breath until Franklin made it across safely. He would have gone himself, except that his wounded leg was still giving him hell. Franklin was faster.

When Franklin was in position, Olivera ducked around the corner and furtively made his way along the front of the buildings, keeping to the shadows. Every few seconds, he stopped and flattened himself against the dark storefronts and empty offices. He reached the end of the block and ducked into a shallow alcove at the door of a Chinese restaurant. Poking his head out from behind a brick column, he peered into the distance and thought he could see short, dark forms moving around in front of the Transit building.

He looked back and signaled to Franklin to begin his advance. Kneeling the way he had been taught in training, Olivera shouldered the heavy plasma rifle and fingered the trigger guard. Franklin was advancing in quick spurts, and had almost reached the corner opposite Olivera when the shots rang out, loud and close by, bringing Franklin down.

Olivera dived past the brick column and fired down the street to his right. The first dazzling bolt hit a parked freight skimmer and burned a hole completely through it, front to back. The second took the head off the naked, fur-covered assassin who had shot Franklin. He saw no one else by the light of the burning lorry.

He got to his feet, kept low, and fired off two more bolts in the direction of the Transit building, then ran across the street to reach Franklin. He almost made it.

The antique bullets ripped through him from shoulder to thigh, and Olivera pitched forward onto the rough cobblestones. He tried to push himself up and found that he couldn't. He looked down at his ruined torso, not quite believing what he was seeing.

Twice in one week. Shot by a thousand-year-old museum piece! That wasn't serious, he thought. Not serious at all. He wanted to laugh at the absolute absurdity of it; but before he could, he died.

ON THE SECOND NIGHT OF HER CAPTIVITY, Gloria slept. But she dreamed.

The second day had been physically and mentally exhausting precisely because absolutely nothing happened. Kleska never came in to speak to them, and their bonds were never released except for meals and necessity. They lay side by side on the floor, close enough to share a kiss or two, but incapable of any useful motion.

They spent the long day talking, at first of the possibility of rescue or escape, but then of other things—anything at all but the grim reality they faced. Hawkes told her about growing up on the hell-for-leather world of Woolamura, and she told him about growing up at Court under Darius IV. She avoided mentioning Charles and her marriage, and he was silent on the subject of other women in his life. In a strange way, they finally got to know each other. For once, they had no other immediate concerns or urgent agendas; they had nothing but time, and neither of them knew how much of that they would have. The Marines might arrive on Mynjhino at any moment.

She drifted off, her forehead up against Hawkes's cheek, and dreamed of her childhood and happier times. The dreams began to change, and then she found herself back at Dexta during those first horrible months, her naked back pressed against the cold tile of the men's room floor, leering faces looming above her. And then she was standing nude in front of Quan at the Palqui, only it wasn't Quan, it was Kleska, pointing an AK-47 at her. He asked her if she wanted another cup of jigli tea before he shot her, and she tried to kick him in the face, only she kept missing and slipping, falling onto the slippery tile floor and sliding down, down, into an incomprehensible and terrifying darkness . . .

"What!"

She couldn't tell if it was Hawkes's voice or her own. She tried to sit up, but couldn't. A series of muffled *cracks!* sounded somewhere outside.

"That's gunfire!" Hawkes whispered.

"Spirit," cried Gloria, "they've come for us!"

But the noises were not repeated, and there was no sound of battle, or of men. They waited in the darkness, and Gloria wished once more that she could hold on to Hawkes.

The door opened and light splashed into the room. A Myn entered and knelt next to them. It was Dilanth, Gloria realized, and he was untying her.

She rubbed her wrists and tried to get to her feet while Dilanth untied Hawkes. He was up a moment later, and they both looked questioningly toward Dilanth.

"What was that gunfire?" Hawkes asked him.

"A disagreement," Dilanth said simply. "But it is ended now. Kleska has gone to join his accursed ancestors. Come, you must go."

He led them out of the room and the house, and they found themselves in a glimmering dawn. Several Myn were standing silently, staring at them, AK-47s in their hands. For an awful moment, Gloria thought that they were going to be shot, but then Dilanth spoke to them.

"You must take the skimmer and get back to the Compound," he told them. "Tell them that the Brotherhood of the Myn-Traha accepts an immediate and unconditional cease-fire. The humans who are here may stay, and we will not harm them. We seek only friendship, and we *must* have the help of the humans!"

"What's happened?" Gloria asked.

"The Jhino have invaded Myn," said Dilanth. "They have taken Dhanj!"

chapter **17**

BEFORE THEY LEFT, DILANTH TOLD THEM WHERE
they were and gave them directions on how to get back
to Dhanj. He apologized for having taken them captive
in the first place. It had been Kleska's idea, he told them,
and he and Quetra had reluctantly gone along with it
only because it was Kleska who had managed to secure
the AK-47s.

"Where did they come from?" Hawkes asked him.
"How did Kleska get them?"

"They simply appeared one day in a freight skimmer. Kleska never told us how he got them. He said that
he could get more."

"How many were delivered?"

"One hundred," said Dilanth.

"A hundred? Is that all?"

"Kleska said that it would be enough, to begin with.
But now, we must have more! The Jhino have thousands
of them! The Myn of Dhanj have told us this, Brianhawkes. They will slaughter our people if we cannot defend ourselves. We must have more weapons and more

ammunition! Can you get them for us?" He looked at Hawkes with hope in his huge eyes.

"No, my friend," Hawkes told him. "I can't."

"Then all is lost!"

"Not yet." Hawkes clapped Dilanth on his shoulder. "We'll get back to the Compound and try to put an end to this."

He and Gloria got into the old skimmer and flew away. They had been traveling for ten minutes when Hawkes suddenly slapped himself on the forehead. "Dammit. We should have gotten our comms back!"

"We can go back and get them," Gloria said.

Hawkes shook his head. "Dilanth and the others probably aren't even there by now. If they have any sense, they've already begun relocating. They can't afford to let the Jhino find them."

"The Jhino." Gloria said it as if it were a swear word. "That bastard Veentro!"

"They gave the Myn-Traha just enough weapons to make a nuisance of themselves and get the humans to evacuate. They probably don't even have much ammunition left. And with the humans gone and the Myn-Traha effectively disarmed, there's no one left to stop the Jhino from marching in and taking over. Lovely."

"But the Marines could stop them," Gloria pointed out.

"The Marines obviously aren't here yet. By the time they arrive, Veentro will present them with a *fait accompli*."

"Nevertheless," Gloria insisted, "this is a clear violation of the Annexation Treaty of 3131. Not to mention about a dozen sections of the Imperial Weapons Code. And Veentro has to know that."

"He must think he has a way around it. He's been pretty damn clever so far."

"We'll see about that," Gloria sniffed.

Twenty miles outside of Dhanj, they encountered the first of the refugees. A few days earlier, it had been humans, mostly in skimmers but some on foot, jamming the narrow, dusty roads as they fled for their lives. Now, it was Myn—thousands of them. They carried bundles on their backs and bags in their arms, salvaging what little they could of their possessions and the lives they had known. Their faces looked desperate, their eyes empty and haunted. They kept looking back over their shoulders, fearful of what might be behind them.

Hawkes landed the skimmer in a clearing by the side of the road and got out. He approached the Myn trudging along the road and watched in silence for a while. The Myn looked at him, then turned quickly away, as if they were somehow ashamed. Many of them had cheered when the humans left, and now, they were running for their own lives. They were confused by all that had happened, and didn't know what to think or what to feel, other than fear.

"Can you tell me what happened in Dhanj?" Hawkes trilled to them. A few Myn stopped and looked at him, then hurried on their way. Finally, one of them approached Hawkes and trilled to him rapidly and at length. Hawkes nodded and thanked the Myn, who shouldered his burden again and resumed his flight.

"The Jhino suddenly showed up last night, about an hour after sunset," Hawkes told Gloria when he returned to the skimmer. "Hundreds of them, apparently downtown."

"The Transit?" Gloria wondered.

"He didn't know, but it makes sense. If they came by sea, they would have to have started a couple of weeks ago, long before the evacuation. Anyway, they've taken most of the city, including the harbor area and the Palqui. Every Myn in Dhanj is on the run by now. A million of them."

"Spirit!" Gloria breathed. "What will happen to them? There can't be enough food in the countryside to feed all of them."

"And they must realize that," Hawkes said. "But

they'd rather face starvation than be taken by the Jhino. That should tell you something."

"This could turn into a catastrophe!"

"Easily," said Hawkes. "Come on, we've got to get back to the Compound."

Hawkes took the skimmer cross-country to avoid the roads, but from an altitude they could see thousands upon thousands of Myn clogging the narrow paths. Clouds of dust from their footsteps rose into the morning air and turned the sky a dirty yellow.

The Compound was in the northwest corner of the city, and Hawkes, coming from the southeast, skirted around the edge of the metropolis to reach it. The suburbs already seemed to be completely deserted. Here and there, a fire burned. Whether they were the result of actions by the Jhino or deliberate sabotage by the fleeing Myn, they couldn't tell.

Hawkes got back onto the now-deserted roadway to make their entrance into Dhanj. As they approached the city limits, they saw a freight skimmer parked diagonally across the road, blocking it, and a group of about a dozen armed Jhino pointing AK-47s in their direction.

"Checkpoint," said Hawkes. "We'd better stop."

Hawkes brought the skimmer down short of the lorry and opened his side window. An armed Jhino walked over to them. Like all Myn and Jhino, he was un-clothed, but this one wore a backpack, a belt, and a sort of garrison cap. He looked at Hawkes for a moment, then said, "Humans should be gone from this area."

"We have to get into the city," Hawkes told him. "To the Compound."

The Jhino shook his head from side to side. "Access denied," he said. "Those are my orders."

"What's your name?" Hawkes demanded.

"My name?"

"Yes, dammit, your name. When I report this, I want to be sure to get your name right."

The Jhino stiffened to attention. "I am Sergeant

Plantha," he said. "Lieutenant Gresklo ordered me to deny access to the city. You cannot enter."

"And I am Brian Hawkes, Imperial Undersecretary for Administration. This is Gloria VanDeen, Imperial Coordinating Supervisor for this jurisdiction. Did your orders tell you to detain Imperial officials, Sergeant Plantha?"

"My orders are to deny access," Plantha repeated.

"Well, Sergeant, if you want to deny us access, you're going to have to shoot us. Do you know what will happen to you if you open fire on Imperial officials? Do you have any idea what the Empire will do to you?"

"But . . . my orders . . ." Plantha stammered.

Hawkes glanced at Gloria. "He doesn't know," he said.

"A pity," said Gloria.

Hawkes turned back to the bewildered Jhino. "We're leaving now, Sergeant Plantha. I suppose you'll just have to do what you think is best. Good luck at your trial."

Hawkes engaged the skimmer and hovered for a moment, then ascended and cleared the lorry by a few feet. No one fired at them.

Five minutes later, they ignored another checkpoint outside the Compound and cruised through the gate. They parked in front of the administration building and got out of the skimmer.

Petra burst out of the office building and ran to Gloria. She hugged her breathlessly, then buried her head against Gloria's shoulder and began to sob. Gloria looked up and saw Melinda Throneberry, an expression of anguish on her face.

"Olivera is dead," Melinda told her. "Franklin, too. Shot by the Jhino."

"Oh, no!" Gloria gasped. She wrapped her arms around Petra and held her close.

Melinda turned to Hawkes, hesitated, then gave

him a tentative hug. "Thank the Spirit you're safe. How did you get away?"

"They released us after they got word about the Jhino," Hawkes told her. "They've offered an immediate and unconditional cease-fire. And they want our help."

"I don't doubt it," Melinda said with a half laugh. "Do you know what's happened?"

"Just that the Jhino have taken the city. And that there are a million Myn on the roads, running for their lives. What happened to Olivera and Franklin?"

"We heard gunfire from downtown. The Jhino had taken the Transit. Ricardo and Franklin went to investigate, and those bastards murdered them. They brought the bodies in a few hours ago. Said it was a terrible but unavoidable accident, and they were very sorry. They also killed three Imperium security people at the Transit."

"How many Jhino are in the city?"

"We don't know. Hundreds, at least. Probably a few thousand by now."

"They've got the city sealed off, but we didn't see any of them in the countryside beyond it. I suppose they need to consolidate their position here before they make an advance. What are they doing in the city?"

"We've heard sporadic gunfire, but we don't really know anything," Melinda told him. "They've got us bottled up in the Compound for our own safety."

"What about Rhinehart? Has he done anything?"

"Oh, yes," Melinda laughed. "He's done something, all right. Come on, why don't you two get inside and get cleaned up, then we'll bring you up to date on everything. We'll fix you a meal while you get a shower. You smell worse than a Myn, Hawkes—but you look awfully good!"

GLORIA AND HAWKES ATE THEIR BREAKFAST at the conference table, while Petra, Throneberry, Blumenthal, and the two remaining Security men, Holst and Quesada, drank coffee and told them the news. The Marines were due to arrive in another two days, and in the meantime, Governor Rhinehart had just declared a state of Unlimited Emergency.

"Well," said Hawkes, "that's good. It gives him the legal authority to tell the Jhino to get the hell out of Myn."

"No," said Melinda, "that's bad. It also gives him the legal authority to declare the Myn to be in a state of unlawful rebellion, which he has already done."

"But he doesn't know we're free," Gloria said. "And that the Myn-Traha have agreed to a cease-fire. We have to tell him!"

"As soon as you finish your breakfast," said Melinda, "we'll go over to the Residence and give him the happy news. But I don't think it's going to make any difference. You see, an hour ago, our distinguished Imperial Governor met with a Colonel Jangleth of the Army of Jhino and gave him the fucking keys to the city."

"What?" Hawkes demanded.

"You heard me," said Melinda. "Rhinehart has declared the Jhino to be our allies against the treasonous Myn. He has put the Imperial stamp of approval on the invasion."

The entire group walked slowly across the Compound toward the Governor's Residence. They heard syncopated gunfire in the distance, and saw several columns of dark smoke rising from different locations in the city. The Compound itself seemed strangely still. All of the Myn staff had fled, and the remaining humans were staying inside the buildings.

They found Rhinehart in the Sitting Room, along with Tatiana Markova. While Tatiana remained seated, Rhinehart sprang to his feet and dashed across the room to give Gloria a hug and a kiss. "Thank the Spirit you're safe!" he cried. "I tell you, I had all but given up hope. And Hawkes—good to see you safe as well, old man." He gave Hawkes a quick handshake.

Rhinehart led them into the Sitting Room and told them to make themselves comfortable. He looked at Holst and Quesada, very junior personnel, and told them to remain outside, where they might be needed. The two Security men looked quickly toward Throneberry, saw her nod, then turned and left. Tatiana stared at Hawkes and Gloria and said nothing.

"Governor," Gloria said, once she was seated next to Hawkes on a small sofa, "the Myn-Traha released us and have accepted an immediate and unconditional cease-fire. They say humans can remain in Myn and will not be harmed."

"Well, that's very big of them, isn't it?" said Rhinehart. "Considering that they've already slaughtered dozens of us and forced the rest to flee for their lives. Well, it won't do! We'll bring the whole treasonous lot of them to justice, and then they can natter all they want about cease-fires. The nerve of them!"

Rhinehart sat down on a sofa next to Tatiana and squeezed her hand.

"You don't understand, Excellency," Gloria persisted. "The Myn-Traha are no threat to anyone now. There were never very many of them, and they only had a hundred automatic weapons in the first place. And now, they don't even have much ammunition left."

"I should think not," Rhinehart said, "considering how much of it they shot at us the other night."

"Governor," said Hawkes, "that's not fair. They let the evacuation come off without ever firing a shot."

Rhinehart's eyebrows rose noticeably. "Fine thing for you to say, Hawkes. They were all set to murder you, and Ms. VanDeen as well, weren't they?"

"That was the doing of their leader at the time, a Myn named Kleska," Hawkes told him. "But they've gotten rid of Kleska. They killed him this morning. Their leader now is named Dilanth, and he wants peace."

"And what happens when they murder this Dilanth

and another bloodthirsty rebel takes *his* place? Eh? Answer me that, old boy."

"Governor," Gloria pleaded, "whatever the Myn-Traha have done, they are only a small minority. Right now there are a million peaceful Myn on the roads outside the city, running for their lives. We know; we saw them. Excellency, those people will starve in the countryside."

"Then they bloody well should have stayed in the city, shouldn't they? The Jhino are a civilized race. They'll do no harm to anyone."

"No harm?" screeched Petra, rising from her chair. "They *killed* Ricardo!"

Gloria reached for Petra, got her by the elbow, and pulled her back down to her chair. Rhinehart frowned, and said, "Yes, my dear. I gather that you two were close. A terrible thing, but an unavoidable accident. If Olivera hadn't gone charging off so recklessly, I daresay, it would never have happened."

"He was doing his *job*!" Melinda said, unmistakable anger in her voice.

"Yes? Well, be that as it may, it was a tragic happenstance, and no blame attaches. I understand your anguish over this tragedy, but I must emphasize to you all that the Jhino are our friends. Colonel Jangleth has given me his personal assurance that all personal and property rights will be respected. Prime Minister Veentro himself will be coming here in a few days, once things have settled down. The Jhino are our allies in this fearful struggle."

"*Struggle?*" Hawkes shouted. "What fucking struggle? The Myn-Traha have quit!"

Rhinehart stiffened. "Really, old boy," he said, "I realize that you've been through a terrible ordeal, but you should try to control your temper."

"Governor," Melinda quickly interjected, keeping her voice under control, "when the Marines get here on

Saturday, you have to tell them to force the Jhino to leave Myn and return home."

"I'll do no such thing!" Rhinehart cried indignantly. "Don't tell me what I *have* to do, Melinda, my dear. Do I have to remind you of the law? Under the present conditions, my word *is* the law. I speak in the name of the Emperor, and no Dexta bureaucrat has the right to gainsay me or contradict me. Remember your place!"

"All right, then," said Gloria, "let's talk about the law. Governor, the Jhino invasion is a flagrant violation of the terms of the Annexation Treaty of 3131. And their acquisition and use of those AK-47s violates Chapter Nine, Paragraphs Fifteen, Sixteen, and Seventeen of the Imperial Weapons Code."

"Let me remind you, Ms. VanDeen," said Rhinehart, "that it was the Myn, and not the Jhino, who introduced those weapons to our formerly peaceful world. Colonel Jangleth tells me that they intercepted a boat full of those rifles just a few days ago, and confiscated them for their own use as a defensive measure against the Myn."

"A few days ago?" Gloria said in disbelief. "Do you really believe that they took those weapons, formed an army, distributed the weapons, and trained their recruits in their use, all in a few days? Governor, that's patently ridiculous!"

"Now, look here, Ms. VanDeen," Rhinehart said, growing impatient, "the fact remains that the Myn introduced those weapons and used them to take forty-odd human lives. Whatever technical violations the Jhino may have committed, they pale to insignificance against the lawless and treasonous actions of the Myn. As for the Annexation Treaty, the Myn are in violation of that, as well. The actions of the Jhino, while precipitous, are entirely legal under my authority as Imperial Governor in a declared state of Unlimited Emergency. Isn't that right, Tatiana?"

Tatiana smiled pleasantly. "Right as rain, Excellency,"

she said. "Look it up, Gloria. *Imperial Code,* Article Ten, Section Five, Paragraph Three, Subsections A through D."

Melinda stared daggers at her Undersecretary for Corporate Affairs. "Tatiana," she said, "when we're finished here, I want to have a word with you in my office."

"Certainly, Melinda," Tatiana replied.

"Governor," Melinda said, "regardless of all the legal ins and outs of this situation, we need to launch a courier for Earth immediately. I'll need your authorization."

"A courier? No, I think not," said Rhinehart. "Inasmuch as one was dispatched without my knowledge during my recent illness, we are down to our last courier. I think it best to preserve it for use in case of an emergency."

"But you just declared an Unlimited Emergency!" Melinda cried in exasperation.

"Relax, my dear. The situation is stable for the moment, and the Marines will be here in two days. We can avail ourselves of their communications facilities at that time." Rhinehart got to his feet. "I believe that covers everything," he said. "Hawkes, Ms. VanDeen, I really am overjoyed to see you here, safe and sound." Rhinehart gave Tatiana a quick smile, then turned and walked resolutely from the room.

"My goodness," said Sonia Blumenthal when he was gone, "what a malodorous pile of shit *that* was."

GLORIA GOT A SPARE WRISTCOM FROM SONIA and tapped in Bryce Denton's code.

"Hey, Gloria!" he said. "Heard you made it back. I want to get your whole story just as soon as you can manage it, okay? Hawkes too."

"Okay, but I need a favor from you."

"And I need one from you. Can you piggyback my invasion story on your courier?"

"There's not going to be a courier," Gloria told him. She got to her feet and went to the window of her office, where she could see smoke from the fires in the city. There seemed to be more of them now. "Bryce, I was going to ask the same favor from you. I need to get a report out, and I thought I could put it on your next messenger to Pecos."

"Isn't that wonderful?" Denton muttered. "Why no courier?"

"In his wisdom," said Gloria, "the Governor is saving our last one for a true emergency. Why no messenger?"

"Same reason. They are being reserved for 'special circumstances which may arise,' per order of Randall Sweet, Regional Director of Servitor."

"What has Sweet got to do with it?" Gloria wanted to know.

"For such a smart, sexy babe, Gloria, you can be pretty naïve at times. Apparently you were not aware that Empire News Service is a wholly owned and operated subsidiary of Consolidated Fusion Enterprises. The aptly named Con-Fusion, in turn, is a holding company controlled by our friends at Servitor."

"So Sweet has the power to censor your stories?"

"No, he can't do that. What he can do is keep me from getting them out."

"Well, what about the Flyer you came in? Can't you take that back to Pecos and report the story in person?"

"Sweet's reserving that, too. Cute, huh?"

Gloria ran her hand through her hair and tried to think. There had to be a way to get the news of the invasion to Earth. The sooner Dexta and the Household knew what was going on, the sooner they could countermand Rhinehart's emergency decrees—or, better yet, fire the son of a bitch.

"Okay," said Gloria, "this stretches the *Code* a bit, but I think I can let you borrow my Flyer and take that to Pecos."

"That's very generous of you Gloria, and I appreciate it, but there's one small problem."

"And that is?"

"Your Flyer is parked up there at the Orbital Station. I'd need a shuttle to get there, and your friend and mine, Vladislav Rhinehart, is not about to authorize a shuttle just to give little old me a ride up to orbit."

Gloria thought some more. There was still a way, she realized. She didn't like it, but she couldn't think of anything else.

"I can get a shuttle for myself on my own authority," she said. "I don't need Rhinehart's approval for that. In fact, he doesn't even have to know about it. But I'd have to go with you to Pecos. Half a day in a Flyer, right?"

"Right," said Denton. "Damn, Gloria, that is a fantastic idea. I can get your story on the way, then you can hold a media briefing when we get to Pecos. With a courier from Pecos, your version of the story will get to Earth ahead of Rhinehart's. In the meantime, you make as big a media splash as you can on Pecos, and everyone else will jump on the story, too. And knowing you, it could be one hell of a big splash, if you play it right. Wear something sexy for a change, huh?"

"Control yourself, Denton," she said. "I'll be in touch about the shuttle. This afternoon, with luck."

Gloria went to Melinda Throneberry's office, just in time to see Tatiana Markova leaving it. Tatiana stopped and smiled at Gloria.

"You should have fucked the old fart when you had the chance, Gloria," she said. "Too late now."

Gloria returned her smile. "You're a Thirteen, right, Tatiana?"

"Uh, yes. Same as you, so don't think you can pull rank on me, Coordinating Supervisor or not."

"Oh," said Gloria, "that's not what I had in mind. I was thinking of something entirely different. See you around the Compound, Tatiana."

Gloria went into Melinda's office and sat down in

front of her desk. Melinda had considerable color in her face, and seemed to be grinding her teeth. "I'd like to kick that little bitch from here to Jhino and back," she said.

"You can't," Gloria reminded her. "You're her superior, and a Twelve. I, on the other hand, am a Thirteen." She grinned at Melinda.

Melinda grinned back at her. "Just let me know when. I could sell tickets to everyone in the Compound."

"Business before pleasure, I'm afraid," Gloria said. She filled in Melinda on what had transpired with Denton. Melinda liked the idea and gave it her unqualified endorsement.

"I should be back here by Friday night," Gloria said. "I want to be here when the Marines arrive."

"And I want you here. Hawkes and I will try to hold things together while you're gone. Actually, I'm not really sure what we can do around here."

"There's something you can do for me," Gloria said. "Take care of Petra. I hate to leave her at a time like this, but there's only room for two in the Flyer. I left her in her room, crying. Maybe she'll get some sleep. I hope so."

"I'll keep her close, Gloria. Try to keep her busy."

"Good, that will help. I'm going over to the Comm Room and set up the shuttle."

"Gloria? This is a clever move, but keep in mind that there's a hell of a lot more at stake here than a bureaucratic fast shuffle on Rhinehart. If he gets his way, all those Myn you saw on the road today are going to starve. If the Jhino don't kill them first."

Gloria nodded. "That's why I'm doing this, Melinda."

chapter 18

WITH BLUE IMPERIAL FLAGS ON THE DOORS
and a flashing yellow light on the roof, the skimmer
moved out of the Compound and didn't pause at the
Jhino checkpoint. Hawkes drove toward the harbor for a
few blocks, then pulled over to pick up Bryce Denton.
He piled into the back with a duffel bag filled with dirty
laundry and imaging equipment.

Hawkes turned to the right and stayed close to the
ground, following back streets out of the city, then
headed northwest along the coast. "Hey," said Denton,
"harbor's the other way."

"We're going to Shanagh, a small port fifty miles up
the coast," Gloria explained. "I arranged for the shuttle
to meet us there. The Jhino aren't there yet, and Rhinehart and his friends won't see it coming or going. I figured we could get a head start that way."

"Smart lady," Denton said. "Hey, Hawkes, you don't
mind about this, do you? I mean, Gloria and I are going
to be alone together in that little Flyer for twelve hours."

"Don't make any sudden moves, and you should be fine," Hawkes advised.

"Don't even make any *slow* moves," Gloria added.

"Hmmpf," Denton muttered. "Some public servant *you* are!"

The shuttle had already splashed down and was waiting for them at the docks when they arrived in Shanagh. Gloria gave Hawkes a lengthy good-bye kiss, then followed Denton into the spacecraft. She said hello to the pilot, found a seat, and strapped herself in. The shuttle's thrusters backed it out of the dock and maneuvered it out into the Roads, where the powerful main engines roared to life and quickly lifted the vehicle out of the ocean and into the sky. Ninety minutes later, they docked at Mynjhino Orbital Station.

The Station Manager was once again disappointed to find that Gloria had no time to have lunch with him. He told her that the Flyer was fueled and programmed for the voyage to Pecos. As she was about to board, a thought occurred to her.

"Jorge," she said, smiling at the Station Manager, "before I return to Earth, I'd like very much to have lunch with you. But I was wondering if you could do me a favor."

"Anything at all," he assured her.

"If Governor Rhinehart orders the launch of a courier in the next day or so, could you see to it that you have a few technical problems? Enough to delay it for at least twenty-four hours?"

The Station Manager's mouth dropped open.

"I know it's asking a lot, but this is one of those nasty little jurisdictional disputes, you know what I mean? Imperial versus Dexta? And I know you'll be loyal to Dexta, Jorge. I'll be sure to mention it when I get back to New York." Gloria gave him her most beguiling smile and stood before him in her tiny, translucent miniskirt and an entirely transparent blouse, unbuttoned to her waist.

What Gloria was asking of him violated any number of Imperial and Dexta regulations. Doing it could get him fired or demoted. On the other hand, who was to know?

He grinned at her. "Funny thing about those couriers," he said. "Sometimes, after they've been in storage a while, the nav systems get a little degraded. It can take hours just to find the glitch."

Gloria blew him a kiss and boarded the Flyer.

ONCE THEY HAD MADE THE TRANSITION TO YAO Space, Gloria sat in one of the chairs in the forward area while Denton sat in the other and aimed his imager at her. She answered his questions about her captivity and subsequent release by the Myn-Traha. It wasn't much of a story, but it gave her a chance to talk about the Myn generally, and discuss the current situation.

She went on to describe in some detail the scene on the roads outside of Dhanj, and the fear and desperation that were driving a million Myn refugees from their homes. "What you have to understand," Gloria emphasized to the people who would be viewing the vid, "is that the Myn and Jhino have been fighting ever since they discovered each other, some five thousand years ago. When humans first arrived on Mynjhino in 3131, they had been engaged in continuous warfare for over five centuries. But their technology at that time was such that they were very evenly matched, and neither side had an upper hand. So the war dragged on, without victory for either the Myn or the Jhino. Then the Empire brought the war to a halt, and the two races have lived in peace for the past eighty-five years. But the ancient rivalry and hatred never disappeared. Now, they have reemerged, and one side, the Jhino, has a decisive advantage in weapons technology. Exactly how they acquired that advantage is under investigation, but the central point is that the potential exists for an unlimited genocide. If the Jhino are not restrained and forced to return to their own continent, there could be a tragedy on a scale not seen in the Empire since the war with the Ch'gnth Confederacy, more than forty years ago."

"And yet," Denton pointed out, "Imperial Governor Rhinehart has, in effect, sided with the Jhino."

"When the Governor made that decision," Gloria said, "he was not yet aware that Undersecretary Hawkes and I had been released, and that the Myn-Traha had accepted an unconditional cease-fire. I think the Governor was reluctant to reverse his decision abruptly, and wants to see how the situation develops. His caution is understandable, under the circumstances. However, I'm confident that Governor Rhinehart will recognize the urgency of the situation and take the appropriate steps to avert a tragedy."

"In that case, why are you making this sudden trip to Pecos?"

"As you know, the majority of our Security staff has been lost to hostile fire, first by the Myn-Traha, then by the Jhino. I need to consult with Governor Hollingsworth on Pecos to arrange for personnel transfers and to address the immediate needs on Mynjhino."

Denton put the imager down. "Spoken like a loyal little bureaucrat," he said.

"What do you want from me, Bryce?"

"I was kind of hoping that you'd tell the Empire that Rhinehart is an incompetent fool who is obviously in bed with Servitor—among others—and that if he gets his way, millions of Myn will die. You know, Gloria—the truth."

Gloria sighed. "Make you a deal, Bryce," she said. "I'll tell the truth if you do. I'll hold the imager while you explain to your audience how the pigs at Servitor tried to keep you from getting your story out. And make sure you mention how Servitor is probably responsible for creating this entire situation in the first place, just to grab GalaxCo's land on the cheap."

Denton scratched his chin thoughtfully. "You know," he said, "I'd almost be willing to do that if I thought there was a chance in hell that my editor would let it go out."

"You could slip the story to some other service," Gloria suggested.

"Sure, why not? I could always learn a new trade. I always thought bricklaying was kind of interesting."

"Empire isn't the only news service."

"Gloria, after I blew the whistle on one of the Big Twelve, do you think the other eleven would fall all over themselves trying to obtain my services? The fact is, every news service in the Empire is run, directly or indirectly, by one of the Big Twelve. The wonder is that any honest news ever gets out, at all."

"So we're both stuck in the system," Gloria said.

"Sometimes," Denton observed, "the system stinks."

"That it does," Gloria agreed.

DENTON CAUGHT UP ON HIS SLEEP WHILE Gloria sat at her work console, writing reports to go out on the courier from Pecos. The first report was entirely factual, stating as clearly as possible what had happened and what she knew to be true. It would be addressed to Zoe Zachary and the other System Coordinators for Mynjhino, with additional copies for her immediate superiors, Balthazar Trobriand and Gladys Pymm, as well as their superior, Grant Enright, who would send a copy upstairs to Hector Konrad. From there, more copies would wend their way upward as far as Lars Ringold, the Sector Administrator, who stood at the top of the Pyramid in Sector 8. Undoubtedly, the central facts of the report would continue to percolate upward, probably all the way to Norman Mingus.

Next, Gloria wrote what was known within Dexta as an Appreciation. In this report, she discussed not only what she knew, but what she suspected. She laid out the known facts that seemed to indicate a link between Servitor, the Governor, the weapons, the Jhino, and the Myn-Traha. The evidence was circumstantial and, she was well aware, proved nothing, but she believed it was important for certain people at Headquarters to get a comprehensive view of the situation on Mynjhino. Sweet's attempt to prevent Denton from filing his story struck Gloria as a strong indication that Servitor had something to hide.

Her original *cui bono* theory was looking a lot better, now. If all Servitor stood to gain was the chance, somewhere down the road, to take over the pharmaceutical business on Mynjhino, their actions would make little sense. And given the attitude of the Myn, her jigli theory didn't make sense, either. But what if Servitor didn't have to rely on the Myn to grow the jigli? What if it would be grown instead by the invading Jhino, or perhaps by enslaved Myn workers?

The pharmaceutical crops were labor-intensive and the actual yield per hectare was quite small. In addition, expensive processing was required to extract and purify the active agents in the plants. But jigli grew naturally in some regions of Myn, and its leaves required no processing at all. The explosive variety of the herb that Sweet had given her would bring a very high price, she was sure. Putting it all together, it seemed to Gloria that Servitor's profit per hectare from a jigli plantation might be worth hundreds of times more than GalaxCo's marginal profits from the pharmaceuticals.

And that would make it all worthwhile. Especially so for Sweet himself, who would stand to reap a substantial "finder's fee" from Servitor. The money involved would be huge, more than enough to give a piece of the action to Rhinehart and—of course—to Tatiana Markova. In the longer term, Veentro and the Jhino would undoubtedly show their gratitude to Servitor in other tangible

ways. The Jhino would run the planet, and Servitor
would become the dominant corporate on their world.

Rhinehart was the key to making it all work. He
could not help but be aware that he was not highly
thought of at Dexta or in the Imperial Household. The
new Emperor owed him nothing, and would undoubtedly dispose of him before long. Past a hundred years of
age and longing for the good old days in Rio, carefully
led into the conspiracy by Tatiana, Rhinehart would
have seen this as his chance to escape from obscure de-
crepitude on a backwater world and make a secure and
comfortable return to the delights of Earth. All he had
to do was embrace the Jhino invasion once the human
population was evacuated and out of harm's way. When
they arrived, the Imperial Marines would be under
Rhinehart's orders, and he would ensure that they
would do nothing to stand in the way of the Jhino conquest. By the time Dexta or the Household could learn
what had happened and attempt to do anything about it,
the continent of Myn would be occupied by the Jhino,
with little or no hope of removing them. A company of
Marines certainly couldn't do the job; it would require at
least a division, and there was absolutely no chance that
the Empire would make such a commitment of its thinly
stretched forces.

Gloria completed work on her Appreciation and addressed it to Zoe Zachary and Grant Enright, marked
Confidential. Zoe needed to know what was really happening, and Grant could use his own judgment about
circulating the Appreciation to the higher-ups. Hector
Konrad would have to see it, but Enright could also take
it directly to Konrad's superiors, including Viveca Kwan.
Konrad would reject it out of hand, simply because it
came from Gloria, but Viveca could be relied upon to
give it serious consideration. She was in a position to
launch her own investigation of the Servitor link, and
might turn up additional evidence at her end.

Finally, Gloria decided to take a chance and write a

letter directly to Norman Mingus, with the Appreciation appended. Normally, a Thirteen would not dream of communicating directly with the Secretary himself—or anyone within ten Levels of him—but Mingus had already made the initial contact. He had come to Gloria's office (a fairly extraordinary thing in itself) and asked for her advice. Well, here it was.

Mingus could put pressure on the Household to remove Rhinehart. According to Althea Dante's informed sources, the Household would probably welcome the opportunity to sack Rhinehart, in any case. Patronage was the principal source of the Emperor's political power, and removing a holdover from the time of Darius and Gregory would open up a new slot to reward one of his own supporters.

The letter to Mingus could backfire, Gloria realized. If word of it got out, Konrad would be outraged, and even people as far up the line as Lars Ringold could be annoyed by her presumption. Going outside of channels was a good way to commit professional suicide at Dexta. But the situation seemed to demand it, and Gloria felt reasonably confident that Mingus would not throw her to the wolves.

Gloria had one more card to play, and she would turn that one over when she met with the media on Pecos. She couldn't tell the whole story publicly, but she could at least arouse public sentiment over the plight of the Myn and the invasion of the Jhino. Parliament might take notice, and although their actual power was limited, Ministers loved nothing better than a juicy scandal to investigate. The more attention Gloria could attract to the story, the better the chance that meaningful action would be taken. And, as Denton kept reminding her, it was within Gloria's power to make a very big media splash. So much, she thought wearily, for staying out of the limelight.

The report, the Appreciation, the letter to Mingus, and the media briefing could add up to a formidable and effective attack on Rhinehart, the Jhino, and Servitor. There was only one problem: timing. The courier would take three days to reach Earth. Assuming that Mingus and the Household acted with blinding speed (a big assumption), a day after Gloria's courier arrived, another courier could be sent to Mynjhino with directives countermanding Rhinehart's actions. That would take another three days to reach Mynjhino. So nothing could result from what Gloria was doing for a minimum of seven days.

And in seven days, the Jhino could conquer all of Myn.

AS SOON AS THE FLYER REENTERED NORMAL space, Denton sent off his accumulated story material to the ENS office on Pecos. Then Gloria transmitted everything she had written to the Imperial Secretary, along with an urgent request to the Governor for the launch of a courier. By the time they reached Pecos Orbital Station, things would be in motion.

The Station was probably ten times larger and twenty times more active than the one orbiting Mynjhino. When the Flyer docked, Gloria was greeted by the Station Manager and several assistants, all of whom were eager to meet their famous Coordinating Supervisor.

Gloria quickly arranged for a shuttle, and she and Denton were on their way down to the surface less than half an hour after reaching the Station. They came down on the day side of Pecos, where it was midmorning in the capital city of New Laredo. Looking out of the shuttle's windows, Gloria saw a modern metropolis spreading out into the distance, in vivid contrast to the backward and sleepy city of Dhanj. Pecos was home to more than 400 million humans and was a principal hub of commerce in Beta Division. Settled two centuries earlier, it was one of the worlds that reflected great credit on the Empire and human expansion into the galaxy. Finding a salutary climate, abundant resources, and no troublesome native species on Pecos, humans had quickly turned it into a showplace world that was virtually free of poverty, crime, and all the other Earthly ills that had prompted expansion in the first place.

The shuttle cruised smoothly to a wheels-down landing on a runway outside of the city. Denton was met by a gofer from the ENS office and told Gloria he'd see her later. Gloria was met by a large delegation of Dexta and Imperial staffers. Even at full complement, counting the consulate staff on Jhino, there were no more than fifty Dexta people on the entire planet of Mynjhino; on Pecos, there were more than five hundred, plus a substantial complement of Imperial personnel. The greeters whisked Gloria through a Transit, and she found herself at the Dexta Building in downtown New Laredo.

She met first with Imperial Secretary Vladimir Vasquez, whom Gloria already knew from his visit to Manhattan a few months earlier. Vasquez was full of questions about the situation on Mynjhino, and Gloria did her best to bring him up to speed. She spared no details; Servitor had a major presence on Pecos, and if they were behind the mess on Mynjhino, Vasquez needed to know about it.

Vasquez didn't seem terribly surprised. "I know Randall Sweet," he said. "He's Servitor's Regional Director, and spends a fair amount of time here. Played a round of golf with him a couple of years ago. He cheats. Doesn't really need to—he's a four handicapper. I think he just enjoys cheating."

Gloria discussed the personnel situation on Mynjhino and asked Vasquez to transfer ten of his Security people. Vasquez said he was eager to help, but resisted as much as he decently could. The size of a Dexta office's staff was a measure of its importance and, therefore, of the importance of its Secretary. Gloria realized how the game was played and settled for six, with a promise of six more as soon as replacements could be brought in from Earth. Vasquez estimated the initial complement could make the transfer within a week.

Then, it was on to the Governor's office for lunch with Ted Hollingsworth, a florid, robust man with a handshake like a drill press and a high-voltage smile. Gloria knew Hollingsworth, as well, from her days at Court. He was a native of Pecos and had been one of Charles's first appointees after his ascension. Hollingsworth had dabbled in a dozen different business ventures and was one of those people who knew everyone, liked everyone, and had an inexhaustible supply of funny, slightly off-color stories to tell. He had once made a play for Gloria, who, at the time, was angered by Charles's many infidelities, and she had very nearly accommodated Hollingsworth out of spite. Nearly every man made a play for Gloria in those days, but Hollingsworth had gotten a lot farther than most. He was, at least, the only current Imperial Governor who had once spread suntan lotion all over Gloria's naked body. At the last minute, she had declined an invitation to spread it all over his.

"Ted," she told him after she had given him a rundown on the situation on Mynjhino, "I know it's an imposition, but I really need a courier just as soon as possible."

"Any old time, darlin', any old time. This afternoon soon enough?"

"That would be perfect. I'm doing a media briefing after lunch, and I'd like to get that on the courier, as well. I want this story to get as much attention as possible."

"I don't think there's any problem on that score," Hollingsworth laughed. "Shitfire, darlin', you ain't wearin' much more than you were the last time I saw you."

"I need to play it this way, Ted," she said, smiling. "I seem to have a public image to live up to now."

"Ain't that just the Spirit's own truth? Gloria, honey, you just play it any way you want. I guess you've been kind of out of touch the last couple of weeks, but the fact is, you gotta be the most famous and popular woman in the whole damn Empire by now. People got a big kick out of the way you took ol' Charles down a peg or two. They kind of like the notion that there are some things even an Emperor can't have anytime he wants. You made it sound like poor ol' Chuck's gonna have to wait another five years 'fore he gets another shot at Gloria VanDeen."

"At least," said Gloria.

"Listen, honey," said Hollingsworth, "just a word to the wise. I know Rhinehart from the Division Governors' Conferences. He's a pompous old ass, but he ain't stupid. You go after him, Gloria, you make damn sure you get him. The Household may not like him, but it don't like the idea of Dexta people taking potshots at *their* people, not one little bit. And Randy Sweet and that Servitor crowd are just plain *mean*. If everything you say is true, they were willing to see a few dozen humans get themselves shot just so they could get the pot stirred up. If you get in their way, they'll get rid of you any way they can. Darlin', you just make sure that your cute little ass stays covered, you hear me?"

"I hear you, Ted, and thanks."

"Of course," Hollingsworth added as they got to their feet and started out of his office, "I was talkin' *metaphorically*, y'understand." He shook his head in admiration as Gloria walked ahead of him, her extremely brief skirt granting him a glimpse of her bare bottom. "Sweetest cheeks I ever did see!" Gloria laughed and gave her hips an extra wiggle for his benefit.

Following lunch with the Imperial Governor, Gloria met briefly with the President of the Republic of Pecos and a delegation from the congress. They chatted amiably if inconsequentially, and the politicians took turns posing for images with Gloria. On most colonies, the local governments—usually democracies of some form—dealt with purely internal matters, while Dexta and the Imperial Governor handled all external and Empire-related concerns. The multitiered system of overlapping jurisdictions was a source of endless legal and bureaucratic wrangling on many worlds, Pecos among them, but it acted as an effective check on the power of each of the contending entities. Hollingsworth worked hard at maintaining his personal popularity on Pecos, with the result that the Empire was well regarded by the citizens.

At the appointed time, Gloria entered the Dexta auditorium and found nearly a hundred local, global, and Empire media reps waiting for her. The PAO told her that she was the biggest story to hit Pecos since Darius IV made a brief visit, twenty years earlier. Her near-nudity caused a considerable commotion, and Gloria stood smiling at the lectern for several minutes until it subsided. If nothing else, she had won their full and complete attention. Now, she had to use that to her advantage.

"As I stand here speaking to you," she began, "more than a million desperate, hungry, frightened refugees are fleeing for their lives from the city of Dhanj on Mynjhino. Their land has been subjected to a sudden, violent, and unlawful invasion from across the sea. The invaders have already taken human lives, including those of Imperial personnel, and have killed an unknown number of the citizens of Dhanj. There is every reason to believe that they intend to conquer the entire continent of Myn and subject its population to slavery or outright extermination. The invaders are Jhino, their victims are Myn, but both races are subjects of the Empire and must be held to account for their actions, no less than the citizens of Pecos or Earth are held to account for theirs."

Gloria paused and moved her eyes slowly and methodically across the room, looking directly into every imager she saw. "The Empire is doing all it can to avert this tragedy, but Mynjhino is small and far away from the centers of power and trade. Imperial Marines have been ordered to Mynjhino and should arrive within the next day. But they will constitute a small force, while the Jhino have unleashed an entire army against the Myn. The situation on Mynjhino is fluid, but I have every confidence that Governor Rhinehart will take every legal step necessary to see to it that the Jhino abandon their invasion and return to their own land.

"The immediate pretext for this invasion was the terrorist activities of a small band known as the Myn-Traha, who were responsible for the deaths of over forty humans. I was recently a captive of the Myn-Traha, but I was released unharmed and given assurances that the Myn-Traha will accept and abide by an unconditional cease-fire. The leadership of this organization has been purged of its violent elements, and is now willing to accept a continuing human presence in their land. The vast majority of Myn never subscribed to the views of the Myn-Traha, but it is they who are being victimized by the actions of the Jhino."

Gloria knew she had gotten off to a good start and had enlisted the sympathies of her listeners. Now, she moved onto dangerous ground, choosing her words with care.

"The Jhino invaders," she said, "are armed with weapons superior to any possessed by the Myn, who do not, in any event, have an army of their own. Those weapons were provided to the Jhino in defiance of the Imperial Weapons Code and the Mynjhino Annexation Treaty of 3131. There is every reason to believe that the weapons were acquired by the Jhino through the active collusion and assistance of human partners. The ultimate goal of the conspirators is the seizure of Myn lands for use in commercial ventures. This entire matter is under investigation, and, at this time, I cannot tell you more than I already have. But I will say this. The conspirators will be brought to justice, and their corporate or Imperial connections, if any, will not protect them. The Empire will not stand idly by in the face of treasonous conspiracy, armed aggression, and genocide. I say this not only as the Dexta Coordinating Supervisor for this region, but as a proud and patriotic citizen of the Empire. If the Empire stands for anything at all, it is equal protection under the law for all its citizens, and I give you my personal pledge that I will not rest until the peaceful citizens of Myn can return to their homes in safety. I'll take your questions now."

For the next hour, Gloria stood there and responded to questions that were, by turns, sympathetic, hostile, informational, technical, rhetorical, personal, and repetitive. She skirted the details of the conspiracy she had alleged, and avoided directly implicating Rhinehart in any wrongdoing. She refused to name the corporate connection she had alluded to, but at one point she did mention that Imperium security personnel had been killed by the invaders. Since GalaxCo was already gone, that left only Servitor to blame. When asked directly if Servitor was the corporate culprit, she simply said that the matter was under active investigation.

But for all that she said, Gloria was well aware that the single statement that would attract the most attention was her personal pledge to secure justice for the Myn. If, as Hollingsworth had said, she was now the most famous and popular woman in the Empire, she was determined to use that popularity in this battle.

She had made it personal. Now, in the eyes of the Empire, it was Gloria VanDeen's war.

chapter **19**

THE IMPERIAL NAVY CRAFT *MYRTLE MCCORMICK* (LASS-374) floated downward on its stubby wings, toward the harbor of Dhanj. The drone of its powerful fusion engines could be heard on the shore as it descended toward the Roads and threw up a long, graceful roostertail spray as it made contact with the water. Its velocity slowed as it followed the buoyed channel and maneuvered toward land. The Land-Air-Sea-Space vehicle was capable of making either a horizontal or vertical touchdown directly on land, but a sea splashdown was easier and more economical of fuel. It avoided the docks and moved toward an open beach area north of the main harbor. A small throng of humans and Jhino watched from one side as the craft engaged its mass-repulsion units, ponderously rose from the surf, and skimmed low over the beach, water pouring from its hull. With a loud, electronic sigh, it settled onto the land and came to a halt.

The LASS was more than four hundred feet long, some eighty feet in diameter, and studded with pods, bubbles, and nacelles along its upper flanks. Some of them burst open, releasing an array of electronic gear and defensive weaponry. From one unfolding pod, a seventy-foot SAL (Sea-Air-Land) skimmer emerged, hovered briefly, then maneuvered away from the huge mother ship and flew low over the heads of the waiting humans and Jhino before descending and coming to rest near the right-front corner of the LASS.

Instantly, doors on both sides of the SAL popped open, and within seconds, forty fully armed Imperial Marines had scrambled out and taken up defensive positions around the perimeter of the LASS. Clad in camouflaged body armor that adjusted itself to the ambient yellow-brown-green surroundings, the Marines assumed a kneeling position and slowly waved their Mark VI plasma rifles back and forth in a distinctly menacing fashion. Helmeted and goggled, the Marines seemed to belong to no species but their own unique warrior race.

Three officers, helmeted but with their goggles up, walked briskly from the SAL toward the knot of onlookers. Governor Rhinehart, decked out in his Imperials, stepped forward to meet them. One of the officers approached him and saluted smartly.

"Major Delbert Barnes, Executive Officer, First Regiment, Fifth Imperial Marine Division, reporting, sir."

Rhinehart returned the salute and extended his hand to the Marine. Major Barnes took it in his own. "Imperial Governor Rhinehart, and I'm mighty glad to see you here, Major. Allow me to present Colonel Jangleth of the Army of Jhino."

Barnes saluted the diminutive Jhino, Jangleth returned it, and the two shook hands. The Major then turned and indicated the two officers standing behind him. "This is Bravo Company Commander Captain Hobart Zwingli, and his Exec, Lieutenant Betty Ann Singh."

Salutes, handshakes, and introductions complete, Barnes looked around at the harborside scene, and observed, "Area seems secure, sir."

"Oh, quite, quite," Rhinehart assured him. "None of those Myn buggers within twenty miles of here. The Jhino have things well in hand."

Barnes looked at Zwingli, said, "Captain," then Zwingli turned to Singh, and said, "Lieutenant." Singh ran off and issued some orders to a sergeant, and the Marines came out of their defensive posture, pulled up their goggles, and got their first good look at Mynjhino.

"Sir," said Major Barnes, "we came in from Hogarth, out on the Frontier, and our orders are at least two weeks old. Am I to understand that the Jhino have occupied Dhanj?"

"That's right, Major. I can see that we need to sit down and have a talk. The situation here has changed considerably since your orders were issued. Of course, you and your troops are now subject to my own orders, but I'll make everything clear. If you would care to join me in my limo, we'll take you over to the Compound and my Residence, where we can discuss this in comfort."

Barnes spoke briefly to Zwingli, then joined Jangleth and the Governor in the limo and sped off toward the Compound.

AS SOON AS THE LIMO WAS OUT OF SIGHT, FIVE humans emerged from behind a low, adobe building and approached Captain Zwingli. One of them was a stunningly beautiful woman who, he realized to his shock, was the ex-wife of the Emperor—the one he had seen in a news-vid before leaving Hogarth. She had been nearly naked in that vid, and she was nearly naked now in revealing, low-cut jeans and a flimsy transparent top that didn't really cover anything. Zwingli reflexively snapped to attention.

Gloria held out her hand and smiled warmly. "Captain Zwingli, welcome to Mynjhino. I'm Gloria VanDeen, Dexta Coordinating Supervisor for Beta-5."

"Yes, ma'am!" snapped Zwingli, taking the soft flesh of her hand in his own. Zwingli was twenty-seven years old, had been on the Frontier for two years, and had not seen a human female in all that time, aside from other Marines, who didn't count. As Company Commander, he could not cohabit with anyone under his command.

"Captain," said Gloria, "I'd like you to meet Melinda Throneberry, Imperial Secretary for Mynjhino, Undersecretary for Administration Brian Hawkes, and my assistant, Petra Nash. Oh, and this is Bryce Denton, of Empire News Service. He's here with my permission, and will not be recording what we say or using it in any reports. You can trust him. Isn't that right, Bryce?"

Denton nodded, and Zwingli shook hands all around.

"Is there somewhere we can talk in private?" Gloria asked.

"Over here in the SAL," Zwingli said. They followed him to the Marine vehicle, ducked slightly to get through the main hatch, then sat down on the benches that lined each side of the compartment.

"Captain," Gloria said, "we wanted to talk with you because there are some things you need to know."

"In a few minutes," said Hawkes, "Governor Rhinchart is going to unload a steaming heap of bullshit all over your Major. You and your troops are subject to Imperial orders, and we're just Dexta, but before you do anything, you should know the truth about what's been going on here. Then you can brief your Major when he gets back. Okay with you, Captain?"

"Sir? Ma'am? I'd welcome any information you can give me. We got here expecting a hot LZ with hostile

Myn crawling all over it. Nobody told us anything about these Jhino. We just saddle up and go where they tell us—first to go, last to know. I don't mind telling you, I'm kind of confused."

"We'll see if we can do something about that, Captain," Gloria told him.

GLORIA AND PETRA SAT IN THEIR BORROWED office, munching bad sandwiches and sipping weak, lukewarm coffee. With the departure of the Myn staff, the quality of food in the Compound had declined precipitously. The Compound itself was far from tidy, and there was no one to make the beds or sweep the floors.

Petra had been uncharacteristically silent all day, and Cloria looked at her with concern. "Are you okay?" she asked.

Petra managed a smile. "I'm fine," she said. "We had a memorial service for Ricardo and Franklin yesterday. It was . . . very nice. Gloria? Don't worry about me. I can handle this."

Gloria reached for her hand. "Are you sure?"

"When we go back to Earth," she said, "I'll have nine days to cry my eyes out in the privacy of the Flyer. Until then, I can be as strong as I have to be. Really. But speaking of going back to Earth, what about Hawkes?"

Gloria shrugged her shoulders. "He says he'd rather be staked out on an anthill than live in New York, and I can't stay here. So I guess we'll go our separate ways."

"Do you love him?"

Gloria had intentionally avoided asking herself that question. "I think," she said, after a moment's thought, "that Hawkes is probably the best man I've ever met. He's handsome, intelligent, strong, brave, and fantastic in bed. What's not to love?"

"But do you *love* him?" Petra persisted. "I mean really love him?"

"What are you getting at?"

"Gloria, if you love him, *don't lose him!*"

"Petra..."

"Yeah, I know, who am I to be giving Gloria VanDeen advice about life and love? I just don't want to see you go through what I'm going through now."

"It's not the same, Petra. I don't know if you loved Ricardo or were only infatuated with him, but either way, his death was a horrible shock to you. Death is so damned final. But if I lose Hawkes now, well, who can tell what the future will bring? At least Hawkes and I *have* futures, whether together or apart. And you have a future too, Petra. Don't let this ruin it for you."

Petra nodded. "I know," she said. "It's a big galaxy, a lot of men in it. But right now...I just have all this *pain*..." A tear ran down Petra's cheek, her chin trembled, and she turned away from Gloria. "I'm all right, dammit!" Petra insisted in a choked voice. "Don't hug me, don't say anything, okay?"

"Okay," said Gloria. She turned and looked out the window at the rising columns of smoke from the city of Dhanj.

A FEW MINUTES LATER, GLORIA RECEIVED THE summons she had been waiting for. Upon her return from Pecos the previous night, she had sent Rhinehart a recording of her media briefing. For good measure, she had sent one to Sweet, as well. Now, the Governor wanted to see her.

She walked across the Compound to the Residence, and was directed to the Governor's office by Preston Riley, one of his Imperial aides. When she entered, Rhinehart, seated behind his desk, did not rise. Gloria took a chair in front of the desk, sat down, and waited. Rhinehart stared at her in silence for several moments. Finally, he said, "Just what do you think you're about, young lady? Just what the bloody hell do you think you're about?"

"Are you referring to my media briefing, Governor?"

"Of course I'm referring to your media briefing. The gall of it. The unmitigated gall! Who told you that you could go to Pecos? Who gave you permission to give that impudent briefing?"

"I went on my own authority," Gloria said calmly. "And I don't need your permission to brief the media."

Rhinehart rose halfway out of his chair, then managed to bring himself back down. "Well, we'll just see about that, Ms. VanDeen! Rest assured that we will. I understand that you've also been talking to the Marines. Well, that will cease, too, as of this moment. Neither you nor my staff will have any further contact with Marine personnel without my express consent, which you are not about to get. Is that understood?"

"I understand that you can give orders to your staff. But I'm not *on* your staff, Governor. I take orders from Dexta Headquarters, not from you."

"While you are here, you will take orders from me and like it!" Rhinehart roared.

"Like hell," Gloria answered. "Look it up. *Dexta Code*, Chapter Twenty-seven, Paragraph Nine, Subsections C, D, and E. You have no authority over me at all, Governor. What's more, if I require assistance in the performance of my duties from resident Dexta staff, I have full power as Coordinating Supervisor for this jurisdiction to enlist their aid, with or without reference to existing local authority, which means *you*."

"This is nothing short of insubordination, Ms. VanDeen. Your superiors in Manhattan will hear of it, you have my word on that."

"Fine," said Gloria. "They'll be glad to see that I know the *Dexta Code*, and they'll probably wonder why you don't."

Rhinehart pursed his lips and stopped himself from responding. Gloria hid a smile; Rhinehart should have known better than to get into a rule-book battle with someone from Dexta.

"Do you understand what you have done, Ms. VanDeen?" Rhinehart asked her in a calmer tone.

"I believe I do. I told the people of the Empire the truth about what has happened here."

"Truth? Fantasies about conspiracies? Scare stories about genocides? It won't wash. Oh, the media always love a scandal, and you certainly provided them with that. But the day will come when you'll have to answer for your words, make no mistake. And it will not be a happy day for you."

"Governor, just what do you think is going to happen here once the Jhino complete their invasion?"

"For one thing," said Rhinehart, "the killing of humans will cease. The terrorists will be apprehended, order will be restored, and we'll all get on with our lives."

"Except for the thousands—perhaps millions—of Myn who will die in the meantime."

"Oh, spare me your lamentations, Ms. VanDeen. The Jhino are a civilized and honorable race. They have given me assurances, and I believe them. There will be no genocide, no mass starvation. At this moment, their army is assembling in Dhanj, and soon they will move beyond the city and provide food and shelter for those panicky Myn you say you care so much about. It's all been arranged, Ms. VanDeen."

"Is that how you eased your conscience, Governor? You told yourself that you could make your little deal with Servitor and the Jhino, but it would be all right because no real harm would be done? Spirit, don't you realize how much the Myn and Jhino hate each other? Do you really think that thousands of Jhino armed with automatic weapons are going to pass up an opportunity to slaughter the Myn? Are you really that naïve?"

"I don't deny that some blood will be shed," Rhinehart conceded. "But it won't be *human* blood, and that's all that really matters to the Empire. If you think the Emperor or the Parliament or anyone else really gives a damn about a bunch of benighted fuzzy-wuzzies, Ms. VanDeen, then it is you who are being naïve. Your attempt to stir up public sentiment against me will accomplish nothing. By the time anyone can even respond to your pathetic bleating, the deed will be done, and so much the better."

"Their first response," Gloria warned him, "will be to remove you from office, Governor."

"Let them!" Rhinehart cried. "Do you think I want to spend the rest of my life on this Spirit-forsaken sinkhole? If the Household disapproves of my actions, they can remove me if they please, but my actions will stand. Neither the Emperor nor the Parliament nor high-and-mighty Norman Mingus himself will be able to reverse what will happen here in the next week."

"And so," said Gloria, "you'll get your suitcase full of crowns, or your secret account on New Helvetia, won't you? You'll have delivered what you promised, Servitor and the Jhino will be satisfied, and everyone will be happy."

"Everyone who matters, Ms. VanDeen," Rhinehart smirked. He was clearly beginning to enjoy himself.

"There will be investigations," said Gloria.

"Of course. There always are, aren't there? But they'll come to nothing, because nothing can be proven. I'm sure you'll have your big moment, Ms. VanDeen, testifying before some Ministerial Inquiry, beating your lovely breast about the monstrous injustice of it all. But the moment will pass, and nothing will have changed. Don't you understand what you're up against? At this moment, I have the full legal authority of the Empire at my disposal, Imperial Marines stand ready to execute my orders, an entire army is prepared to march, and a colossal corporate entity is coordinating a plan that cannot possibly fail. I suggest to you, Ms. VanDeen, that attempting to oppose me at this late date would accomplish nothing, and would be neither wise nor safe."

Gloria got to her feet. "Are you threatening me, Governor?"

"You're so fucking smart, dear Gloria," he replied. "What do *you* think?"

GLORIA PACED AROUND MELINDA THRONE-
berry's office, mumbling curses under her breath. Melinda, Petra, and Hawkes watched her perambulations and kept a safe distance.

Outside the Compound, the *Myrtle McCormick* had arrived, and Marines were busily securing the area. Two hundred of the deadliest warriors in the galaxy stood ready to defend them from a nonexistent threat, while three miles away in the center of the city, an army was preparing for a massacre. And 862 light-years away, no one on Earth even knew what was happening.

"We need a plan," said Melinda. "We need to think this through and make a plan."

A plan for *what?* Hawkes wondered. Incapable of coping with the larger crisis, he focused on a smaller and more immediate threat. Gloria had made herself a target, and somehow, he had to keep her out of harm's way. But he couldn't even conceive of a way to accomplish *that*. They were effectively prisoners in the Compound, and between his Imperial aides, the Jhino, and the Marines, Rhinehart could do just about whatever he wanted.

Hawkes didn't know quite what to make of Gloria. She was a primal force, like some quantum anomaly ripping through the fabric of space-time. She distorted what Hawkes had come to think of as reality. Her body warped his mind, and her mind almost frightened him. Gloria knew what she wanted and always found a way to get it; the fact that she wanted *him* was more than a little unsettling. Part of him was relieved that when this was all over, one way or another, she would be returning to Earth, where distance would insulate him from the power she had over him; and part of him utterly refused to accept the thought of losing her. Whatever happened, he was determined that he would *not* lose her to the threats and machinations of Rhinehart or Sweet or any other malicious bastard. He would do *anything* to prevent that from happening.

Something like a plan began to take root deep in Hawkes's mind.

He knew that he had to protect her. It wasn't even a choice—it was something he *had* to do. Hawkes took in the subtle curves of her golden body, overflowing from her low-cut jeans, and the dark, jutting protrusions of her perfect nipples spilling free from the minimal confinement of her clothing as she moved. He studied her face, felt the hypnotic, gravitational pull of her too-blue eyes, and sensed the determination in the set of her jaw and thin, tightly drawn lips. She was *his,* dammit—at least, as far as she would ever be any man's. If the Emperor couldn't keep her, what hope could Hawkes have? And yet he knew that he would do anything—*anything*—to protect her.

His plan began to take a tangible form. It was becoming real.

Rhinehart had threatened her. There was, he realized, a way to deal with Rhinehart. He was appalled to find himself thinking such a thought, but looking again at Gloria, he knew that he could do it if he had to. To protect Gloria, he could do whatever was necessary—no matter what it might cost.

A Marine sergeant entered the office and looked at Melinda. "Ms. Throneberry, ma'am," he said, "Major Barnes would like to have a word with you."

"Sorry, Sergeant," Melinda told him. "I can't speak

with the Major or any other Marine. I'm under strict orders from the Governor."

"I'm not," said Gloria. "Where is he?"

"Just outside the gate, ma'am," said the sergeant. "If you'll follow me."

"Gloria," said Hawkes, "be careful."

"Hey," Gloria laughed, "I'll be surrounded by two hundred Marines. What could happen?"

"A PLEASURE TO MEET YOU, MS. VANDEEN," Major Barnes told her. Pleasure didn't even begin to cover it, he thought. It was damned lonely out on the Frontier. "You're the Coordinating Supervisor for Beta-5?"

"That's right, Major. And you command these troops?"

Barnes nodded. "Captain Zwingli is the Company Commander and is in effective command of this detachment. I'm actually the XO for the First of the Fifth, but Colonel Bradshaw decided to send me along to handle the diplomatic niceties and higher-level horsesh—uh, pardon me, ma'am—the higher-level complications."

"It's all right, Major, I know what horseshit is."

"Seems to me," said Barnes, "that there's a fair amount of it around here. My orders tell me one thing, Governor Rhinehart says everything has changed and tells me something entirely different, and you Dexta people gang up on my Company CO and tell him to tell me not to believe anything the Governor tells me. It was a hell of a lot less confusing pacifying Hogarth. All we had to deal with there was intelligent lizards who liked to have humans for lunch. Around here, seems like the humans want to have each other for lunch."

"Then you understand the basic situation," Gloria said. "Is there anything I can do to clarify things further?"

"What I'd like to do," said Barnes, "is take a look for myself and see how things stand. I'm going up in a scout skimmer and reconnoiter the area, and I could use a local guide. Would you care to come along, ma'am?"

"Unfortunately, I'm something of a stranger here myself, Major, but I'll do the best I can. Undersecretary Hawkes could give you a much better picture, but he and the rest of the resident staff are under orders from the Governor not to talk to you or any other Marine."

"I heard," said Barnes. "Mighty strange order. As you know, ma'am, we can only take orders from the Governor, not from Dexta. But I'd be mighty interested in hearing anything you might have to tell me."

"Let's go, then," said Gloria. "I'll give you an earful."

GLORIA AND BARNES GOT INTO THE BACK OF AN open scout skimmer and belted themselves in. A corporal served as pilot, and a sergeant with a plasma rifle at the ready rode shotgun. The skimmer whined into life and quickly rose two hundred feet above the Compound. Gloria could see armed Marines patrolling the entire perimeter, while isolated detachments of Jhino troops watched from a distance.

"If I could make a suggestion, Major," said Gloria, "I think it might be a good idea to go inland, east of the city, and get a look at the Myn refugees."

"My thought as well, ma'am. We've got a recon satellite up there, and the images show at least a million of them in camps and on the roads. What they don't show is anything that looks like an army or even anything that looks remotely organized. What we seem to have out there is nothing but chaos."

"The only army here belongs to the Jhino, and they are armed with repros of AK-47 assault rifles. The Myn don't have any weapons at all, except maybe some flintlock muskets left over from their last war, nearly a century ago."

"Yes, ma'am. I saw those Jhino AKs. Beautiful, mint-condition museum pieces. Where the hell did they get them?"

"They've got a factory cranking them out somewhere over on Jhino. Best guess is that Servitor smuggled in rolling mill and machine tool equipment on an Imperium freighter, and the software to run them. I don't suppose your satellite could spot the factory?"

"We'll get right on it." Barnes tapped his wristcom and rattled off a series of orders to his Intelligence Officer, who would reprogram the recon satellite to begin a search of Jhino. "I can't promise quick results," Barnes said. "We've only got the one satellite, and Jhino's a pretty big place. But we might get lucky."

"If you find it, could you take it out?"

"We could if someone gave us orders to," said Barnes. "But I get the impression that we wouldn't get such orders from the Governor."

"Rhinehart is in bed with Servitor and the Jhino," Gloria told him. "I can't prove it, but he as much as admitted it."

"You get me proof, and maybe we can do something. Without it . . ."

"I know."

"As things stand, my orders are to protect human lives and stand by while the Jhino do whatever they want. I don't like it much, but orders are orders."

The skimmer cruised over deserted suburbs and abandoned small towns. Every Myn within twenty miles of Dhanj seemed to have vanished from the face of the planet. Finally, they began to see small groups of stragglers on the dusty roads, which were lined with meager bundles of possessions that had grown too heavy for the tiny Myn to carry any farther. As they skimmed onward, the isolated pockets of Myn turned into a steady stream, then a broad, sluggish river of them, moving steadily eastward, away from the Jhino.

In what had once been a field of GalaxCo pharmaceuticals, they came upon a sprawling encampment. A few tents were visible, and a low haze of smoke from a thousand cook fires clung close to the ground in the humid air.

"Jesus Christ!" exclaimed Barnes, who followed the old religion. "There must be a hundred thousand of them."

"And this is just one spot," said Gloria. "There are eight main roads leading out of the city, and every one of them is probably just as crowded as this one. There were a million Myn in the city itself, with probably another million in the nearby suburbs and towns. And it looks as if every one of them is a refugee."

"Can they get food out here?" Barnes wondered.

"I don't see how," said Gloria. "Myn is mostly just small towns, once you get away from Dhanj. Even if they were organized, which they aren't, they don't have the transport to get a significant amount of food to these people. And when the refugees come to a town, odds are that everyone in that town will start running, too. When the Jhino start marching, it will get even worse."

"Lord above." Barnes sighed. "Okay, I've seen enough. Corporal, take us back to the city. I want to get a look at the Jhino forces."

Smoke rising from the fires in the city was visible from ten miles away. In the open skimmer, the breeze blowing off the ocean brought an acrid scent to their nostrils. Gloria had grown accustomed to the stench of the Myn, but this was something different.

"Over there," Gloria said, pointing to the left. "That's the Palqui, the Myn government center. We haven't heard anything from them since the invasion began."

"Give us a look, Corporal," Barnes instructed. The

skimmer swooped down and left, and from above, the intricate nested walls and gardens of the Palqui looked incomparably peaceful. But in the broad plaza fronting the Palqui, Gloria could see what looked like several thousand Jhino troops assembled in parade-ground order, with neat rows of tents forming a bivouac ground. Sunlight glinted off the barrels of their weapons. Gloria couldn't see a single Myn anywhere in the area.

"Must be close to five thousand of them in this one spot," said Barnes. "Any idea of the total?"

"Not really," said Gloria. "They're bringing them in via Transit from Jhino. By now, they could easily have ten or twenty thousand in Dhanj."

"They'd have to bring in supplies as well as troops," Barnes pointed out. "From what I see here, it looks like they're concentrating on establishing a supply depot. Once they have an adequate stockpile built up, they'll be ready to move. Two or three more days, at a guess." Barnes sniffed the air. "What the hell is burning around here? Corporal, see that smoke column on the left? Take us over there."

The skimmer cruised over the low buildings of Dhanj toward an open area of parkland, where black, greasy smoke billowed upward from what looked like a stack of yellow-brown bundles. They looked like duffel bags, or rolled-up carpets from a distance, but as the skimmer approached, the truth of what they were seeing hit them with a force that was almost physical in its impact.

"Spirit!" Gloria gasped.

"God damn," breathed Barnes. "Corporal, take us down!"

The skimmer landed at the edge of the parkland. The sergeant leaped out and leveled his plasma rifle at the Jhino troops in the area. Barnes and Gloria followed him out. Gloria nearly gagged from the smell.

A hundred yards away, the Jhino were dragging the

small, yellow-brown bundles toward the fire and tossing them into it.

The yellow-brown bundles were the bodies of Myn.

The Jhino troops started toward them, and the sergeant looked expectantly toward his Major.

"For two cents..." Barnes muttered.

"Major!" Gloria said sharply.

Barnes looked at her, then nodded his head. "Corporal," Barnes barked, "get us the hell out of here!" And then he added, "Before I puke."

chapter 20

RED-FACED AND STEAMING, MAJOR BARNES
emerged from the Governor's Residence and shook his
head forlornly at Gloria. He had just spent half an hour
in a shouting match with the Governor, all to no avail.

"At first, the son of a bitch refused to believe me
when I told him what I saw," said Barnes. "And then he
said that the Myn had probably just killed each other in
their panic, and that the Jhino were only performing a
necessary act of public sanitation. *Public sanitation!*"
Barnes spat on the dirt of the Compound.

"There must be some way..." said Gloria.

"Find one, then!" Barnes snapped. "Find me just
one scrap of legal authority, and those fucking Jhino will
wonder what hit them. But I've *got* to have that authority, Ms. VanDeen. I'm an Imperial Marine, and my father before me. No matter what, I have to follow the
chain of command. If the Marines ever started freelancing, the whole Empire would fall apart. Rhinehart is the
biggest four-flushing bastard I've ever met, but I'm un-

der his orders, and if he tells me to jump, all I can do is say, 'Which way and how high, sir?'"

"I understand, Major," Gloria told him. "I'm not blaming you."

"I'm going back to the *Myrt*," he said, "and order up a recon skimmer. If I can't do anything else, then goddammit, at least I can document this horror show."

"Good idea," said Gloria. "In fact, would you mind taking along a journalist?"

"For once in my life, Ms. VanDeen, I would be overjoyed to take along a journalist. You got one stashed away around here?"

"Bryce Denton of ENS. I'll reach him on the comm and have him meet you at your ship."

"Fine," said Barnes. He started to walk toward the gate, then stopped and looked back toward Gloria. "Find me that authority, Ms. VanDeen!" he pleaded. "Find it!"

"IF THE GOVERNOR WERE INCAPACITATED," said Melinda, "then I would be empowered to act in his place. But I suppose it's too much to hope that he'll come down with another migraine."

Melinda was meeting with Gloria, Petra, Sonia, and Hawkes in her office over a dinner of stale sandwiches and bad coffee. The miserable food had not improved anyone's mood, and so far, little had been accomplished. Melinda had appointed Hawkes as acting Undersecretary for Security, since legally the position needed to be filled, and she thought Quesada was too inexperienced for the job under the present circumstances. In any case, Hawkes had little to do these days as Undersecretary for Administration, since there was nothing left in Myn to administer.

"Couldn't we have him declared, you know, incompetent or something?" Petra asked. "I mean, his migraines are a matter of record. Couldn't we get a doctor to say that he's too sick to do his job?"

"Good idea," said Melinda, "but the only human doctor left in Myn is Levin, and he's a personal friend of Rhinehart's. No chance that he would do it."

"What about the Marines?" asked Gloria. "They have a Medical Officer with them, don't they?"

"But he'd have to examine Rhinehart," Melinda pointed out. "Which means that both Rhinehart and Levin would have to consent to it, which they won't."

"Well, then," Petra persisted, "couldn't we find a way to *make* him sick? Slip something into his food?"

Everyone looked at her.

"I know, I know," she said, feeling the force of their gaze. "But we have to do *something*!"

"I'm not saying that I object to the idea in principle," Melinda said at last, "but I think the actual execution would be a problem."

"Execution," said Hawkes. He said nothing more, but he didn't have to. He looked at the faces staring at him. "He's already threatened Gloria. And Myn are dying by the thousands. I've already thought about it—and unless we can come up with something else, I'd be willing to do it."

"Hawkes," Gloria cried. "You *can't*!"

"Dammit, Gloria, what choice do we have? If you could go back in time and kill Hitler before the Holocaust, or Fukajima before the Nardoni Massacre, wouldn't you do it?"

"Come on, Hawkes," Gloria replied. "That's Ethics 101 bullshit. This isn't some theoretical time-machine exercise. We're talking about a real situation and a real person."

"That's my point," said Hawkes. "Real lives are at stake here. By taking one, we could save thousands, maybe millions."

Melinda got to her feet. "Philosophical debates bore me," she said. "I think I'm going to take a walk.

Continue your theoretical discussion, if you wish, but I don't really care to know how your debate turns out. Sonia, maybe you'd like to join me?"

"Not me," said Sonia. "I *love* philosophical debates. Don't worry, Melinda, we won't tell you anything you don't want to hear."

The Imperial Secretary left the room. There was an extended silence, finally broken by Gloria.

"I just finished talking with Major Barnes," she said. "He very wisely pointed out to me that if the Marines were to start freelancing, the whole Empire would fall apart. That applies to Dexta, too, Hawkes."

"Now who's talking sophomore-year bullshit?" Hawkes demanded. "I pull the trigger on Rhinehart to prevent a genocide, and suddenly the whole Empire crumbles as a result? I don't buy it."

"Maybe not immediately," Gloria conceded. "And there have been plenty of assassinations in Imperial history. More than you realize, in fact. But that doesn't make it right, and I don't feel comfortable being a part of it."

"Take a walk, then," Hawkes suggested. "Better yet, *I'll* take a walk, then nobody else has to know a thing about this. We had dinner, we talked about the Empire Cup soccer matches, then we all went our separate ways."

He got to his feet and started toward the door. "I like Ortega," he said. "Those high-gravity teams always have an advantage when they play on a one-G world. And they've got a goaltender who's about the size of a house. I wouldn't be surprised if—"

Hawkes, going out the door, ran into Melinda, coming back in.

"Short walk," said Sonia.

"I hate to interrupt your theoretical discussion," Melinda said, "but I think it just became moot. Take a look out the window."

Everyone went to the windows. Out in the

Compound, they saw a limo parked near the Residence being loaded with luggage by Rhinehart's aides. A moment later, Rhinehart emerged from the Residence and quickly got into the limo. The aides followed him into it, and the skimmer rose straight up fifty feet. Ignoring the northwest gate, it spun around and sailed out of the Compound over the southeast wall. It headed into the city and out of sight.

"I think Rhinehart just figured out the same thing we did," Sonia said. "He'll hide out with the Jhino until it's all over."

"Well, I'm relieved," said Gloria. "I think."

"Isn't he abandoning his post or something?" asked Petra.

"Not if he stays within fifty miles and maintains communication," said Melinda as she sat down again. "We're going to have to come up with something else."

"I'm sick of the way the *Dexta Code* keeps telling us what we *can't* do," said Petra. "Isn't there something that we *can* do?"

"We can tear up the fucking *Code!*" Hawkes snarled. "A minute ago, we were ready to kill the bastard—or, at least, I was. I say it's time to ignore the rules and start playing dirty. If we can't find a legitimate way for the Marines to act, then let's make something up."

"Barnes is no fool," said Gloria. "It would have to look awfully good, and even then, I'm not sure he'd bite. He knows the *Marine Regs* as well as we know the *Code.*"

"It doesn't have to stand up after the fact," Hawkes insisted. "I'm willing to take the consequences of an Inquiry Board if it comes to that. All we need is something that will convince Barnes that he has the authority to act, whether he really does or not."

"Maybe we could doctor the *Code*," Petra suggested. "Insert some bogus paragraph that Barnes would accept as legitimate."

"That has possibilities," Gloria admitted. "If we could—"

"Hey, kids!" Sonia called out abruptly. They all looked at her. "If you don't mind a suggestion from a half-drunk old woman, you're going about this in the wrong way. About twenty years ago, I was on staff on Beringia. We had a Governor who was totally paranoid and losing his grip, but we couldn't force him out because the only doctor on the planet was his own brother, who was even crazier than he was. So we wound up making his paranoid fantasies come true. We hit him from all sides with about a dozen different obscure rules and regulations from the *Code*. Forced him into doing truly insane things that he would never have done otherwise. Finally, he went stark raving mad, and even his brother had no choice but to declare him *non compos mentis*."

"And your point is?" asked Melinda.

"My point is, don't tear up the *Code*—use it! If we can't find something in three thousand pages of the densest, most prolix and persnickety prose in the history of civilization, then we just aren't trying. And remember, Rhinehart isn't our only target here. There's also Sweet and Servitor, and the Jhino."

"And Tatiana," Melinda added thoughtfully.

"And dear Tatiana," Sonia agreed. "Plus the Marines. If we go at this hammer and tongs, we just might be able to hit someone where it hurts with three thousand pages' worth of *Dexta Code*. Let's remember who and what we are, folks. We're Dexta *bureaucrats*! We make the galaxy go 'round."

TATIANA MARKOVA ROAMED AROUND THE Governor's spacious bedroom, feeling trapped. She had wanted to leave the Compound with him, but Rhinehart told her that she had to stay. She would be his legally necessary point of contact, as well as his eyes and ears in the Compound. That was all very well for Rhinehart, but Tatiana was left here all alone, surrounded by people who detested her.

She picked up her pad and again reread her letter of resignation from Dexta. If things got too ugly, she would transmit it to Throneberry and be on her way. She had done everything Sweet had asked of her, and more. The secret account in the bank on New Helvetia was already set up, and Sweet could transfer the promised payment with a couple of keystrokes. Delaying it any longer was unfair and unreasonable. The outcome was no longer in doubt. She would go to him and demand that he send the transfer order; he couldn't refuse her.

Without knocking first, Gloria and Melinda barged into the bedroom. "Good evening, Tatiana," Gloria said pleasantly. "I think it's time we had a little talk."

"I have nothing to say to either one of you," Tatiana said, a defiant edge in her tone. "Get out."

"You can talk now, or you can talk later, Tatiana. Personally, I hope it will be later, because later will be a lot of fun for me and a lot of pain for you."

"What do you mean by that?"

"You're a Thirteen, I'm a Thirteen," Gloria said. "If we can't resolve our differences calmly and rationally, Dexta has a time-honored alternative."

"You can't be serious!" Tatiana was aghast. "Do you seriously expect us to fight it out like a couple of moronic Fifteens in a restroom? That's Manhattan bullshit. I won't do it."

Gloria walked toward Tatiana, who involuntarily backed up until she bumped into the Governor's huge bed. "You don't have a choice, Tatiana." Gloria gave her a very dangerous-looking smile.

Tatiana looked toward Melinda, who was still standing by the door. "You can't let this happen, Melinda. Tell her!"

Melinda shook her head. "None of my business," she said. "This is between you Thirteens. I'm just here to make sure everybody abides by the rules. No permanent damage allowed, gals. Gloria, that means you can't break her neck or turn her pretty face into something that resembles a sackful of potatoes."

Gloria slipped out of her shoes. "No problem," she said. "All I'm going to do is kick her ass. Like so."

Gloria sprang forward, caught Tatiana by the shoulder, swung her around, and gave her a sidewheeling Qatsima kick in her hindquarters. Tatiana cried out as she flew forward onto the bed. Gloria grabbed her, pulled her back to her feet, and administered another boot to the backside.

Tatiana recovered her balance and ran into a corner of the room, her back to the walls. Anger had momentarily bested her fear, and she snarled, "Come and get me, bitch!"

"Gladly," Gloria answered. She spread her arms to keep Tatiana cornered, feinted left, went right, got Tatiana by the upper arm and elbow and swung her out into the room, where she let fly another kick. Tatiana hit the rich Myn carpet face-first, scrambled back to her feet, and ran for the door. Melinda stood there, her arms crossed, and refused to budge.

"Get out of my way!" Tatiana screamed.

"I don't think so," Melinda said placidly.

Tatiana looked behind her and saw Gloria approaching. Frantically, she started to grab Melinda and shove her out of the way, but some deep-seated bureaucratic instinct stayed her hand.

"Smart," Melinda observed. "I'm your superior. Lay one hand on me, and you'll spend the next ten years on a prison world."

"Fuck this shit!" Tatiana screamed. "You can't do anything to me. I quit!" She dashed past an unresisting Gloria and grabbed her pad. She ran back to Melinda and held the pad up to her face.

"There!" she shouted. "That's my resignation, and I just transmitted it to you. I'm out of Dexta and there's not one fucking thing either of you can do about it, so leave me the hell alone! Touch me again, Gloria, and it's not some bullshit Dexta matter, it's criminal assault!"

"Nice try, Tatiana," said Melinda. "But your resignation does not become effective until it is officially approved and endorsed by your immediate superior, which is me, such approval and endorsement not to be unreasonably withheld or delayed. Resignee may file a formal protest if approval is not granted within five working days of receipt by said superior, pursuant to exceptions noted below, see Subsections F, G, and H."

"What?"

Gloria grabbed Tatiana by her long, dark hair, spun her away from Melinda, and gave her the best kick yet. It sent her sprawling onto the floor. Before she could get up, Gloria nailed her again.

Sobbing and gasping, Tatiana screamed, *"Stop it! Stop it!"*

But Gloria didn't stop. She thought of the dead Myn, and of the dead humans, and of Ricardo, and she went right on kicking. Finally, she felt Melinda's hand on her shoulder.

"That's enough, Gloria," she said.

"No, it's not," said Gloria, and she lashed out one more time, connecting with such force that she lost her balance on the follow-through and fell on her own backside. She pushed herself back up, looked down at the sobbing Tatiana, and realized that she didn't feel as good about this as she had thought she would. She turned away and went to lean against the door and catch her breath.

Melinda stepped forward. "Tatiana Markova," she said formally, "you are hereby charged under the provisions of the *Dexta Code,* Chapter Seven, Paragraphs Eleven through Eighteen, with malfeasance of office, accepting bribes and other illegal emoluments, conspiracy to commit a breach of *Code,* and such other instances of misconduct as may be determined by subsequent investigation. Pending resolution of these matters, your resignation is moot. You are further advised that pending the convening of an appropriate board or panel, subject to the laws governing this colony and the provisions of the *Dexta Code* and the *Imperial Code,* you are to be held in administrative confinement under suspicion of having participated in felonious criminal acts, to wit, treason, conspiracy to commit murder, and accessory before and after the fact in the murders of Ricardo Olivera and James Franklin, Dexta officials then engaged in the lawful performance of their duties. Now get up, bitch."

TATIANA DIDN'T TALK. SAFELY LOCKED AWAY in a room in the basement of the administration building, she stood in a corner—it would be quite some time before she sat again—and brooded in ill-tempered silence.

The threat of criminal charges was bullshit. There was no evidence and they couldn't prove anything. But the internal Dexta administrative complaints could be a problem. They could keep her locked up almost indefinitely, pending a hearing sometime in the nebulous future. She was entitled to an advocate within Dexta, but there wasn't a single Dexta staffer on the planet that she could trust. Sweet could get her a lawyer to handle the criminal charges—if any were actually filed—but internally, Dexta washed its own dirty laundry. One thing was certain: The only people who could get her out were Rhinehart and Sweet. She would be cutting her own throat if she said a word against either one of them.

TWO FLOORS ABOVE HER, THE GROUP IN Melinda Throneberry's office had reached much the same conclusion. They had hoped to frighten Tatiana into talking, but it seemed that they had accomplished exactly the opposite. Eventually, they might hope to wear down her resistance; administrative detention could go on almost forever under the *Dexta Code*. But they had no time for such a strategy.

The criminal charges would also take time to process. With a human population of barely ten thousand, Mynjhino didn't even have a legal system, as such. Routine civil matters were adjudicated by the Imperial Secretary. In the rare event of a felony charge, the entire case would be transferred to Pecos, where lawyers, judges, and juries were available. Filing charges against Tatiana would get them nothing.

"Well," said Melinda, "at least we've removed a pawn from the board. Rhinehart has to communicate directly with me now, and won't have Tatiana spying for him."

"I doubt that she really knows very much anyway," said Hawkes. "She was just a go-between. Sweet aimed her at Rhinehart and she roped him into the plot, but I can't see Sweet telling her anything important."

"What we need," said Sonia, "is to get Rhinehart and Sweet pointing fingers at each other. I have a feeling that our distinguished Imperial Governor would sing like a bird if we could apply a little pressure."

"How are we going to do that?" Melinda asked. "He's safe with the Jhino, now. We can't touch him."

"So that leaves Sweet," said Hawkes. "Unless he's holed up with the Jhino, too."

Petra had been staring at her pad for hours, until her eyeballs felt like hot lumps of molten metal. The *Dexta Code* had apparently been written by sadists, for the use of masochists. But she was nothing if not persevering, and her effort finally turned up something that might prove useful.

"Hey, Gloria," Petra said. "When Sweet gave you that jigli tea the other day, did he tell you what it was?"

"No. Why?"

"Then I think we've got him!" Petra grinned. She

held up her pad for Gloria and the others to see. "Check it out. It seems that it is illegal to administer psychotropic, hallucinogenic, or erotogenic substances to Dexta personnel engaged in the lawful performance of their duties, without the informed consent of the recipient."

The others huddled around and read the relevant section of the *Code* on Petra's pad while she smiled triumphantly. But Melinda shook her head and frowned. "It won't do," she said. "For one thing, that happened several days ago, and no complaint was filed at the time. More importantly, the alleged act was not tied to any other criminal activity, which makes this, in itself, nothing more than a misdemeanor. We couldn't even take him into custody based on this."

"Why not?" Hawkes demanded. "The charge doesn't have to stand up in court. We just need an excuse to pull Sweet in for a few hours until his lawyer can spring him. Once Tatiana sees that we have Sweet, she might decide to open up and give us something we can actually use against him. We offer her immunity, get her talking, put the screws to Sweet, and hope he says something that we can use to arrest Rhinehart. Then we send in the Marines."

Melinda shook her head. "We can't risk stepping too far over the line," she cautioned. "If we bring Sweet in on charges that are too obviously bogus, he can turn around and have his lawyer slap us with a dozen different complaints. That would give Rhinehart all the legal ammunition he needs to suspend the lot of us and get us out of the way until it's too late."

"But if we could tie the jigli business directly to an overt criminal act," said Gloria, "then we'd really have him, wouldn't we?"

"But there *was* no overt criminal act," Melinda reiterated.

"Maybe there will be," Gloria said.

"What do you have in mind?" Melinda asked her.

"Sweet wants me," said Gloria. "I think it's about time to let him have me."

SWEET HAD BEEN CERTAIN THAT SHE WOULD come back. She was too full of herself, too proud and arrogant and overconfident, to deny herself a dramatic confrontation. Sending him that vid of her media briefing on Pecos had been a warning shot across his bow, a declaration of her intent. Now, with time running out, she was maneuvering in for what she hoped would be the kill. A comm call, a request for a late-night meeting in his office—her tactics were as obvious as her clothing. Gloria VanDeen, Dexta's very own *femme fatale,* would confront the villain in his lair, tempt him with her body, dazzle him with her charm, and trip him up with her steel-trap mind. He would be putty in her hands.

In fact, it was going to be just the reverse. Sweet was neither stupid nor naive. He was not about to babble closely held secrets just to gratify his ego or gain access to that magnificent body. There was no need.

Two cups of jigli tea had had an obvious effect on her. She had certainly warmed to him, but she had left before giving in to the impulses that must have been coursing through her mind and body. Perhaps she even suspected something, although it was unlikely that she had ever heard of jigli or knew what it could do. The important thing was that even if she did suspect something, she was now certain that she could handle two cups of the stuff without losing control. She would smile and flirt, and maybe even ask for some more of that delicious tea, thinking that nothing could go wrong.

What she couldn't know or suspect was that the jigli tea he had given her was medium-grade, unrefined product. Tonight, Sweet had brewed up a kettleful of processed, refined, high-grade, maximum-potency jigli. Two cups of it would make a saint want to fuck an army. She meant to have him, but he would have her.

The only question in his mind was what to do with her afterward. It was unlikely that she would be foolish enough to come alone. She would have backup, someone out on the street waiting for her to come out of the office. If she didn't within a reasonable time, they would come in after her. Very well, that could be handled. Once he had finished with her, a quick comm call would bring a squad of armed Jhino to sweep the immediate area and detain or scare away any snooping Dexta people.

Afterward...well, accidents were easy to arrange. On the other hand, it would be easy enough to take her to the Transit, only a block away, and spirit her off to Jhino. There, she could be kept on ice until after the plan for Myn had been accomplished. Then, it would simply be a matter of waiting a few weeks until Captain Pulsipher arrived in Phanji on his next run for Imperium. For a reasonable fee, Pulsipher would take her off Mynjhino. He would never even know what cargo he was carrying.

Then, Sweet knew, it would be easy enough to transfer her to one of several worlds where, despite the halfhearted efforts of the Empire, traffic in human flesh continued unabated. And Gloria VanDeen's flesh would be priceless. With a chained collar around her neck and an implanted neurostim providing measured doses of pleasure and pain, even the haughty ex-wife of the Emperor could be turned into a docile and willing slave. Sweet smiled as he imagined the auction—the bids would go right through the roof. He might easily realize a price that would match his profits from the entire Mynjhino operation.

She would be missed, of course. There would be searches and investigations, but it wouldn't really matter. In the end, she would just be one more missing person in a war zone.

• • •

SWEET WAS STANDING IN FRONT OF HIS DESK waiting for her when Gloria arrived. He smiled at the sight of her and she smiled back at him. She was wearing nothing but a completely transparent white dress, buttoned only at her waist. Her blond pubic delta at the junction of her long, silken thighs, and her round, firm breasts were entirely uncovered. She stood before him and let him get as good a look as he wanted.

"Always a pleasure to see you, Gloria," he said.

"Good of you to agree to meet me, Randy," she told him. "We have a lot to talk about."

"Do we? Then why don't you sit down and get comfortable? Would you care for some tea? I just brewed a fresh pot."

"I'd love some," Gloria said. She sat down on the chair in front of his desk and the fabric of her dress fell away to the sides, giving Sweet a full view of what she knew he wanted.

He poured a cup from the kettle and handed it to her. "I do admire the way you dress, Gloria. High Imperial, isn't it? Is that what the ladies of Rio are wearing these days?"

"Thank you, Randy. Actually, it's more of a tribute to the Myn. To them, this signifies that I'm an honest woman who has nothing to hide." She sipped some of the tea.

"Are you, now?" asked Sweet as he leaned back on the corner of his desk and took in the view. "Well, then, suppose you tell me what brings you here tonight."

"I think you already know that."

"Ah, yes, your grand conspiracy. Very interesting media briefing, Gloria. Sam LeMoyne, our corporate legal counsel, tells me that you cleverly managed to avoid saying anything that was actionable. Didn't quite cross the line, he says, although you certainly gave everyone the impression that we at Servitor are a bunch of malicious thugs. Very nicely done. Is the tea all right? Not too strong?"

"Oh, no," Gloria said, drinking some more, "it's just fine. Tell me, did Mr. LeMoyne also happen to mention to you what the penalty is for illegal traffic in arms, bribing Dexta and Imperial officials, and conspiring to commit treason and murder?"

"No," said Sweet, "I don't believe he said anything about that. But then, why would he?"

"Then he's not part of it? This is strictly your own personal enterprise?"

"Everything I do, I do for Servitor. I'm a loyal, devoted, and honest representative of my firm."

"So Servitor is branching out, from services and software to gunrunning?"

"You have such a charmingly unsophisticated view of things, Gloria. Take this hypothetical gunrunning. Do you think anyone at Servitor would actually be so stupid as to go carting antique weapons from planet to planet?"

"How would Servitor do it, then—hypothetically?" Gloria took another sip of the tea and smiled at him.

Sweet returned her smile. "Speaking hypothetically," he said, "I would suggest that a smart operator would begin by legally importing the rolling mill equipment and machine tools necessary to manufacture the weapons in question. All quite aboveboard. Then, it would be a very simple matter of providing the software required to operate the machinery and produce the weapons. You see? No heavy lifting involved. No romantic midnight rendezvous on a windswept beach. No skulking in dark alleys. Hypothetically, it would be a very clean and businesslike transaction."

"I see," said Gloria. She finished her tea and held out the cup to Sweet. "Delicious. May I have some more?" Sweet laughed out loud at that and happily refilled her cup.

She took it from him, sipped, and said, "If I understand you right, Randy, if Dexta were to initiate a thorough check of all import manifests for Jhino in the last year, say, then we would find clear evidence that you—

or someone—brought in a load of the appropriate manufacturing equipment."

"Oh, tons of it!" Sweet laughed again. "Jhino is industrializing its economy and imports vast quantities of machinery, from many different sources. As a service provider, Servitor facilitates the process, gets them the best prices, arranges for delivery, and gives advice on implementation. It's what we *do*, Gloria! Surely, you don't intend to bring us up on charges simply for conducting our usual business."

Gloria had another drink of the tea. She was feeling it, now, no mistake about it. She looked at Sweet's piggy little eyes and tried to stay focused. "How did you get the weapons across the ocean to the Myn-Traha?"

"Hypothetically, you mean?"

"Of course."

"Hypothetically, I imagine it would be a breeze to sneak in a hundred or so weapons under the noses of the sleepy Myn."

"Interesting that you knew there were only a hundred of them, Randy."

Sweet nodded, conceding the point without actually acknowledging it.

Gloria began to feel something like a fire igniting within her. It smoldered in her gut and sent waves of heat racing through her groin and limbs. She thought of Hawkes, just outside, of his strong hands, and of how good it would feel when they stroked and caressed her waiting body. Sweet's hands were small and fat.

She took some more of the potent tea; it seemed stronger than she remembered, but perhaps that was just the cumulative effect. Servitor would make a fortune on it. Could it be addictive? She finished the cup and stared at the pattern of the tea leaves in the bottom of it.

"Was there anything else, Gloria?" Sweet asked solicitously.

Focus, dammit!

"Yes, Randy," she said. "Tell me, when does the big show begin? When do the legions of Jhino march out of the city to subdue the barbaric Myn hordes?"

"Oh, military matters are beyond my competence," he said modestly. "But I gather that Prime Minister Veentro himself will be arriving day after tomorrow. I expect there will be some sort of flag-waving, drum-beating affair to get the thing properly launched. Politicians of every species seem to love that sort of thing."

"Have you thought about how many Myn will die?"

"Appealing to my humanitarian instincts now, Gloria?"

"My mistake," she said. "I should have realized that you don't have any."

"Ogre that I am."

"Ogre that you are," she agreed. She noticed again that her cup was empty. That seemed a shame, somehow. She held it up to him.

"You want more?" Sweet asked, frankly astonished. "Certainly," he said, taking the cup from her and refilling it. "I have lots more."

Gloria felt herself beginning to dissolve into a vague, sexual haze. She took the refilled cup from him and allowed herself just one more sip. Well, two.

"Where was I?" she wondered.

"You were telling me what an ogre I am."

"Ah. Yes. Randy the Hun. Scourge of the Myn and all things furry and helpless."

"It hurts me deeply to hear you say that about me, Gloria. I'm really not such a bad sort. And I think the world of you." He reached for her, cupped her cheek in his hand, then slowly brought it downward across her neck, down her sternum, and to her left breast. He squeezed it tenderly and stroked her stiff, erect nipple. She shuddered at his touch.

"What are you doing, Randy?" Gloria protested vaguely.

"You don't like it? But it feels so good, doesn't it? I think you like it a lot, Gloria."

"What if I do? You're still an ogre." She pushed his hand away from her, slid the chair back, and got to her feet. The office suddenly tilted from side to side, and she noticed that she was spilling tea. Waste not, want not, she thought, and gulped down the rest of it. She handed Sweet the empty cup. "Here," she said. "I think I've had enough."

"Are you all right, Gloria? You don't look well. Perhaps you should lie down on the couch. Here, let me help you."

Without being quite sure how she got there, Gloria found herself stretched out on the couch. Sweet was leaning over her. He kissed her on her lips, and Gloria trembled from the intense pleasure of it.

"No," she said. "Don't do that, Randy."

"Why not?" he said. "You know you want it. Right now, Gloria, you want it more than you ever wanted anything in your life. You want *me!*" Sweet licked her earlobes and her neck, then moved downward to suckle at her ripe nipples. Gloria gasped and moaned.

"No," she forced herself to say. "Stop it."

"Stop? But we've just begun!" Sweet unbuttoned her dress and pushed the fabric out of his way. He tongued the shallow cavity of her navel and continued onward across the smooth, cocoa-colored flesh of her belly.

Gloria cried out involuntarily as he reached the blond tangle of her pubic mound. She felt his wet, slick tongue on her, and then his short, pudgy fingers, stroking and probing and finally penetrating her.

"No," she said mechanically. "No." It had become a meaningless mantra. Any second now, she realized, she would explode. But there was something she had to do first, she remembered. Something important. If only she could remember what it was.

Sweet stood up and unfastened his belt. He lowered

his pants and pushed his shorts down, and Gloria watched him as he leaned forward and prepared to enter her.

"No," she said again, and finally remembered. As Sweet maneuvered like a boat approaching a slip, she reached for the comm on her left wrist and pushed a button.

Sweet arrived at his goal and had just begun to push his way into her when the office door swung open and Hawkes, Denton, and Petra charged into the room.

"Help," Gloria said with languid disinterest. "Rape. Help. Rape."

Sweet abruptly withdrew, stood straight, and reflexively covered himself with both hands. Hawkes grabbed him by the collar, spun him around, and shoved his face down onto the desk.

"Randall Sweet," said Hawkes, "as Acting Undersecretary for Security in this jurisdiction, I hereby place you under arrest for criminal sexual assault on a Dexta official engaged in the lawful performance of her duties. Also for slipping her a mickey, you shithead."

"This will never stand, Hawkes," Sweet bellowed. "Never!"

"We recorded the whole thing," Petra said proudly. "She said 'no' or 'stop it' seven different times. You should have listened."

"And I got the—if you'll pardon the expression—climactic moment on my imager," said Denton.

Gloria staggered to her feet and weaved across the room to a cabinet behind Sweet's desk. She opened it, rummaged around for a moment, and pulled out a thick, heavy, tightly wrapped bundle that reeked of jigli. She held it against her breasts.

"Evidence," she said, smiling dreamily. "Mustn't forget the evidence!"

chapter 21

PETRA STEERED A PROTESTING GLORIA INTO
her bed, put out the lights, and left. Her head swimming, her body tingling, Gloria felt miffed that Hawkes
would leave her alone at a time like this. She had been
no less frustrated than Sweet when they had burst into
the office and put an end to what had barely begun.
Technically, legally, she had been penetrated and therefore, raped; it just didn't feel like it. Letting that awful
man have his way with her had been bad enough, but
being left there, hanging on the brink, was downright
maddening. Hawkes had been willing to kill for the
cause, and Gloria had been willing to let herself be violated for the same noble end, but somehow, she felt simultaneously soiled and unsatisfied. She tossed and
turned in her bed until finally she found relief on her
own and sank into a warm, sensuous sleep, filled with
the sexiest dreams she'd ever had.

• • •

MEANWHILE, IN THE BASEMENT OF THE ADMIN-
istration building, Hawkes, Quesada, Blumenthal, and
Denton listened to the conversation between Sweet and
Tatiana—or rather, the absence of it. They had locked
Sweet in with Tatiana for the time being, then retired to
an adjoining room to listen to their bugs. But it had all
been chaste and innocent so far. It was "Mr. Sweet" and
"Ms. Markova," and beyond a short recitation of the alleged crimes for which they were being held, they had
said little to each other.

"This is going nowhere," Hawkes declared. "Let's
pull him out and go to work on them individually." They
transferred Sweet to the adjoining room and Hawkes sat
down to chat with him while Sonia Blumenthal went in
to commiserate with poor, dear Tatiana.

"My lawyer will be here before long," Sweet
pointed out. "He's in Jhino, but it won't take him an
hour to get here. In the meantime, I have nothing to say
to you, Hawkes, except that your little ploy is going
to get you nothing but a suspension. You and the whole
damned lot of you."

"Maybe," Hawkes conceded. "But we've got you
cold, Sweet. The whole thing was recorded, imaged, and
witnessed."

"The whole thing was also a blatant setup."

"Nevertheless, we've got you. Do you know what's
going on next door? Right now, Sonia Blumenthal is im-
pressing upon Tatiana just how deep the shit she's in is.
The only way she can save herself is by ratting you out.
Rhinehart, too. Tatiana just doesn't strike me as the kind
of person who could stand up to that kind of pressure for
very long. What do you think she'll tell us, Sweet?"

"If you've set her up with the same skill that you set
me up, she'll be out of here fifteen minutes after I am.
I'll give her the loan of my lawyer."

"That could turn out to be a conflict of interest,
don't you think?"

"I'm content to let the Bar Association sort that out," said Sweet. He crossed his legs and folded his arms.

Hawkes got up and paced around the small room in what he hoped was a prosecutorial manner. "You see, Sweet, the thing is, whether you walk out of here tonight or not, this is only the beginning. No matter how things turn out with the Myn and the Jhino, and no matter how much you make on the deal, you'll never be able to spend a crown of it in peace. Dexta will hound you for the rest of your miserable life. Not only did you rape one of our people, but you were directly responsible for the deaths of five others, as well as forty more humans. Do you really think we're going to let you get away with all of that?"

"Events on this world have been disastrous, no question," said Sweet. "And following every disaster, there is a predictable pattern of events. The first is always the search for a scapegoat. You seem to have nominated me for that role. Very well, then, do your worst. I have nothing to hide and nothing to fear."

"You're wrong about that," Hawkes told him. He leaned down and looked Sweet in the eye. "You've got *me* to fear."

"I tremble at the very thought," said Sweet.

"Even if somehow Dexta doesn't get you, I will. I liked Ricardo Olivera and the other people you killed. What's more, I actually like the Myn, bad smell and all. Some humans smell a hell of a lot worse."

"Is that a personal threat, Hawkes? I'll be sure to mention it to Sam LeMoyne when he gets here."

"While you're at it, mention this. If a genocide happens, everyone connected with it is going down, one way or another. If LeMoyne is stupid enough to try to defend you, he won't be able to get so much as a skimmer citation case anywhere in the Empire. This is the kind of dirt that you can never wash away, Sweet."

"Big words, Hawkes," Sweet said defiantly. "But

words are all you have. And I'll remember them. So you go play the Lone Avenger if it makes you feel good, but I don't expect to lose a moment's sleep over it. You've got words, Hawkes—but I've got an army."

"And should I take that as a threat?"

"Take it any way you like."

SONIA BLUMENTHAL WAS MAKING LITTLE MORE progress with Tatiana. Her initial fear had given way to a stubborn resentment and a determination to outlast her tormentors. They could kick her in the ass and threaten her all they wanted, but they would never get her to talk. The instant she said one word against Rhinehart or Sweet, that secret account on New Helvetia would vanish like the morning dew. That was what it had been all about, and she would be damned if she would give it up.

"You don't have much time, you know," Sonia pointed out to her. "You can walk out of here tonight with complete immunity, Tatiana, but the minute those Jhino troops start to march, all bets are off. Think about that."

"You think about it. Better yet, why don't you go get yourself a drink, Sonia? It's been a long day, and you must really need one by now."

Sonia smiled grimly. "You're right," she said, "I do. But that's nothing compared with all the things you're going to want and need during ten years on a prison world. Have you ever seen those places, Tatiana? I have. Dexta inspection tour, about fifteen years ago. Ghastly beyond description. It was hard for me to believe that such places still exist in a civilized Empire. But they do."

"Is that supposed to scare me?"

"It should. It would scare the pants off me."

"I'm not going to any prison world. Not for ten years and not for ten minutes. You don't have any evidence. I'll get myself a Dexta advocate and walk out of the hearing a free woman." And, she thought, a rich one.

* * *

"NOTHING?" MELINDA ASKED. "YOU GOT NOTH-ing out of them?"

"Tatiana surprised me a little," said Sonia. "She showed more spine than I thought she had."

"And Sweet was smug and confident," Hawkes said.

"So all this was for nothing?" Melinda retied her robe and ran her hands through her sleep-disheveled hair.

"You might as well get up and get dressed," Hawkes said. "Sweet's lawyer is with him now. You'll have to hear his complaints."

"And I'll have to do it honestly," Melinda said. "I can't fudge this, Hawkes. Yes, I know what's at stake, but there are other issues involved. If you don't have a legitimate case and I keep Sweet in custody anyway, LeMoyne will go straight to the Governor. He'll file a dozen complaints charging me with abuse of my author-ity and the rest of you with conspiracy. Rhinehart will have the Marines put *us* in custody, where we'll be of no use to anyone. He may try to do that in any case."

"I don't think Barnes would go for that," Hawkes said. "He'd say it's a dispute between Dexta and the Im-perial Governor, and that the military should stay out of it. At least, I *think* he would."

"Well, I for one am not willing to take that risk. Now go away and let me get dressed. I'll meet you in my of-fice."

"Should we get Gloria?"

"No," Melinda said after a moment's thought, "let her sleep. *Somebody* around here ought to get a decent night's rest."

"IT'S THE FLIMSIEST, MOST BLATANTLY OBVIOUS case of entrapment I've ever seen," lawyer LeMoyne told Melinda when the principals had gathered in her office. "I won't even mention these other allegations of gunrunning and conspiracy. No one has presented even a scintilla of evidence concerning any of them."

"Agreed," said Melinda. "In the absence of additional evidence, no charges will be filed in these other matters." Hawkes started to protest, but Melinda gave him a threatening look and he remained quiet.

"However," Melinda continued, "there is substantial *prima facie* evidence in support of the criminal sexual assault charge, as well as the Chapter Twelve violation involving the nonconsensual administering of an erotogenic substance to a Dexta official. What have you to say on these points, Mr. LeMoyne?"

LeMoyne was a compact, dapper-looking man who didn't seem to realize or be bothered by the fact that it was three o'clock in the morning. "First," he said, "I find it strange that the alleged victim is not present at this proceeding."

"She's asleep," said Sonia. "Recovering from her ordeal."

"Hah!" snorted Sweet.

"That will be enough out of you, Mr. Sweet," Melinda warned him.

"Be that as it may," LeMoyne continued, "on the question of the alleged erotogenic substance, just what are we talking about here?"

"Jigli," said Hawkes. "It's an herb that grows in some regions on this continent. The Myn use it for essentially spiritual purposes, but it has a very powerful erotogenic effect on humans."

"Is that so?" LeMoyne asked sarcastically. "Well, I'll tell you, Mr. Hawkes. I called up the *Imperial Pharmacopoeia* on my pad, and I found a list of a hundred and seventeen substances, both natural and artificial, known to possess erotogenic properties. Everything from Spanish Fly to Orgastria-29. But nowhere on that list did I see reference to or mention of a substance by the name of jigli."

"Jigli is a nondescript species," Hawkes said, "largely unknown to humans. Nevertheless, it has—"

"Nevertheless *nothing*, Mr. Hawkes," LeMoyne interjected. "Legally speaking, this jigli stuff doesn't exist. Charging my client with its use, with or without the alleged victim's knowledge or consent, is nonsense, Ms. Throneberry."

Melinda sighed. "Agreed," she said. "That charge is dismissed. Which leaves us with the criminal sexual assault. Mr. LeMoyne, on that charge there is substantial evidence."

"All of which is a patched-together mishmash of entrapment and outright conspiracy on the part of the alleged victim and her friends."

Hawkes turned to Denton, who handed him a hard copy of the image from Sweet's office. "Denton," Hawkes whispered, "if this thing ever turns up anywhere in the Empire outside this room, I will personally feed you to a Mondavian blood-spider."

"You don't scare me, Hawkes," Denton responded defiantly. "It's *Gloria* that scares me."

Hawkes handed the image to LeMoyne. "In addition," he said, "there's the audio recording, which you've already heard, and the statements of Ms. Nash and Mr. Denton."

LeMoyne examined the image with great interest, then handed it back to Hawkes. "Ms. Throneberry," he said, "confronted with such graphic evidence, I can hardly deny that *something* of a sexual nature occurred in my client's office last evening. However, I reiterate that the whole thing was entrapment and does not constitute criminal sexual assault. I would point out Ms. VanDeen's extremely provocative attire, her reputation as, shall we say, a libertine, and the demonstrated animus shown against Mr. Sweet by Ms. VanDeen in her recent public statement on Pecos. If this case were ever to come to trial, I would relish the opportunity to get

Ms. VanDeen on the witness stand. It would be like shooting fish in a barrel."

"Mr. LeMoyne," said Melinda, "the purpose of this hearing is to determine whether sufficient evidence exists to support the charge, not to characterize that evidence or the witnesses and participants in the matter. It remains an uncontested fact that on the audio recording, Ms. VanDeen can be heard telling Mr. Sweet to stop, seven different times. When you get in front of a jury, you'll have plenty of opportunity to drag Ms. VanDeen through the mud, but for now, I find that sufficient evidence does exist to support the charge."

LeMoyne nodded obediently. "Very well, Madame Imperial Secretary. I request that Mr. Sweet be released on his own recognizance, pending the next stage in this matter."

Melinda looked toward Hawkes. "Unacceptable," he said flatly. "Mr. Sweet is a dangerous man who needs to be kept incarcerated."

"Oh, come on, Hawkes!" cried LeMoyne. "You're really reaching."

"I'm afraid that I have to agree with Mr. LeMoyne," Melinda said. "Mr. Sweet, you are hereby released from custody. However, you are instructed to remain within the city of Dhanj, pending further action in this matter."

Hawkes gave Melinda an exceptionally dirty look, while Sweet and LeMoyne shook hands.

"Ms. Throneberry," LeMoyne said, "I would also like to address the charges against Ms. Tatiana Markova at this time."

"You're out of order on that, Mr. LeMoyne," Melinda told him. "No criminal charges have been filed against Ms. Markova at this time. The existing charges constitute an internal Dexta matter, in which you have no standing. Ms. Markova will remain in custody. I believe that concludes our business here."

Smiling smugly, Sweet made his triumphant exit

from the office, followed by his attorney. Melinda looked at the fuming Hawkes.

"Don't say it, Hawkes," she warned him. "Don't say anything."

GLORIA AWOKE THAT MORNING FEELING RE-freshed, invigorated, and sexually voracious. The jigli was still in her system, and in her mind. Her first order of business for the day: find Hawkes. She pulled on a band-skirt, set for minimum coverage and near-maximum transparency, adjusting it so low on her hips that it was in real danger of falling off. Her choice of a top was tight and sleeveless, with a U-neckline so wide and deep that the garment was essentially superfluous.

Outside her room, there was no sign of human activity. She opened Petra's door to peek in, and found her assistant sound asleep, snoring softly. She scoured the rooms in the building, but could find no sign of Hawkes or anyone else. Finally, she found Melinda in her office, head down on her desk, quietly dozing. Gloria cleared her throat. Melinda looked up groggily.

"Where is everyone?" Gloria asked her.

"Asleep, if they have any sense."

"What is this? The sun's up. There's work to be done!"

"Gloria," Melinda said wearily, "while you were sleeping, the rest of us were up all night. Would you like to hear what happened?"

Gloria heard, but she didn't like it. "You mean I went through that for *nothing*?" She wanted to kick something. "How in hell could you let him walk out of here?"

"I didn't have any choice, Gloria. I'm sorry, but I was more concerned with keeping all of us *out* of custody than I was with keeping Sweet in it. The rape charge still stands, if you want to push it. I wouldn't recommend it, though."

"What about Tatiana?"

"Oh, we've still got her. After the hearing, Hawkes and Sonia took turns browbeating her until the sun came up, for all the good it did."

"Where's Hawkes?" Gloria demanded.

"Sleeping. Leave him alone, Gloria. He needs sleep more than you need sex."

"Want to bet? Where is he?"

"Gloria..."

"Oh, all right, all right. If he ever wakes up and wants to know where I am, tell him I've joined the Marines."

GLORIA FOUND MAJOR BARNES STANDING near the grounded LASS. He was watching a steady stream of skimmer traffic coming in from all points of the compass. The skimmers all descended and parked in an open field on the far side of the LASS. There were a few hundred of them.

"Opening up a used skimmer lot, Major?" Gloria asked brightly.

Barnes saw her and swallowed hard. "Morning, Ms. VanDeen," he said.

"Please, call me Gloria. And you're Delbert?"

"Only my mother calls me that," he said with an embarrassed grin. "But I kind of like the way it sounds coming from you."

"Delbert it is, then." She pointed toward the field with all the skimmers in it. "What's going on?"

"Well," said Barnes, "within the confines of my orders, I'm doing my level best to give the Jhino a hard time. Those recon skimmers we sent up yesterday found that most of the Jhino were engaged in moving supplies from the Transit to their depot. Those that weren't busy killing Myn and burning their bodies. They've grabbed all the freight haulers they could find, and they've also been collecting abandoned skimmers. By now, they've got maybe a couple hundred of them."

"And so you're going into competition with them?"

"Exactly. I've had my people out all night in the SALs and scout skimmers, rounding up every skimmer we could find within twenty miles of Dhanj. War is not just about destroying the enemy, Gloria. It's about moving troops and their supplies into a position where they are *able* to destroy the enemy. The Jhino have no transport except what they've been able to confiscate in and around the city. Right now, they don't have nearly enough skimmers to do more than haul a minimal quantity of supplies. Wherever they go, their troops are going to have to walk. The fewer skimmers they have, the more supplies they'll have to hump on their backs. Maybe we can't stop this invasion, but we can sure as hell slow it down."

"That's great, Delbert." Gloria gave him a warm, approving smile. "It would be even better if you could find a way to delay it. We've learned that their Prime Minister is arriving tomorrow, and he'll probably give the signal to begin their troop movements to the interior. Tomorrow's Monday; if we could find a way to make them delay until Friday, maybe we could prevent the whole thing."

"What happens Friday?" Barnes asked.

"That's the earliest day that we could receive a courier from Earth. There's a good chance it will carry instructions countermanding Rhinehart's orders to cooperate with the Jhino. In fact, there's a good chance it will bring word that Rhinehart has been sacked. That would put Melinda Throneberry in charge, and she could give you orders to block the Jhino."

"It's a long time till Friday," Barnes said. "But I've already given some thought to a way we might be able to slow the Jhino down even more."

"How?"

Barnes smiled. "By enlisting the oldest, most

powerful enemy any army in history has ever had to contend with. It's a force that has delayed, dragged out, and lost more battles than anything else you can name."

"Really? What?"

"Mud," Barnes said, grinning.

Gloria grinned back at him. "Tell me more, Delbert."

"Glad to, Gloria. Maybe you'd like to join me in the *Myrt* for some coffee?"

"I'd love to. In fact, I'm ashamed to admit it, but I haven't even had breakfast yet. Do you suppose...?"

"Steak and eggs all right?"

Gloria slipped her arm around Barnes's elbow. "Delbert," she said, "I think I'm falling in love with you."

In the wardroom of the *Myrtle McCormick*, Barnes introduced Gloria to the Imperial Navy personnel who ran the vessel, including the Captain, a twenty-year veteran named Miles Weatherby, who was only too happy to sit down and have a second breakfast with her. Gloria's steak and eggs arrived promptly, served by a mess attendant who hung around so long staring at Gloria that the Captain finally had to order him back to the galley.

"The swabbies treat us like cattle," said Barnes, "but they do feed us well."

"And the Marines treat us like cab drivers," said Weatherby. "Only we don't get any tips."

"Major," Gloria asked between bites, "what's this about mud?"

"Well," said Barnes, "Captain Weatherby and I have been kicking around a few ideas, but I can't say that we've come up with anything definite yet."

"I have my Engineering Officer, Lieutenant Mbunda, working on it full-time, Ms. VanDeen. She's got most of the brains on this ship, and if anyone can come up with a way to do it, she will."

"Do what, exactly?"

"If we could arrange for a good rainstorm—a real gullywasher—we could turn these dirt roads around here into gumbo," said Barnes. "That wouldn't bother the skimmers much, but the Jhino infantry would have to slog through the stuff. They've got short legs anyway, and if they had to march through six inches of mud with full packs and weapons, I think it might stop their invasion before it got started."

"I love it," said Gloria. "But you'd have to do it within the next day."

"We're not sure we can do it at all," said Weatherby. "The problem is that it's the dry season around here. Won't be any rain for another two or three months. At this time of year, the trade winds take all the wet weather well to the south. There are plenty of storms about six hundred kilometers off the coast, but we have to figure a way to bring them here in a hurry."

"We're computer-modeling some ideas," said Barnes, "but nothing looks very good at this point. Differential heating, atmospheric ionization, even a large-scale plasma discharge to divert the ambient winds. If we had time, I think we could come up with something that would work. But doing it within a day is a tall order."

"I see," said Gloria, trying not to sound disappointed. She appreciated the way the Navy and Marines were working so hard for the same goal as Dexta. She had never had many dealings with the military, but she was beginning to admire these people.

A Marine sergeant came into the wardroom and saluted. "Excuse me, Major," he said, "but there's a Jhino colonel outside who wants to see you. Says he's got orders for you."

"He does, does he? Very well, Sergeant, go tell him I'll be out in a few minutes. Under no circumstances should you let him aboard the ship."

Barnes eyed Weatherby. "*He's* got orders for *us?*"

"I think you need to educate this colonel of theirs, Del," said Weatherby.

"I can think of several lessons I'd like to teach the son of a bitch. Care to audit the class, Gloria?"

Gloria accompanied Barnes out of the LASS and found Colonel Jangleth and two aides waiting impatiently in the shadow of the immense vehicle. Barnes confronted him and pointedly failed to salute; instead, he folded his arms across his chest and stared contemptuously at the Jhino commander.

"Major Barnes," Jangleth said, "I have orders for you from Governor Rhinehart." He held out a folded piece of paper.

"Colonel Jangleth," Barnes said, "apparently you and the Governor are not familiar with how we do things. You are not in our chain of command. We don't take our orders from you."

"But these orders come from your Governor!" Jangleth protested. "Here. See? They are in writing."

"I don't care if they are written in the Governor's own blood. I can't accept them from you. If the Governor wants to give us orders, he'll have to do it in an officially approved manner. That means he'll have to come himself, or send the orders via one of his aides."

"But these orders concern the skimmers that you—"

"Colonel!" Barnes cut him off. "I don't care what they concern. I can't accept them from you." Barnes did a brisk about-face and marched back into the LASS. Gloria followed him.

Once inside, Barnes told her, "They want me to give them the skimmers we've collected, and if Rhinehart orders it, I'll have to do it. Don't worry, they won't get the ones we already have. I've got a way of dealing with that. But if we had another hour, we could bring in another couple hundred of them."

Gloria thought rapidly. "Delbert," she said, "maybe I can buy you that hour. I'll need to borrow a skimmer. And could you give me a flare?"

"Do I want to know what you intend to do with them?"

"No"—Gloria smiled—"you don't."

* * *

GLORIA HOVERED PATIENTLY, TWO HUNDRED feet above the city. She was a quarter of a mile from the Jhino encampment in the plaza fronting the Palqui, and had an unobstructed view. Rhinehart had to be inside the complex of buildings that made up the Palqui, she figured. The next skimmer that departed the Palqui would be the one she wanted.

Fifteen minutes after she arrived on station, she saw a maroon skimmer ascend from the plaza. It slowly accelerated and moved toward the Compound, passing below her own. Gloria steered down and left in a wide, swooping arc that brought her to the angle she needed. She gunned the skimmer and took aim on her target.

At an altitude of forty feet, Gloria's skimmer slammed into the maroon skimmer, taking the brunt of the impact on its underside, smashing the left rear of the other vehicle. The internal mass-repulsion safety system held Gloria rigidly in place at the instant of impact, and she felt no more than a sudden jar as her skimmer crumpled around her. Both skimmers plunged toward the ground, coming in at a thirty-degree angle. They bounced off a rooftop and caromed forward, plowing a shallow groove into the hard-packed dirt roadway before piling into the side of another building and coming to an abrupt halt.

Gloria popped open the damaged door on her left and snaked her way out of the ruined skimmer. Preston Riley, one of the Governor's aides, emerged from the wreckage of his own vehicle, looking shaken but unharmed. Gloria ran up to him.

"You maniac!" she screeched hysterically. "You could have killed me! Who the hell ever taught you to drive a skimmer? Whaddya think you're doing, you moron?"

Already stunned, and now thoroughly confused, Riley managed only a weak, "What?" in response.

"Whaddya mean, *what*, you fucking asshole? Look

what you did to my skimmer!" Gloria's years in New York had not been wasted.

"What I did to *your* skimmer?" Riley stammered. "Hey, *you* crashed into *me*! I was just—"

"You were just asleep at the fucking controls, is what you were, pal! How did a moron like you ever get a license? Hey—would you look at that!"

Gloria pointed off into the distance with her left hand. Riley reflexively looked in that direction, but didn't see anything. He also didn't see Gloria's lightning Qatsima move, or her right elbow as it smacked into his temple. Riley silently collapsed.

Gloria checked his pulse quickly, making certain that she hadn't done more damage than she had intended. As far as she could tell, he was fine, aside from having been knocked out cold. She dragged him across the roadway and deposited him against the side of a building. Checking through his pockets, she came up with the Governor's signed orders for Barnes. She also removed his wristcom.

She ran back to Riley's smashed skimmer and dug around under the hood for a few moments until she found the pressure relief valve on the fuel tank. She unscrewed it and stepped back as hydrogen gas hissed out of the tank. Then she dropped the orders into the front seat of the skimmer and fetched the flare from her own wrecked vehicle. She struck it, watched it sputter into life, then pitched it toward the skimmers and ran. They exploded with a satisfying *whump!* Gloria looked back and saw the barely visible blue flame engulfing the two skimmers. Quickly, orange flame and black smoke began to boil up out of them as plastic and fabric started to burn.

Gloria walked the mile back to the Compound and went up to Melinda's office. "I thought I should let you know," she said, "that in a little while you're going to get a complaint about my driving."

Melinda started to ask a question, but seemed to think better of it.

"That idiot Riley, the Governor's aide," Gloria explained. "The man shouldn't be allowed behind the controls of a skimmer! Don't believe a word he tells you—it was all his fault. He was knocked out when the skimmers exploded after the crash, but I think he'll be okay. And it really was all his fault."

"I'm certain of it," Melinda agreed.

"What's this about an explosion?" Hawkes had come into the office behind her.

"It's about time you woke up!" Gloria grabbed him by one arm and practically dragged him out of the office, out of the administrative building, and into the other building where her room was.

"Have a good sleep?" she asked him as they went up the stairs.

"Uh, yeah. Where the hell have you been?"

"With the Marines," she told him. "I'm sorry, Hawkes, but you missed your chance with me."

"I did?"

"While you were sleeping, the Second Platoon offered me their hands in marriage. We're thinking June."

She opened the door of her room, shoved Hawkes in ahead of her, then slammed the door behind her. Hawkes started toward the bed, but Gloria didn't let him get that far. She wound up with rug burns on her backside, but it was worth it.

AN HOUR LATER, FEELING MUCH MORE RELAXED, Gloria went back to see Barnes and the Marines, with Hawkes in tow. "I don't know how you did it," said Barnes, "but you got us that hour. An hour and a half, actually."

"I see you've made good use of the time," said Gloria. In the field beyond the LASS, there were now at least five hundred skimmers, stacked four and five deep in places.

"But you're just going to have to turn them over to the Jhino when the orders arrive," Hawkes pointed out.

"Leave that to me," Barnes said. He looked toward the city and pointed. "Here they come," he said. Gloria and Hawkes looked up and saw three skimmers approaching in an abbreviated V-formation. They landed nearby, and Jangleth, Riley, and half a dozen armed Jhino troops got out.

"Major!" Riley called as he approached, waving a paper in his hand. He saw Gloria standing next to Barnes and started to say something, but discretion won out over valor.

"Be with you in just a second, Mr. Riley," Barnes said. He turned toward the *Myrtle McCormick* and waved his arm toward Marines in the defense nacelles atop the LASS.

An instant later, four brilliant blue bolts of plasma sizzled through the air and carved incandescent arcs through the mass of skimmers in the field. Explosions began to multiply like cooking popcorn, and by the time the gunners ceased their fire, the skimmers were completely engulfed in a scorching inferno.

Jangleth and Riley watched in outraged disbelief for several moments, then turned on Barnes.

"What have you done?" screeched Jangleth. The natural pitch of Jhino speech was high to begin with, and now Jangleth's pained outburst ascended to a frequency that was barely discernible to human ears.

"The Governor ordered you to turn those skimmers over to the Jhino!" Riley roared.

"Did he?" Barnes asked. "Fine." He turned to Jangleth. "They're all yours, Colonel," he said with a satisfied smile.

"Why have you done this?" Jangleth piped. "You have destroyed them!"

"It's a funny thing, Colonel," Barnes explained.

"Would you believe it? Every last one of those abandoned skimmers had a coolant leak. You know how noxious that stuff is? It's a dangerous pollutant, and we couldn't just let it foul the environment. We didn't have enough people to fix them all, so we figured this would be the safest way to dispose of the problem."

"Barnes!" Riley shouted. "I'm going to report this to the Governor!"

"You do that, Mr. Riley. Just tell him that it was a matter of public sanitation."

They stood and watched the skimmers burn for several minutes. Finally, Jangleth, Riley, and the Jhino troops stomped back to their skimmers and flew away.

"Wish I had some marshmallows," said Hawkes. "Major, I admire the way you build a bonfire."

A sergeant trotted out of the LASS and saluted Barnes. "Major," he said, "Lieutenant Mbunda asks if you could come. She says she's got something. Something that will work!"

"Thank you, Sergeant." Barnes looked at Gloria and Hawkes. "Come on," he said, "let's go make some rain."

chapter 22

THEY JOINED CAPTAIN WEATHERBY AND LIEU-
tenant Carol Mbunda in the wardroom of the *Myrtle
McCormick* for coffee and cake. Mbunda was bright-
eyed and excited, bubbling over with the joy of discovery, but Weatherby maintained his calm reserve.

"You know how we say that when a ship turns on its
Ferguson Distortion Generators, it has gone into Yao
Space?" Mbunda asked. "Well, that's not really a precise
description of what happens. In fact, the ship stays inside
a bubble of normal space that is contained within an
eleven-dimension membrane composed of Yao Space.
The membrane slides through normal space at trans-c velocities, carrying the trapped bubble of normal space—
and the ship—along with it."

"I never knew that," said Gloria, whose grasp of
technical matters tended to be hazy, at best.

"It has to be that way," Mbunda explained. "If we
were actually *in* Yao Space, we'd get all folded up and
squished. So the membrane of the bubble is always kept

well away from the ship itself. On the *Myrt,* our bubble is about a kilometer in diameter."

"I see," said Gloria.

"What I propose to do," Mbunda said, glancing at Weatherby, "is to expand our bubble to a diameter of about twenty-five kilometers. If we were sitting in the middle of a thunderstorm cell when we turned on the Fergusons, that would trap the entire storm inside our bubble of normal space. Then all we have to do is bring the bubble to a point above Dhanj, turn off the Fergusons, and *voila*! Instant deluge." Mbunda grinned at them.

It sounded clever to Gloria, but she looked at Weatherby and saw concern on his face.

"We can do it repeatedly," Mbunda added, "and bring in as many storms as we need to get the job done."

Weatherby nodded slowly. "Good work, Lieutenant," he said. "I assume you've run simulations of this?"

"Yessir, a half dozen. Everything checked out."

"That's comforting," said Weatherby. "And what are the hazards?"

"There might be some pretty big static electricity discharges when the bubble is relaxed," Mbunda said. "But there would be lightning from the storm in any case, so I don't see that as a problem."

"And what about the hazards to my ship?"

Mbunda's bright smile faded just a bit. "Well, sir, I admit, this is an unusual procedure."

"Unusual? Lieutenant, I'm not even aware that anyone has ever tried to turn on a Ferguson inside an atmosphere."

"Oh, it's been done, sir. Lots of times. It's true that it was always done under controlled conditions for the purpose of various tests, but they had no problem forming the bubbles."

"And just how big were these bubbles?"

"Well, sir," Mbunda admitted, "they were only a

few hundred meters in diameter. But in theory, there's no reason why the bubbles couldn't be as large as necessary."

"I see." Weatherby took a sip from his coffee mug.

"We can do it, sir. Really!"

"I believe you, Lieutenant. But it strikes me that the power requirements to form a bubble twenty-five kilometers in diameter would be enormous. And what about fuel consumption?"

"Sir, my calculations show that we have enough fuel to do this nine or ten times and still have a big enough reserve to get us to Pecos for refueling."

"And what about the strain on the engines and the Fergusons?"

"Uh...that would be considerable, sir, but still within design specs. And we're due for a refit, anyway."

"Overdue, in fact," said Weatherby. He stared at a bulkhead in silence for several moments.

"I don't understand," said Hawkes. "If you have enough power and fuel to go interstellar, I'd think you'd have more than enough for a six-hundred-kilometer shuttle back and forth to the storms."

"Lieutenant?" Weatherby fixed his stare on her. "Explain it to Mr. Hawkes, if you would."

"Yessir," said Mbunda. "You see, sir, it's a matter of the mass involved. It's no problem to push the *Myrt* up to .92 c in the vacuum of space. Not much resistance out there. And when we turn on the Fergusons, the bubble doesn't trap any mass at all, aside from a few stray atoms of hydrogen. But expanding the bubble to twenty-five kilometers inside an atmosphere would mean we'd have to generate the power to push an enormous amount of mass around. The mass of a thunderstorm is...well, I don't have precise figures, but it's—"

"Huge," said Weatherby. "That's what bothers me, Lieutenant. I'm concerned about what the strain would do to the Fergusons. If one of them cut out, even for an instant, you know what would happen."

"Yessir," Mbunda answered meekly.

"What?" Gloria asked.

Mbunda looked at her and hesitantly explained. "Well, ma'am, you see, the Yao bubble has to be perfectly uniform—a geometric sphere, precise to within a tolerance of microns. And, well...if one of the six Fergusons were to cut out, the bubble would become asymmetric, and it would collapse on itself."

"And?"

"And," Weatherby answered, "the Yao membrane would come into contact with the ship. The *Myrt* would be crushed. At least, it would be crushed up to the point where the Fergusons were disabled entirely, and the fusion reactors exploded."

"Oh," said Gloria.

"Sir," Mbunda said, "we'll keep an eagle eye on the Fergusons throughout the operation. If there's the slightest sign of trouble, we'd shut them down immediately."

"You're damned right you would, Lieutenant," Weatherby told her. "Look, there are some worrisome aspects to this, but I'm willing to give it a try. The first thing we have to do is reduce the mass of the ship itself as much as possible. We can begin off-loading all the Marines' stores and equipment this afternoon, as well as any of our own stuff that is not essential for our immediate purposes. That includes people, as well. We can do this with a skeleton crew, no more than twenty people. If you say it can be done, Lieutenant, I'll go along with you on it. However," he added, looking at Gloria and Hawkes, "I still have some questions about the operational aspects of this. If Governor Rhinehart gives us an order telling us to stop raining on his parade, we'll have to obey it."

"But he won't even know what's going on," said Gloria. "At least not until the first storm hits."

"And if you wait until night," put in Hawkes, "they

won't even notice that the *Myrt* has gone. Not right away, at least."

"I'll extend the perimeter out to two klicks," said Barnes. "That should keep prying eyes at a respectable distance."

"Fine," said Weatherby. "But if we're going to have a worthwhile effect with all of this, I'd say we'd need to bring in a minimum of five or six storms, maybe seven or eight. We'll need to saturate the ground for a radius of twenty to thirty kilometers around the city. Won't Rhinehart catch on after the first couple of storms and order us to knock it off?"

"Rhinehart's holed up at the Palqui," Hawkes said. "He doesn't have the communications equipment he'd need to get in contact with your ship. He'd have to come into the Compound to use the Comm Room, and I don't think he'd do that himself. And if he sent one of his aides, we might be able to...delay him." Hawkes glanced at Gloria, who grinned guiltily.

"What if he just uses his comm to call Barnes, and tells him to relay the order to us?" asked Weatherby.

"Well, Miles," Barnes said, "rain does funny things to our comm equipment. I think we might have a hard time communicating with anyone in the middle of a thunderstorm."

"Sir?" Mbunda said. "There's another thing. Once the *Myrt* is inside the bubble, communications with us will be impossible anyway. All we have to do is restore a normal-sized bubble after we release the storm, and stay in it on our return trip out to the storm systems. Unless someone transmitted to us at the precise instant when we were in between bubbles, they'd never get through."

Weatherby smiled at his Engineering Officer. "Didn't I tell you that Lieutenant Mbunda has most of the brains in this ship? All right, unless anyone has further thoughts on the subject, I think we should get started lightening the ship. We'll plan to be under way an hour after sunset."

• • •

HAWKES WENT BACK TO THE COMPOUND TO TELL
Melinda about the local weather forecast, while Gloria
accompanied Barnes in a scout skimmer on a tour of his
expanded perimeter. Meanwhile, other Marines and the
crew of the *Myrtle McCormick* kept busy off-loading
equipment and stores, building up small mountains of
crates in a ring around the vessel.

The Marines on the perimeter were still in full combat gear, and looked jumpy to Gloria's eyes. They were
accustomed to combat and pacification, but this was a
situation charged with ambiguity, and Marines didn't
like ambiguity. Most of them were aware of what was
happening and understood the conflict between the
Governor and Dexta; they knew that their officers would
side with Dexta if they could, but were bound by the
Governor's orders. Those who hadn't actually seen the
pyres of burning Myn bodies had heard about them, and
everyone would have enjoyed the opportunity to un-
leash their firepower on the Jhino.

Barnes and Gloria strolled around one of the checkpoints. Barnes introduced Gloria to the lieutenants and
sergeants in charge, and they, in turn introduced her to
the members of their squads. Gloria shook hands with
each of them and exchanged some light banter.

"At a rough estimate," Barnes told her, "I'd say
you've improved morale around here by about 87,000
percent."

"Just doing my part." Gloria laughed. She hooked a
thumb in the top of her skirt and tugged it downward
another inch, until her buttocks were nearly half-
exposed and a blond fringe curled over the fabric in
front. Around her, Marines grinned happily.

"We've been on Hogarth for two years now," Barnes
said. "We should have rotated out six months ago, but
we're stretched so thin on the Frontier that we just don't
have enough troops and ships to go around. The more the

Empire expands, the bigger the Frontier we have to patrol. Then, something like this happens, and it puts even more pressure on us. These are good people, Gloria, but they've been away from civilization for a long time. It does them good to see a pretty girl. Hasn't done me any harm, either."

Maybe it was just the aftereffects of the jigli, or the sight of so many strong, muscular men, or maybe it was her profound gratitude and respect for the Marines, but Gloria found herself wishing that she could make love to every last one of them. She fingered the seam contacts on her top and skirt, rendering them 100 percent transparent. She took Barnes by the hand.

"Delbert," she said, "I'm kind of involved with Hawkes at the moment. If I weren't . . ."

"No explanations necessary, Gloria," he said.

She gave him a firm, passionate kiss on his mouth. Around them, Marines whooped and applauded. Gloria released her hold on Barnes, tugged her skirt downward yet another inch, and waved to the ecstatic troops. "That was for every one of you!" she shouted. "I love you guys!"

The Marines went crazy.

Barnes led Gloria back to the scout skimmer. "I'm not sure whether you've just completely undermined my authority," he said, "or turned me into a Marine Corps legend."

They skimmed back to the LASS, where the offloading was proceeding at a brisk pace. As she walked with Barnes toward the ship, she said, "Captain Weatherby has been awfully good about this. I'm just sorry we had to put him to so much trouble."

"Gloria," said Barnes, "you should understand what's really going on here. A few hundred tons of mass more or less isn't going to make much difference. Miles is just making sure that we have all of our supplies and equipment with us, and he wants to get everyone he can off the ship. What they're going to do tonight is incredibly dangerous."

"Oh," Gloria said, suddenly sobered by his words.

"Miles knows what's at stake here, so he's willing to take the risk. And he wouldn't try it at all if he didn't think that the odds were in our favor. But this cloud-catching maneuver has never been attempted before, and a lot of things could go wrong."

Gloria considered the implications of what Barnes had said. Her appreciation and respect for the Navy and Marines, already considerable, multiplied tenfold. She felt small and useless as she watched the crew members perform their labors; life at Dexta suddenly seemed pretty soft.

Taking her cue from Barnes, she went around the ship doing whatever she could to improve morale and show her gratitude. Her near-total nudity proved to be as much an inspiration as a distraction, and the Marines and swabbies lifted, heaved, and hauled with broad grins on their faces. She insisted on being introduced to each of the sixteen men and four women who would be going along with Captain Weatherby on tonight's mission, and gave each of them a kiss and a hug as sincere and passionate as any she had ever bestowed on Hawkes. She only wished that she had the time and opportunity to do even more.

By early evening, the preparations were complete. Barnes huddled with Weatherby in private, while Petra and Hawkes joined Gloria outside on the perimeter of the mountains of supplies. Gloria was beaming with pride and affection for the men and women she had come to know during the busy day.

"Is it just my imagination," Petra asked, "or do you have fingerprints all over your body?" In fact, there were a couple of somewhat greasy handprints on Gloria's bare buttocks, and other smudges on the now transparent fabric of her revealing top. Gloria just smiled. Hawkes shook his head and said nothing. Jealousy wasn't his style and, in any case, he was not about to challenge two hundred Marines to a duel.

Barnes emerged from the *Myrt* and joined them after the sun had set. He communicated with each of his checkpoints and learned that all was quiet. The Jhino troops had withdrawn as the Marines advanced, and no one had even seen a Jhino for hours. "I think Rhinehart and Jangleth are bending over backwards to avoid any incidents," Barnes said. "If just one of those bastards would oblige us by firing a shot in our direction, I could supersede Rhinehart's orders and take any action I deemed necessary to protect my people."

"What could you do, if it came to a fight?" Hawkes asked him.

"Right now," said Barnes, "with the *Myrt* here and all of the Jhino concentrated in one place, I could mop them up in a few hours. Once they get out of the city and start dispersing in the countryside, it would be a different story. There are twenty thousand of them, and only two hundred of us."

A warning Klaxon sounded from the *Myrt,* and a moment later the huge vehicle pushed itself off the ground and into the air. It hovered at an altitude of twenty feet for nearly a minute as the skeleton crew checked every system. Then the LASS swiftly rose straight upward to two hundred feet and moved forward, arcing away from the city and northward along the coast as it began to climb. Only one of Mynjhino's three moons was up, and it was in a crescent, so the night was dark and soon the watchers could only follow the *Myrt*'s progress from the way it eclipsed stars in the background. Then it was gone.

"Satellite images showed a whole line of thunderstorms about five hundred kilometers due west of us," Barnes said. "There ought to be enough water in them to turn this whole area into a quagmire."

"How long will it take for the ship to get there?" Petra asked.

"She's already there." Barnes grinned. "But I imagine the Captain will take a while to check everything out before he blows the first bubble. Then, once they've got a storm cell, they'll bring it back here at subsonic speed. So it could be forty-five minutes or an hour before anything happens here. It'll give you ladies time to go and fetch an umbrella."

"Not me," said Gloria. "I intend to run around naked in the raindrops and make mud pies to throw at people. This is going to be fun!"

"I just wish we could see Rhinehart and Jangleth when this hits," said Hawkes. "Now, *that* would be fun."

NEARLY AN HOUR LATER, BARNES POINTED toward the western horizon, and said, "Here they come." Gloria looked where he had pointed, but at first, saw nothing. Then she noticed that a small, circular area of stars was being obscured. The size of the circle steadily expanded, until the entire western half of the sky was blotted out.

"Spirit!" Petra exclaimed. "It's *huge!*"

The sphere of Yao Space was impervious to normal matter and energy. Photons striking the surface of the sphere bounced off, making it perfectly reflective. As the sphere approached, the ocean below it could be seen mirrored on its precise curves, and scattered lights from the city speckled its surface. The reflections added a sense of depth and scale to what would otherwise have been an unblemished void cruising majestically through the night sky.

With the sphere centered some eight miles high, at the altitude of the storm cells, the lower edge of it was only a few thousand feet above the surface of the planet. It was passing a few miles to the south of the Compound, but the northern underside of the sphere was directly overhead. Seeing something so immense, so close, in motion above them was an utterly unique experience. Even though she knew what it was, Gloria felt a vague, unsettling sensation of fear. She couldn't imagine what the surprised Jhino must be feeling at this moment.

The sphere slowly moved inland until it was centered a few miles beyond the eastern limits of Dhanj. Then it came to a halt and hovered in absolute silence for more than a minute.

And then, it was gone.

In an instant, the immense sphere vanished and was replaced by a roiling tower of cumulonimbus clouds, illuminated from within by dazzling discharges of lightning. Jagged bolts of electricity stabbed at the ground for miles around; the first thunderclaps reached them seconds later and were followed by a continuous, bone-shaking reverberation that went on for minutes. It sounded like an artillery barrage, or a symphonic percussion section gone mad.

At first, the clouds conformed to the spherical shape of the bubble that had contained them, but they quickly began to spread downward and outward. Whirling vortices formed along the margins of the storm, as winds rushed in toward the center of the intruding low-pressure system. Dust clouds swept across the ground and gathered up small bits of debris, stinging the onlookers in the Marine encampment. Blinded and deafened by the onslaught, they could only crouch and face downwind, trying to shield themselves from the natural forces that had been unleashed by the unnatural intervention of the *Myrt*.

Then the rain hit them. It was as if someone had turned on a fire hose. They gasped for air, sputtering and spuming like shipwreck survivors in a heavy surf. The first stunning inundation quickly gave way to a steady, insistent downpour. They straightened up, turned their faces skyward, and grinned to one another as the heavy drops of water pelted them.

"*It worked!*" Gloria shrieked. She jumped up and

down, hugged Hawkes, then turned her attention to Barnes and gave him a very wet kiss on the lips. "They did it!" she cried.

All around them, Marines were spreading their arms, spinning around dazedly, and laughing raucously. They had never been so impressed with their own power as they were at this moment.

The water came down faster than the dry ground could drink it in, and rivulets and puddles quickly formed. Gloria, as good as nude anyway in her drenched, plastered-down togs, lived up to her promise and stripped off her clothes. She bent down to a puddle, scooped up a handful of mud, and searched for a target. Petra backed away and Hawkes gave her a threatening look, so she attacked the smiling Marine major and scored a direct hit. She rubbed the gunk around on his face, then quickly reloaded and nailed Hawkes. She was laughing triumphantly when Petra came up from behind her and slapped a load of fresh mud in her boss's face. Gloria brought Petra down with a Qatsima move and both of them were soon rolling around in a puddle, shrieking and giggling madly. Gloria gained her vengeance, ripping Petra's clothes off as the delighted Marines watched. Soon they were both standing there in the pouring rain, gasping for breath in the midst of their laughter, as naked and innocent as two devout Spiritists on a Visitation day.

AS HE WATCHED THE TWO WOMEN, BARNES reached down and scooped up some of the mire. "I'll tell you one thing," he said to Hawkes. "I wouldn't want to have to march through this stuff. Especially if I were only five feet tall and covered with fur."

"Then we've done it!" Hawkes declared.

"Well," said Barnes, "we've sure as hell done *something*." He looked up to see if he could catch sight of the *Myrt,* but saw nothing except the swirling, lightning-illuminated clouds. The ship was probably already back at the offshore weather system, preparing to grab another storm.

"What do you mean?" Hawkes asked him. He had detected an undertone of caution in the Major's words.

"Well," said Barnes, "if the Jhino were planning to march out of the city tomorrow, this'll force them to rethink their plans. And that's the problem. They do have some other options."

"Such as?"

"If it were my job," said Barnes, "I'd think seriously about revising my tactics. They've still got several hundred skimmers at their disposal. They could use them to ferry a few hundred troops inland and occupy some of the bigger towns in the plantation region. With no organized local opposition, that would be enough to hold the towns and the road net. They could live off the land until forces advancing from Dhanj established direct contact. It might take a couple of weeks or so, but in the meantime, they could bottle up the refugees and keep them from escaping. You don't need to occupy every acre of ground in order to take control of a region. The mud will delay them and make things more difficult for them, but it won't really stop them."

"I see," said Hawkes. He wiped some mud off his face and frowned.

"It's not as bad as all that," Barnes said. "This gunk is going to cause them some major headaches. At a minimum, it ought to keep most of the Jhino forces concentrated around Dhanj for several more days. If they're still here when we get orders from Earth telling us to stop them, we should be able to manage it."

"Assuming we actually get those orders."

Barnes shook his head. "Not my department, thank God," he said. "I'm counting on you and Gloria to handle that."

"Not me," said Hawkes. "That's entirely up to our water sprite." They watched as Gloria and Petra took turns happily sliding through a long, shallow mud puddle. Half-clad Marines were joining them in their sport.

"I wouldn't bet against her," said Barnes. "You're one lucky son of a bitch, Hawkes."

"Don't think I don't know it." Hawkes laughed. Marines were smearing mud all over the naked bodies of his lover and her assistant, and Hawkes watched with benign approval, enjoying the sound of their laughter.

They'd all needed this, he thought.

THE RAIN BEGAN TO SLACKEN AS THE STORM drifted away to the east, but before it could stop entirely, another immense sphere moved overhead, shoving the first storm out of its way. The sphere vanished abruptly, and another round of wind and lightning commenced. They watched the show again in unabashed awe, then shielded themselves from the first torrential blasts of the storm. By the time the *Myrt* delivered the third storm, the mud was ankle deep.

Petra had hardly stopped laughing and giggling the whole time. It was as if the rain and mud had somehow washed away her pain, and for the first time since Ricardo's death, she felt whole again. Thoughts of Ricardo made her pause in the middle of her rain dance, but she found that she was smiling. She only wished that he could be here with her, to see her frolicking naked and happy in the welcome downpour.

A Marine began applying a fresh coat of mud to her bare breasts, and she spread her arms wide as he smeared it over her belly and down to her groin. She let him take liberties, and felt a surge of sexual thrill and visceral satisfaction in the realization that she was able to give something back to these brave men who had come so far to help them. She knew Ricardo wouldn't mind, and the Marine's eager attentions gave her a renewed sense of life and purpose. Naked and unashamed in a cloudburst 862 light-years from New Jersey, Petra realized that her life was still worth living. She threw her head back and laughed at the absurdity and wonder of it all.

The world suddenly turned white.

The impossibly bright flash froze them in place for an awful instant. Petra felt a surge of heat penetrate her bare flesh.

As the ghastly light slowly faded, they turned and looked out toward the ocean. The sea had become red, and the sky above it burned. Far out, above the distant horizon, a second sun had risen in the west, boiling in crimson and gold like a hellish cauldron of brimstone. They watched in stricken silence as it consumed the night.

chapter **23**

BY THE FIRST LIGHT OF DAWN, THE RAIN HAD stopped and two hundred muddy Marines and sixty-five orphaned crew of the *Myrtle McCormick* began loading their supplies onto the four SALs and six scout skimmers that remained. With the *Myrt* gone, Barnes realized that he needed to establish a defensible base, which meant the Compound. He disliked herding his entire command into what could become an Alamo or a Dien Bien Phu, but he could see no other option.

Inside the Compound, Gloria and the other staffers watched forlornly as the procession of Marine vehicles entered, disgorged their cargoes in designated areas, then departed to pick up another load. The giggling hilarity of last night had vanished in an instant, replaced by the numbing consciousness of twenty-one more deaths and the loss of the irreplaceable LASS. Gloria tried to remember the faces and names of those who had been lost; she felt responsible for all of them.

Leaving Captain Zwingli to supervise the transfer operation, Barnes met with the senior Dexta staff in

Melinda Throneberry's conference room. He surveyed the faces he saw gathered around the table and realized that the civilians were unprepared to cope with the sudden catastrophe. That was the difference between them; Barnes had lost troops under his command before and accepted the inevitability of it. The Dexta people, despite their recent losses, were accustomed to bloodless battles in which victory and defeat were no more painful or final than a losing hand in a game of poker.

"We were lucky," Barnes told them. "I know it doesn't feel that way now, but it's true. The *Myrt* was at least a hundred kilometers offshore when she exploded. If it had happened above the city, we wouldn't be having this conversation. And Weatherby and those swabbies accomplished everything they set out to do. Those three storms they delivered will delay the Jhino by at least two or three days."

"Will that be enough?" Melinda asked.

"That depends on when we get orders from Earth and what they say. If we get a courier on Friday that countermands Rhinehart's orders, I think we may still be able to stop the Jhino before they get very far."

"What if they send out their skimmers to seize the towns in the plantation region, like you said last night?" Hawkes asked him.

"That would complicate things," Barnes conceded, "but if the bulk of their forces are still on the roads, I think we could contain their advance. The first thing we'll do—assuming we get a go-ahead—is to seize or destroy the Transit. That will cut off their supply line and prevent reinforcements."

"Not entirely," Hawkes said. "They could already have ships at sea to bring in more supplies and troops. They could land them anywhere along the coast."

Barnes nodded. "We could track them by satellite and try to be ready for them when they come ashore, but you're right. We just don't have enough troops to defend the entire coast and at the same time oppose their main force. There's also another ugly possibility that you should be aware of. Once we start actively fighting them, they could decide to attack the Compound."

"But you can defend it," said Melinda.

"It depends on what they've got," Barnes responded. "If all they have are those AK-47s, they wouldn't stand much chance against us. But for all we know they may have other simple but effective antique weaponry. Mortars, bazookas, light field artillery. If they have that capability, we'd take losses. They could bottle us up in here, defending the Compound, while their infantry marches out into the countryside and secures their major objectives. There just aren't enough of us to stop an entire army once it's on the move."

"That being the case," said Melinda, "even if Rhinehart is removed, I would have to give very careful consideration to the orders I give you, Major. If we can't mount an effective defense, there's not much point in initiating hostilities. How soon could we expect more help?"

"I've already dispatched the last courier from the Orbital Station," said Barnes. "A military emergency takes precedence over anything else. It will reach Earth by Thursday. Assuming the Navy has another LASS available and in the region, and Marines to put in it, I don't think we could expect it to get here in less than two to three weeks from Thursday."

"Could we survive a three-week siege?" Melinda asked.

"Again," said Barnes, "it depends on what kind of weapons they have. Artillery could do some serious damage around here, although with our ballistic-tracking capability, I think we could take out their field guns almost as fast as they could fire them. But something like mortars would be a real problem. If they fire a shot and move, fire another shot and move again, they would be very hard to find."

"And so, your answer to my question is . . . ?"

Barnes looked Melinda in the eye. "We can hold out three weeks, ma'am," he said. "We have supplies for six weeks, so that's the limiting factor. But three weeks is doable. I just want you to realize that it's not simply a matter of hunkering down inside the Compound walls and waiting for help to arrive. We would be in a combat situation, and we would take losses."

Melinda nodded slowly. "Thank you, Major," she said gravely. "I'll have to give this some thought. In the meantime, do everything you think necessary and proper to prepare for a siege."

"Yes, ma'am."

"There's something else we have to consider," said Hawkes. "There are still something like two million Myn out there in the countryside. They must be getting pretty hungry by now. As soon as you have a free skimmer, Major, I'd like to take it out and get a look at the situation. Maybe there's something we can do to help them."

"Make that two skimmers," said Gloria.

"All right," said Barnes. "Although it beats me what we can do to help two million refugees."

"Maybe we could go fishing," Sonia Blumenthal said. Heads turned to look at her.

"What do you have in mind, Sonia?" Melinda asked her.

"The Myn depend on seafood for most of their protein," Sonia said. "They may be able to scavenge the countryside for fruits and greens, but they'll need fish and crustaceans from the sea or the freshwater rivers and lakes if they're going to avoid malnutrition. It occurred to me, Major, that you might have the capability of harvesting a substantial quantity of fish. Don't people sometimes drop explosives in the water to kill fish?"

"They do," Barnes said, smiling as an idea struck him, "but we can do something better than that. We can rig a SAL to emit a very powerful submarine sonic burst. It would probably kill every fish in a hundred-meter radius. But we'd still need to collect them and deliver them."

"No problem," said Hawkes. "There are hundreds of abandoned fishing boats in the harbor. All we'd have to do is salvage some big nets. Attach the nets to the bottom of a SAL, and then just fly low over the water, scooping up all the fish you've killed with your sonic burst. After that, we just fly them out to the refugee camps, dump them, and go back for more. Sonia, you're a genius!"

"No," she said, "I just happen to like fish."

"It should work," said Barnes. "I'll get it in motion as soon as the supply transfer is complete, which should be before noon. Hawkes, Gloria, I'll give you those scout skimmers right now. You go out and find the position of the biggest concentrations of refugees and tell them to get ready for a fish fry."

"I feel better," Gloria announced. "At least we're *doing* something."

"I'd feel better if I knew what Rhinehart and the Jhino are doing," said Barnes. "As of the moment, we have no effective intelligence. And I don't like fighting blind."

"And I," said Melinda, "would feel better if I knew what was happening back on Earth. They should have Gloria's courier by now. Spirit knows what they'll decide to do."

RHINEHART WAS BEGINNING TO HATE THE Palqui. It was dusty and dark, and it smelled of Myn. All the comforts of his Residence were just a few miles away, but they might as well have been back on Earth. He had considered sending his two aides, Riley and Pomfrit, back to the Compound in a freight skimmer to retrieve his bed, a few comfortable, human-sized chairs, and a supply of decent food. But he realized the idea was impractical, since Riley and Pomfrit would have to do all the loading themselves. No one in the Compound was likely to lift a finger to assist them, and he couldn't very well send Jhino into the Compound. Anyway, Riley was reluctant to go anywhere near Gloria VanDeen.

Another reason he disliked the Palqui was that he had absolutely nothing to do there other than pace around his room and fret. He was still the Imperial Governor of Mynjhino, but he no longer had any effective power. The Dexta people were in open rebellion, and the military, although still subject to his orders, were clearly not on his side. They had proven that last night with their disastrous rainmaking operation.

Jangleth and Sweet had raged at him, as if it were somehow *his* fault. As if he should have thought to order the military not to change the weather! Maybe he should also have ordered them not to move the moons or tamper with the tides.

"It will be at least two days, possibly three, before we can begin the operation now," Jangleth complained. "I've already spoken with Prime Minister Veentro and advised him to delay his visit. I can tell you, he was *extremely* upset to hear this."

"We can't afford any more delays," said Sweet. "They could get orders pulling the plug on you as early as Friday, Rhinehart. We *have* to be under way before then."

"We shall be," Jangleth assured him. "And thanks to the foolishness of the hu—of the Marines—we have an advantage now. With their ship gone, even if the Governor is removed and the Marines oppose us, their effectiveness will be limited. We are many and they are few."

"True," said Sweet. "That was a lucky break for us, all right."

Rhinehart looked at Sweet and didn't like what he saw. The man was positively gloating about the loss of an Imperial Navy vessel and the deaths of an unknown number of crew. Sweet's plan would make Rhinehart a wealthy man if it worked, but that didn't mean that he had abandoned every last shred of decency and loyalty. The holy plan—the plan that Tatiana and Sweet had assured him would be nearly bloodless—had already cost far more human lives than Rhinehart had countenanced. If he had known in the beginning what the price would be, he would have turned them down flat.

He had given up everything for the sake of one roll of the dice, and Sweet had promised him that the dice were already fixed. The plan could not fail. And yet here he was, forced out of his comfortable home by a pack of maddened, possibly murderous bureaucrats, and counting the days until word arrived that the Emperor had sacked him. The invasion, upon which everything depended, would be two or three days late, and timing was critical to the plan. If he was removed from office before the thing was properly under way, the Marines—even without their ship—might still manage to repel the Jhino onslaught. And Sweet had made it perfectly clear that unless the Jhino could take and hold the vital plantation lands, there would be no payoff.

It was insane to rely on these vile Jhino in the first place. True, they were more efficient—more human, in all essential respects—than the dreamy, backward Myn. But they were also vicious, hateful creatures, arrogant, cruel, and depraved. No one talked about it, but on the flight over from the Compound, Rhinehart had caught a glimpse of what the Jhino were doing to the Myn. The acrid odor of those fires permeated the city and sickened Rhinehart. Jangleth had looked him in the eye and sworn to him that there would be no unnecessary killing; he supposed that Jangleth, by his own lights, had kept his word. To Jangleth, it was necessary to kill every Myn.

"Have you heard anything about Tatiana?" Rhinehart asked Sweet.

"As far as I know," he said, "she's still in custody. I wouldn't worry about her. She wants to be paid just as much as you do. Anyway, there's not much she could say against either one of us that would stand up in court."

"But if she talks at all," Rhinehart pointed out, "that could give Throneberry the pretext to arrest me and start giving orders to the Marines."

"Markova won't talk and Throneberry wouldn't risk it even if she did. What's more, the Marines wouldn't risk disobeying your orders in favor of hers. Anyway, it's far from certain that the Emperor will remove you. Servitor has some clout in the Household, and Charles might just surprise everyone. After all, just look who our main opponent here is—his bitch of an ex-wife! She all but humiliated him in public with that media briefing— made him look like some impotent wuss who couldn't satisfy his woman. You think he'll be sympathetic to any of *her* complaints?" Sweet cackled contentedly. "The lovely Gloria VanDeen may just turn out to be *our* biggest asset!"

SOMETIMES, NORMAN MINGUS REFLECTED, THE system worked too well. Over the course of forty years, he had tweaked and refined the procedures and protocols of Dexta until the entire apparatus fairly hummed with purpose and efficiency. Standing atop a pyramid of a million bureaucrats administering twenty-six hundred planets, Mingus was both master and servant of the system. He snapped his fingers, and things happened; yet sometimes, the reverse was true, and things happened that ultimately forced him to snap his fingers. The system facilitated the flow of information and imperatives in both directions, and Mingus was as much a prisoner of that system as any Level XV drone.

Just now, Mingus was reading a smart-ass memo produced by one such drone, a Level XV named Gordon Chesbro. In the normal course of events, Mingus would remain happily unaware of Chesbro's existence, and Chesbro's words wouldn't get to within ten levels of him. But sometimes the system propelled flotsam like this memo all the way up to the highest levels, driven by winds of institutional paranoia, personal loyalties and rivalries, and circumstantial quirks. During this memo's journey upward, Chesbro's name had, of course, been deleted by successive layers of superiors whose own names, in turn, had been deleted by their own superiors. Typically, that process continued until the balance between the desire for credit and the fear of blame shifted in favor of blame. At that point, a superior either halted the memo's progress or sent it onward with no endorsement and the subordinate's name undeleted.

In this instance, that point had been reached at Level X, when Sector 8 Supervisor Hector Konrad passed the memo along with Deputy Supervisor (Level XI) Grant Enright's name still affixed to it. But Mingus's console had a function that allowed him to restore all the deleted names and thus follow the progress of the memo, from its lowly origins onward. He could trace the intricate workings of the system by such means, and gain a feel for how well or how poorly it was functioning. Like a spider at the center of a web, Mingus remained sensitive to every subtle vibration of each silken thread.

Today, the vibrations were troubling. Far away, on a backwater world of no intrinsic importance, Dexta people had died in the performance of their duties. The vibrations had reached Manhattan and quickly propagated upward. Mingus charted their course to his desk.

Gloria VanDeen's report and Appreciation from Mynjhino, by way of a courier from Pecos, had spurred her own subordinates into action. Zoe Zachary (Level XIV), acting in place of VanDeen, had ordered Gordon Chesbro (Level XV) to prepare this memo in support of the VanDeen report. Zachary had quickly filtered it through the Beta-5 Coordinating Supervisors, all Level XIII, adding footnotes from Fresco Terwilliger (Agriculture), Nancy Nfumi (Corporate), Raoul Tellemacher (Banking), Phillip Benz (External Security), and a catty personal observation from Althea Dante (Imperial).

Zachary then sent the revised and amended memo

onward to Beta Division Associate Supervisor Balthazar
Trobriand (Level XII), a flashy but efficient nonentity,
who added his own name to the memo and promptly
dispatched it to Deputy Supervisor for Beta Division,
Grant Enright (Level XI). According to the time hacks
on the memo, Enright spent a full hour with it, adding
revisions, corrections, and a rather bold personal endorsement, before sending it upward to Sector Supervisor Hector Konrad (Level X).

Konrad also spent time with the package, taking the
trouble to add a negative and unflattering assessment of
Gloria VanDeen and the reliability of her initial report.
Given the importance and inflammatory nature of the
subject matter, he could not risk squelching it, so he sent
it onward without endorsement. It was clear to Mingus
that VanDeen had the loyalty and respect of her subordinates and peers, the support of her immediate superiors, and the unqualified animosity of Konrad.

From Konrad, the package quickly passed through
the hands of Deputy Assistant Sector Administrator for
Administration Nigel Raines (Level IX), who apparently
didn't even take the time to read it, and Assistant Sector
Administrator Viveca Kwan (Level VIII), who seemed
to have read it quickly and attached a brief note com-
mending VanDeen for her diligence and willingness to
stand behind her controversial and potentially dangerous assessment of the situation on Mynjhino. Kwan sent
it on to Sector Administrator Lars Ringold (Level VII),
who pondered it for nearly an hour before adding a
very brief note ("This needs immediate attention!—
LR") and sending it out of Sector and upward to Quadrant, where Deputy Assistant Quadrant Administrator
Sylvia Twining (Level VI) read nothing but Ringold's
note before transmitting it to Assistant Quadrant Administrator Giselle Mirabelli (Level V).

Mirabelli wasted no time in bringing the matter to
Quadrant 2 Administrator Manton Grigsby (Level IV).
Grigsby, a good man, a fastidious administrator, and a

fair golfer, promptly took it to Assistant Secretary for Administration Theodora Quisp (Level III). Theodora, who reminded Mingus of the loving but imperious governess he'd had as a child, alerted Executive Assistant Secretary Hiroshi Kapok (Level II) that something important was happening off in the far reaches of Sector 8. Loyal, brutally efficient Hiroshi read through the entire package and decided that there was no time or need to reduce it all to a short, easily digested précis. Hiroshi had the virtue of knowing what Mingus needed to see, whether he wanted to see it or not, and making certain that he did, in fact, see it.

So, now, the smart-ass memo, originally generated by Gordon Chesbro hours earlier, resided in the console of Norman Mingus, who read it and the rest of the package with a growing sense of displeasure. He had already read the VanDeen Appreciation, which the stunning young woman had recklessly sent directly to him. Her brains were obviously as good as her breasts, and it seemed that she had courage and convictions, as well. Mingus wondered about her judgment, but could not fault her overall assessment of the mess on Mynjhino.

The Marines would have landed on Mynjhino by now, and would be subject to the orders of Imperial Governor Vladislav Rhinehart, a political hack who owed his office to the departed Darius IV. According to VanDeen, Rhinehart was apparently in league with a corporate assassin from Servitor named Randall Sweet. Mingus had never heard of Sweet, but knew the type all too well. Each of the Big Twelve had them, of course, but Servitor had more than its share. That was a faithful reflection of the personality of Servitor's Board Chairman, Govert Magnusson, whom Mingus had known for fifty years. Magnusson was as charming as he was detestable, and almost always found a way to get what he wanted. The best thing Mingus could say about Magnusson was that he was not quite as detestable as his children.

But the immediate problem was Rhinehart. The

much-traveled memo from the previously and deservedly anonymous Gordon Chesbro was nothing less than an indictment of Rhinehart. It cataloged every mistake, misjudgment, error, lapse, lie, and boneheaded act of sheer stupidity attributable to Rhinehart during the course of his administration on Mynjhino. The list was long, detailed, and depressing. If even half of it were true, the man should have been retired years ago.

Combined with the VanDeen Appreciation of recent events on Mynjhino, the memo made a powerful case against Rhinehart. If it were up to Mingus, Rhinehart would be consigned to the oblivion he had so thoroughly earned. To let such a man issue orders to Imperial Marines was like giving a charged plasma pistol to a certified idiot. If the plot alleged by VanDeen was real, Rhinehart would be in a position to do serious and lasting harm to an entire planet. And if the plot turned out to be nothing more than the product of VanDeen's overactive imagination, the Jhino invasion of Myn certainly *was* real. As the various addenda to the original memo made clear, the Jhino and Myn were blood enemies, and the potential for a tragedy existed. Rhinehart was hardly a man who could be relied upon to prevent it. He had already given at least tacit approval to the Jhino invasion and was in a position to provide the enterprise with direct aid and support.

Rhinehart had to be removed. But Rhinehart was an Imperial appointment, and Mingus had no power over Imperial personnel. During his stewardship of Dexta, Mingus had dealt with three different Emperors, and not one of them had welcomed his interference with Imperial prerogatives. Except in matters of war and external relations, Emperors were a rather toothless lot. Hamstrung by constitutional strictures and Dexta's vast bureaucratic inertia, Emperors played little role in purely internal affairs; on a day-to-day basis, Norman Mingus ran the Empire, and not Charles V. The one area in which Emperors did have meaningful power within the Empire was in the matter of Imperial appointments. Twenty-six hundred and forty-three Imperial Governors owed their positions to the Emperor and no one else. Consequently, Emperors tended to regard any attack on their Governors as an attack on the Household itself. Not even Norman Mingus could tell an Emperor to fire a Governor. All he could do was advise.

Mingus reluctantly pressed a button on his console. "Hiroshi? Where is Charles today?"

"Still in Rio," Kapok told him.

"Very well. Call the Chamberlain and tell him I'm coming. Tell him it's urgent."

"Mynjhino?"

"Mynjhino."

"You know, of course, that Gloria VanDeen—"

"I know," Mingus said, "I know." One more complication. Norman Mingus hated complications.

EMPEROR CHARLES V, STILL DRESSED FOR tennis and perspiring, welcomed Norman Mingus to the Residence and showed him to a seat on the veranda overlooking the swimming pool. Servants instantly provided them with cold drinks, then quickly vanished.

"We don't see enough of you around here, Norman," Charles said affably. "Missed you at the Levee."

"I'm too old for those things, Highness," Mingus told him. "All those undressed women give me heart palpitations."

Charles glanced toward the pool, where three undressed women were lazily sunning themselves. "We can move inside, if you'd like," Charles said.

"I'm just fine, thank you, Highness. I said I was old; I didn't say I was dead."

"In that case, if you would care to meet my friends..."

"Thank you, Highness, but I'm afraid we have some rather urgent business to discuss. A crisis has developed on Mynjhino, and I believe that it requires your personal attention."

Charles leaned back in his chair to get comfortable, idly scratched his bare knee, and took a sip of his drink. "A crisis," he said. "Very well, then, Norman. Give me the particulars, if you would."

Mingus proceeded to give the Emperor a five-minute briefing on the history, ethnography, geography, and politics of Mynjhino, the dubious accomplishments of Imperial Governor Vladislav Rhinehart, the activities of the Myn-Traha, the evacuation of Myn, the Jhino invasion, the assignment of a company of Marines to the planet, the deaths of five Dexta personnel, and the outlines of the possible conspiracy involving the Governor and a representative of Servitor. He managed not to mention Gloria VanDeen, but Charles had his own sources of information.

"Gloria always had a very active imagination," Charles commented. "You don't really believe this scenario of hers, do you, Norman?"

"I find it plausible, Highness, although not proven. In any event, whether or not such a conspiracy exists, the Jhino invasion of Myn is an accomplished fact. The two races have been enemies for thousands of years, and if the Jhino have superior weaponry, they will undoubtedly use it to enslave or destroy the Myn."

"Surely the Marines can handle them," said Charles.

"A single company of Marines would be hard-pressed to deal with an entire army, Highness," said Mingus. "And if Rhinehart is truly plotting with Servitor and the Jhino, then the Marines would be powerless to intervene. If you were to remove Rhinehart now, it might still be possible to handle this situation with a single company. The invasion is still in its early stages, and a show of force could be enough to deter the Jhino from further aggression. If we delay until the Jhino have actually conquered Myn, it would require a division or more to reverse the outcome."

"Impossible," Charles declared. "I'm not about to order a division of Imperial Marines to go sort out an internal squabble on some two-crown planet inside the Empire."

"Yes, I suspected as much, Highness. But by acting now, you could prevent that from ever becoming necessary."

Charles nodded thoughtfully. "So you want me to remove Rhinehart."

"The man is an incompetent, and quite possibly a criminal, Highness. He did a few favors for Darius, and I presume that he has survived this long only by virtue of being inconsequential and invisible. You'd have gotten around to replacing him eventually in any case, Highness. Why not do it now, and possibly save us all a great deal of trouble?"

"I'm reliably informed," said Charles, "that Rhinehart is an ass. However, Norman, at the moment, he is an Imperial Ass. I value your advice, but you have your own garden to tend to. Let me tend to mine."

"Highness—"

"Thank you for coming, Norman." Charles was on his feet and extending his hand. Mingus rose and took it.

"This requires immediate attention, Highness."

"Indeed," said Charles. "Have a good day, Norman. I'll let you know what I decide."

CHARLES WATCHED THE DEXTA SECRETARY make his reluctant departure, then returned to his seat and his drink. Mingus had been in power far too long, but he was a fixture of the Empire and knew where too many important bodies were buried. He had all the support he needed in Parliament, and his public image of steadfast reliability was unassailable. Charles could not remove Mingus; the best he could do was to remind him of his place, whenever possible.

So, thought Charles, Gloria has unraveled the Servitor plot. A shame, really. Freddy Magnusson had given him some of that jigli weed from Mynjhino only a couple of weeks ago. It was quite extraordinary stuff, and Charles had managed to satisfy no fewer than five different women in a single night while under its powerful influence. Servitor would undoubtedly make billions on it, once they got into production. *If* they got into production.

Freddy had outlined the general plan by which his father's company intended to exploit the discovery of this marvelous herb. Apparently the first part of the plan had come off as expected, and Servitor had snapped up GalaxCo's holdings for a song. There had been some unfortunate human casualties in the process, but there were casualties in every war. And the Big Twelve were at war—that was an immutable fact of life in the Empire, even if the reality of it eluded the vast majority of the population. Servitor had scored a victory at GalaxCo's expense on Mynjhino, but GalaxCo would make up the loss somewhere else against some other opponent. Emperors, and even Dexta Secretaries, came and went, but the Big Twelve endured and the war continued. All Charles could do was attempt to referee the contest with a modicum of impartiality and make sure that the casualties were kept within acceptable limits.

But now, these Jhino characters were threatening to blow the lid off the game and do some serious damage. Servitor should have known better than to make them key players in their little plot. Charles was willing to put up with a lot from the Big Twelve, but he had no intention of standing idly by while a genocide occurred. History tended to dwell on such events, and Charles didn't want a stain like that on his own record.

It seemed that he would have to do something to prevent the Jhino from running riot. They had already killed two Dexta people, and Spirit only knew what they would do to the Myn if they got the chance. Freddy had assured him that the invasion would be swift and relatively bloodless, since the Jhino had been provided with some antique weapons that were better than anything the Myn had available. The logic, he supposed, was that the Myn would simply surrender and the Jhino would impose a civilized and enlightened occupation upon them. Idiocy. It was a shame, but Servitor was going to have to do without its jigli plantations for the sake of the greater good.

As Mingus had suspected, Rhinehart was already on the list of future ex-Governors, so he would be no loss. If the Jhino invasion were to be forestalled or reversed, swift action would be required. He could sack Rhinehart and let the local Imperial Secretary take over for the time being, and the Marines would be freed to do whatever was necessary. If one company wasn't enough, he could always send another.

A solution to the problem was at hand, then. Simple. Effective.

Perhaps, he wondered, too simple, and too effective?

Was it really necessary to give up those jigli plantations? If he could save them for Servitor, somehow, Charles was certain that Freddy Magnusson could be induced to express his gratitude in some tangible, untraceable form. It wasn't cheap to run the Household, and Parliament could be contentious and parsimonious concerning appropriations for Imperial perquisites. Charles already received payments of one sort or another from each of the Big Twelve. There were limits to how much he could reasonably extort from them, but there were always new possibilities. How much would the jigli plantations be worth to Servitor?

Could he have his jigli and smoke it, too? As long as he was able to prevent a genocide, did it really matter to anyone whether those plantations were run by the Myn or the Jhino? According to Freddy, Jhino administration was essential because the Myn, for bizarre religious reasons, would never agree to grow the stuff for export. So the question was how to put the Jhino in control of the plantation regions without letting them massacre millions of Myn in the process. If Freddy's projected schedule was accurate, the Jhino would already have seized the plantations before any new orders could reach the planet. If they managed to do it without a wholesale slaughter, perhaps it might be possible to let them keep what they had taken while preventing them from extending their conquest to the rest of the continent.

Charles tapped his wristcom. "Baxter? Get Burke, Rahim, and Tsao in here in an hour. And get the most detailed maps available for Mynjhino. I also want to speak to Freddy Magnusson as soon as possible."

The Emperor promptly met with his senior staff and laid out the situation for them. Poring over the maps and the detailed information from Freddy Magnusson on the precise locations of the new Servitor plantations, they worked out a feasible plan. It would preserve the Myn from extermination while giving Servitor everything it wanted and the Jhino most of what they wanted. And it could all be justified as a fair and equitable means of avoiding a direct conflict between the Empire and the armed forces of Jhino. Charles was certain he could find enough support for the plan in Parliament to make it palatable to the public, who, in any case, had scarcely heard of Mynjhino and had no reason to care about it.

As they were putting the finishing touches on the orders that would be sent by courier to Mynjhino, Baxter, the Emperor's fussy and efficient Chamberlain, came in with a look of distress on his pinched face. "Sire," he said, "I think you ought to see this. We took it off the ENS feed."

Charles and his staff looked toward the vid screen on one wall and spent the next hour watching Gloria VanDeen's media briefing on Pecos and an interview she had granted to an ENS reporter. The Emperor silently fumed while his staff stole anxious glances at him. When the presentation was complete, Charles finally erupted.

"Damn that woman. Damn her!" He slammed a clenched fist on the map table, then got to his feet and kicked a trash basket halfway across the room.

"Did you hear her?" he demanded of his staff. "She gave her *personal* pledge that the Myn could return to their homes in safety! Her *personal* pledge, mind you. The personal pledge of a Level XIII Dexta drone! It's not enough that she tells the whole Empire that I'm not man enough for her! No, now she has to stick her little nose into policy, and give her *personal* pledge that she'll make everything right again on some backwater world that nobody ever heard of in the first place. Damn her!"

When he had calmed down somewhat, several minutes later, his staff pointed out to him that the VanDeen statements didn't really change anything. She was speaking purely on her own, and not even on behalf of Dexta. Her veiled accusations of corporate and Imperial conspiracies were unsupported by hard evidence. Nothing she said could prevent the execution of the plan they had just agreed upon.

"You don't get it, do you?" Charles said when they were through. "That bitch just made the whole thing *personal*! If I do anything at all now that goes against what *she* says should be done, then it will look like *I'm* being personal too. I'll have sacrificed the lives of the noble Myn just to get even with my shrew of an ex-wife. Did you see her? Did you see those tits of hers? How in hell can I compete with *that*?"

No one had an answer.

Suddenly, Charles laughed. His staff soon laughed nervously too, although they weren't quite sure why.

"Gentlemen," he asked them, a broad, satisfied smile on his face, "what is the one thing I can do that will annoy her the most? What is the one thing I can do that will cause the most problems for that arrogant witch?

What can I do that will bring down the high-and-mighty bitch-goddess of Dexta once and for all?"

The staff men stared at him and shook their heads.

"Don't know, boys?" Charles said. "Don't worry— *I* do!"

chapter 24

GLORIA STOOD IN THE MIDDLE OF AN OPEN
field, surrounded by chaos and fear. Thirty-five miles
beyond the city they had fled in panic, more than a hundred thousand Myn had come to a halt because they had
nowhere left to go. Ten miles ahead of them, Jhino
troops, ferried by skimmers, had already occupied the
town of Khoti. As Major Barnes had feared, the Jhino
had hopscotched ahead of their projected line of advance and seized key locations along the roads to the
plantation region. Two days after the unexpected downpour on Sunday night, the main Jhino force, now num-
bering more than thirty thousand, was still stalled in
Dhanj, waiting for the mud to dry. But in the meantime,
they had not been idle.

All around her, Gloria saw Myn clumped together in
family groups, sitting around piles of their meager possessions, staring off into space with big brown eyes devoid of
hope. Other Myn wandered aimlessly through the encampment, searching for friends or family, trilling from
time to time, like lost birds in a cloud bank. Some Myn

simply sat by themselves, heads tilted back, eyes closed, evidently communing with their ancestors. Gloria only hoped that their ancestors could offer them some reason for optimism; she certainly couldn't.

Now in its second day, what the Marines were calling Operation Flying Fish had at least managed to offer the Myn a reprieve from hunger. The SALs were working day and night, delivering hundreds of tons of fresh fish to a dozen different refugee camps, some of them even larger than this one. Because of a scarcity of fuel, most of the Myn were forced to eat the fish raw, but they didn't seem to mind. That was the truly astonishing thing to Gloria; despite their fear and despair, the Myn never complained, never protested. They accepted the handouts from the humans with gratitude and shared the fish as fairly as possible, never asking for more, never begging for help. Either they were resigned to their fate, or their ancestors had persuaded them to remain calm and patient.

For her part, Gloria felt anger and frustration. The tragedy unfolding before her eyes was overwhelming, and her inability to do anything meaningful to prevent it left her cross and impatient. When Corporal Hadaad, the driver of her scout skimmer, came up to her and offered her a candy bar from his ration pack, she simply shook her head and turned away from him.

"Come on, ma'am," Hadaad insisted, "you have to look after yourself. I know it's hard, but if you don't eat, you're not going to be able to do anything to help these poor folks."

"What makes you think I can do anything for them anyway?" Gloria snapped at him, and instantly regretted it. She stuck her hands into the pockets of her jeans, stared at the trampled-down grass beneath her feet for a few moments, then raised her head and smiled wanly at Hadaad. "I'm sorry, Corporal."

"No sweat," said Hadaad. "I'm just as pissed off as you are, ma'am. I've seen some shitty things since I've been in the Corps, but this tops 'em all. One thing I've learned, though."

"What's that?"

"A candy bar never hurts, and sometimes it can even help a little." He held out the bar to her, and she smiled and took it from him.

As she was opening the wrapper, a young Myn, barely three feet tall, wandered over to her. It was sucking on what appeared to be a dry stick. The child looked up at her and reached out with its tiny hand. It poked its forefinger into her navel and trilled in curiosity. The Myn didn't have belly buttons. Then it ran its hand over the strange, smooth flesh of her bared belly until it found a stray pubic hair curling over the top of her low-slung jeans and tugged on it experimentally. It reached for its own belly fur and pulled on that, trilling happily. It had found something in common with the tall, furless alien and seemed delighted by the discovery. Gloria laughed and handed the child her candy bar. It stared at it in confusion for a moment, then stuck the candy into its mouth and sucked on it instead of the dry twig. The child's huge eyes widened, it gave a loud, shrill trill, then dashed off to find its parents.

"Can't do that, ma'am," Hadaad chided her. "Can't feed 'em all. Here, take this dried apricot bar. Eat it yourself, ma'am—it would be downright cruel to give this crap to the Myn. They're suffering enough already."

Gloria was choking down the apricot bar, which was every bit as bad as Hadaad claimed, when a SAL arrived overhead. Beneath it was slung a long, bulging fishnet, overflowing with a wet, silvery bounty from the ocean. The fish of Mynjhino looked remarkably like fish on Earth—evolution had solved the same design problems in the same way on both worlds—except that instead of scales, they generally had a thin, tough, leathery skin. An open area quickly materialized beneath the SAL as Myn scampered out of the way. Two of the lines holding the net in place slackened, and an avalanche of seafood spilled onto the field below.

Thousands of Myn raced for the drop site, and an excited trilling filled the air. Yet the confusion was remarkably polite, and no one was trampled or seriously hurt in the crush. The Myn scooped up whatever they could hold and made their way back to their own spots in the field, giving others a chance to share in the meal. Within fifteen minutes, the pile of fish had vanished, and throughout the camp, Myn were gnawing contentedly on the raw seafood.

Gloria watched from a distance and felt a small measure of satisfaction. The Myn in this camp would survive for at least a few more days—or until the Jhino army began its march.

A Myn child ran up to her, and Gloria realized that it was the same one she had given the candy bar; she was beginning to be able to tell the Myn apart, now. The child trilled something, then held up its tiny hand to her. In it, there was a small, silvery fish, about the size of a sardine. Gloria hesitated, then accepted the offering from the child. The child stood waiting expectantly, so Gloria could do nothing but raise the fish to her lips and pop it into her mouth. The Myn child seemed to smile at her, then ran off again, trilling excitedly.

Gloria reluctantly began to chew the fish, and was pleasantly surprised. It was better than the apricot bar.

A few minutes later, a scout skimmer swooped in from the east and landed next to Gloria's skimmer. Major Barnes got out of it and walked over to her, pausing to return Hadaad's salute.

"How's it going here?" he asked.

"Another delivery about twenty minutes ago," Gloria told him. "I hate to think what they'd be doing without it. What about the other camps?"

"Everything is working pretty well," said Barnes. "No significant problems on that score. However, I'm afraid I have some bad news. The Jhino have staged another airborne assault, this time on Prazhdi, about a hundred klicks inland from here."

Barnes removed his pad from his belt, tapped a few buttons, and held up the map display for Gloria to see.

"It's obvious that they're making for the plantations," said Barnes. "They've already secured the bridge over the river at Prazhdi, and I'd guess that their next target will be ninety kilometers farther on, at Skashji. Once they take it, they'll have effective control of the whole lower piedmont region and all the plantations in that area. If they have enough skimmers, they can move on from there to Krajhni, and get a foothold in the upper piedmont. By the time they march out of Dhanj, they'll have clear sailing all the way to their objectives."

"And what happens to all the Myn caught in their path?" Gloria asked, gesturing to the encampment surrounding them.

"If they take to the countryside and stay away from the roads, they should be all right for the immediate future. Jangleth will keep his troops on the march and worry about mopping up later."

"But if they all scatter, we'll never be able to feed them!"

Barnes nodded. "That's the choice they face, I'm afraid," he said. "Starve or get shot."

"Were there any casualties at Prazhdi?" Gloria asked.

"There was some gunfire," said Barnes. "But most of the population ran as soon as they realized what was happening. I suppose we'll need to reconnoiter the area and try to set up a fish drop out that way. We're already stretched pretty close to our limit, though. We can't go on indefinitely feeding millions of Myn with just four SALs at our disposal."

"Three more days, Delbert," Gloria said. "If we can hang on for three more days, we'll get that courier and maybe we'll be able to stop those bastards."

"Maybe," said Barnes. "But the roads are already

firming up around Dhanj. They'll be ready to march by tomorrow morning. Once they get out of the city, I don't see how in hell we can stop them. There are two major roads that lead to the plantation district, and they'll be spread out along both of them. Add in the towns they've already taken or will take, and there's just too much ground for us to cover. We don't have enough vehicles, and we don't have enough troops. Anyway, this morning Riley delivered an order from the Governor, instructing me to keep the Marines at least five miles away from the Jhino line of march. I can't disobey it, and even if I did, there's no way we can be everywhere we need to be."

"We'll find a way," Gloria insisted as she gazed at the crowds of Myn around them. "We've *got* to find a way!"

THE SCOUT SKIMMER LANDED INSIDE THE Compound, and as Gloria got out of it, Bryce Denton ran up to her. "We got a messenger from Pecos this morning," he told her. "And that's not all we got."

"What do you mean?"

"The competition arrived on a shuttle. Right now, Hawkes is busy briefing a dozen media reps. Thanks to you, Mynjhino is the biggest story in the Empire."

"It *is*?" Gloria was more than a little surprised by the news. She had hoped to stir up enough interest to generate some public support for the Myn; that would create pressure on Dexta and the Household to take at least some measures to deal with the situation. "Aren't you exaggerating a bit?" she wondered. "I mean, you couldn't have heard anything from Earth yet."

"Nothing from Earth," Denton affirmed, "but the whole Beta Division is buzzing. Between my intrepid reporting and your fabulous body, Mynjhino is all anyone is talking about."

"Spirit, Bryce, do you have to hype everything?"

"No hype, Gloria," Denton said, holding up his hand as if to swear an oath. "Listen, there are two ancient axioms that the news business has lived by for centuries. One is 'Sex sells,' and the other is 'If it bleeds, it leads.' The Jhino are providing the blood, and you're providing the sex. It's an irresistible story. Everyone is waiting to see what that gorgeous Gloria VanDeen is going to do next. Hell, on Pecos, people are even coming into the Dexta office and volunteering to come to Mynjhino and help the poor Myn."

"They *are*?"

"Hundreds of 'em! And it's all because of you, babe. If anyone else had given that briefing, or if you had done it dressed like some gray Dexta drone, people would have paused for about five seconds, and said, 'Oh my goodness, those poor Myn,' then forgotten all about it. But you made the whole thing personal—a human interest story with a sexy, courageous heroine. You already stood up to the Emperor, and now you're standing up to the savage hordes of Jhino. You made people want to get involved and come here to help—not just help the Myn, but help *you*!"

"People are really volunteering? You're not just hyping this?"

Denton shook his head emphatically. "No, ma'am. A couple of freighter captains have even offered their ships to take the volunteers here. They'd be on the way already, except that the Dexta officials on Pecos say that they have no authority permitting them to accept volunteers for duty on another planet. If you don't believe me, just go in and meet with those media reps. But do me a favor and give me an exclusive first, okay?"

"There's something I've got to do first. Bryce, go get Hawkes and bring him to Melinda's office."

"For you, anything." Denton hurried off to the administration building.

Gloria tapped a code into her wristcom. "Delbert? Where are you?"

"On my way back to the Compound, Gloria. Why?"

"Can you meet me in Melinda's office in ten minutes?"

"Can do," said Barnes. "What's up?"

"I'll tell you when you get here." She closed the connection, then tapped in Petra's code.

"Petra's Laundry Service," she answered. "How may we serve you?"

"What are you babbling about?" Gloria demanded.

"Hi, Gloria. I'm in the basement of the administration building, doing my laundry. And yours too, I might add. No, don't thank me, I do this for all the Thirteens who hold my future in the palms of their hands."

"The future is now, Petra. Drop your duds and grab your pad, then get over to Melinda's office. There's something I want you to look up for me."

GLORIA, MELINDA, HAWKES, BARNES, DENTON, and Petra assembled around the conference table in Melinda's office. "Major Barnes," Gloria said to him, "what could you do with a thousand volunteers?"

"Volunteers? Gloria, there aren't a thousand humans left in all of Myn."

"These volunteers are on Pecos," Gloria said. "Bryce, tell them."

"It's true," Denton said. "Gloria's media briefing stirred up a regular hornet's nest. People are lining up to come and help the Myn, especially since they got the news about the loss of the *Myrt*. And my images of those funeral pyres in Dhanj also had some effect. The problem is, Dexta says they have no authority to send volunteers to Mynjhino, even though ships are available."

"It's not a problem any longer," Gloria said. "Petra?"

Petra held up her pad and read from it. "*Dexta Code*, Chapter Twenty-four, Paragraph Nine, Subsection A. 'During a declared state of Unlimited Emergency, or in the event of natural disaster, civil unrest, armed rebellion, or foreign invasion, Dexta officials may deputize such persons within their jurisdiction as may be necessary to perform services essential to the preservation and maintenance of public safety. Such deputies may include, but are not limited to, police, fire, emergency, and unattached military personnel. Said deputies shall be subject to the lawful orders of Dexta officials or such other legally constituted authorities as may be designated.'"

"As Coordinating Supervisor for Beta-5," Gloria said, "both Pecos and Mynjhino are within my jurisdiction. I can give the word to the media, then piggyback specific instructions to the Dexta office on Pecos aboard their messenger. Bryce, how soon could they get here?"

"The messenger will reach Pecos late tonight. If the word goes out early tomorrow, the ships could be on their way by late afternoon. They ought to arrive here no later than early Friday morning."

"There you are, Delbert," said Gloria. "Now, what could you do with them?"

Barnes took a deep breath and let it out in one big puff. "Look, Gloria," he said, "this may sound good to you, but what I see is a thousand well-meaning but incompetent civilians running around loose, getting in the way, and endangering themselves and everyone else."

"Not civilians," Gloria objected. "We'll accept only police, fire, and emergency personnel, all of them trained to deal with crisis situations and accustomed to taking orders. The police can even bring their own weapons, and probably supply them to the others. And they won't be alone. They'll have a core of active-duty military personnel to lead them."

"Not from me, they won't," Barnes said firmly. "I have explicit orders to keep the Marines away from the Jhino line of march. And if I can't order the Marines in, I sure as hell am not going to order in a bunch of civilians, no matter how well trained they are."

Gloria smiled, and said, "Petra."

"*Imperial Code*," Petra read, "Article Fifty-seven,

Paragraph Three, Subsection C. 'Naval personnel whose assigned ship has been lost are considered to be un-attached until such time as they may be reassigned to another vessel or to other positions.'"

Barnes looked at Gloria. "The swabbies?"

"Why not? They may be nominally under your com-mand, but technically, they are unattached. Therefore, they can be deputized. And as deputies, they will no longer be subject to your orders—they'll be subject to *mine*."

Barnes scratched his head and frowned. "I don't know," he said doubtfully.

"Come on, Major," Denton prodded him. "Take a chance."

"That's easy for you to say, Denton. It would make a hell of a good story either way for you, wouldn't it? A thousand civilian volunteers getting shot to pieces would be lead-screen stuff, right?"

Denton looked offended. "Hey, give me a little credit, would you? A hundred thousand Myn getting shot to pieces would be a great story too, but it's not one that I want to report."

"Look," Gloria said quickly, "the volunteers could even bring along extra skimmers, so we'd have addi-tional transport."

"And just what do you propose doing with them?" Barnes asked her.

"According to your map," said Gloria, "there are five major refugee camps along the two roads the Jhino will be using. We could send two hundred armed volun-teers to each of them, along with a dozen of the Navy people to command them. They could take up defensive positions along the side of the road, between the Jhino and the Myn. I don't think the Jhino would dare to try anything."

"You realize, don't you," Barnes said, "that all it would take is one panicky Jhino or one hotheaded vol-unteer to turn it into a bloodbath?"

"It's a risk I'm willing to take," Gloria said. "I intend to be there with them. After all, I'll be their commanding officer."

"I don't like it either," Hawkes put in, "but I don't see that we have any choice. If we don't try it, the Myn will either be massacred in the camps or starve in the hills. And if something does go wrong, Major, then all bets are off, and you'll be free to send in your Marines."

Barnes ran his hand through his short, spiky hair. "I can't begin to tell you all the things I hate about this," he said. "But there's a chance that it could work, and I guess I'm not willing to ignore that chance with so much at stake. Okay, Gloria, count me in."

"Me too," said Melinda, "although I hate this even more than Major Barnes does. Gloria, I really think this whole thing has gone to your head. Who the hell do you think you are, Joan of Arc? In the long and checkered history of Dexta, I seriously doubt that any Level XIII bureaucrat has ever led an army into battle."

"If we do it right, Melinda," Gloria replied, "there won't *be* a battle. By midday Friday, the Jhino will march past the camps and nothing will happen. And maybe by that afternoon, we'll have a courier that tells us Rhinehart has been fired and that you have been appointed Acting Governor. Then you can give Major Barnes orders that let him do whatever needs to be done to turn back the invasion. With the volunteers and Navy people guarding the camps, he'll have his entire force available. We can *do* this, Melinda!"

"Maybe," Melinda agreed. "But I still hate it. As Acting Governor, my first order will be to see to it that you have your head examined. If it's still attached to your shoulders by then."

AS SHE SPOKE TO THE MEDIA REPS OUTSIDE THE administration building, Gloria wondered if there might be some truth to what Melinda had said. Maybe it *had* gone to her head. She couldn't honestly deny that there was a tangible thrill associated with being the darling of the media and the heroine of vid-watching masses throughout the Empire. If they wanted a sexy and courageous leading lady for their real-life melodrama, she was willing to play the part if that was what was necessary. She could only hope that she had the courage, but the sexy part was something she knew she could handle. Before meeting the reps, she tugged her jeans down even lower and spread the unbuttoned front of her floppy blue shirt open far enough to half expose her nipples.

If she was secretly enjoying herself—and why not?—she was also deadly serious in what she said. She emphasized to the potential volunteers that they would be entering an extremely dangerous situation. This would not be a holiday outing. On her authority as Coordinating Supervisor for Beta-5, she instructed the Pecos office of Dexta to accept only those volunteers who were members of recognized police, fire, or emergency organizations, or military veterans. She didn't want any yahoos from private militias—of which Pecos had more than its share—or starry-eyed, thrill-seeking romantics.

"The Myn need you," she said, "the Empire needs you, and I need you. I ask you to stand with me and help us prevent a tragedy. Too often in history, good people have been content to watch from the sidelines while evil triumphs. Afterward, they turn to one another, and ask, 'What could we have done?' Today, we *know* what can be done, and it needs only the courage and commitment of good and dedicated people to see to it that it *is* done. I ask you to join me on Mynjhino, as we strive to write a new page in history, one that our descendants will be proud to read. Thank you, and I look forward to seeing you here on Mynjhino."

She turned and strode purposefully away from the media and their imagers, taking care to sway her hips as she did so. Sex and rhetoric made a powerful combination.

"Wow," said Petra as she joined her in her walk across the Compound. "Where do I sign up?"

"*You* don't," Gloria informed her. "Friday morning, you are going to be holed up in the Comm Room. If anything goes wrong, notify the Orbital Station, ask for a shuttle on my authority, then get on the Flyer and get the hell out of here. Understand me, Petra?"

"Why is it that us cute little people never get to be heroes?"

"There's a minimum height requirement. You'll do as I said, right?"

"I don't even want to think about that."

"Petra?"

"Yes, dammit, I'll do it. Sir."

"Good. Now go and finish the laundry. I want to look devastatingly glamorous for my big day." Because, she added silently, it might be my last.

chapter 25

THE NEXT MORNING, PRIME MINISTER VEENTRO
stood on a raised platform in front of the Palqui and addressed thousands of Jhino troops assembled in orderly
ranks on the plaza. A hovering skimmer transmitted images and sounds to humans in the Compound, but none
of them understood the language of the Jhino. If they
had, they would have found Veentro's speech depress-
ingly familiar. Over the past few millennia, countless human leaders had delivered essentially the same speech
on similar occasions. Veentro spoke passionately of
things like honor, glory, racial purity, and destiny. The
Jhino responded to the speech in the same way that human armies always had, and soon marched out of the
plaza suffused with feelings of pride and bloodlust.

The Jhino army split into two columns, following
the northern and southern roads leading eastward, out
of the city. They passed resolutely through abandoned
suburbs, pausing only to commit random and meaningless acts of vandalism. Few of them indulged in looting,
since they would have been forced to carry their booty

on their own shoulders. With the available skimmers providing only a minimum of transport for the army's supplies, each soldier was weighed down by an over-loaded backpack. Between the weight of their packs and the heavy, awkward AK-47s they carried, the troops moved slowly over the soft, narrow roads. Their short legs carried them forward at a steady but limited pace. By day's end, the lead elements of the two columns made camp in and around small towns barely a dozen miles from the borders of Dhanj.

They covered more ground on the second day of the march. With no speeches to delay them, the army got an earlier start and there were fewer towns and villages along their route. The troops were buoyed by news that their skimmer-borne units had successfully taken the town of Skashji, some 110 miles ahead of them. The cowardly Myn had run, of course, just as they had run from Dhanj. The Jhino troops were disappointed that they had yet to see even a single Myn anywhere along their line of march. But they knew that, not far ahead, vast numbers of the enemy lay waiting for them in great encampments. The glory Veentro had promised them was soon to be theirs. When they came to a halt at sun-set, they were nearly thirty miles from Dhanj, and the Myn were barely five miles to the east. Tomorrow would be a day of destiny.

GLORIA AND HAWKES ROSE EARLY THAT MORN-ing, sharing coffee and fruit before the sun came up. They spoke sparingly, each of them absorbed with thoughts they would rather not have been thinking. They were not warriors, by nature or training, and overnight a hard knot of fear had formed within each of them. When they were captured by the Myn-Traha, nothing but their own lives had been at stake, but today they would bear responsibility for the lives of hundreds of humans and hundreds of thousands of defenseless

Myn. Their own safety now seemed somehow less important than the way they performed their duties, and yet self-preservation remained a powerful and unpredictable instinct. Will I stand? Will I run? They couldn't know until the moment was upon them.

They rose from the table in the administration building and went outside into the Compound, where the Marines and Navy were already busy readying SALs and skimmers. Hawkes took Gloria's hand and squeezed it. They looked into each other's eyes for a long moment, smiled silently, then, by mutual consent, released their hold on each other and walked briskly toward the Command SAL, where Major Barnes was conferring with his officers.

"Good morning," Barnes greeted them. "We've received word that the two freighters are already in orbit. They'll be landing in less than an hour."

"Then I guess we should get down to the docks to welcome them," said Hawkes.

"First platoon is already down there, clearing space for the SALs and skimmers. When they showed up, the Jhino guards pulled out. They'll be watching us, though."

"Let them," said Gloria. "There's nothing they can do to stop us now."

"I like your attitude, Gloria," Barnes told her, "but the fact is, there's a lot they could do to stop us. If they're on the ball, they could put a picket line of patrol boats into the harbor and prevent the freighters from docking."

"That would constitute interference with official Dexta traffic," Gloria said. "I could legally order the Navy people to take the SALs out and sink those boats."

Barnes and Hawkes stared at her.

"Well, I *could*," she insisted.

"Do they teach you Dexta people military tactics," Barnes asked, "or are you just making this up as you go along?"

"Hell hath no fury like a bureaucrat scorned," Gloria answered.

"And here I thought you were all nothing more than glorified filing clerks."

"We give out Purple Hearts for paper cuts and field promotions for meritorious alphabetization. If you're ready, Major, let's go to the docks."

Four SALs and six scout skimmers slowly rose from the Compound and into the pink sky of dawn. They cruised quietly toward the harbor, circled the neighborhood once, then set down in the open landing area that had been marked off by the first platoon of Marines. Gloria stepped out of the SAL and looked around at the nearby warehouses and sheds. Jhino snipers might be hiding in them, for all she knew, and could already have her centered in their crosshairs. But she could see no patrol boats in the harbor, and the early-morning quiet was broken only by the low buzz of conversation among their own forces. An odd sense of calm descended on her. She felt ready for anything.

The Marines and Navy people all greeted her with warm smiles, and some of them even saluted her. They knew her now, and she knew them. Over the past two days, she had met with all of them in small groups, explaining in detail their mission and their responsibilities in the coming operation. They understood the legalities and the tactical situation, and appreciated the danger inherent in what they would be attempting. The Marines were disappointed that they would be left out of it, but the Navy people were determined and enthusiastic. After the loss of the *Myrt,* they had felt devastated and useless; now, they would be playing a vital role, and welcomed the opportunity.

If they felt uneasy about being under the command of a civilian bureaucrat instead of one of their own officers, they didn't betray it. Gloria had made it clear that, while she bore overall operational responsibility, the tactical leadership would devolve on the Navy officers. She would defer to their judgment once they actually reached the encampments they would be guarding, and would not interfere in the normal chain of command.

The distant rumble of a sonic boom reached them, and everyone looked toward the western sky. Two bright streaks caught the early-morning sunlight high above the darkened ocean. The streaks soon resolved themselves into distinct objects as the two freighters descended toward the harbor of Dhanj. The first of them splashed down in the Roads, followed a minute later by the second. A scout skimmer flitted about them like a mosquito harrying two hippopotamuses, and led them along the channel toward the docks. The first freighter—a fat, well-experienced beast painted a dull red and bearing the logo of Garibaldi Brothers Freight, Ltd.—maneuvered into the designated slip and came to a halt flush against a pier on the left side of the slip. The second freighter, smaller, a bit sleeker, and a dirty white in color, the property of the New Laredo Trucking Company, came into the slip smoothly and clamped onto the pier on the right.

Hatches popped open and people began pouring out of the two vehicles. After some initial confusion, they began to organize themselves, aided by the naval officers and petty officers who greeted them. In Gloria's instructions to the Dexta office on Pecos, she had requested that the volunteers organize themselves into groups of two hundred, and that officers be appointed or elected to command each unit. As they assembled in twenty-by-ten blocks on the piers, skimmers began to float out of the open hatches and proceed to landings in the designated areas ashore.

Major Barnes and Lieutenant Pelleu, the senior naval officer, stood with Hawkes and Gloria on the lateral dock connecting the two piers and waited while the volunteer leaders were escorted to them by their naval liaisons. There were salutes and handshakes all around, and the volunteer leaders couldn't help grinning as they were introduced to their commanding officer.

Gloria had more than lived up to her desire to look devastatingly glamorous on the big day. She was wearing her white bodysuit, set at 80 percent transparency, with the pressure seam open down the front from neck to crotch. If the volunteers had come to Mynjhino because of her request—or because of *her*—she was determined not to disappoint them.

The volunteers' leader was Captain Frank Culpepper of the New Laredo Police Department. After ten years in the Marines, with combat experience late in the war against the Ch'gnth, he had been a cop for thirty-five years. He had a weathered face and a no-nonsense look in his gray eyes. The commanders of the individual units—henceforth to be known as Alpha, Bravo, Charlie, Dog, and Easy Companies—were also police officers, except for the Alpha Company leader, a retired Imperial Marine colonel named Beauregard ("Call me Bo!") Dunston.

After the introductions were complete, Barnes showed each of them the map display on his pad. The five refugee camps, which had been given designations corresponding to the companies assigned to them, were strung out along the two roads ahead of the advancing Jhino. Alpha, on the northern road, would be the first camp they reached, followed by Dog on the southern route. Gloria would be in overall command at Alpha, while Hawkes would play that role at Dog. Lieutenant Pelleu would be in tactical command at Alpha, and Bo Dunston and his volunteers would take their orders from him. Captain Culpepper would also be at Alpha, acting as second-in-command to Pelleu. Thirteen Navy people from the *Myrt* would be assigned to each company as squad leaders.

"We brought along our own weapons," Culpepper said. "It works out to twenty Mark V and VI plasma rifles for each company, and plasma pistols for everyone. We're loaded for bear, Ms. VanDeen."

"Well," Gloria told him, "the Jhino may look a little like bears, but they aren't. They have AK-47 automatic rifles, and they are a trained and disciplined army. Make sure that your people realize that, Captain."

"And also remind them," Barnes added, "that our goal here is to *avoid* a fight. If you've got any cowboys or crusaders in your ranks, Captain, make sure you keep them under control."

Culpepper nodded. "I had a long talk with my people on the flight over," he said. "And they had that same conversation on the other ship. I think they all understand the situation. These people are mostly police and fire officers, and they know how to take orders. They won't let you down."

"How are we fixed for skimmers?" Barnes asked.

"We've brought a total of thirty twelve-passenger utility vehicles," Culpepper told him. "Everyone already knows his skimmer assignment. We also brought along enough tents for everyone, and food for two weeks."

"Excellent," said Barnes. "Now, what I'd like you to do is return to your companies and get them ready to move. We'll deploy Alpha and Dog first, since they'll be at the most advanced positions. We have two SALs for each company, and the rest will go in your skimmers. They'll drop off the first two companies, then come back here for the rest. When everyone is deployed, we'll keep a SAL and the skimmers at Charlie and Easy. That way, if fighting breaks out at Alpha or Dog, we can bring in reinforcements quickly. The other two SALs will be with the Marines in the Compound. Any questions, gentlemen?"

No one had any. "All right, then," Barnes concluded. "You know that the Marines and I have to stay out of this. But we'll be back at the Compound and ready to roll if fighting should break out. Let's just pray that it doesn't. Good luck, gentlemen, and I'll turn you over to Ms. VanDeen and Lieutenant Pelleu. They're good people, and you can rely on them. Thank you all for coming."

Barnes saluted smartly, shook hands one more time, then left them to return to the Compound.

For a moment, Gloria suddenly felt very much alone. But as she looked into the faces of Culpepper, Dunston, and the others, she felt a warm surge of confidence flowing through her.

"They tell me," Gloria said, "that the men of Pecos are the bravest, toughest, handsomest, orneriest sumbitches in the Empire."

"Now what damn fool told you a thing like that, ma'am?" Dunston drawled.

"It isn't true, Colonel?"

"Shitfire, ma'am, it's a damned slander, is what it is. We're the bravest, toughest, handsomest, orneriest sumbitches in the whole damn *galaxy*! And I told you to call me Bo, ma'am."

"They call me Gloria, Bo. Gentlemen? Let's get to work."

ALTHOUGH SHE WAS SURROUNDED BY TWO hundred humans and more than a hundred thousand Myn, Gloria watched the SALs and skimmers depart and felt lonely again. She had read about "the loneliness of command," and now she was experiencing it. The lives of her troops and the fate of an entire planet rested on her shoulders, and the weight would have crushed her if she had let it. She had always enjoyed the sense of responsibility that went with being a Coordinating Supervisor, and felt proud that five planets and a billion lives had been entrusted to her. But that was mere bureaucratic sophistry, she now realized. Juggling boxes on an organizational chart could not compare with the cold reality of leading troops into what could easily turn into life-and-death combat.

She watched passively from the road as the volunteers went about their work. First, all the Myn had to be cleared from the south side of the road and herded into the larger encampment to the north of it. Pelleu and Culpepper wanted everyone on the same side of the road and at least a quarter of a mile away from it. The Myn were confused by what was happening, but went where they were told without protest. They accepted without question the humans' authority over them, and a few who spoke English even thanked the volunteers for coming to protect them.

With the Myn safely out of the way, Alpha Company set about constructing a rude breastwork thirty yards from the road. The line was at a slight angle to the road, permitting a clear field of fire for the troops at the eastern end. They scraped together whatever bulky debris from the encampment that would serve, and soon had put together a nearly continuous line more than two hundred yards long. At the western end of the line, the breastwork bent at a right angle to the north as a minimal precaution against any flanking maneuver by the Jhino. The defenses could not be called formidable, but they would offer at least some protection against bullets or grenades.

When Pelleu and Culpepper pronounced themselves satisfied, the volunteers took up their positions behind the breastwork. Bo Dunston prowled the line, offering advice and encouragement. The Navy people, in their blue denims and work shirts, could be seen at regular intervals among the volunteers, who were dressed in everything from camouflage hunting jackets to baseball caps and colorful tee shirts.

Gloria walked back from the road and squeezed through a gap in the defensive line. Lieutenant Pelleu came over to her and saluted. Feeling self-conscious and a little ridiculous, she returned his salute.

"Just got word from the scout skimmer, ma'am," Pelleu reported. "The Jhino are about a kilometer down the road, just beyond that rise. And *that*," he added, pointing to a dark-colored skimmer in the distance, "would appear to be a Jhino scout. They know we're here."

Gloria nodded. "If you were in the Jhino commander's shoes—well, they don't actually *wear* shoes—but if you were in his place, what would you be thinking now?"

"I'd be thinking that I'd want to consult with my superiors, ma'am," said Pelleu.

"Which means Jangleth. I don't think Jangleth wants a fight, but he won't want to be stopped, either. I think we can expect a visit from the Colonel before long."

Culpepper and Dunston joined them. Gloria was aware that every one of the volunteers of Alpha Company was looking in their direction.

"We've got our fields of fire straightened out," Culpepper said. "Everybody knows where to fire and where not to. Which leaves the question of when. If you want, Gloria, we can pick them off as soon as they come over that rise."

"I *don't* want, Captain," Gloria told him.

"Whatever you say, ma'am. But I'd like to be clear on the rules of engagement."

"Nobody fires unless fired upon," Gloria said. "This isn't Lexington Green, gentlemen, and our troops aren't embattled farmers. I don't want any anonymous shots heard 'round the world. Is that clear to everyone in the line?"

"If it ain't," said Dunston, "I'll go around kickin' asses until it *is* clear."

She looked at Pelleu. "Lieutenant, I'm a little concerned about what happens if they get off of the road and swing around to the north."

"The scout will give us plenty of warning if they do, ma'am," Pelleu said. "If it looks like they intend to try it, we'll have the eastern half of the line double-time it to the west end and extend the perpendicular in that direction."

"That covers us if they try a left jab," Culpepper said, "but what if they try a left hook?" He pointed at the open fields to the northwest. "If they get a sizable force all the way over on our right rear, they can go straight for the Myn and we won't have enough people to stop them."

"He's right, Gloria," Dunston put in. "I know you don't want us to fire first, but we can't exactly afford to sit here suckin' our thumbs while they get the drop on us."

"I'd say that we have to consider any flanking maneuver to constitute an aggressive act on their part, ma'am," said Pelleu.

"So you're saying that we should open fire if we see them coming through that field?" Gloria was beginning to realize that things were not quite so clear-cut as she had envisioned.

"I don't think we'd have any choice," said Culpepper.

"I agree with the Captain, ma'am," said Pelleu.

"Make it unanimous, Gloria," said Dunston.

The last thing Gloria wanted was to be forced into firing the first shot. But she felt protective of her volunteers, and wasn't willing to sacrifice them just to be able to score debating points about who was the aggressor. Anyway, they were here to protect the Myn, who would be completely exposed by a Jhino move around to the right.

"All right," Gloria said at last, giving a reluctant nod. "If they try that flanking maneuver, we'll open fire if they get within half a mile of the Myn. How does that sound to you?"

"Sounds right to me, Gloria, honey." Dunston grinned. Culpepper and Pelleu nodded their agreement.

"But nobody fires until I give the word," Gloria added. "And Lieutenant, the instant *any* shot is fired, I want you on the comm to Barnes and the troops at Charlie. If this does turn into a firefight, we'll need all the help we can get. Let me remind you, there are two hundred of us, but about twelve thousand of *them,* just over that hill."

"Sounds like a fair fight to me," said Dunston. "I reckon those critters ain't seen what a plasma rifle can do. If they get frisky with us, we'll educate 'em real fast."

"Assuming they don't try to flank us," Gloria said, "I expect that they'll come to a halt somewhere short of our line and wait while Jangleth comes to talk. I'll be out in the road the whole time, and I'll handle the explanations. I want the three of you back here in the line. If anything goes wrong, I'm expendable but you aren't."

"Gloria, honey," drawled Dunston, "far as I'm concerned, ain't *none* of us expendable. If that Jangleth tries anything funny, you dive into the ditch and let us handle the rest."

"I appreciate the thought, Bo," said Gloria, "but I *am* expendable, if it comes to that. Specifically, if Jangleth or his troops try to take me hostage while we're out there talking, you are *not* to attempt any rescue. Just open fire and Spirit be with you."

"And you, ma'am," said Pelleu.

Gloria looked to the west and saw no sign of Jhino activity. Rather than simply stand there waiting and fretting, Gloria walked to the eastern end of the line and met her volunteers, being sure to shake hands with each of them. She moved slowly down the line, thanking everyone for responding to her call. The volunteers grinned and stared at her, feeling proud and fortunate to be part of Gloria's Brigade, which was what they had decided to call themselves. Gloria, embarrassed and flattered, upped the transparency of her bodysuit to 90 percent and let her troops get as good a look at her as they wanted. They had come to serve a noble cause, but they had also come for *her,* because she had asked it of them and because she had made it a personal matter. Before this day was over, some of them might die because of her.

Gloria's Brigade. Spirit!

It was a terrible responsibility—and the greatest honor she could imagine.

Gloria wiped tears from her eyes as she moved down the line. She saw Bryce Denton and the other media reps imaging the scene, recording their first draft of history. Whatever happened here today, Gloria realized, her life would never be quite the same afterward. The Empire was watching, and would remember.

She said a silent prayer to the Spirit she had never quite believed in as she looked into the smiling, eager faces of the volunteers she had brought to this place. Let me be worthy of them, she thought.

Lieutenant Pelleu ran up to her as she completed her tour of the line. "Bad news, ma'am," he said. "Scout reports that the Jhino are sending about a quarter of their force off to the north, just beyond that ridgeline. They're trying to flank us."

Gloria felt a sinking sensation in the pit of her stomach. Spirit, it was really going to happen!

"Thank you, Lieutenant," she said, trying to sound calm and professional. "Have the scout keep an eye on them. For now, we'll watch and wait, but make sure that the people at the east end of the line are ready to move in a hurry. See that tree line there, to the right of the ridge? If they start moving east from there, we'll fire warning shots in front of them. *Warning shots*, Lieutenant—understood?"

"Yes, ma'am."

"If that doesn't stop them...you have my permission to open fire for real when you think it's necessary."

"Yes, ma'am. And if I may say so, ma'am, I think you're playing this exactly right."

Gloria gave a muffled laugh. "I guess we'll find out about that soon enough," she said.

The scout reported that the main column of Jhino had resumed their march along the road. A minute later, they caught sight of the first troops coming over the rise and descending the slope to the flat plain where the volunteers lay waiting. Skimmers darted back and forth above the advancing troops.

"I guess it's time," Gloria said. She offered her hand to Pelleu. "Good luck, Lieutenant."

"And to you, ma'am. Don't worry, we won't let you down."

Gloria squared her shoulders and walked forward to a gap in the line. Volunteers gave her words of encouragement and a few comradely pats on her back as she crossed through the line and walked on toward the road. She mused on Pelleu's parting words to her—they wouldn't let *her* down. If only she could be sure that she wouldn't let *them* down!

She reached the center of the dusty road and turned to face west, where the eight-wide column of troops was marching toward her, barely a third of a mile away. Off to the right, she saw the glint of sunlight on metal, and knew that the flanking force had reached the tree line. They seemed to have paused there.

The Jhino continued their advance along the road. They were close enough now that Gloria could see the individual faces and hear the high-pitched trills of the officers. She could sense a stir of heightened tension moving along the line of volunteers. The two forces were within range of each other now, and anything could happen. Gloria felt a tightness in her chest, and each breath seemed to require all of her energy. Her legs felt weak and she tried to keep them from trembling.

A Jhino officer at the head of the column shouted something, and the troops came to an abrupt halt, just two hundred yards from where Gloria stood. For an endless moment, nothing happened, and the two armies stared at each other in brittle silence.

A black limo skimmer suddenly flew forward from above the column. It hovered just ahead of Gloria, then descended to the road thirty feet from where she stood, throwing up a small, diffuse cloud of dust. Before the dust settled, six Jhino jumped from the vehicle and advanced slowly in her direction, their AK-47s held at port arms. Behind them, Colonel Jangleth emerged from the skimmer. He paused, stared intently at the line of volunteers and the two hundred plasma weapons aimed in his direction, then walked through the cordon of Jhino guards and approached Gloria. He stopped five feet away from her and looked up into her eyes.

"Ms. VanDeen," he screeched in high-pitched, Jhino-accented tones. "What is the meaning of this?"

"I think the meaning of it is perfectly clear, Colonel," Gloria said, sounding calm and resolute. "We are here to protect the Myn. If you make any hostile moves, we will open fire on you and your troops."

"But this is an outrage," Jangleth protested. "Your Governor has given orders that your troops are to stay away from our line of march!"

"Those orders apply only to the Imperial Marines, Colonel," Gloria informed him. "These people"—she gestured toward the volunteers with her right arm—"are not Marines. They are here under my authority as Coordinating Supervisor for this jurisdiction. Under the provisions of the *Dexta Code* and the *Imperial Code,* they are empowered to do whatever is necessary to preserve and maintain public safety. Your troops may continue their advance, but they may not leave the roadway. Any threatening or provocative actions on their part will be regarded as sufficient cause for defensive measures. Do you understand, Colonel?"

Jangleth emitted a squeaky, ear-piercing trill. Gloria wondered if that was how Jhino cursed. "You have no right!" he sputtered in English.

"I have every right," Gloria replied, in calm counterpoint to Jangleth's rage. She pointed in the direction of the tree line to the northwest. "As for those troops attempting to flank us, Colonel, if they don't return to the roadway immediately, we *will* open fire."

"You wouldn't dare!" Jangleth screeched.

Gloria turned to her right, motioned to Pelleu, and called, "Lieutenant!"

Pelleu replied, "Yes, ma'am!" and gave a crisp order to the Navy people on the northern angle of the line. Instantly, two brilliant bolts of sizzling blue plasma burst into being and neatly cleaved the tops off two trees in front of the flanking forces. The limbs crashed to the ground, accompanied by the characteristic thunderclap of the plasma discharges. Startled, Jangleth squeaked another Jhino curse while the troops in column on the road rustled nervously, like dry leaves before a storm.

"Move them back to the road *now*, Colonel," Gloria told him, raising her voice slightly. "We won't waste another shot on trees."

"You have no right to tell me what to do!" Jangleth shouted. "These are my troops, and only *I* can give them orders!"

"Then you'd better order them to get back on the road, Colonel. If you don't within the next ten seconds, you'll never give another order."

Jangleth started to protest again, but one look into Gloria's eyes was enough to cut him short. He nervously tapped his wristcom and trilled at it angrily. A few seconds later, Gloria saw the flanking troops begin to move in a Jhino approximation of a double-time trot toward the road.

"Your troops may continue on their march now, Colonel," Gloria said. "But I should caution you that we have set up defensive positions at each of the camps to the east of here, and at the camps on the southern road, as well. When you reach those positions, you will not halt, pause, or attempt to maneuver. Is that clear, Colonel?"

Jangleth looked up at her, his bristly brown fur standing on end. His large eyes narrowed slightly, and he muttered a high-pitched trill under his breath.

"You have not heard the last of this," he promised her.

"We'll look forward to receiving your formal protest,

Colonel. In the meantime, I suggest that you get your furry little butt out of here."

Jangleth growled at her, then turned and stomped quickly back to his limo. The guards backed up, then followed him into the skimmer. It ascended swiftly, pivoted, and zipped back toward the Jhino column. A moment later, the column began to move forward again.

Gloria watched them approach, then stepped to the side of the road to let them past. The Jhino troops, their weapons shouldered, turned their heads to stare at her as they marched by in sullen silence. It took thirty minutes for the column to pass her, and in all that time, no one—human or Jhino—uttered a single sound.

When the end of the Jhino column was a hundred yards beyond the eastern end of the defensive line, Gloria turned back toward her troops, grinned, and raised her right hand high, in a thumbs-up salute.

The Gloria Brigade roared.

"Alpha Company!" Gloria yelled, *"I love you!"*

THREE HOURS LATER, GLORIA HAD SHOUTED out her love for Bravo and Charlie Companies, as well. Meanwhile, Hawkes had reported that the southern column had cleared Dog and Easy without incident. The last of the northern column disappeared in a dust cloud to the east, and Gloria finally allowed herself to relax.

They had done it. The Myn, at least for now, were safe.

Culpepper, Pelleu, and the Charlie Company Commander gathered around her, smiling ear to ear. Denton and the media reps encircled them and began shouting questions. Gloria smiled wearily at their imagers, but ignored their questions. She suddenly realized that she was very tired.

Her wristcom beeped at her, and Gloria tapped it.

"Congratulations, Gloria," Melinda said. "Now, if

you're finished playing soldier, we need you back here at the Compound. The courier just arrived."

"On my way," Gloria said. Leaving Pelleu and Culpepper to handle things at the camps, she boarded the scout skimmer and headed for home. On the flight back, she closed her eyes and realized that she had never felt happier in her life.

When the skimmer landed in the center of the Compound, Gloria roused herself and stepped out to find Melinda, Petra, and Sonia there to welcome her. Petra came to attention and saluted her.

"Barnes gave us all the details," Sonia said. "You did Dexta proud, Gloria."

"It wasn't me. It was the volunteers. They were fantastic."

"Well," said Melinda, "enjoy it while you can. Petra, give her the news."

"Something bad from the courier?" Gloria asked.

"I suppose that depends on how you look at it," Melinda replied.

Petra held up her pad to Gloria, who took it and scanned the message. Her mouth dropped open, and her features froze as she read it a second time to be sure that she hadn't made a mistake. But she hadn't; the mistake was the Emperor's.

Gloria looked up into the sky and shook her fist at him across the light-years. "Charles, you bastard," she roared. "You can't do this to me!"

"He already did," Melinda told her. "Congratulations, Madame Acting Imperial Governor."

chapter 26

"YOU MIGHT AS WELL MOVE INTO THE RESI-
dence," said Melinda. "A very comfortable bed, according to Tatiana."

Gloria gave her a sour look. Hawkes had returned
from the southern road and joined them at the conference table in the administration building, along with
Major Barnes. Gloria was relieved to see Hawkes safe,
but her joy over the events of the morning had evapo-
rated in the wake of the news from the courier.

"I'm truly sorry, Melinda," Gloria told her. "The appointment should have been yours."

Melinda shrugged. "To tell the truth," she said, "I'm
kind of relieved that you got it. The rest of the instructions are going to make things very difficult for you."

"He did it on purpose," Gloria growled. "He knew
that the one thing I didn't want was for him to intervene
on my behalf at Dexta. He knew how much trouble this
would cause for me in Manhattan."

"I'd be a little more concerned about the trouble
it's going to cause for you here, dear," Sonia said, not

unkindly. "Those instructions don't leave you much wiggle room."

"None, as far as I can see," Gloria agreed. "That bastard."

In addition to the appointment of Gloria VanDeen as Acting Imperial Governor, the message from Earth contained a number of specific orders regarding the situation on Mynjhino. The Emperor had explicitly forbidden her to make any arrests or file any charges in connection with the alleged Servitor plot to bribe Rhinehart and arm the Jhino, "pending a thorough investigation by appropriate authorities." Further, the Imperial Marines were not to take any action against the armed forces of Jhino, other than necessary defensive measures to protect the Compound and human lives.

Most troubling of all, the Emperor had instructed the Acting Governor to arrange an immediate "cease-fire in place" in the "conflict" between "the forces of Jhino and the forces of Myn." In a concession to justice, the instructions did require the Jhino to evacuate the city of Dhanj, except for a "defensible corridor" permitting them free access to the Transit facility.

"*What* forces of Myn?" Gloria wondered aloud as she read over the instructions for the tenth time. "What the hell does he think is going on here? I made it perfectly clear in my report that the Myn don't even *have* an army to oppose the Jhino. Yet he talks about the 'conflict,' as if there were some sort of military confrontation here. And how am I supposed to arrange for a cease-fire if he won't let me use the Marines to enforce it? That incredible bastard!"

"Calm down, Gloria," Melinda counseled. "Calling the Emperor names isn't going to help anything."

"But he did this on purpose!" Gloria persisted. "He gave me the job just so he could set me up to fail in it. He doesn't give a damn about the Myn *or* the Jhino—he's just trying to get back at me. The son of a bitch made it *personal*!"

"And didn't you already do that with those media briefings?" Sonia asked.

"Yes, but—" Gloria stopped herself. Sonia was right, she had to admit. But even if this had turned into a personal pissing match between her and Charles, the mess on Mynjhino still had to be resolved. Somehow.

"Servitor should be happy about this," Hawkes said, hoping to divert the subject from Gloria's personal battle with Charles. "This gives the Jhino—and therefore, Servitor—effective control of the plantation regions."

"Does it?" Petra asked. "I thought they only had troops in two or three towns out there."

"But they control the road net," Barnes explained. "They don't have to physically occupy a piece of ground in order to control it."

"Yes," Petra persisted, "but the instructions say, 'cease-fire in place.' Doesn't that limit them to the ground they're actually standing on?"

"Well," Barnes said patiently, "that's not realistic. I mean, if you want to interpret it literally, yes, I suppose that would be true, but as a matter of—"

"And what's wrong with that?" Gloria said, suddenly smiling.

"What do you mean?" Barnes asked her.

"Petra, you're a genius!" Gloria gushed.

"It's about time you noticed. I should have started doing your laundry months ago."

"Gloria," Barnes said, "you can't actually mean that you intend to interpret those instructions in a strict, literal sense."

"Why the hell not? By my reading, 'cease-fire in place' means exactly that! The Jhino can keep those towns and whatever piece of road their troops happen to be occupying at the moment—*but nothing else!*"

Barnes wasn't buying it. "That's clever, but it would never work," he said. "The Jhino would never accept it. I mean, how would they be able to survive if they were restricted to nothing but their immediate surroundings?"

"They wouldn't," Gloria declared triumphantly. "They'd have to leave Myn entirely."

"But how would you enforce it?" Barnes asked, exasperated by Gloria's literalism. "As soon as they got the word, they'd simply spread out into the countryside around those towns and the road, and establish a viable perimeter. If you're being literal, according to those instructions, the Marines wouldn't be able to lift a finger to stop them."

"Who needs the Marines?" Gloria asked, grinning. "You're forgetting, Delbert—I've got my own army now."

Barnes was aghast. "You can't mean... but that's crazy, Gloria. The volunteers got away with it this morning because all they had to guard was a few hundred meters of roadway. You can't ask them to guard perimeters around three towns."

"Why not? There are a thousand of them. We could put them into a loose line around each of those towns on the edge of the plantation region. And we back them up with *your* troops and a SAL or two. Your instructions order you to defend human life, and the volunteers are all human. If the Jhino opened fire on them, you would be *required* to come to their assistance."

"Yes, but those instructions clearly refer to the Compound and whatever human civilian population remains on Myn. They don't say anything about defending a force of armed vigilantes."

"That's right"—Gloria smiled—"they don't. They don't say that you can't defend them. Forgive me for being so literal again, but as Acting Governor, my reading of those instructions tells me that I have the authority to order the Marines to protect human life anywhere on this planet. It's not my problem if Charles didn't know about the volunteers when he wrote those instructions. You'll be acting on my legal authority, Delbert, and if anyone gets in trouble for it, it'll be me and not you."

"Yes, but—"

"But me no buts, Major," Gloria insisted. "All I need

to know from you is whether you can do it. You have an effective force of 200 Marines, and I have 1,065 volunteers and Navy people. We have plasma weapons, they have thousand-year-old antiques. They're bottled up in those small towns and along the road, while we have freedom of movement. Can you do it or not, Major?"

Barnes pursed his lips as he thought about it. "It would have to be a mighty loose cordon to stretch all the way around those towns," he said. "And if it came to an actual fight, they could concentrate their forces and we couldn't."

"But you could fly the SALs to the point of danger," Gloria said. "The more they concentrate, the more vulnerable they would be to the plasma cannons on the SALs."

Barnes nodded. "That's true," he conceded. "It might be possible to prevent them from penetrating our perimeter, but it would be awfully dicey. And if they did make a breakout into the countryside, beyond your volunteers, then they would no longer be threatening human life and I'd have to stand down my forces."

"But then they'd be in violation of the cease-fire in place, and you could pursue them, if necessary, on my orders. Again, it's my responsibility, not yours."

"I'll be sure to mention that at my court-martial," Barnes said glumly. "Look, I'm with you in spirit on this, but I need to know where this is leading. We can't just stick our troops out in the middle of nowhere and hope for the best. What's your endgame, here? What are you trying to achieve?"

"Those troops in the towns will have to be supplied, won't they?" Gloria asked. "I mean, sooner or later, they'll get hungry, right?"

"The Jhino could supply them by skimmer," Barnes pointed out.

Gloria shook her head. "The instructions make no reference whatsoever to skimmers. Therefore, by my interpretation, the Jhino have no right to fly their illegally confiscated skimmers over territory that their troops don't already occupy. In order to reach the towns they hold, they'd have to fly over territory that, according to the instructions, belongs to the Myn. If they venture out of their own airspace, I would be within my authority to order the volunteers to send up their own skimmers and force down the Jhino skimmers. Or shoot them down, if necessary."

"So you intend to starve out the Jhino?" asked Barnes.

"Unless someone has a better idea," Gloria said. She looked around the table.

Melinda looked at the ceiling and sighed. "All I can say is, I'm overjoyed that the Emperor didn't give the job to *me*. The weight of authority has already driven Gloria stark, raving bonkers. The whole idea is just plain crazy. The hell of it is, I think it might just be crazy enough to work. I say, let's try it and see what happens."

"I think we have to spring it on them right away," said Hawkes. "I mean now, this afternoon. If we use the SALs and every skimmer we have, we can move those troops from the camps to the interior towns before dark. We'll also have to set up roadblocks ahead of the two main forces, far enough ahead so that they won't bump into them until tomorrow morning. That way, we can have a SAL available at each roadblock."

"And while all of this macho muscle-flexing is going on," Sonia said, "you, Gloria, are going to have to go into the Palqui and explain the situation to Rhinehart, Sweet, and the Jhino. I think you should tell them that you want to meet with Veentro himself. If you can make them see that their position is hopeless, maybe they'll decide to go home without a fight. They didn't fight this morning; maybe they won't want to fight tomorrow, either."

"Good ideas, people," Gloria said. "Then it's settled." She looked at Barnes. "It is, isn't it, Delbert?"

Barnes rubbed his hands over his eyes, then puffed some air out. "I never thought I'd miss Hogarth," he said. "It was so much easier when all I had to deal with was a bunch of intelligent lizards who wanted to eat me. God save us all from bureaucrats!"

Gloria smiled. "I'll take that as a 'yes,' " she said.

GLORIA HAD ANOTHER IDEA. SHE HAD GOTTEN it from Colonel Jangleth and his high-pitched Jhino curses that morning. She discussed her idea with Barnes on the way out of the administration building. He liked this one.

"Why not?" he said. "It worked with the fish, maybe it'll work with the Jhino. If it does, we can put it to use out in the boonies tomorrow. I'll tell you what. I'll give you the loan of Tech Sergeant Hooper and a scout skimmer—assuming that's not a violation of the Emperor's instructions."

"No problem," said Gloria. "As Acting Governor in a declared state of Unlimited Emergency, I'm entitled to a military aide. Hooper's got the job—if he wants it."

"He'll love it. Come on, I'll give him his orders and you can fill him in on the details."

Gloria spent fifteen minutes with Hooper, discussing what she wanted and how it might be employed. Hooper was enthusiastic and eager to give it a try. As they talked, four SALs filled with Marines rose into the sky and headed east.

When she was finished with Hooper, Gloria returned to the administration building, found Sonia, then went downstairs to pay a visit to Tatiana Markova. She was still confined in the small room in the basement, and not happy about it.

"Game's over, Tatiana," Gloria cheerily informed her. "Your side lost."

Tatiana glared at her suspiciously. "What do you mean?"

"Well, let's see. Rhinehart is out, I've been appointed Acting Governor, the Jhino have been stopped in their tracks, and they didn't get to the plantations. That about cover it, Sonia?"

"I think you hit all the highlights," Sonia said. "You see where this leaves you, don't you, Tatiana?"

"I don't believe any of it!"

"Facts are facts, whether you believe them or not," Sonia said. "But just for the sake of argument, why don't you assume that what we've told you is true, then think about your position?"

"You still don't have any evidence against me," Tatiana insisted. "All you've got is your bullshit Dexta administrative charges, and they won't hold water, either."

"Maybe, maybe not," Gloria conceded. "But your friend Vladislav just lost his job, and Sweet's little plot just went belly-up. No plantations, no payoff, right, Tatiana? Do you really think you'll ever see a crown from Sweet now?"

That plainly got to her. Tatiana sat down on her bed and looked thoughtful and worried. "That bastard *swore* it would work!" she muttered.

"I imagine Sweet's career at Servitor is about to end," Sonia said. "No money, no job, no future for either one of you."

"I'm *still* not going to say anything!" Tatiana resisted. "Maybe I won't get any money now, but I'm not going to wind up on some Spirit-forsaken prison world, either."

"Don't count on it," Gloria told her. "The Emperor has decided that this whole matter needs to be investigated by 'appropriate authorities.' I intend to call for an Imperial grand jury on Pecos. They'll get to the bottom of it, sooner or later. You see, Tatiana, Rhinehart doesn't want to wind up on a prison world, either. You know how grand juries work, don't you? One of you sings, one of you sinks. Think about it."

Gloria and Sonia started to leave. As they were going out the door, Tatiana screamed at them in frustration.

"You bitches think you're so fucking smart! You think you've got this all figured out, don't you?"

"Yes," Sonia said pleasantly, "we do."

GLORIA AND SERGEANT HOOPER HOVERED FOR a few moments, observing the Jhino on the plaza fronting the Palqui. Two or three thousand troops were still bivouacked there, and half a dozen limo skimmers were parked next to the outer wall of the Palqui. Petra had called ahead to announce Gloria's visit and learned that Veentro was already present.

"Land wherever you think your coverage will be best," Gloria told the sergeant.

"Right in front of the entrance ought to do it," said Hooper. "If this thing works at all, that will do as well as anywhere."

"Look, Alvin," Gloria said, "I don't know how things are going to go in there. If I don't come out, or if the Jhino start shooting, just get the hell out of here, understand?"

"I'll do what needs to be done, ma'am."

That wasn't exactly what Gloria had ordered, but she decided not to press the point. This morning, she'd had hundreds of troops covering her, but this afternoon, she would have only one. Fear tickled the edges of her consciousness, and she took a few deep breaths to steady herself.

"Okay, Alvin," she said. "Let's do it."

The scout skimmer descended toward the plaza. Hooper circled it once at a low altitude, then brought them down directly in front of the Palqui, between the parked limos. As Gloria got out, Jhino troops all around her looked toward her and hefted their AK-47s expectantly.

Gloria recognized Veentro's aide, Kenthlo, standing at the front gates. He looked at her warily, and said, "This way, ma'am, if you please." His polite, PR man's veneer was entirely absent. Gloria followed him along the crushed-stone path toward the inner buildings of the Palqui. She noted that the meditation gardens between the inner walls appeared to have been taken over by the Jhino officers, who had pitched their headquarters tents willy-nilly among the small trees and grassy glades. Kenthlo halted at the entrance to the hexagonal inner building and gestured for Gloria to go ahead. "The Prime Minister will be with you shortly, ma'am," he said.

Inside, the customary candlelight had been replaced by powered lamps attached to the walls. In the brighter illumination, the place looked more threadbare and age-worn. The central raised platform where Quan had greeted her was empty; even the cushions on which he had sat were missing. Souvenirs for the Jhino, she supposed. There had been no word at all concerning Quan since the invasion.

"Pathetic, isn't it?"

Gloria turned around and saw the Jhino Prime Minister entering from a door at the rear of the chamber. Jhino facial expressions and body language were difficult to read, but to Gloria, Veentro seemed to be angry.

"They tried to govern an entire continent from here," Veentro said. "Do you suppose that was arrogance, or simply ignorance?"

"Parts of this building are nearly five thousand years old," Gloria observed. "They must have been doing something right."

"Times have changed," said Veentro, "and one must change with them, or be swept away on the unforgiving tides of history. At least, that was what the Empire kept telling us when they came to our little planet. We learned the lesson; the Myn didn't."

"And what has become of Quan?" Gloria asked him. "Did you kill him, or was he just swept away on the tides of history?"

Veentro gave an approximation of a shrug. "Who

can say? I expect he simply ran with the rest of his cowardly people."

"Or wound up on one of your bonfires."

Veentro looked at her and said nothing for a moment. He seemed so small and inoffensive that Gloria had to remind herself of who and what he was. In the context of Mynjhino, Veentro was another Alexander, another Hitler. He meant to conquer his world, and might already have done so if not for Gloria's intervention.

"I expect you'll want to see Rhinehart," Veentro said at last. "Follow me."

Gloria trailed along behind him as he walked to the rear of the chamber and went through a low doorway. Gloria had to duck slightly to get through it and the narrow hallway beyond it. After another doorway, she emerged into a more comfortably sized room filled with terrestrial furniture and a large desk. Rhinehart was staring out a window, his back to her; in one of the chairs along the right-hand wall sat Randall Sweet.

"Congratulations, Governor VanDeen," Rhinehart said, without turning to look at her. "I still have my access codes, so I know the news from the courier. I suppose you must be very proud of yourself."

"I guess it pays to fuck the Emperor," said Sweet.

Gloria ignored him. "Rhinehart," she said, "I'm calling for a grand jury on Pecos to investigate everything that's happened here. I expect you to remain in Dhanj until you are called to testify."

Rhinehart stepped away from the window and looked at her. He seemed to have aged about twenty years since the last time Gloria had seen him.

"A grand jury," he said. "Indeed. However, I believe that your instructions from the Emperor preclude you from arresting me or filing any charges."

"They do," Gloria agreed. "However, inasmuch as you are a key witness, it is within my authority to restrict your movements. You can't leave this planet without an exit visa, signed by me. And you might be interested to know that I just had a little chat with Tatiana Markova. She'll be testifying, as well."

"Ignore her," said Sweet. "She doesn't know anything."

"You'll be testifying, too, Randy," Gloria told him.

"How charming," said Sweet. He got to his feet and took a few steps toward her. "Forgive me for not offering you a cup of tea. I'm a little short of jigli, at the moment, but that situation will be rectified as soon as our first crop comes in. You see, Ms.—excuse me—*Governor* VanDeen, you haven't really changed anything. You've been an inconvenience, nothing more."

"Stick around, Randy," Gloria said, "and you'll see just how inconvenient I can be." She turned to Veentro. "Prime Minister, if you've seen the instructions from the Emperor, then you know that I am declaring an immediate cease-fire in place. Your troops will remain where they are as of this moment, with the exception of troops in Dhanj. They will evacuate the city immediately, except for a corridor leading to the Transit. I'm defining that corridor as Seventh Avenue. That street leads directly from here to the Transit and connects with both highways to the east. Anyone straying from that street will be in violation of the cease-fire order and subject to immediate arrest."

"I see," said Veentro. "And you expect us to pack up and leave Myn, do you?"

"No," said Gloria, "under the strict terms of the cease-fire, you and your troops may stay on the ground you now occupy. That ground, and no other. Your two troop columns are restricted to the highways, as far as they have advanced to this point. If they leave the roads, for any reason, they will also be subject to immediate arrest. As for the troops you landed in Khoti, Prazhdi, and Skashji, the same restrictions apply."

"You can't be serious!" Veentro squeaked in a high

pitch that went almost beyond the range of human hearing.

"I'm entirely serious. Your troops can remain precisely where they are now, or they can march back to the Transit and go home. As for the troops in the interior towns, I'm afraid they'll simply have to remain where they are. They have no right to march out through Myn territory, and I'm grounding all your skimmers. You have no right to violate Myn airspace."

"But that's impossible," Veentro sputtered. "Those troops have to be supplied!"

"Not by you," Gloria told him. "However, if they lay down their arms, the Imperial Government will be happy to fly them back to the Transit. You see, Prime Minister, as we speak, our forces are establishing a cordon around each of those three towns. If your troops attempt to leave the towns and spread out into the surrounding territory, they will be fired upon. We are also establishing roadblocks along the northern and southern highways, which will prevent any advance by your ground columns."

"But that's...that's...*illegal*!" Veentro screeched. "The Emperor's instructions specifically forbid the use of Imperial Marines against us."

"I'm not using Marines," Gloria said. "The cordons and roadblocks are being established by legally authorized deputies, subject to my orders. However, if your troops should open fire on those deputies, the Marines are authorized—under the Emperor's orders—to come to their defense."

"This is intolerable! You are exceeding your authority! I intend to file the strongest possible protest."

"Be my guest. However, there are no couriers remaining at the Orbital Station, so you'll have to make use of a messenger. That's six days to Earth, Prime Minister. Any formal protest would require a hearing, which would take a minimum of another three or four days to organize and conduct. Then three more days back to

Mynjhino for a courier. So I'd say you're looking at a minimum of two weeks before you can expect any sort of response to your protest. In the meantime, my orders stand, and your troops will stay where they are."

"She's bluffing," Sweet snarled. "She can't possibly enforce this."

"Prime Minister," Gloria said, "if you think I'm bluffing, I suggest you have a talk with Colonel Jangleth. Ask *him* if he thinks I'm bluffing."

"I'll do just that!" Veentro sniffed. "He commands more than thirty thousand troops! We will not be intimidated by your posturing, Ms. VanDeen." Veentro stormed out of the room as fast as his stubby legs could carry him while maintaining a modicum of dignity.

Gloria turned to Sweet and smiled. "I'm afraid you'll have to do without that jigli, Randy."

"Bullshit," Sweet raged. "Total fucking bullshit! You'll never get away with this. Servitor has influence in the Household, maybe even more than you. We'll see about this!"

"Freddy Magnusson!" The name popped into Gloria's mind like a long-forgotten bad odor. Suddenly it all made sense. From the look on Sweet's face, she knew she had struck pay dirt.

Freddy had been one of Charles's more obnoxious sycophants when they were in school, and afterward. His father was the Chairman of the Board of Servitor, so Charles had cultivated the relationship. Now that Charles was Emperor, Freddy was probably one of his inner circle of old and detestable pals.

"That explains the cease-fire in place order," Gloria said. "He *knew*! He knew all about this. Except that Charles thought that the invasion had gone off on schedule. He didn't know it was delayed, so he thought that by the time I got his orders, the Jhino would have physically occupied the entire plantation region. He thought he was giving Servitor everything it wanted! I'm right, aren't I?"

Sweet looked as if he had bitten into something exceptionally foul and rancid. "We'll *still* get everything we want," he told her.

"Not a chance," Gloria said proudly. "Even if Charles grants Veentro's protest, by the time word of it gets back here, the Jhino will have cleared out of the plantation region. If they haven't, they'll have starved by then. No plantations for Servitor, Randy. And no big payoff, either, right? I imagine that's bad news for you, Rhinehart."

Rhinehart seemed to have aged another twenty years. "Spirit," he breathed. "Dammit, Sweet, you *assured* me—"

"Don't listen to her! I tell you, it's all a bluff."

"I'd start thinking about what you're going to say to the grand jury, Rhinehart," Gloria advised him. "If you handle this right, you might still avoid going to a prison planet, where you'd probably wind up sharing a cell with Randy, here."

"I'm not going to any fucking prison," Sweet said with calm assurance. "And neither will you, Rhinehart, if you just show some spine. She can't prove anything! As long as you keep your mouth shut, we'll be fine."

"Fine?" asked Rhinehart. The corners of his mouth curled into a bitter smile. "Disgraced, impoverished, blamed for the sickening atrocities on this Spirit-forsaken world? Even if they don't convict us of anything, we'll be ruined. You call that 'fine,' Sweet?"

"Oh, get a grip! Worst case, we just pick up our marbles and start over someplace else."

"That's easy for you to say. You're still a young man. But I . . ." Rhinehart's eyes seemed to turn inward upon himself, as if examining his own condition. He sat down abruptly and stared off into empty space.

Sweet watched Rhinehart's physical and emotional collapse with a growing sense of horror. It was obvious that he had just lost his hold over the wreckage of what had lately been his tame Imperial Governor.

"Maybe you should come back to the Compound with me," Gloria said to Rhinehart. "I don't think it will be safe for you to stay here." Rhinehart didn't seem to notice her words.

Veentro came back into the room, Colonel Jangleth at his heels. Jangleth stopped short and stared at Gloria, squeaking incomprehensibly to himself.

"The Colonel tells me," Veentro said, "that the cease-fire conditions you propose are entirely unacceptable."

"Too bad," said Gloria. "You'll abide by those conditions, Colonel, or suffer the consequences."

"I shall do no such thing!" Jangleth screeched. "My troops will destroy your so-called deputies. I should have done it this morning, but I foolishly hoped that you would come to your senses. Now, you will learn the power of the Army of Jhino! We have modern weapons—"

"You have thousand-year-old antiques, Jangleth. You won't be murdering defenseless Myn this time around, you'll be facing disciplined troops with plasma weapons. Your entire army will be slaughtered if you try anything stupid."

"Never!" Jangleth shouted. "You will never—"

"Colonel," Veentro cut him off. The Colonel looked warily at his Prime Minister and was treated to two minutes of harsh, peremptory trills. When he had finished with his subordinate, Veentro turned to look at the new Imperial Governor.

"Madame Governor," Veentro said smoothly, "it seems that you have the advantage, for the moment. I still intend to file that protest, and we shall see whether the final outcome of this unfortunate affair is quite what you expect. Nevertheless, I have instructed Colonel Jangleth to issue the appropriate orders to his troops. There will be no fighting, and our army will begin its withdrawal tomorrow morning."

"You can't do that," Sweet bellowed.

"Oh, shut up, Sweet," Veentro said, without bothering to raise his voice. "You've become tiresome. I should have known better than to listen to you in the first place."

"I'm glad to see that you've decided to be reasonable," Gloria told Veentro. "However, I'm afraid that you'll have to give those orders to your troops yourself. Colonel Jangleth won't be giving any more orders to anyone. Colonel, I am placing you under arrest for ordering the murder of an unknown number of Myn citizens of the city of Dhanj. You will accompany me back to the Compound and remain there to await trial before an Imperial Court."

Jangleth erupted in an angry symphony of high-pitched trills that escalated far beyond Gloria's ability to perceive them. While Jangleth continued his outburst, Gloria turned to Sweet, whose face had turned tomato red.

"Our satellite has found the weapons factory in Jhino," Gloria lied smoothly. "And between what Rhinehart and Jangleth are going to tell us to save their own necks, I expect we'll be able to connect you to those weapons soon enough, Randy. And the moment we do, you'll be arrested for complicity in the murders of more than forty humans and thousands of Myn. In the meantime, you are still restricted to the city of Dhanj in connection with the sexual assault charges."

"Do you really think you're going to get away with this?" Sweet shouted.

Gloria didn't bother to answer him. She turned to Veentro, and said, "Prime Minister, I'm quite sure that the atrocities committed by Jangleth and his troops were without your knowledge or permission. At least, I suppose that's how you're going to play it. If you pursue your protest, of course, the entire matter will have to be investigated very thoroughly, and who knows what new evidence might turn up?"

Veentro stared at Gloria in silence for a moment, then nodded slightly. "Very clever, Ms. VanDeen. And, I admit, effective. Very well, then, there will be no protest. And as for Colonel Jangleth's unauthorized—"

"Enough of this bullshit!" Sweet suddenly shouted. A plasma pistol had appeared in his hand, and he pointed it directly at Gloria's heart. "It'll be a shame to kill you," Sweet told her. "I could have gotten a hell of a good price for you on Shandrak Four."

"Sweet," Gloria said, trying to remain calm, "if you walk out of here without me, my aide will send a signal to a Marine SAL, and two seconds later, the Transit will be a pile of burning rubble. You can't get out of the city."

"Is that so? Then I guess I'll have to take you with me." Sweet reached out with his left hand to her shoulder and spun her around before she could come up with a Qatsima move that would safely counter a man with a plasma pistol at the ready. He slipped his fingers under the microscopically thin fabric of her bodysuit and grabbed a fistful of it just behind her neck. "You'll love it on Shandrak, Gloria," Sweet said. "You'll get to fuck the entire royal family. There are a couple hundred of them, I think."

Sweet shoved her toward the doorway, then looked back. "Jangleth," he said, "I've got a small freighter waiting in Phanji. I think you ought to come with me. You can make sure there's no trouble with your troops between here and the Transit."

Jangleth considered this for a moment, then turned and screeched a bitter farewell to Veentro.

"Don't worry about *him*," Sweet told Jangleth. "I'm not leaving any witnesses behind." A thin, blue plasma beam blossomed over Gloria's right shoulder, and Veentro's brains suddenly spilled out of the gaping hole in his forehead. Before his body had fallen to the floor, another plasma bolt burned through Rhinehart's chest. He had an instant to register his surprise before toppling face forward.

"You go first!" Sweet ordered Jangleth. He started Gloria moving ahead of him, still holding her by the knot of fabric at her neck. They made their way, crouching, through the hallway into the large hexagonal chamber where Quan had once presided over his people.

Gloria didn't try to resist Sweet. She tried to remain calm and focused, knowing that she would have only one chance, and that she had to get it right. They followed Jangleth out onto the crushed-stone path through the meditation gardens. Two Jhino soldiers saw them and registered confusion on their faces until Jangleth sharply trilled something to them. They backed away from the path.

"Open that limo," Sweet told Jangleth as they approached the last wall. Jangleth ran ahead and did as Sweet instructed, then stood next to the skimmer and looked back at them. Immediately next to Jangleth and the limo, Sergeant Alvin Hooper in the scout skimmer caught sight of Gloria, with Sweet behind her and a plasma pistol in his hand. Hooper fingered a control button with one hand and reached for his pistol with his other.

Two thousand Jhino troops, crowding the plaza, stopped what they were doing and turned to watch as their commanding officer trilled something at them. "Straight into the skimmer," Sweet told Gloria, "and don't try anything stupid." He shoved her forward, and Gloria used the momentum to launch herself into a flat dive to the right. The bodysuit fabric, stretched to its limit, disintegrated in Sweet's fist.

"*Alvin!*" Gloria hollered as she hit the ground and rolled.

A high, intense tone pierced Gloria's ears and reverberated inside her skull. It stunned her momentarily, but when she finished her roll and looked, she could see thousands of Jhino soldiers clutching their ears, collapsing to the pavement, and writhing in agony. Jangleth had fallen half into the limo and was stiffening in rhythmic spasms.

In the scout skimmer, closest to the source of the

hypersonic tone, Sergeant Hooper appeared to have been knocked unconscious. Sweet staggered forward, his free hand held up to his head. Gloria scrambled behind another limo as Sweet looked for her and fired an off-target burst from his pistol. Gasping at the pain, Sweet wanted nothing now but to escape. He grabbed Jangleth by the scruff of his neck and tossed him into the limo, then scrambled into it himself.

A moment later, the black limo rose from the ground and hovered for an instant. Gloria ducked as another plasma bolt cut an arc through the roof of the skimmer she was hiding behind. The limo hovered another moment, then darted across the plaza and headed west, toward the Transit.

Gloria pulled away tatters of her bodysuit that still clung to her as she popped open the door of the limo she had used as a shield. She started the engine, ascended to four feet, then pivoted the vehicle sharply and shot out across the plaza in pursuit of Sweet. She looked back over her shoulder and saw that Hooper had come around. The scout skimmer rose and followed her.

Sweet was a good two blocks ahead of her. Gloria kept low, clearing the street by no more than six inches as she sought to gain the maximum power of the mass-repulsion unit. The limo was bulkier and less responsive than her Ferrari back on Earth, and twice she nearly lost control as she accelerated to three hundred miles per hour, but she was gaining on Sweet. The low, ochre buildings of Dhanj flashed past her, and ahead, at the far end of the street, she could see the modern structure of the Transit facility, with its glass doors, guarded by a handful of Jhino troops.

Sweet's limo slowed rapidly, but not rapidly enough, and slammed sideways into one of the building's walls. Gloria could see Sweet scrambling out, dragging Jangleth along with him. The guards opened the double doors and the two of them darted into the building.

Gloria decelerated with maximum power, and

rocked forward even against the force of the mass-repulsion safety field that enveloped her. She took careful aim, then instinctively ducked as her skimmer shattered the glass doors and scraped through the entrance into the building. Ahead of her, Sweet and Jangleth dived to the left as Jhino troops dived to the right or ran from her path. The skimmer slammed down onto the polished floor and rebounded back into the air. It glided forward and sailed straight through the ring of the Transit.

JHINO GUARDS AT THE TRANSIT IN PHANJI WERE astonished to see a smashed limo skimmer come hurtling through the ring. It crashed to the floor and skidded crazily as Jhino scattered in every direction. The skimmer finally crunched into a wall and came to a halt. A moment later, a nude human woman wormed her way out of the wreckage and began sprinting back toward the ring. As the dumbstruck Jhino watched, she disappeared into it.

GLORIA RETURNED TO DHANJ AT A FULL RUN. Fifty feet away from her, Sweet was on his hands and knees, crawling after the plasma pistol that he had dropped when Gloria had come crashing into the building. Gloria ran for him.

Sweet had just managed to put his hand over the pistol when Gloria launched herself at him, feetfirst. She clipped him in the chin on her way past. Hitting the floor, she rolled through a somersault, springing instantly back to her feet. A dazed Sweet was still fumbling with the plasma pistol; Gloria knocked it out of his hand with another kick. The next kick caught Sweet flush in the face. He abruptly collapsed, arms and legs splayed out to his sides, as if he were attempting to swim.

Gloria looked for Jangleth. She saw him, running after the plasma pistol that had skittered away from Sweet. He was too far away, and had the pistol in his tiny hand before she could reach him. He aimed it at her.

Another piercing tone stabbed at her. Jangleth's entire body went into a spasm, and he fell backward, writhing in hypersonic agony as the pistol clattered to the floor. Gloria took a deep breath and went to retrieve it.

A moment later, Sergeant Hooper stepped gingerly through the broken glass at the doorway and entered the building. He surveyed the wreckage, then looked at Gloria and shook his head.

"Where'd you learn to drive, ma'am?" he asked.

"New York," Gloria answered with a proud grin.

chapter 27

THE FLYER SLIPPED BACK INTO NORMAL SPACE
and announced its presence to Earthport, two hours
ahead. Gloria looked at Petra and smiled. "It'll be good
to be home again," she said.

"Easy for you to say," Petra replied. "You don't have
to go back to Annex Fifteen."

"Neither will you. At least, not for long. I promise,
you'll be a Fourteen as soon as the paperwork is done."

"Likely story," Petra sniffed. "You bureaucrats are
all alike."

"You've been spending too much time with Bryce
Denton," Gloria observed. In fact, before leaving
Mynjhino, Petra had spent five days with Denton at a
beach resort, acquiring an all-over suntan that had faded
somewhat, and a happy, satisfied smile that hadn't.

"He's not such a bad guy, for a weasel," Petra said.
"You have to admit, he did right by both of us with those
stories he filed."

Denton, who had been the first media rep on the
scene at Mynjhino, had artfully exploited his advantage

over the competition and gotten exclusive interviews with all the *dramatis personae*. The glamorous, heroic Gloria VanDeen had dominated the Empire's lead screens for weeks, and had not been shy about exploiting her position. She knew she would need all the public support she could muster when she returned to Earth and faced the wrath of an embarrassed and angry Emperor.

When there was nothing left to say about Gloria, the media reps focused on her cute, suddenly sexy assistant. Petra's tragic affair with Ricardo Olivera was an irresistible story, and Denton's surprisingly sensitive and respectful interview with her had established Petra as a media darling in her own right. At first, she was hesitant to discuss what had happened, but she soon came to realize that Ricardo would have loved being eulogized across the Empire as a dashing, romantic figure. So she shared her story with the masses, and willingly played the part of the tragically bereft lover, teardrops falling on her heaving bosom, which she took care to conspicuously display in plunging necklines and transparent bits of nothing borrowed from Gloria. Bryce Denton took note, and before long, Petra had a new lover.

By now, two months after the end of the Jhino invasion, the story had become old news, and the media had moved on to other matters. Following the departure of the Jhino army and the return of the displaced Myn to Dhanj, events had settled into a less tumultuous routine, and something like normalcy returned to the Compound. As Acting Governor, Gloria presided over the affairs of the planet with proper Dexta efficiency.

The Tandik, Myn's ruling tribal council, had selected a new Primat to replace Quan, who was presumed to have died in the initial occupation of Dhanj. Jhino, meanwhile, had chosen a new Prime Minister, who deplored the shocking conduct of his predecessor and pledged renewed fealty to the Empire and obedience to the law. The AK-47 factory was dismantled and the now-disarmed army was dispersed.

Sweet and Jangleth were quickly tried and convicted by an Imperial Court on Pecos. Both were sentenced to spend the rest of their lives on a sweltering, high-gravity hellhole of a prison world. Tatiana Markova wound up talking, but it was too little and too late to save her from a ten-year term. Meanwhile, Imperium, Ltd. snapped up Servitor's now worthless plantation leases for pennies on the crown. Julius Omphala met with the Myn tribal leaders and promised to resume the production of pharmaceuticals through a sharecropper system that would please the Myn and make the land happy once again.

New faces began to appear in the Compound, as replacements arrived to fill the vacancies in the reshuffled Dexta hierarchy. On the strength of Gloria's reports, Melinda Throneberry was promoted to a Level XI Deputy Sector Administrator slot, and happily returned to Manhattan. Sonia Blumenthal, on the basis of her seniority, was offered the Imperial Secretary position, but turned it down. She also declined offers of a job back on Earth. She was happy where she was, she insisted, and, anyway, someone who knew which end was up on Mynjhino had to stick around to educate all the newcomers.

One of the newcomers was Zoe Zachary. Newly promoted to Level XIII, she came to Mynjhino—a world she had managed as System Coordinator but had never seen—to fill Brian Hawkes's vacated Undersecretary for Administration slot. Hawkes had moved up to Level XII and become the new Imperial Secretary. He groused about the move, complaining that it would keep him tied down in the Compound and prevent him from getting out into the countryside, but Gloria knew that he was secretly pleased. He soon found that Zoe Zachary was a capable and dedicated administrator, freeing him from his desk often enough to make extended forays into both Myn and Jhino.

On one such trip, Hawkes and the Acting Imperial

Governor went to the province of Dhabi to visit their old friends, Pakli and Dushkai. Pakli's health had improved; the land was happy again and his ancestors had instructed him to remain in Myn, where he was needed, instead of joining them. Now that he had been selected as the new Primat, Pakli could only accept his ancestors' wisdom and do his part to help the Myn recover from their tragedy. Still, he preferred to spend his time at home in Dhabi, and ventured into Dhanj to assume his seat at the Palqui only with great reluctance.

For Gloria, the past two months had been a confusing whirl of events large and small, and she was far too busy to dwell on the larger significance of all that had happened. She bore the responsibilities of her exalted but temporary position with relative ease, relying on her new Imperial Secretary for both professional and personal support. Knowing that their time together was limited, she and Hawkes had focused on the present and made the most of each moment. The intense pleasure they found in each other was magnified by judicious use of the potent jigli that had been seized from Sweet as "evidence." They didn't really need it, they assured each other, but as long as it was available, they would be foolish not to avail themselves of it. Gloria found that she could handle a record four cups of jigli tea with no ill effects, although the experiment nearly destroyed Hawkes. They went easy on the jigli after that, and most of the remaining "evidence" was safely packed away in Gloria's luggage.

When Gloria reflected on her time on Mynjhino, it was the farewells that touched her most deeply. After two weeks on the planet, Gloria's Brigade returned to Pecos following a gala banquet in Dhanj. The volunteers gathered outside the Compound for an open-air, Pecos-style barbecue that featured more beef and beer than the planet normally consumed in a year. Gloria, wearing nothing but her low-rise jeans and a cowboy hat, had circulated among her reveling recruits, hugging and kissing each one of them, until her lips were chapped and her breasts and half-bared butt were smeared with barbecue sauce. Her farewell speech left the hard-crusted men of Pecos weeping.

A month later, she hosted another parting banquet, this one for the Marines and Navy. Another ship had arrived to take them back to Hogarth, where there were still lizards to be pacified. This gathering was more somber, as they solemnly toasted their lost shipmates and the courageous captain of the *Myrtle McCormick*. During their entire time on Mynjhino, they had never fired a shot in anger nor taken a single life, yet they felt more proud of what they had accomplished here than of any campaign they had fought on the Frontier. Major Barnes handed out newly created Mynjhino service ribbons, which his troops would wear with pride for the remainder of their military careers. The final ribbon, he personally pinned to Gloria's blouse, then stood at attention and saluted her. From that day forward, Gloria VanDeen would be an honorary member of Bravo Company, First Regiment, Fifth Division, Imperial Marine Corps.

And finally, she had said good-bye to Hawkes. They had managed a cheerful, no-tears parting, with promises that they would see each other again, somewhere, someday. Neither of them quite believed it. He was the best man she had ever been with, but he wouldn't be the last. Life would go on for each of them, and eventually their time together would recede into the realm of fond memory and nostalgic passion. It had to be that way.

Now, as the Flyer maneuvered into a dock at Earthport, Gloria shook off the aura of the past and forced herself to consider the future. There had been a flock of promotions in the wake of the Mynjhino affair; even Gordon Chesbro had been rewarded for all his smart-ass memos by a bump to Level XIV and assignment to fill Zoe Zachary's vacated slot as System Coordinator for

Mynjhino. But there had been no word from Headquarters regarding Gloria's own fate.

In the absence of news to the contrary, she could only assume that she would simply return to her position as Coordinating Supervisor for Beta-5. She had a right to expect more, she told herself, but as a matter of practical politics, she supposed that she should feel lucky if she wasn't shunted off to some dead-end assignment. She had frustrated the Emperor's schemes with Servitor, and neither Charles nor the Big Twelve behemoth was likely to forgive or forget.

Moreover, she had ruthlessly exploited her personal fame in a way that made Charles look like an ineffectual loser. After one night with Charles, she had let it be known that she had no desire for another. She supposed that, sooner or later, she would have to confront Charles and have it out with him. Their personal conflict had almost contributed to a tragedy on Mynjhino, although Gloria didn't believe that Charles was deeply involved in the Servitor plot. More likely, he had simply seen a chance to gain some easy graft by supporting Servitor as far as he decently could. Nevertheless, he had knowingly made things as difficult as possible for her and would probably continue to do so whenever a suitable opportunity arose.

Then, there was Dexta. By appointing her Acting Governor, Charles had lifted Gloria out of the normal chain of command in the sprawling bureaucracy. By holding an Imperial office, even temporarily, she had been consigned to a kind of bureaucratic limbo. It was far from clear that she could even hope to return to her previous rank and position. Hector Konrad would certainly do his best to punish her, and throughout the bureaucracy there would be many who would remember and resent her special treatment by the Household. And even Norman Mingus himself might not be pleased by the way Gloria had stretched the limits of Dexta authority. A rogue bureaucrat was something that Dexta could never tolerate.

THE FLYER DOCKED AT EARTHPORT AND GLORIA and Petra readied themselves to venture out and confront their future, whatever it might prove to be. Gloria knew that her return would be another media event, and decided that she might just as well continue being the glamorous and sexy siren that the Empire now expected her to be. She wore the same sheer, wide-open, white dress she had worn the night she had tried to entrap Sweet. If there was any part of her body that the people of the Empire had not yet seen, this dress unashamedly remedied that omission. Meanwhile, Petra wore a borrowed miniskirt and a Dexta-gray shirt, dangerously unbuttoned. The Heroines of Mynjhino were back.

They emerged from the Flyer and saw a crowd of media reps being restrained by Dexta people. An aide to Secretary Mingus came forward, introduced himself, and told them that they would be escorted back to New York, where Petra could go home, while Gloria would meet with Mingus. If they didn't want to meet with the media, he assured them, they didn't have to.

They did anyway, and spent five minutes responding to the usual questions with the usual answers. Gloria had left New York hoping to avoid the media spotlight, only to return and find herself caught in its glare. She stood there smiling as the media imagers captured every detail of her famous face and body. If she was destined to be public property from now on, she was determined to enjoy the experience and play the part to the hilt. She hoped Charles was watching; there was something deliciously satisfying about making herself available to everyone in the Empire *except* the Emperor.

For her part, Petra enjoyed the attention she was getting. When the session had gone on long enough, Gloria had to put her arm around Petra and subtly shove her to get her moving. Petra knew it would probably be her last time in the spotlight, and she regretted having to leave it.

The VIP Transit quickly returned them to New York. Gloria and Petra looked at each other before going their separate ways for the moment, and realized that their grand adventure had come to an end. They spontaneously hugged each other and had to wipe away a few tears. "Petra," Gloria told her, "I couldn't have done it without you. You can be on my team for as long as you want."

"I don't know," Petra said, "maybe I'll get a better offer. Say hi to Norman for me, and ask him if he needs a cute little Level XIV assistant."

Five minutes later, Gloria was ushered into the office of the Secretary, high above the streets of Manhattan. Mingus got up from behind his desk and greeted her with a handshake and a warm smile. "Welcome home, my dear," he said. "You've had quite a time of it, haven't you?"

"Yessir, I guess I have."

"And none the worse for wear, I see," Mingus said, unabashedly ogling her from head to toe. "Well then, come share a couch with an old man. Can I get you anything to drink?"

"I'm fine, sir," she said, sitting down next to him.

"Yes, I can see that you are. You are positively glowing, my dear, and well you might be. Your escapade on Mynjhino has made you the Sweetheart of the Empire—every man's dream and every woman's envy. You may recall that I warned you that it might be difficult for you to go back to being an anonymous Level XIII Dexta bureaucrat. Well, I suppose we'll have to take care of that, won't we?"

"Yessir," Gloria answered. She wasn't certain that she liked the implications of the word "escapade," and Mingus had yet to say anything unambiguously favorable about what she had done on Mynjhino.

"You can have your old job back, if you want it," Mingus said, "although I expect it would seem a trifle tame for you now. But I have something else in mind for you, if you are interested."

"Very," Gloria said.

"Before I tell you about it, there is a condition to my offer. Think about it very carefully. The condition is me."

"Sir?"

"You heard me, my dear. I'm an old man, but a man nonetheless, and I find you intoxicatingly desirable. I've had many women in my life, but none to compare with Gloria VanDeen. You would gratify an old man's ego, and you may find that experience has much to recommend it. What do you say, Gloria? If I am the condition of the job, will you accept it?"

Gloria didn't know what to say, or think. She was shocked but not entirely surprised. Why should Norman Mingus be different from men a hundred years younger and fourteen levels lower in the Dexta hierarchy? She had put out for Fifteens to save her job during those first, awful months at Dexta, and now, the one and only Level I was insisting that she do the same to secure her advancement. It was the same old Dexta game, but at a different level.

And yet, Gloria suddenly realized, she was no longer the same old Gloria.

"Well, my dear?" Mingus prodded. "I'm waiting for my answer."

"The answer is no," she said.

"No? Truly? Do you realize what you are turning down, Gloria? Such an opportunity will not come your way again."

"I think I know," Gloria told him. She shook her head emphatically, and said, "I don't need to do this anymore. Maybe I never did."

Mingus surprised her by smiling. He took her hand and squeezed it.

"I can't tell you how pleased I am to hear you say that," he said. "It's not often that one so young as you comes to understand that. Forgive me for putting you on the spot, but it was necessary. I needed to take your measure, you see. I needed to know if the Gloria Van-Deen who performed so magnificently during the crisis on Mynjhino was as smart, self-confident, and courageous as she seemed to be. I know now that you are. I'm very pleased, my dear."

"And I'm . . . uh . . . confused."

Mingus chuckled. "Don't be. You see, what goes on at the lower levels in Dexta is a necessary trial, but it should not be taken as a preferred way of life. We get so many applicants, so many would-be Imperial administrators, that we must be utterly ruthless in our treatment of them when they first join us. We try our best to make them fail, and vast numbers of them do. We intentionally subject them to psychological, physical, emotional, and sexual abuse and intimidation, all with the sole intention of weeding out the weak sisters and the crybabies—people who may be found wanting at a critical moment. We want winners at Dexta, so we manufacture losers by the score in the hope of finding a few genuine winners—as we clearly have in your case."

"Thank you, sir. But I—"

"Bear with me a moment, if you would. It's so seldom that I get a chance to pontificate about the realities of Dexta."

"Yessir," Gloria said obediently. "Pontificate away."

"You see, Gloria, the problem is that the system by which we identify losers also tends to create a certain number of winners who misunderstand the reasons for their own success. They believe that they have achieved advancement through their manipulation of the system and their ability to exploit the weaknesses of others. And, to an extent, that's true, particularly at the lower levels. But the only sure way of succeeding and advancing within Dexta is quite simply by doing good work.

Those who come to rely on their sexual games and manipulative stratagems seldom advance much beyond the lower levels. You know Althea Dante, of course? Have you ever wondered why, for all her native intelligence and womanly wiles, she is still a Thirteen? It's because her games have become an end in themselves, rather than a means by which she can contribute to the overall performance of Dexta. But you, dear Gloria, seem to understand what she doesn't. You realized that you needn't sleep with a wicked old man just to promote your own ambitions. You've grasped the essence of the matter. It is your performance, Gloria, that determines your future at Dexta. It always was."

"I don't know what to say."

"Gloria," Mingus went on, "you succeeded at Mynjhino because you managed to mobilize all your resources *to get the job done*! Not to advance yourself or come out of it looking good, but to save the Myn and restore order. You used every arrow in your quiver, my dear, and hit the bull's-eye with each of them. Your sexual appeal, to generate public support and attract volunteers to the cause; your raw intelligence, to find and creatively employ the appropriate provisions of the *Dexta Code*; and your very great personal courage, to stand up to that Jhino army the way you did."

"To tell you the truth, sir," Gloria admitted, "I was scared to death."

"I know you were," Mingus said. "If you examine the vid of that confrontation on the road very carefully, it's possible to see your knees knocking, in what I assume was sheer terror. And yet, there you stood, my dear. Dexta is proud of you. *I'm* proud of you. In fact, I've rarely been so happy to see my own judgment proven faulty."

"Sir?"

"You see, Gloria, when you first came to Dexta, I didn't want you here, and I did my level best to see to it that you left."

"I'm afraid I don't understand, sir."

"It wasn't anything personal, I assure you. I didn't know you and didn't want to know you. I simply wanted you *out*. Naturally, I can't examine the backgrounds of all one hundred thousand new Fifteens each year, but when one of them turned out to be the former wife of a member of the Imperial Family, it was brought to my attention. Dexta must maintain its absolute independence from the Household, Gloria, or it will become no more than a personal tool of the Emperor. That would be disastrous, for Dexta and for the Empire. The last thing we need here is Imperial dilettantes who think it might be fun to wield real power in the Empire. So when I discovered that you had joined our organization, I took steps to have you expelled. I saw to it that you were subjected to the most extreme forms of abuse that Dexta has to offer—physical, sexual, psychological, emotional—the entire gamut. You can thank me for the hell you went through in your first year, Gloria. I'm not proud of what I did, but considering the results, I'd do it all again."

Gloria was slightly stunned by the revelation. "I never realized."

"You weren't meant to. You were meant to fail, to quit, to get the hell out of my organization. Instead, you fought to stay and found a way to survive and succeed. And, really, can you honestly say that you would have performed as you did at Mynjhino if you *hadn't* been subjected to that ordeal? Would you have been as tough and resilient and self-confident as you needed to be if you hadn't already gone through that trial by fire?"

"I don't know," Gloria replied.

"I do," Mingus said. He smiled at her again. "Now, as to that job."

"Sir?"

"You presented a rather serious challenge, you know. What the hell was I going to do with you? You have become the most famous, glamorous, desirable, and thoroughly remarkable woman in all of Dexta—

indeed, in all of the Empire. How am I to employ such a unique asset? I asked myself. But I believe that I have found an answer."

"I can't wait to hear it," Gloria said. She was practically blushing after hearing his words of praise.

"Gloria," he said, "I want you to do on a regular basis precisely what you did on Mynjhino. Use your wit and your wiles in the service of Dexta. I want you to be my number one troubleshooter, my fixer, my chessboard queen. I want to send you wherever there is a problem that needs solving or a looming disaster that needs to be prevented. What do you say? Are you game?"

"I . . . I'm not sure. It's . . . it's kind of staggering."

"I realize that I'm asking a great deal of you. It will be a difficult and possibly dangerous assignment. And frankly, Gloria, you won't always succeed. Indeed, it is inevitable that someday you will fail, and probably in full view of the Empire. And then the public and the media, which have put you on a pedestal, will take great delight in pulling you down from it. Depending on the circumstances, I may find myself unable to help you. The risks are real, Gloria, but so are the rewards. Oh, practically speaking, you'll be promoted to a Ten to give you some clout within Dexta, but I'm referring to the intangibles. Not to put too fine a point on it, the truth is that you saved millions of innocent lives on Mynjhino. What I'm offering you is the opportunity to save millions more."

"When you put it like that, sir, then I suppose I can't say no."

"You can say it, my dear. I hope you won't, but if you decline my offer, I'll understand. I'm asking you to put everything you have on the line. Don't say yes just because you think that you have to."

Gloria was silent for several moments.

"Sir," she said at last, "I joined Dexta because I didn't want to spend my life being just another useless rich person. I wanted to make a difference in people's lives, to play a part in the greatest adventure in human history. It seems to me that you're offering me the opportunity to do that on a scale beyond anything I ever imagined. My answer, sir, is *yes*. A definite, emphatic yes! And thank you."

"Wonderful," cried Mingus. "But the day may come when you'll damn me instead of thanking me. This won't be easy."

"I can handle it."

"I know you can. Of course, it won't just be you, all by yourself. I intend to set up an Office of Strategic Intervention, with you as its head. You can choose your own staff, and I'll give you all the support I can. When I send you off to solve some dreadful problem, you won't be alone, Gloria. Wherever you go, you'll represent Dexta in all its awful power and majesty. And I know you'll make us proud."

"I'll try to live up to your expectations, sir," Gloria said. "But I do have one question."

"And what is that?"

"What would have happened if I had said yes to your offer... I mean, your *first* offer?"

"Then," Mingus said, "I would have happily fucked you to the best of my limited ability; and then I would have sent you off to some show-and-tell position in Public Affairs, where you would never have borne real responsibility or faced a meaningful challenge. You made the right choice, my dear, much as it grieves me."

Gloria leaned toward him and gave him a passionate kiss on the mouth. "You never know," she said, smiling slyly. "Play your cards right, Norman, and you may still get a chance."

"Oh, now you're just shamelessly sucking up to a superior. Don't play games with me, young lady, or I might just surprise you. I don't suppose you brought any of that jigli stuff back with you?"

Gloria threw her head back and laughed. "Sir, that would be a violation of the *Dexta Code,* Chapter Thirty-seven, Paragraph Nineteen, Subsection D, which specifically prohibits Dexta personnel from importing psychotropic, hallucinogenic, or erotogenic substances which have not been approved for general use in the *Imperial Pharmacopoeia,* subject to the exceptions noted in Subsection E, below."

"Hmmm," said Mingus, "so it would, so it would. In any event, we have no time for such foolishness at the moment. You and I are expected in Rio in a few minutes."

"Rio?" Gloria gasped.

"Didn't anyone tell you? Oh, I suppose not. Well, my dear, it seems that Emperor Charles V, in his wisdom—with which I, for once, wholeheartedly concur—has decided to present you with the Distinguished Service Medal for your exploits on Mynjhino, in recognition of your conspicuous gallantry and service to the Empire. Come, my dear, stop gaping and get a move on. We mustn't keep the Emperor waiting."

About the Author

C. J. Ryan lives and works in Philadelphia.

Be sure not to miss the next exciting Dexta
novel featuring Gloria VanDeen:

GLORIOUS TREASON

C. J. RYAN

On Sale December 2005

Here's a special excerpt

GLORIOUS TREASON

On Sale December 2005

THEY CALLED HIM OLD ABEL, AND HE HAD BEEN there since the beginning—before the beginning, really. He wandered freely, almost randomly, through the valleys and forests, finding shelter when he needed it in natural caves and depressions or in the flimsy lean-tos he built and then abandoned as his moods and whims dictated. No one knew his age, but it was considerable, and it was a mystery where and how he obtained his food, clothing, and other presumed necessities of life. Not that he needed much.

He was a small, stoop-shouldered man with a scraggly white beard, long tangled hair, and sharp, suspicious eyes the color of the evening sky before a storm. His voice, on the rare occasions when he used it, sounded like a stick being dragged through dry leaves. He appeared and disappeared without preamble, and although he was recognized throughout the mining camps and sparse clusters of tumbledown shacks that dotted the slopes of the valley, no one could claim to know him. He seemed neither alien nor entirely human, a species unto himself, indigenous and mysterious.

Sylvania was his world, as far as it was anyone's, and even the nabobs in the Lodge and the swaggering boom-rats in the town and the camps treated him with a wary, deferential respect. When they saw him coming, leaning heavily on his wooden staff and lugging a sackful of Spirit-knew-what over his shoulder, the miners paused in their work and nodded to him. Some even ventured a greeting, perhaps receiving a nod of recognition in return, perhaps not. The bolder souls among them occasionally invited him to share their dinner, and sometimes he did. He might even engage in something that passed for conversation, exchanging a few words about the weather: a topic on which he was considered—in the absence of meteorological satel-lites—the ultimate local authority. He knew to the hour when rain would begin or end, and precisely how high up the slopes it would turn to snow. On other subjects, he had little or nothing to say, but he listened carefully to the words of the boomrats about the progress of their diggings, the latest troubles with Grunfeld and his thugs, or the new whore down at Elba's.

He rarely bothered with the town these days, and when he did, people made way for him and whispered be-hind his back, telling the newcomers—and there were many of them now—that this strange, threadbare appari-tion was just Old Abel, the local "character," as if that ex-plained everything that needed to be known about him. Elba gave him food and drinks and sometimes joined him at his table. He was even believed to spend time in the rooms upstairs—but if he did, the whores didn't talk about it. Some of the older boomers might buy him drinks in re-turn for a few minutes of his almost wordless company. And then he would be gone again, quietly retreating to his silent wilderness.

A few of the boomrats actively sought him out in the forests, convinced that Old Abel knew better than anyone just where to find outcrops of the glimmering green crystals that had lured them here across the light-years, three years past. But Old Abel could seldom be found unless he wanted to be, and he had nothing at all to say on the sub-ject that obsessed the boomers. His silence only served to convince them that he was in possession of secret knowledge that, if they had it, would make them wealthy beyond calculation. But it was no easier to find Old Abel than it was to find the crystals themselves; in fact, it was more difficult, for the Fergusite crystals rimmed the broad valley and littered its streambeds, but there was only one Abel, and he moved as he would.

Exactly what Abel knew, or might know, was a subject of endless debate around the campfires and cookstoves. Some advanced the opinion that he knew nothing at all and was, in fact, simply the ignorant, witless old hermit he appeared to be—but no one could really bring themselves to believe that. Others were convinced that Old Abel had a secret cache somewhere up in the mountains, and lived a life of luxury and ease when no one was looking. A few even suggested that he was really an Imperial agent, spying on the boomrats for the Empire, or for Dexta. Or for the Lodge, or one of the corporate titans.

The oldsters—men like Bill McKechnie and Amos Strunk—knew better, but made no attempt to dispute the opinions of the latecomers. They kept their own counsel, and merely smiled as they listened to the theories come gushing forth like water through a sluice. But Bill and Amos had heard the Voice, and most of the newbies hadn't.

They didn't talk much about the Voice. Those who hadn't heard it were convinced that the Voice was simply the delusion of men who had spent too much time in the silent hills of this lonely world, and some of those who had heard it feared that the doubters might be right. The easily frightened among them had taken heed of the Voice and quickly packed up their meager belongings and left the planet as soon as they could. Others, with stronger spines and a more resolute nature, had defied the Voice and remained at their diggings, but kept an ear to the wind and tended to jump at sudden noises.

The Voice seemed to come from everywhere and nowhere, and whispered to them at odd moments as they squatted in the cold, rushing waters, panning for crystals, or sat among the high crags, fussing with their plasma drills. It came to them in the dead of night or in the blaze of noon, on the shining outcrops of the cliff faces or in the gloom of the forests, and it spoke different words to different men. To most, it breathed in soft, insistent tones, "Go away. Leave me alone." To Bill McKechnie and Amos Strunk, it had said only, "Don't hurt me."

Old Abel wouldn't talk about the Voice. "I hear what I hear," he had said one night at Bill McKechnie's campfire. "And you hear what you hear."

WHAT ABEL HEARD ONE MORNING IN MARCH OF 3217, as the Empire reckoned time, was not the Voice but a cry of pain and outrage. It echoed down from the high reaches of the slopes, up near the snow line, where some of the newbies had been testing their luck. Abel peered upward from the edge of the forest, where he had spent the night, and saw two men he recognized even from this great distance, and a third that he didn't know—and never would.

The two he knew were Karl Cleveland and Hank Frezzo— big, tough, distinctive men who worked for the mayor, the Honorable Kevin Grunfeld, tsar of the town of Greenlodge and anything else he cared to be tsar of. Cleveland and Frezzo held a third man between them, grasping each arm at the shoulder while their victim's feet kicked frantically at empty air. With a minimum of effort and only a final dying scream to mark the moment, the two tossed the third over the edge of the cliff face, sending him pinwheeling downward a hundred meters or more to the jumbled pile of scree at the base of the precipice. They peered over the edge for a few seconds, evidently satisfied with their work, then walked away and out of Abel's line of sight.

Abel waited awhile to be sure they were gone, then laboriously picked his way upward through the scree to the place where the shattered body of the newbie had finally come to rest. Even if Abel had known the man, he would not have been able to recognize the smashed face that stared sightlessly upward toward the cold sun of Sylvania. Abel didn't touch the body or attempt to scavenge anything useful from his kit, although others undoubtedly would when they found him. Nothing was easy to get or hold onto on this planet, and even life itself was but a slippery possession.

He liked the newbies even less than he liked the oldsters, but Abel found himself feeling sorry for the dead man. Somewhere, perhaps a thousand or more light-years away, at the other end of the Empire, this man had once had a home, maybe even a family. When they heard the news—and they would, eventually, for Dexta was remarkably efficient in such matters—they would be saddened and mournful. Or perhaps not; perhaps the dead man was a good-for-nothing sonofabitch, like so many of the boomers, and the Empire would be a better place without him in it. Abel didn't know, and didn't really care.

But he cared about Sylvania, and was disheartened by what this and other such incidents must inevitably mean for his world. Sooner or later, the Empire would have to do something about it. More boomers were already on their way, and now they must be joined by the grim, gray bureaucrats of Dexta, who ran the Empire and enforced its rules. And Dexta, in turn, would soon be followed by the corporate behemoths, who would rape this quiet valley and then kill it, as surely as Grunfeld's men had killed this sad specimen crumpled at his feet.

And what, Abel wondered, would the Voice have to say about *that*?

THE TWO MOST POWERFUL MEN IN THE EMPIRE stared at themselves and each other in the gently rippling waters of the reflecting pool, the replica of the Taj looming above them in carefully crafted splendor. The original had been destroyed in an alien attack more than seven years earlier, in pre-Imperial days, before the men of Earth had come to dominate this corner of the galaxy. Reconstructed as one of six Imperial Palaces scattered around the terrestrial continents, the Taj Mahal no longer seemed a monument to love, but to human persistence, ingenuity, and arrogance. The two men embodied those same qualities.

Norman Mingus was the first to break the spell of the reflection and look away. Tall, spare, slowed but unbowed by his years, Mingus had a face that was pink and unlined, and that might have belonged to a retired and much-loved schoolteacher. Instead, it belonged to the Secretary of the Department of Extraterrestrial Affairs.

The Emperor Charles V, forty-seventh in an unbroken line stretching back nearly seven centuries, lingered another moment with his reflected image. When at Agra, he affected garb of flowing white robes and rather fancied the way they set off his athletic frame and regal features. He imagined that Alexander the Great, when he came East, might have cut a similar figure. With his closely cropped beard, longish curling locks of dark blond, and pale blue eyes, he knew that he *looked* like an emperor, just as Mingus, a hundred and two years his senior, with his dark business suit and beady, censorious eyes, looked like a bureaucrat.

"I do love it here," Charles said, finally looking away from the reflecting pool. "Next to Rio, I think Agra is my favorite Residence. Of course, Paris has its own particular charms, as well. And there's much to be said for Colorado. Tell me, Norman, which do you prefer?"

"I suppose, Highness," Mingus replied after a moment's thought, "it depends on what business brings me to them."

"It's always business with you, isn't it, Norman?" The Emperor shook his head regretfully. "Very well, then, business. We may as well go inside, then, lest we be distracted by this beautiful day and magnificent setting. Four walls and a couple of chairs will do, I suppose."

CHARLES LED THE WAY INTO THE RESIDENCE, slowing his normally brisk gait to accommodate a man who was nearly five times his age and had been Secretary of Dexta ten times longer than Charles had been Emperor. Mingus followed at his own pace, feeling no need to match the Emperor stride for stride. He had been walking with Emperors for forty years now, and was no longer impressed by their company—never had been, in fact.

Charles was Mingus's third Emperor, and probably his

last, although even that was far from certain, given the casualty rate in that office. His first had been Darius IV, bumbling and benign, who had somehow managed to die of old age in spite of his occupational hazards. Dour, dark-visaged Gregory III had come next, his brief reign cut short by a botched coup known as the Fifth of October Plot, which had swept the Emperor and the next five in line to the throne from the board, leaving the callow and untested Charles to carry on in their place.

It was far too early to judge Charles in any historical sense; it was entirely possible that he might yet wind up with "Great" affixed to his name. Possible—but in Mingus's view unlikely. Still, Charles's flaws—self-absorption, self-indulgence, and outright selfishness—were the flaws of youth. If he lived long enough, he might outgrow them. But the early signs were not encouraging, and Mingus didn't much care for the young Emperor. He had a streak of meanness in him, more appropriate to a small-town bully than the leader of an Empire encompassing a sphere of space two thousand light-years in diameter, with 2,645 planets populated by three trillion sentient beings. And Charles had surrounded himself with a retinue of truly detestable young chums, who lent the Household a pungent and unmistakable air of decadence.

On the other hand, Charles was intelligent and reasonably industrious when motivated, and had an excellent grasp of the complexities and realities of his realm. What he needed was guidance—which Mingus was prepared to offer but which Charles was just as prepared to reject. Mingus knew that Charles resented him, just as every Emperor resented every Dexta Secretary, but at least Darius and Gregory had been willing to listen. And today, of all days, Charles needed to listen to what Mingus had to say; the very future of the Empire might depend upon it.

THEY SAT OPPOSITE EACH OTHER IN COMFORT-able chairs, surrounded by a profusion of elegant tapestries and opulent bric-a-brac, which they ignored as completely as they ignored the tea that had been brought by silent and quickly vanishing servants.

"As you know, Norman," the Emperor began, "I asked you here today to discuss the situation on Sylvania. We had expected to commence large-scale mining operations there at least six months ago. In that expectation, we have been disappointed. We would appreciate an explanation."

When Charles said "we," it was not necessarily the Imperial We. In this case, Mingus knew, the use of the plural pronoun referred to Charles and his coterie of intimates from the Big Twelve corporates, who were drawn to him like iron filings to a lodestone. Or like flies to shit, Mingus thought. It was an unworthy thought—but in this case entirely apt.

"Highness," said Mingus, "it is a complicated problem."

"Of that, I have no doubt. I was hoping that you would uncomplicate it for me."

"Very well, then. In a nutshell, Sylvania—in a legal sense—is neither fish nor fowl. It is, at this moment, still an Unincorporated Imperial Territory. Normally, that would entitle you to make whatever deals you wish with the corporates and begin mining operations at your pleasure. However, the planet has been continuously inhabited by a population of over one thousand for nearly twenty years. Under the provisions of the *Imperial Code*, those residents have certain rights that date back to the Homestead Acts of 2697 and supercede the provisions of the *Code* which would otherwise apply here."

Charles nodded vaguely.

"However," Mingus continued, "because the population is still under five thousand registered voters, you have no legal authority to incorporate the territory and appoint an Imperial Governor, thus bringing it under the aegis of other provisions of the *Code*. Specifically, the Eminent Domain Statutes. Without Eminent Domain, large-scale mining operations of the sort you and the corporates envision would not be permissible unless you could somehow gain the consent of the entire resident population, as defined by the Homestead Acts."

"Which I'm not going to get," Charles acknowledged.

"I understand all of that, Norman. What I don't understand is why, in spite of the economic boom that has begun on Sylvania, we don't yet have five thousand registered voters. I gather that people are flocking there as fast as they can. A rough count of the freighter traffic implies that there are already at least seven thousand people on that planet." Charles leaned forward and smiled unpleasantly. "So why hasn't Dexta been able to get them registered?"

Mingus pursed his lips for a moment. He didn't quite sigh.

"I confess, Highness," he said, "to a certain amount of embarrassment in that regard."

"Why is the Imperial Historian never around when I need him?" Charles wondered. "Certainly, this must be a historic first. Norman Mingus, embarrassed?" Charles gave a snort that might have been a genuine laugh, of sorts. Whatever his shortcomings, Charles did, at least, have a sense of humor.

Mingus shrugged. "Embarrassed is the only word that applies, I suppose. The awkward and, yes, embarrassing truth, Highness, is that at the moment, the Department of Extraterrestrial Affairs has not a single representative on the planet of Sylvania. You see, sire, they keep quitting on us."

"Quitting?" Charles raised an eyebrow.

Mingus nodded. "We send people there, and before they've been there a month, they come down with what you might call gold fever. All around them, they see people striking it rich. Dexta staffers are as human as anyone else, and sooner or later—generally sooner in this case—cupidity trumps institutional loyalty. They stop shuffling papers and start digging for Fergusite. We can't chain them to their computer consoles, you know. Every Dexta staffer we've sent to Sylvania in the past year has resigned and headed up into the hills to make a fortune. And I gather that some of them have done just that, which only encourages the others to follow. I can't really blame them, I suppose. If I were a young man, I'd probably do the same thing."

Charles got to his feet abruptly, shuffling his sandals on the glistening tile floor. He walked around behind his chair, leaned against it, and peered at Mingus. "I have difficulty picturing that," he said, a bemused smile flickering across his handsome features. "You as a young man, I mean. Somehow, I always imagined that you were carved from a block of marble, fully formed."

Mingus returned the half-smile. "I wasn't," he informed the Emperor. "I just feel that way. Complete with cracks."

"You know, that gives me an idea. I'm going to have the Imperial Sculptor do a bust of you, Norman. I'm going to put it right behind my desk in Rio. You'll be there forever, staring down at me and all my successors, like Poe's raven, croaking 'Nevermore' at us whenever we get a notion that you'd disapprove of. Keep us honest, I'd think."

"Forgive me, Highness, but that's what I'm trying to do now. The problem we have to deal with is not the Dexta staff on Sylvania or getting voters registered. The problem is the damn Fergusite itself—and you know that as well as I do, Charles."

Charles cocked an eyebrow at him. "Do I, Norman?"

"Well, dammit, you should," Mingus responded, raising his voice slightly.

"Whenever you call me 'Charles,'" the Emperor said, "I get worried. Don't try to get fatherly with me, Norman. I had a father once, and he was a scoundrel and an idiot. As for the Fergusite, it's not a problem. It's a once-in-a-lifetime opportunity!"

"Gold fever," Mingus sniffed. "You've got it, too, I see."

"What if I have? Spirit's sake, Norman! A quadrillion crowns' worth of Fergusite, and you want me to leave it in the ground?"

"That's where it belongs, Charles," Mingus said evenly. "For the sake of your Empire, leave it where it is."

FERGUSITE WAS THE STUFF THAT MADE THE EM-pire possible. First synthesized in the twenty-second century—atom by atom and at great expense—the precisely structured latticework of Fergusite focused the immense energy generated by fusion reactors inward upon itself, until the strain ruptured the very fabric of space-time and formed an eleven-dimension membrane of Yao space, which squirted through normal space at transluminal velocities and thus made the dream of interstellar travel a reality.

It was long believed that Fergusite could only be created artificially, but three years earlier, in 3214, the Imperial Geological Survey had stumbled upon a vast deposit of Fergusite on the small and neglected world of Sylvania, 542 light-years from Earth. Natural Fergusite could form only when the most precise combination of factors came into perfect alignment—mineral content, time, pressure, temperature, and gravitational force, all as delicately balanced and tuned as a symphony orchestra with a billion different instruments all playing the same music at the same instant. The Sylvanian deposit of Fergusite was nearly as pure as the artificial version that the Big Twelve corporates had been brewing in their factories for eleven centuries. With a minimum of processing, it could be used in the Ferguson Distortion Generators that rode on every starship—at a tenth of the price of the artificial Fergusite. The discovery would dramatically reduce the cost of interstellar travel, and might usher in a new Golden Age for the Empire.

But there was a problem . . .

"IT IS *NOT* A PROBLEM!" CHARLES INSISTED VE-hemently. "It's a minor . . . *inconvenience*. Nothing more."

"You call being crushed into a soup of subatomic particles an *inconvenience*?" Mingus demanded.

"There's no need to over-dramatize it. Yes, a few more ships may—*may*—be lost. But what of it? Boats have always sunk, aircraft have always crashed, starships have always disappeared. It's just the price of doing business, and everyone accepts that. Except you, apparently."

"Using the Fergusite on Sylvania would raise that price significantly, Highness."

"It would do just the reverse! Dammit, Norman, just look at the figures my economists prepared. The Empire spends 30 trillion crowns on interstellar trade each year.

Fergusite production represents nearly a third of that cost. Using the Sylvanian Fergusite, even allowing for processing costs, would save something like seven trillion crowns—a twenty-three percent reduction! Think of what that would mean. Reducing the cost of interstellar travel by nearly a quarter should lead to a fifty to one hundred percent increase in the total volume of trade. How can you claim that would be bad for the Empire?"

"I have economists too, Highness," Mingus reminded him. "And they've factored in some things that your economists didn't bother to include. The loss of an additional ten to one hundred starships each year would cost—here, let me bring it up on my pad." Mingus reached into his pocket.

"Oh, don't bother," Charles told him. "I've seen those numbers. I just don't believe them."

"All right, then. But there's another factor that you cannot assign a number. The loss of confidence in the safety of interstellar travel would have devastating consequences for the entire Empire."

"Spare me, Norman. Do you really think anyone would care—or even notice? How many notice now, when we lose a ship? There are three trillion people in the Empire, and fewer than one hundredth of one percent of them ever get anywhere *near* a starship. A few more losses—and it will be a lot closer to ten than a hundred, my people assure me—won't make a damn bit of difference."

"Except to the people who are on those ships," Mingus replied. "And their families. And the insurance carriers; rates will go up substantially, you know. Did your economists bother to mention that? Then there's the cost of replacing the losses and training new crews. But the *real* cost—"

"Is unknown! No one knows—not your economists and not mine. Why must you assume the worst?"

"Because of the consequences. Highness, if I am wrong, there are no consequences. The Empire simply goes on doing business as it has always done. But if *you* are wrong, the consequences could be catastrophic. If—"

"Nonsense!"

"Dammit, Charles, just shut up and listen!"

No other person among the three trillion in the Empire could have told the Emperor to shut up. Even for Norman Mingus, it was a close call. Charles stared at him in suppressed rage for a moment, then crossed his arms, balanced his right ankle on his left knee and sulkily sat back in his chair.

"All right, Norman," he said. "I'm listening. Make it good."

Mingus took a deep breath. "Highness," he said, "as you pointed out, it is impossible to determine with certainty the quality of those Fergusite deposits on Sylvania. The initial reports suggest that the level of impurities lies in a range between one and ten parts in a billion, but we have a very limited number of samples. And, as you know, we cannot test every piece of Fergusite that comes out of Sylvania because the very process of testing destroys the sample and makes it useless. So all we have to go on is a statistical procedure that, by its very nature, is suspect. The process we use to fabricate Fergusite is rigidly controlled, but nature is random and sloppy. One chunk of Fergusite might be perfectly pure, and another right next to it might be dangerously impure. There is simply no way of knowing except by putting it to work in a distortion generator and hoping for the best."

Charles nodded. "Go on."

"Any impurity in the structure of the Fergusite can cause the bubble formed in the FDGs to become asymmetrical, resulting in the collapse of the bubble and the destruction of the ship. Even with the process we use now, impurities are believed to result in the loss of some ten to twenty ships each year. We can live with that. But could we tolerate the loss of one or two hundred?"

"It would be nowhere near that high," Charles protested. "Maybe another ten or twenty, worst-case."

Mingus stared at the Emperor. "You said you'd listen."

Charles retreated back into his chair.

"Aside from the direct consequences of those losses," Mingus continued, "consider this. Of the Big Twelve, only seven actually manufacture Fergusite. Prizm takes seventy percent of the commercial market; the others make it mainly for their own use. Now, what happens if tons of Fergusite start flowing out of Sylvania? For one thing, Prizm would take a huge loss and be forced to shut down most of their Fergusite facilities."

"That's their problem," Charles said. For hundreds of years, emperors had routinely pocketed vast sums collected from the Big Twelve. Charles pursued the practice with more diligence and enthusiasm than most of his predecessors, but his relations with Prizm were not especially close. What he lost from Prizm, he would more than make up with revenues from whichever corporate wound up with the Sylvania concession.

"It could become *everyone's* problem, Highness," Mingus pointed out. "What happens if, after Prizm shuts down its fabricating plants, we find that the level of impurities in the Sylvania deposits is simply too high to be sustained? The Empire would be crippled for years, perhaps decades. Without reliable interstellar travel, the Empire might very well break up. You couldn't even depend on the Navy to hold it together, because they'd have the same problems as everyone else."

"Purely hypothetical."

"Hypothetical or not, it is a consequence which cannot be ignored. And," Mingus added, "there's this. The confidence of the population in the reliability of interstellar travel would be ruinously, perhaps fatally, weakened. They would turn inward and rely upon their own resources, pursue their own goals. The very concept of the Empire would come into question. You want to run the Empire on the cheap, Charles—but if that's the kind of Empire you want, you may find yourself with no Empire left to run."

The Emperor nodded thoughtfully, then leaned forward again.

"Is that it, Norman? Anything else you care to say?"

"Not just now, Highness."

"Good," Charles said, a cold edge coming into his voice. "Now, *you* shut up and listen, Norman, and listen very carefully. In the first place, exploiting the Sylvanian deposits will not weaken the Empire, but strengthen it. Do you know what per capita interstellar trade amounts to?

Barely ten kilograms per year. Ten kilograms! That's a pittance. It could—and should—be ten times that. The only reason it's not is because interstellar travel is so fucking expensive. We're going to change all of that, and the key to doing it is those Fergusite deposits on Sylvania. The geologists tell me there's enough to last at least a century. And that century—*my* century!—is going to see a historic increase in trade, prosperity, and Imperial strength. It's going to be a fucking Golden Age, Norman, and I am not about to let you stand in the way of it."

"I see," Mingus said.

"Just in case you don't, let me paint you a picture. You are going to get those five thousand people registered in the next three months. And about ten minutes after that, we are going to begin large-scale mining operations on Sylvania. If you try to drag your feet on this, or employ your usual bureaucratic bullshit to obstruct, delay, or impede this operation, I'll drag your ancient ass before Parliament and have it booted out of Dexta once and for all. There are plenty of M.P.'s who would like nothing better than to have one clean shot at you, and by the Spirit, I'll make sure they have it. I'll go public with this and let the people of the Empire know that the only reason they can't have cheaper trade, lower taxes, and a chocolate fudge sundae with cherries on top for breakfast every morning is because of *you*, Norman Mingus. You understand me?"

Mingus locked eyes with the Emperor for a long moment, then nodded slowly. "I believe that I do, Your Majesty."

Charles's body, as tight as an old knot, abruptly relaxed. He sat back in his chair and offered a thin smile. "Now, then, Norman, suppose you tell me how you intend to solve our mutual problem on Sylvania?"

Mingus returned the smile. "I have a possible answer, Highness," he said. "But you won't like it."

"If it works, I promise you, I'll love it."

"I doubt that, Charles," Mingus said. "I sincerely doubt it."